CHALK LINE

A Ben Gallagher Mystery

CHALK LINE

Paula LaRocque

Marion Street Mysteries

Portland, Oregon

Published by Marion Street Mysteries,
an imprint of Marion Street Press
4207 SE Woodstock Blvd # 168
Portland, OR 97206-6267
USA

Printed in the United States of America
ISBN 978-1-933338-95-8

Copyedited by Lorna Gusner
Author photo © 2011 Mei-Chun Jau

Library of Congress Cataloging-in-Publication Data

LaRocque, Paula.
  Chalk line : a Ben Gallagher mystery / Paula LaRocque.
    p. cm.
  ISBN 978-1-933338-95-8 (hardcover)
  1. Murder—Investigation—Fiction. I. Title.
  PS3612.A737C47 2011
  813'.6--dc23
                              2011026752

For PAUL

Readers familiar with the Texas and Michigan settings in this novel will recognize much in those locales. But there is no Knowlton Arms along the tourist route in Dallas that follows John F. Kennedy's motorcade the day of his assassination; no cul-de-sac called Aycliffe Court in northwest Arlington; no Last Resort bar in Battle Creek; no 1160 Undermain or Village Apartments in Winnesaka, the village near Kalamazoo—nor, indeed, is there a Winnesaka. The places touching the characters' personal lives—like the characters themselves—exist only in the author's imagination.

CHALK LINE

A chalk streak stops a hen.
—Friedrich Nietzsche

PART ONE

Hush, little baby, don't say a word,
Mama's gonna buy you a mockingbird.

CHAPTER 1

Friday morning, February 21, 2003

The best way to get there from Dallas is to go straight down I-45. Takes three hours or so. The terrain's more rolling and wooded than you might expect, especially around Corsicana. It levels off as you head south, going to heavy underbrush and open fields and farmlands.

When you get close, you can see the compound's big guard tower from the I-road, a bit of wall, some chain-link fence. Not much foliage, they probably keep it down. You can also see that huge statue of Sam Houston towering nearly eighty feet above I-45—twenty-five or thirty tons of steel mesh covered with white concrete, tall as a steeple.

Take the US 190 exit, and go east. Turn right on Avenue J and left on Twelfth. You'll see it on your left. You wouldn't think it would need an address, but it has one:

Texas State Penitentiary
815 12th St.
Huntsville, Texas

The first time Ben laid eyes on Huntsville's white concrete colossus commemorating Sam Houston, he thought, *Jesus Christ, isn't that just pure-damn Texas—make it big!* But that was many trips ago, the first hellish drive down to see Andrew. Now he didn't even notice it. Nell had been with him that first time: alternately huddling in the passenger seat, crying quietly—then staring morosely out the window, a lonely bundle of melancholy—then chattering brightly, falsely, taut as piano wire.

A decade ago.

He'd never been here this early in the morning. He pulled his new cherry-red Porsche into the almost empty parking lot and took a spot close to the entrance, twenty-five or so feet from the Walls Unit's little portico, concrete landing, and stone steps. Andrew should see him right away. The smooth-as-glass finish of the 911 GT3 glittered. He'd wanted the car to gleam like a beacon in the drab parking lot. *Andrew! Over here!* And so it did, its sparkle undimmed by the trip down, even with dust blowing from the west and intermittent rain from the south.

He turned off the ignition and sat in the sudden stillness—the engine ticking away its heat into the chill, the wind sweeping across the parking lot and softly buffeting the car. He opened the door and hauled his six-foot-six frame out of the driver's seat, stood, stretched, looked around. Only the Porsche met his expectations for this particular morning. The featureless terrain lay sprawled beneath a low dome of February sky, overcast and opaque, lighter smears of gray daubed along the eastern horizon. Over the years, when Ben had imagined this day, greeting Andrew after three thousand, six hundred and fifty days and nights of lockup, he'd imagined it bright with sun, bluebonnets maybe banking the I-road.

Shivering in his bomber jacket, he zipped the front, pulled his cell phone from a pocket, flipped it open, and punched in Nell's speed-dial number.

"Ma. I'm here."

"Oh dear. Already?"

"Couldn't sleep."

"You have a long wait."

"Some other cars here already, though. Friday's a big parole day."

Nell paused. "Getting them out in time for the weekend, I guess . . ."

Her words drifted away, dry and aimless as dead leaves. Now why would that be, today of all days? She was fine last night, bright as a brand-new penny. What could have happened overnight to change that? He pushed away his surprise and didn't ask. Nell hated questions. He'd ask Dayton.

God, what would they do without Dayton?

"Dayt there yet?"

"Not yet. He's closing on the Knowlton Arms this morning. Ben . . . will you call me when you start back?"

"Andrew can call."

Nell breathed a shuddery *ohh*. Ben recognized in the syllable a small *eureka!* Andrew would call. No special provisions or permissions. Pick up a phone, punch in a number . . . free at last. Free at last! Thank God almighty.

"Pretty soon, Ma," Ben said.

He snapped the mobile closed against his thigh, dropped it into his pocket, and got back into the car. She was right—he had a long wait.

———————

He'd pulled out of his garage in Arlington this morning while it was still full dark—at the same instant the newspaper guy's jalopy swung into the cul-de-sac. Ben had braked on the drive and trotted over to retrieve his paper, rolled and wrapped in its plastic sleeve. He'd tossed the newspaper onto the passenger seat. It landed alongside his sketchbook and a thermos filled with freshly brewed French roast. He could catch up on the news, maybe work the crossword puzzle while he waited.

Now he unscrewed the top from the thermos, and the steaming coffee's fragrance filled the Porsche—vying with its new-car smell. He carefully poured the hot liquid, set the cup into the dashboard cup-holder, and shifted sideways to lean against the door. Stretching his long legs, he made room for his right foot on the passenger seat and stuck the other in the well, elbow resting on the steering wheel. He adjusted his shoulder holster to keep it from touching the wheel. He'd had the Glock strapped in place this morning before reminding himself this was no usual day. But he left it. All told, he'd be on the road a minimum of six hours round-trip, and this was Texas. And he was a cop. He didn't want to be the only guy out there not packing.

He took up his coffee and sat loose and brooding in the dull morning, the sun rising somewhere behind the gray flannel sky, and waited. Or tried to wait. For Ben, waiting was an acquired rather than natural skill, and his mind flitted from one uncertainty to another, restless as a fly.

Was Andrew ready? Were they?

At least he wasn't in the middle of a case. But maybe that would be better, something to work on, discuss. That was the question—which was better? He'd thought about bringing Bood. Andrew loved dogs. Then thought again—sturdy little dreadlocked Bood in Andrew's lap, licking him to death all the way to Dallas.

Good? Bad?

He didn't know. Chief of Detectives Ben Gallagher, razzed by the other cops as a boy wonder, didn't know. Doctor Gallagher—holder of a PhD in Fine Arts, accomplished artist, king of certainty—didn't know. Not where Andrew was concerned.

Other early arrivals were pulling into the lot. Some parked near Ben. Others stayed well back from the entrance and remained in their cars—as though if they got too close, the jaws of those opening doors might clamp down on them, jerk them inside, close with an iron clang. Ben knew the feeling. How many times had he driven into this lot and passed uneasily through the Walls Unit's glass doors? Seemed like a thousand. But a couple hundred, anyway.

Dayton almost as many, coming all the way from Kalamazoo. And Nell even more. Their tightly knit little unit. Family.

Ben supposed it was true that friends were the family you *chose*. But family, by God, were the friends he chose. In any case, family was what he had. Nell had mentioned it once—after Andrew went to prison. Maybe it seemed to her that Ben was more alone—he'd certainly felt more alone.

Benny? You don't have, like, drinking buddies, do you.

Nope.

Andrew always did.

He'd paused a beat.

True enough. And look where it got him.

The exchange was just that brief, but it made Ben think. And he'd finally settled on the plain truth. He had what he needed. He had Nell, who was in her way another Ben—solitary, private, independent, intense—with the big difference that she couldn't help showing her emotions, and he couldn't help hiding his. He had Dayton, longtime family friend, father he'd never had, all that—the source of calm he most admired and emulated. And now—again!—he would have Andrew, like the self Ben would never be: gregarious, impulsive, a sunny counterpoint to moody Nell and brooding Ben.

He saw that some drivers were out of their cars and wandering toward the entrance, where they milled around restlessly at the foot of the stone stairs—near a little patch of straw-like grass flanked by a large old oak that rattled in the wind, a scatter of dead leaves clinging to its barren branches. Men and women in jackets and puffy vests, exchanging a few words. One walking a little way from the group to light a cigarette, exhale a plume of smoke, yawn, hack into a fist. Like a motley, scruffy UN delegation—blacks, browns, whites, in-betweens.

Waiting for their ex-cons—ex-cons lucky enough to have someone to wait.

Ben studied Walker County's lockup as if he'd never seen it: tall brick walls bearing warnings, iron doors bleeding rust, spiraling razor wire. At length, he took a drawing pencil from the door pocket and opened his sketchbook. Chattering mind quiet at last, he began to draw. Leaving out the milling crowd, he rapidly sketched the face of the Walls Unit. He laid in shadow with the side of the pencil lead and blurred and softened the edges with his thumb. When he was satisfied, he printed across the bottom of the drawing in his small, vertical script:

"Huntsville's Walls Unit. February 21. The Day."

He closed the pad and stowed it behind the passenger seat. Someday he'd show the sketch to Andrew. After all, however many times *they'd* seen it from this point of view, Andrew was about to see it for only the second time: going in and now coming out.

He checked his watch. As always when sketching or painting, he'd lost track of time. With a breathless little leap inside his chest, he realized it could be any moment now, and excitement strummed within him like a plucked string. He emptied the passenger seat and slipped the thermos and newspaper alongside the sketch pad. He sat awhile with his eyes on the entrance, chewing his lip. In a queue, someone had to be first. Someone—just never you or yours, so it seemed. But still, someone. And after that, sooner or later in the flow of freed men, would come Andrew. He would pass under the Walls Unit's portico and down the stone steps in his weightless, loose-jointed way, dressed in the clothes he wore when he went inside ten years ago, his hair somewhere between the color of brass and copper, as stocky and well-muscled as Ben was tall and slender. Andrew a good six or seven inches shorter than Ben and still only a fraction of an inch away from six feet himself.

Andrew Gallagher, good kid, his twenties down a Huntsville prison drain.

Two guards appeared inside the Walls Unit's glass doors, and Ben sat up abruptly, pulling his legs back into the well of the driver's seat. A third guard appeared, unlocked the double doors, and came through to stand on the concrete landing. Ben extricated himself from the driver's seat and scrambled from the car. His heart in his throat, he watched as the Walls Unit's heavy glass doors swung open.

His brother was the first man to push through to the outside.

CHAPTER 2

Friday morning, February 21

avid Dayton Slaughter crossed the foyer of his top-floor suite at the Knowlton Arms, the heels of his Italian loafers clicking smartly against the marble floor, and paused at the mirror above the console table. He set his bulging briefcase on the floor beneath the skylight, its overhead brightness filtered by cloud cover and the surrounding Dallas skyline. He examined himself—smoothed his silver hair, adjusted his tie, inspected his eyeglasses. Their lenses sparkled, but he breathed on them anyway and gave them an unnecessary rub with the small chamois square he kept in the inside pocket of his suit coat. The house phone on the console rang once, then stopped. He glanced at his watch, although he knew exactly what time it was and that it was too early for Ben or Andrew to call.

He glared at the phone. He'd begun the day with a twenty-minute telephone wrangle with that interior decorator, and he didn't need a postscript. So far it had been a morning of aggravations. He'd sure as hell never planned for the Knowlton closing to fall on the same day as Andrew's parole. But that's what happened, and he didn't want any further delay, didn't want Andrew buried in an avalanche of detail. He wanted to ease Andrew in, make sure he wanted this. He didn't want to railroad him. But he felt urgency pressing at him from all sides. Things change, fine. So *life* is what happens when you're making other plans—who said that, John Lennon? But he had to consider Andrew. And Nell. And his own . . . predicament. He didn't want to think of it as any more than that.

The phone rang again. He looked at the digital readout. An inside call.

"It's Abner, sir. Just checking when you want your car brought round."

"Not till after the signing, Ab. I'll let you know."

"Big doin's today, huh, Mr. Slaughter . . . er . . . sir." Abner was having trouble dropping the *mister.*

If Ab only knew.

"Uh . . . that fellow Novak is here."

Ah—the *real* reason for the doorman's call.

"He's in the building?"

"Yessir."

"What's he up to?"

"Just here in the lobby. Waitin' for you. All worked up, too. Face all red, like he gets. Wants to see you before you sign them papers. Wait—" The phone went quiet, then Abner said, "Now, where'd that bugger get to?"

"Thanks for the heads-up, Ab. But don't worry. Pretty soon, I'll own the Knowlton, nothing he can do."

"He can cause a right smart nuisance in the lobby."

Dayton's lips twitched. A ruckus in Abner Zeeck's lobby. No, that would never do.

"And some lady was looking for you," Abner added. "Left a message at the desk."

"Lady?"

"I don't know her name. That lady with an accent like . . . ."

At his hesitation, Dayton said, "Like mine?"

The doorman sidestepped the question.

"That lady who likes to wear green."

"Ah. That . . . lady."

"She seemed sorta in a temper."

Of course.

Dayton replaced the phone, his cuff catching the corner of a picture frame and slamming it facedown against the console's polished surface. He winced and picked up the picture. The glass was unbroken, good. The photo was one of his favorites, an enlargement from an old shot, and framed in a heavy rectangle of etched bronze. Andrew's eighteenth. Nell and the boys at the dining room table in the old place, saluting the camera with their glasses, the table littered with birthday stuff, Andrew wearing a paper crown and a goofy grin. Dayton wasn't in it—as with most shots of the three of them, he'd been the photographer.

He stared at the photo in the silence of the foyer, remembering, conscious only of the sound of his own breathing. Happy faces, innocent and oblivious. Nothing wary in Nell's tranquil countenance, no trace of foreboding in Ben's smile, nothing in Andrew's rakish grin to suggest he'd shortly be an inmate in Huntsville prison. Dayton had flown down from Kalamazoo especially to join the celebration—Andrew having graduated and leaving soon for Texas A&M University, Ben focusing on art at Southern Methodist but already talking about law enforcement. And Ben and Andrew clinking their glasses, putting their heads together and singing gruffly in their most exaggerated French an Edith Piaf song Nell had played incessantly when they were growing up.

Non, je ne regrette rien.

Another night swept unbidden through Dayton's mind, and he removed his spectacles and dragged a palm across his eyes. Why was it, when you looked back on one of life's big events, it seemed like both yesterday and a lifetime ago? There wasn't a single part that wasn't stamped indelibly upon his memory, but the whole now seemed smeared across time—that pivotal March night more than three decades ago and the years that followed. Keeping Nell's secret, and in the keeping, creating more secrets. Never finding the right time to tell her, doing what he could—and what he didn't believe in. Putting away the thought that it had to turn out badly. Sooner or later.

And now it had.

I regret nothing or I regret everything. Either way.

His doorbell chimed, and he crossed the foyer and peered through the peephole. There stood Karl Novak. So this was where Abner's bugger had got to.

Dayton snatched the door open. "Goddammit, Karl, I don't have time for your shit this morning."

Novak worked his lips as if he had a hot coal in his mouth but said nothing. Then, breathing hard, a curtain of dyed yellow hair from his comb-over swinging into his face, he put a thick hand on the door and shoved. Thickheaded, too, Dayton thought—thick-set, thick-skinned, thickskulled, thick. Dayton still had the heavy bronze frame in his left hand and, for a millisecond, fought the urge to bang it hard into Novak's face. But he didn't want to damage the picture. So, with the ambidexterity of most left-handers, he hit Novak with his right fist instead. The blow landed squarely between Novak's eyes, Dayton's ring scoring the skin between his brows. Blood sprang from the cut and ran in a rivulet alongside a flared nostril.

Novak put a hand to his nose and stared at his bloody fingers with eyes as vacant as a church on Monday.

"I *said*—" Dayton hustled the dazed Novak down the carpeted stairs to the fifth floor and into the waiting elevator, punched the button marked *Lobby,* and ducked back out through the closing doors. He took the stairs back up to his foyer two at a time for another look-see in the mirror. No blood on him, good. Shoot, he wasn't even breathing hard. And Novak hadn't said a word during the entire transaction.

David Dayton Slaughter, he thought wryly, action hero.

He pulled a gold money clip from his pocket, extracted a couple of bills, and tucked them in his suit coat pocket so he would have a tip handy when Abner brought the car around. He picked up his car keys and patted his wallet pocket. First, the signing. Seal the deal on the Knowlton—priority item number one. Tell Nell— priority item number two.

———————

Dayton loved the Knowlton Arms, a stately old sandstone apartment-building-cum-hotel punctuated with red awnings. It occupied a busy corner along downtown Dallas' tourist route, and that it sat at odds with the steel and glittering glass surrounding it only made Dayton love it more. The Victorian building had begun life more than a century ago as a posh hotel featuring the fanciest lobby in town and five floors of roomy suites—just twenty suites in those days. Today, it had twice that number, but they were still spacious, even with the whole sixth floor given over to a single residence. A recent nod to modernity was a new silent and swift guest elevator. But if the building still had its clunky service elevators and clunkier radiators, it also still had windows that actually opened—a rare premium in Dayton's eyes. For well over three decades, the Knowlton had been his home on his frequent trips to Dallas—first for business, then because Nell and the boys moved there when they left Michigan. And several years ago, when the old building's uppermost floor was renovated into a luxury suite, Dayton jumped at the chance to lease it. He'd planned to stay there when he retired from his law firm in Kalamazoo, either until he found a permanent place or persuaded Nell to marry him.

But now . . . he shook off the thought.

He settled his large frame behind the wheel of his Jaguar and pulled away from the curb—unaware of the commotion in his wake. At the front desk, a rangy, horse-faced woman with oxen-yoke shoulders and hair the color of ashes accosted the clerk. She spoke in an agitated nasal twang and wore a suit of such an acrid green that it struck the eye like neon even in the lobby's subdued light.

"I've been waiting right here for over an hour," she complained. "How'd he slip by me without—" She threw up an exasperated hand. "When will he back? I need—"

"A moment, Madam." The clerk crooked a finger at Abner Zeeck. "You know when Mr. Slaughter's coming back? This lady's been waiting for him."

Abner looked at the woman and back at the clerk.

"He said he wudn't gonna be gone long."

"Said he wudn't gonna be gone long," the woman mimicked, a nasty edge in her voice. "Goddammit!"

Sighing dramatically, she turned on her heel and shoved through the revolving door onto Houston Street, looked back and forth—up toward the old train station and back toward the grassy knoll and book depository.

But Dayton had already turned off Houston and was on his way to McKinney Avenue, his heavy briefcase beside him. It was full of folders, not only the originals of the documents for the closing but also of everything else, witnessed, notarized, and copied, the copies already winging their way to his Kalamazoo law office.

Done and delivered. Airtight.

Now for priority number two. The hardest part. Today of all days.

He had to tell Nell.

CHAPTER 3

While Dayton Slaughter was in his sixth-floor suite at the Knowlton Arms chatting with Abner Zeeck, scrapping with Karl Novak, trying to decide whether he regretted everything or nothing, and preparing to face Nell, Jimmy Thatcher Snipes was three floors down, preparing for his day. He hummed at his image in the large mirror in the living room. He admired his retro three-button black suit—accented at chest and ankle with saffron tie, socks, and pocket silk—and stopped humming abruptly.

That friggin' song again.

When he was five or six, a little girl down the hall named Natalie had an antique music box. Atop the box, a tiny man with a black handlebar moustache and painted hair posed in a white jersey and black tights on an even tinier trapeze. The daring young man! He twirled endlessly to the music—or for as long as you wound his little key.

Jimmy had wanted that music box. He'd wanted that daring young man. And Natalie, to his surprise, had handed it over.

But his mother had laughed—bared her jumble of gray teeth and *laughed!* A *girl's* toy, she'd said, maybe we can get you a little dolly, too, a little *dolly*. Jimmy glowered in the mirror, remembering. His mother's laughter in his ears, he'd taken the music box into the hall, set it on the floor, raised his knee, and stomped. The daring young man popped off, and a second stomp smashed the tiny figure. But the music had played on until it wound down. Even after that, when he touched the box, it emitted a few slow, clear tinkles, *With the . . . greaaatessst . . . offfff . . .*

Now, Jimmy sang a few bars under his breath, Ohhh, he floats through the air with the greatest of ease . . . Then he remembered it was that stupid song again. Falling silent, he stood back from the mirror to get the full effect, thinking maybe one of the Beatles when they first got out of Liverpool. No, Sean Penn. A young Sean Penn. Dollie had brought up Robert F. Kennedy, but no, stick with Penn. Tighter mouth. Yeah. Sean Penn, maybe a little RFK thrown in, just in the way he swooped his hair back, that's all. He tried it in the mirror. Yeah.

Dollie had said she'd seen old clips of Robert Kennedy on the History Channel and that RFK had a "Jimmy gesture." She'd scooped the hair from her forehead with four fingers.

"Like that," she'd said. "Something you do."

Jimmy had run his thin fingers through the lank brown hair that fell over his forehead. Felt right. RFK. Yeah.

"How tall was he, you know?"

She'd shot him a look. "Not tall, I don't think. Kinda short, maybe."

Now, at the mirror, Jimmy peered into his own gold-flecked hazel eyes and stood back to give each shirt cuff a tug—until it showed precisely a quarter inch of white—and buttoned his jacket. Top button *sometimes*. Middle button *always*. Third button *never*.

He crossed the room and switched on the CD player. Linkin Park *Live in Texas*. Yeah. No punk, no funk.

Jimmy Snipes was strumming an air guitar with narrow hands and bitten nails when his mother—stocky, late fifties—strode into

the room on a wave of Lily of the Valley. Her ash blonde hair—
more ash than blonde now—was set in frizzy curls resembling tiny
sausages. She wore a geometric print dress in taupe and gray—
buttoned front, belted waist, shallow lapels making a deep V for
her ample cleavage. Her pale hazel eyes, as golden and reflective
as a lemur's, were nearly the same color as the amber frames of
her spectacles.

She watched as Jimmy made a show of holding his nose and
marching to the window—raising it wide, letting in a rush of
chilled air and the hiss of tires on the wet street below.

"Close it," she said. "It's raining."

"Not much. And you're stinking up the place."

She crossed to the CD player, lowered the volume, and turned
to her son, who pulled his finely etched brows into a frown.

"Why why why," she asked, "do you jump out of bed and
get decked out so early? It's not like you have a job to go to or
anything."

"I want to be ready. If the bar comes my way, I want to grab
it. With the greatest of ease. Readiness is all. Etcetera."

"Bar? What bar? What are you talking about?"

"Never mind, Mommy-O."

"Music blasting, rainy morning and all, somebody might want
to sleep in."

She plopped onto a beige sofa and watched him go to the CD
player and turn up the volume again.

"Let me ask you something, Miz Snipes," Jimmy said. "In fact,
two things."

She rose from the sofa again and plodded across the room.
One, the volume. *Two,* the window. *Three,* the lamp.

"Lights in the middle of the day," she said. "I pay the bills,
remember."

She moved to the window's gray light and half-sat on the sill,
squinting at a slip of paper in her pudgy hand.

"I got a manicure coupon from the beauty salon downstairs."

Still perched on the sill, she frowned at the room's pale walls, bleached oak tables, beige furniture, sand-colored carpeting. "I don't like this Hollywood look, everything kinda light."

"Yeah, I really miss the sooty old stuff we left behind, too. Brown and maroon. Black and gray. Had the advantage of looking dirty right from the start. If you don't like this place, what are we doing here?"

The apartment faced west along the front half of the Knowlton's third floor. Like most of the floors in the building, this floor had ten suites, all arranged at the building's perimeters and boasting plenty of windows and light. The central space was given to corridor and foyer, elevator in the middle. Most of the floors followed this plan—except the freshly remodeled sixth floor with its single suite, and the second floor, which was divided into individual rooms suitable for business and overnight travelers.

Mrs. Snipes visualized the old apartment. Her things. The shiny black laminate tabletops, the faux marble lamps with ruffled shades. And her Hummel figurines, all she'd kept of a lifetime of belongings. She could almost call up the sound and smell of the old neighborhood, the tipsy burst of laughter or snatch of conversation, the stale beer and tobacco wafting from the bars, the grease and onions of the burger joint.

"You wear black and gray all the time," she said, breaking her reverie. "Your Infiniti is black."

"*Obsidian*, Miz Snipes. And my leather interior is a color called *willow*. *And* I spice up my wardrobe with my socks and silks." He crossed to the mirror. "Today, saffron. Other days, terra-cotta, fuchsia, sienna . . ."

"You must mean orange, pink, and brown."

He glanced at her reflection in the mirror and made a farting noise with his lips. "Back to this whatcha might call conversation. *First,* I need a hunnert bucks."

"Why?"

"Bluuhhhh. Because I don't have any dough, Miz Moneypenney."

"Why a hundred?"

"Let's say I want to buy a new car."

"You have a new car. Thanks to me—thanks I never got."

"Thanks a heap, Mommy. But the only reason you bought it's because I had pneumonia and you got scared I'd maybe croak. And you, I mean the same day, bought yourself a new Caddy. You already had one, nearly new, too. Like you couldn't stand to see somebody get something unless it was you."

She slid off the sill and returned to the sofa, plunking one chunky-heeled oxford on the footstool. "And you think you had pneumonia, eh?"

"I had pneumonia."

"You're a klepto—what is it, hydro—no, hypo something."

"I had pneumonia."

She said nothing but continued to regard him, her golden eyes as intent as if he were a specimen in a jar. He picked up one of the largest Hummels on the coffee table and held it aloft with two fingers.

"What's this called?" he asked. "Seven creepy kids on a slab? Maybe I'll take it down to the pawn shop."

"Put that down! You know not to touch those." She grabbed the figurine. "This piece is worth five thousand bucks, for your information."

"*That* crap?"

"Hummel figurines. Depictions of youthful innocence," she recited, turning the figure this way and that.

He tossed back his head and laughed at the ceiling. "Musta read *that* brochure more than once. And this from someone who doesn't know the difference between klepto and hydro and hypo. Thinks it's the Marx Brothers."

He fired off another round of laughter.

She narrowed her gaze. "What's so funny?"

"Ahh, fuck it," Jimmy said, wiping his eyes. "As I said before, bluuhhhh."

"And as I said before, what's so funny?"

"What was that again? Depictions of youthful innocence, yeah. Gives me a case of whatchacallit dissonance. Like when a fatso blimp has a scrawny little Chihuahua in her elbow."

"Maybe I shoulda got a Chihuahua instead of you."

He put his head back again and sent up a hee-hee-hee.

"Well, we're just having a hell of a good time here, aren't we, Jimbo."

"Be better if I could get me some dough."

She stepped to the desk between the windows, reached into the V of her neckline like an ol' timey madam at a brothel, pulled out a key, and unlocked the uppermost drawer on the right. Turning her back, she fished something from the drawer and spent a moment fiddling with it.

Jimmy sighed. "We both know where the real money is, Miz Snipes."

Still with her back turned, she reached into her cleavage again, brought out a roll of bills wrapped with a rubber band, and peeled off five twenties. He rolled his eyes heavenward. He'd never known a time when she didn't keep a wad of cash in her bra. He saw it as a metaphor—not so much for being old-fashioned as for wanting to stay close to her resources.

She turned and fixed her eyes on him; he stared back unflinchingly.

"You ever think of getting a job?"

He held out his hand. "No. Did you?"

"Maybe you can help out in the salon downstairs. The Cachet Day Spa. Since you're always down there anyway, hanging around that Dollie person. Oh! A little blush on the young man's cheeks!" She rubbed her plump little hands in front of her with relish, like a housefly considering a turd. "Over a beautician. Just your speed. Swabbing hair from drains, sanding old ladies' calluses."

"She's the manager. And her name's Dollie Varnes, not Dollie Person."

"Beautician, manager, whatever." She held up the twenties. "She why you want this money?"

Jimmy didn't answer.

"She live here? At the Knowlton? Bet she gets a break on the rent."

He waved a hand vaguely skyward.

"Not the sixth floor," she said.

"What do you know about it?"

She knew it was premium space. And she knew it belonged to one Dayton Slaughter—as of today, the new owner of the Knowlton Arms. She'd sneaked up there a few times. The elevator stopped at the fifth floor—you had to go up carpeted stairs at either end of the landing, past brass plaques announcing "Private." That took you to an outer foyer, a small round room with a brandy-colored marble floor and pale double doors with wide moldings and brass fittings.

She put the twenties back around the roll and slipped it into her cleavage.

"She gets a break on the rent," she said, "she can pay for your date."

His face went scarlet. She retrieved the roll of bills, again peeled off five twenties, reconsidered, and took back two.

"Sixty's plenty. Take her down the street to the Ripe Olive. Cheap drinks, burgers. Why pay hotel prices for food and booze with a place practically next door."

Jimmy took the bills, his complexion still apoplectic, and glared at her.

"Chrissakes! These greenbacks are damp. From your tits. Where do you put your *change,* for chrissakes."

"My boobies to Jimbo's bimbos." Her smile looked more like a baring of teeth, but she kept it going.

"What."

"Have you seen my umbrella?" She went to the closet and extracted a maroon wool coat.

"*What,*" he demanded.

"You said you had *two* questions."

He combed his forelock with four fingers. "You're baiting me."

She sighed.

"You are. Baiting me." He took a last turn in the mirror, shot his cuffs again, headed for the door, and stopped. "Say, Miz Snipes. How tall you think Sean Penn is?"

"Taller than you, Jimbo." She hustled past him, getting to the door before he did. "Isn't everyone?"

CHAPTER 4

On the main floor of the Knowlton Arms, doorman Abner Zeeck was in the Cachet Day Spa helping Dollie Varnes put up a new shipment. He'd shed his cap. His gray jacket—which sported gold buttons and braid, epaulets, and a stand-up collar that hid his scrawny neck—hung on the back of a chair.

Dollie stood on a stool in front of the cosmetic racks and looked toward the glass-doored entry.

"Zora's in the lobby, Ab," she said. "Better go see. Don't let her try to pass out those religious pamphlets. Especially with Mr. Slaughter and Mrs. Delacourt and those lawyers here for the closing."

Abner looked uneasy. "It's raining a bit."

"Then bring her in here for a while."

The glass doors swung open, and Zora the street woman stood there like a block of granite in varying vintages of clothing, her soiled gray curls wrapped in a plaid scarf. She carried a plastic bag full of paper and a tattered umbrella that had once been bright yellow.

"Zora Sanda," she announced, her rough voice like waves washing over pebbles. "Romanian, defender of the church."

Dollie turned on her stool.

"Come in and get dry, Zora."

The older woman fired up a smile that revealed several bad teeth and a few vacancies. Dollie turned back to Abner and made a show of peeking at him through her fingers. "Ab. Seeing you in a T-shirt instead of your uniform is like seeing a priest without his collar."

"*Priest* rhymes with *beast*," commented Zora, sudden distress flooding her pale mother superior face at the word *beast*.

"*Feast* would rhyme okay, Zora," said Dollie. "And it's a prettier word."

Zora's face relaxed.

Abner had loaded his thin arms with little gold boxes. He didn't return Dollie's grin. "You want all these kinda boxes on the top shelf?"

She took the boxes. "What's the matter, Ab? Something on your mind?"

He shook his head.

"Tell me. Unless it's none of my business, I mean."

"It ain't none of *mine*."

She considered. "I'm making it your business, Ab."

Dollie liked the doorman to be his cheerful self. He was twenty-five years her senior, but his naiveté made him seem younger, and she loved his kindness and gift for happiness.

Abner seemed about to speak but slid his mud-colored eyes toward Zora.

"Zora," Dollie said. "There are fresh donuts in the back room."

She watched Zora's broad back disappear through a pink-curtained doorway then turned to face Abner again.

"That Jimmy Snipes is here a lot," he said, hitching up the wide brown belt that held his pants on his thin hips. "I think there's something wrong with him."

She waited again.

"That's all I'm sayin'."

"Something wrong how?" She saw that Ab had resumed loading his arms with boxes, his face closed. "His mind, you mean?"

He didn't meet her eyes. "His soul."

She laughed.

"I think he may be mean," he said. Abner, without meanness himself, was baffled when he saw it in others.

"And I had a bad dream about him," he added.

"Are you worried about me, Abby?"

"Yes, ma'am," he said. "I am."

"I'm not seeing Jimmy again, Ab. I already decided."

He smiled now, showing a row of little square teeth, like kernels on a corncob.

The first time Dollie went out with Jimmy Snipes, she'd thought him quirky but fun. He'd talked non-stop, an entertaining patter of sardonic observation and flight of fancy. The second time, she thought he was eccentric. Well, okay, weird. He'd bent to rub a smudge from the shining black leather of his shoe, and something had fallen to the floor, Dollie picking it up, thinking at first it was a pen. But it was a thermometer in a round plastic case.

He'd taken it from her without comment and stuck it in his breast pocket behind a brilliant bit of flamingo pink silk.

"Why the thermometer?" she'd asked. "You sick?"

"I may be," he'd said. Seeing her puzzlement, he'd added, "My temperature isn't normal. It's never normal."

"What do you mean, Jimmy?"

"I just said. It's never normal."

"How do you know?"

"Because I take it, and it's never ninety-eight-point-six."

"Why are you taking it?"

"To see if it's *normal*," he'd said with annoyance. "Is *yours* normal?"

"I guess so. I mean, I don't know. I don't take it. Unless there's a reason. And if there's a reason, it might not be normal because I'm sick. I don't see why you're taking your temperature if you're not sick."

"So I can see it it's ever normal. So far it never is."

"What is it?"

"Ninety-eight. Sometimes a little lower."

"So that's normal for you, I guess."

"That's just it. Say the doctor takes my temperature. It's ninety-nine and he says, fine. But it's at least a whole degree off for me. I have a fever and nobody knows it." He had sounded angry, fearful. "I just want to be normal, that's all."

Dollie studied him, thinking, *good luck with that.*

On their third—and last!—date, he'd treated her to a monologue, and she'd seen another Jimmy: the sickly, undersized kid, plagued by allergies, abused at school by the other boys and at home by a drunken father.

Yeah, he was sixty-one when I was born. Choked to death on his vomit when I was twelve. Serves him right. Anyways, he didn't beat me after I was ten. That was the last time. Yours truly got stronger and the old man got weaker. Tried to hit me with a broom handle and I marched right into him, took the handle out of his hands and bopped him a good one in the face. With the greatest of ease, yeah! Ma had to take him for stitches. After that, I used to raise my hand near the old man's face, just to see him flinch. The daring young man . . .

He'd laughed at that part.

Coupla times he even raised up his own hands, trying to protect his sorry ass, fuckin' chicken shit bully. Anyway, he died after that.

His voice had quavered, and Dollie sent him a quick glance. "But you must have loved your daddy, Jimmy."

"I never gave a fuck about him. He was an asshole. So don't try to get me to say something sad, like he was my daddy just the same, boo hoo."

Dollie thinking some problems *here*. But that wasn't the end of it.

Only superior people have allergies, he'd said abruptly, *you know that? Yeah, a historical fact. Just like the most superior men are short, the greatest contributions to the world have been made by short men. Yeah,* he'd said angrily when she'd raised her brows, *a fuckin' fact.* And he'd reeled off some names. *Napoleon, of course. Lawrence of fuckin' Arabia. Aristotle fuckin' Onassis. Bob fuckin' Dylan. Yeah, and Dustin Hoffman. Woody Allen. Jason Alexander. Robert Blake—fuckin' Baretta, don't pretend you don't know who he is. All under five feet six.*

Somewhere in there he'd told her, chuckling, about putting a cat's head in a vise when he was a kid and turning the handle until the animal's skull cracked. She'd stared at him, her fingers to her lips and throat tightening, but he hadn't noticed. Then he'd brought her back to her fifth-floor apartment at the Knowlton and—can you believe it?—stepped inside to kiss her. She'd be damned if she'd let that happen; she'd had her last date with Jimmy Thatcher Snipes. But when he reached for her, her little Pekingese, Snazzy, had dashed into the foyer growling and grabbed him by the pant leg. Jimmy had raised his knee to kick, and she'd cried in a voice rich with fury, *Don't you dare!*

But the worst part, and she wouldn't be telling Abner this, was the next day, when he flipped aside his jacket to show her a pistol shoved into his waistband. She'd seen only the handle, but her heart had jumped, and Jimmy had grinned, as though hearing.

Yes. She'd had her last date with Jimmy Snipes.

CHAPTER 5

Nell sat on the ivory sofa in her McKinney Avenue townhouse and stared at Dayton's broad back as he poked at the fireplace—stared at him as if she'd never seen him, as if memorizing him.

I've known him longer than I've known my sons, she thought, and known him better. Dayton was nine years her senior. A big man, but trim. Gravelly baritone, headful of silver hair, clear gray eyes behind spotless lenses. Dapper. Today, a navy blue suit and a navy-and-white striped tie with a gleaming white shirt. On his wrist, the same gold Rolex he'd had for the more than thirty years she'd known him. He'd been using the same gold money clip for just as long. Dayton had always been good at taking care of things.

Nell had chosen Dayton to handle the legal affairs of her estate when she took possession of her inheritance at eighteen, nine years after her parent's fatal auto accident and five years after her grandmother's death left her a ward of the state. Nell was drawn to Dayton not only because he, too, had no family but also because she felt safe in his hands. Dayton was at the time the youngest lawyer at Gold, Gladstone, and Dunne—the Gallaghers' Kalamazoo law firm. That firm would shortly thereafter be re-christened

Gold, Gladstone, Dunne, and *Slaughter*. And later still, *Slaughter,* Gold, Gladstone, and Dunne.

When Nell graduated from high school, valedictorian of her class, she watched her school chums excitedly prepare to fly so-lo—to leave home and family for some distant campus. The idea left her cold. She already knew how to fly solo. And she'd already lost the very things her friends were so eager to shed. So, able by finances and academic performance to go to school anywhere, she chose to go nowhere. She stayed home. Western Michigan University. Besides, where was she going to go? She had no ties to her distant relatives in Ireland. Her only ties were to this town, to the memory of her parents, and to David Dayton Slaughter, who had become both friend and family to her.

But of course, she had not yet met Benjamin Ryan.

Dayton stopped poking at the fire, and she stared at him a moment longer, eyes filled with tears. Exactly when had his hair gone silver? She couldn't remember for sure. When did—

He restored the poker to its stand, and she looked away.

———————

Dayton took his seat on the sofa beside Nell and touched her cheek. It had been even harder than he'd feared—the hardest thing he'd ever done.

"Your coffee's getting cold," he said. He drained his own cup and set it on the cocktail table fronting the sofa.

She gazed out the glassed east wall of the townhouse, a narrow four-story building with long balconies on the east side.

"I wish it were better weather."

He took her hand, and they sat in silence a moment, the softly crackling fire blending with the quiet tick of the grandfather clock on the stair landing. At length she returned his gaze. Those blue, blue eyes—like Ben's, a shade hard to name. Cobalt, electric, even more so against her creamy skin and within the frame of her black lashes and hair—once almost as dark as her lashes but fading now to auburn lights and occasional silver strands.

"Was Benjamin Ryan's hair blue-black like Ben's?" he asked.

"What?"

"I was just wondering if Ben got his father's hair."

She regarded him with a small smile, but her hand was listless in his.

"Exactly. Horse-mane hair so black it shone blue under the lights."

"Nellie. Please don't cry anymore. I wish to God I—especially today. But it can't be helped. We have a decision to make."

She gave a shuddering sigh.

"Main thing," he said. "Andrew's set." He rose and opened his briefcase, removed a fistful of folders. "These are originals. Copies are on the way to the firm, but let's put this bunch in your safe for the weekend so we can go over them with Andrew if we need to."

"I'll do that. But what if—"

"He'll want it, Nell. It's exactly the right thing for him—plays to all his strengths. Monday morning, he'll need to start his life. This way he'll have a life to start. If he wants to shed the Knowlton Arms later and do something else, fine. But it will be a bridge. And it's all his either way. His responsibility. What he needs."

"What was the hassle with Karl Novak?"

She was borrowing time, he knew, something they didn't have much of right now. But he laid the folders on the table at her elbow and took his seat next to her.

"He's been trying to bully me into changing my mind about the Knowlton deal. I stopped him before he even opened his mouth. Almost banged him on the head with a picture of you and the boys." He paused. "Notice the symbolism. Then decided a personal touch was better."

"You *hit* him?"

"Damned straight."

Nell was quiet for a moment. "You remember my visit to Karl's high-rise, when I was fund-raising for the foundation?"

"I do."

Nell had described Novak's apartment as a stage setting for the rich and criminal: monkey lamps with hide shades, leopard-skin seats, walls adorned with safari kills that once roamed the plains of Sapkamma—beautiful in life but now dusty stuffed heads with glass eyes decorating a river-rock fireplace in Texas. She'd asked Karl if he mounted the heads of human conquests as well, and Novak, deaf to her disgust, had laughed—supposing her to be joking, Nell had said. Or worse, flirting.

"Why was he so set on the Knowlton?" she asked.

"My guess is he needs a quick yield on something. Planned on snowing Maisie Delacourt after the old man died, and closing a fast deal on a precious piece of downtown land. Then I got in the way."

Dayton had known he had an edge with Maisie Delacourt, the young widow of Winfield Delacourt III and owner of the Knowlton, but he'd made a fair, even generous offer. For years, he'd watched Winfield refurbish the old building, each time improving it while maintaining its Victorian uniqueness. He knew about old man Delacourt's engagement to Maisie and had seen their wedding photos in *The Dallas Morning News:* a stooped man with thick white hair and thicker lenses, a busty blonde forty years his junior on one side and a glowering heir, Winfield IV, on the other.

Nell had peered at the grainy news photos, Dayton remembered now, and mused, "There must be a template for women like that. They all look alike. Why are you smiling?"

"An old joke. This guy asks a seventy-year-old friend how he got his sexy young wife to marry him. And the old fella says he lied about his age by a couple of decades. 'What, you told her you were only fifty?' the guy asks. And the old fella says, 'No, I told her I was ninety.'"

Nell cut into his reverie. "Sounds like it was one hell of a morning."

"Everyone spoiling for a fight." He gave her a sidelong glance. "I also got into it with Sylva Kaye."

She looked at him sharply.

"Don't ask."

A chime tinkled outside, herald of a north-turning wind; a hanging pot swayed on the balcony, incongruously filled with bright blooms.

"Those pansies have survived the whole winter," Nell said. "That's what I want to do, Dayt. Bloom in snow."

"You have," he said. "You do."

She surveyed the room. "Will Andrew like this place?"

"Considering his former digs?" He laughed shortly. "What's not to like?"

In Dayton's view, the new sofa with its ivory crewel cover sat agreeably beside Nell's old family pieces—pieces Andrew would remember. The clock on the landing. The ancient Aubusson, with its muted colors, warming the polished oak floor. Silk-shaded lamps casting pools of light on gleaming tabletops.

"Everything was my fault," Nell announced abruptly.

"Don't be crazy."

"Even Huntsville."

"Crazy, crazy."

"You think he's grown up over the last ten years?"

"Nothing wrong with Andrew, Nell."

"I mean you think what happened taught him not to be so impetuous?"

"Andrew did a foolish thing, Nellie. We all do foolish things, especially when we're young. And if we're lucky, the universe forgives. Andrew wasn't lucky. But it was a one-off."

"He did lots of foolish things, Dayt. You know he did. You know I was always worried. But I was too soft on him. Too protective. You said so, and you were right. Thing is, Andrew hasn't always considered consequence."

He gave her a long look. "And you have?"

She shook her head ruefully. "I'd say touché if it weren't so trite."

He rose and patted his pocket for his car keys. "I have another meeting, then I'm running over to Arlington. I want to pick up Bood and bring him back to your place. Then Ben won't have to worry about walking and feeding him."

Nell looked pleased. "Ah. I should have thought of that. Bood is family, too."

"This way, we'll all be in one place, and Ben and Andrew will be free to do whatever they want. I also bought some welcome-home stuff to leave at Ben's for whenever they do show up over there. Want to go over with me?"

"Depends on what time you go." She was staring at him again, eyes brimming. "Dayt. I wish—I wish we'd married years ago. I wish—why didn't you . . ."

He sat back down and pulled her close.

"Why didn't I *what*, Nellie? You know why. You've always known. I made my feelings clear, as I recall. The word had to be yours to say."

"Benjamin Ryan."

"Of course. But this is old news." He exhaled heavily. "I couldn't compete with Benjamin Ryan when he was alive, and he was even more formidable in death . . . the perfect young hero, frozen in time." He tucked an errant strand of auburn-touched hair behind her ear. "Have you read Housman's 'To an Athlete Dying Young'?"

"The boy who was wise to die while still a hero."

Dayton pondered Housman's words. *Smart lad, to slip betimes away.*

"Oh my God," Nell said abruptly, "the waste."

"Yes."

"I didn't mean Benjamin. I meant us!" she said hotly.

"What waste, Nell? We've been together. Life happened, and we were together. You raised your boys, and we were together. Where's the waste?"

He rose again, and she looked up at him, face ravaged.

"It's as though my life were partitioned, Dayt. Everything that happened before that St. Patrick's Day, and everything after—"

"Decide, Nell."

"I don't want to play into anybody's hands. But I—"

"Decide."

"The boys can't know—"

"Decide."

"All right." Her voice was muffled. "No more."

"There could be, as you just put it, consequence."

"Agh!" She jerked her head back and flung a hand away. "There mustn't be!"

CHAPTER 6

Ben watched Andrew come down the stairs, leading the queue, moving the way Ben remembered. Loose-jointed and light as a leaf, almost as if falling from step to step, letting gravity bring him down. His brother. Well, his half-brother, but he never thought of it like that.

Ben saw with a jolt that he was thin. The prison jumpsuit had hidden that.

He swung the car door closed behind him and raised a hand. Andrew caught the movement, the freed men swirling around both of them now but Ben's height making him easy to spot. Ben made a move in Andrew's direction but checked it and waited beside the car, watching Andrew pushing through the crowd, nodding to this man or that, closing the distance between them. Ben flashed on something he'd read—something about prison life teaching inmates not to touch. But Andrew had always been a toucher, and Ben was having none of that. He wrapped his brother in a bear hug, briefly, until Andrew broke away with a barrage of back and shoulder claps.

They stood without Plexiglas between them for the first time in ten years, and studied each other. Tiredness lay on Andrew's face like a mask—up close, Ben could see tiny pleats of tension fanning from the corners of his eyes. Ben's gut clenched. The square jaw, the cleft chin, the spatter of freckle—those were the same. But a bump widened the bridge of his brother's nose and the tip was askew. Ben remembered a long-ago visit when Andrew had taken his place on the other side of the Plexiglas with his nose in a splint and both eyes blacked.

"You still look like Brad Pitt," Ben had said. "Only meaner."

"That all you got?" Ben asked, indicating the brown paper bag Andrew carried. "God, those clothes. Been a while since I saw those."

Andrew looked down at his baggy cords and slipover and wind-breaker in Texas A&M maroon and showed Ben a thin smile.

"Me, too."

The ex-cons straggled past, most heading for the Greyhound station, fifty bucks from the state in their pockets. They eyed Ben in passing, eyed his sparkling new cherry-red Porsche, his Napa leather jacket, his custom-cut trousers. His shoulder holster bulge.

So did Andrew, and Ben felt the intensity and curiosity in his gaze. When he went to prison, they were both college students—academic standouts vying with each other, each at their chosen universities. Their choices had been odd in and of themselves: Ben the bookworm at the pricey private institution with a "party school" reputation, and Andrew the fun-lover at a state school known for rigorous standards of discipline and hard work. Ben's nose a little closer to the grindstone than Andrew's, undeniably, but nothing new there.

Ben read it in Andrew's expression: what was new was Ben himself.

Detective Ben Gallagher . . .

"They know you're law," Andrew said, his eyes on the almost imperceptible bulge beneath Ben's bomber jacket.

Ben shrugged. "Force of habit."

Andrew nodded at the parolees, his smile broader now. "They know you're law, and they're trying to figure out how you got a new Porsche."

"Trying to figure out how to get it away from me, more like."

"Looks like we know some of the same people."

"Anyone you want to say goodbye to?"

Andrew ran a quick survey of the ex-cons surging past and shook his head. He moved around to the passenger side of Ben's car and turned slowly on his heel for a one-eighty view of the landscape. Ben's eyes followed his brother's to the horizon. Dallas' chill drizzle had dried as he'd driven south, and right now it wasn't raining. But you could see a new storm brewing in the southwest.

"Wish it were better weather," Ben said. "Few more weeks, we'd see some bluebonnets."

"Bluebonnets," Andrew said delightedly—as if bluebonnets were a good idea he'd almost forgotten.

They settled themselves in the car.

"No Bood?"

Dang. "Should I have brought him?"

"I just thought—well, he's my only nephew!"

"He loves to ride, but I thought he'd make you crazy wriggling in your lap for three hours. Plus he'd lick the eyeballs right out of your head."

Andrew peered at Ben. "You been drawing?" He swept a hand in a wave that encompassed the Walls Unit. "You make a picture of this?"

Ben frowned, then angled the rearview mirror so he could see his reflection. He took a tissue from the console, moistened it with saliva, scrubbed at the dark smudges on his cheek, and wiped his blackened thumb. Then he took his sketchbook from behind Andrew's seat and wordlessly handed it over.

Andrew inspected Ben's drawing, looking up at the Walls Unit and back at the sketch several times.

"This is really good. Can I keep it?"

"Sure."

Andrew studied the drawing again. Then he carefully closed the sketchbook's cover and glanced at Ben.

"Not a bad place to visit, but you wouldn't want to live there."

Ben laid a hand on his brother's shoulder for a second, then pulled away from the Walls Unit and headed for an exit.

"It's not a good place to visit, either."

They sped north on I-45 toward Dallas, storm clouds pushing them from behind. They'd been largely silent, but Ben welcomed the quiet, not really knowing what to say. Odd. They hadn't wondered what to say during ten years of Plexiglas between them—not then or on their sometimes marathon telephone conversations, whenever Andrew could squeeze the privilege from the prison staff.

Andrew rode with eyes closed, square hands quiet in his lap. Ben thought he seemed wary even when relaxed.

He realized he was seeing Andrew through the filter of a decade—as if the Plexiglas were still there—impenetrable, shatterproof. *Behind this transparent wall lies a world I know but that you don't and haven't and never will.* Ben had dreaded that truth. As unthinkable as losing Andrew had been, they had adjusted—Ben and Nell and Dayton. It was Andrew who was displaced, ripped from his environment, captive among strangers. Somehow he'd remained the star of their lives. But they'd stayed in the world while he removed to an alien place. And life happened for all of them—Andrew finishing his degree through the prison program, working at the library, becoming a computer geek. Nell, who didn't need to work at all, working her way to the directorship of her agency. Ben receiving his doctorate in Fine Arts but choosing police work anyway, becoming the Arlington PD's chief of detectives before he was thirty, moving to the Mid-Cities—a thirty-mile or so stretch between Dallas and Fort Worth, the whole area now a megalopolis. And Dayton—building his

Kalamazoo law firm just to abandon it, to retire and move to Dallas to be with Nell. After all these years.

Ben and Nell and Dayton, they tried to keep everything the same, for Andrew. And largely failed. Life happened. And there was no moment when they didn't believe—try as they may to forget it—that the real challenge was always, and would always be, Andrew's.

Ben tried to thrust aside time and absence, tried to see his brother in this faded stranger. And what came to mind was the child. Andrew might have been five again, standing in the schoolyard, tears glistening in his dusty lashes, not wanting to go to kindergarten, Ben saying, *It'll be all right.*

Andrew felt this awkward distance, too, Ben knew. Would Dayton? And Nell, waiting at the window? Ben considered Nell's preparations: the townhouse Andrew had never seen, the third-floor guest suite bristling with whatever she thought Andrew might enjoy. The garage housing a new Lexus SC luxury coupe convertible—white gold, ecru leather, aluminum top that lowered into the trunk in twenty seconds. And Dayton's preparations: the Knowlton Arms—for Andrew to manage, to own.

The Knowlton was a dignified old Dallas building and a fixture along the tourist route: nearby the book depository and the sixth-floor window where an assassin waited, the grassy knoll, the street where a president was slain. Now, its stolid sandstone accented with bright red awnings but still imposing in all its Victorian solemnity, the Knowlton served as both apartment building and hotel to its permanent and semi-permanent, tourist, and business clientele. From the past, the gift of a future. Nothing could undo Andrew's last ten years, but they'd do what they could. And their money would do what money could.

And maybe none of it would be enough.

Andrew stirred and stretched, and Ben cast about for something to say, something that wouldn't make him sound like an asshole. It was as if Andrew had been at war and had come home with hooks instead of hands, with Ben, the brother who didn't go, wondering what to say besides those empty words *I know how you feel.*

Andrew spoke first. "What's up with your nemesis these days?"

Ben rolled his eyes. "Malone. Cracko Jacko. Gone now, sort of. At least officially. Dirty to the end, though. Taking drugs from dealers in return for letting them be. When he couldn't get it free, he busted them and stole it. I offered him a Hobson's choice—retire or I'll turn you in."

"How'd that sit?"

"About how you think. But Jack Malone's—" he broke off. He wasn't going to dump his problems on his brother. Andrew had a full plate.

"What?"

Ben waved a dismissive hand. "Malone's Malone. He tails me from time to time in his big black Chevy pickup. Sometimes he calls in the middle of the night, hangs up, shit like that."

Ben didn't say the rest, that Malone always had to have an enemy, a goal, someone to hate and hound. Jack Malone. The unearned features of an ascetic. Faded blonde hair, flaxen lash and brow, flesh the waxen color of a plucked chicken. And just enough skin to cover the bone. In Malone's taut face, what might have been bright Irish eyes were glacial instead, and narrowed to gun slits.

Ben recalled one of Malone's outbursts, rare only because it was directed at him.

"What do you know about real detective work?" He'd hurled the question at Ben furiously. "Or the tough choices real cops have to make? You just dabble. And why not, with Momma's dough and your degrees and artwork? Run into a rough patch, just run to Momma, or sell another picture." He'd affected a limp-wristed stance and with an imaginary paintbrush between thumb and forefinger, daubed at an invisible canvas. "I was a cop, and a good one, Gallagher, while you were a still a squalling infant."

Malone's attack, unsettling as it was, had also been a revelation. Before this outburst, Ben hadn't fully realized Malone's hatred, nor its source and depth. And he wondered: How many of the other cops felt the same?

"Meantime," he said to Andrew. "I have to deal with Jack's buddies. Ramsey Ratzlaff, for one. I'm not sure how closely I need to watch him. Kenechi says he's a good cop. So does the chief. But I—" He shook his head. "I sound as paranoid as Jacko."

"Kenechi."

"My new partner. And going from Jacko to Kenechi Akundi is like going from Little League to major league. Or, no—let's make that from *bush* league to major league. Kenechi's from Nigeria. Educated here, though. Has a doctorate in chemical engineering." He glanced over at Andrew. "You have breakfast?"

"Hell, no. Get stoked up on prison food?"

"We'll stop. What are you in the mood for?"

Andrew gave the little falsetto chuckle that Ben loved.

"Let's see. No chicken-fried steak. No grits and gravy. No black-eyed peas. No Tex-Mex. No Jell-O. No white bread. No limp, gray-green string beans. No—" He looked at Ben. "Is it true there's a restaurant near the Walls Unit that serves what they call Killer Burgers?"

Ben nodded. He'd seen the sign.

"Okay, no Killer Burgers," Andrew said. "Seafood? I mean real seafood?"

"For breakfast?" Ben grinned. "Well, why the hell not. Good place up here in a bit. Shrimp, catfish, crawfish." He drew his cellphone from his jacket pocket. "You need to call Ma."

"When we stop."

That needed to be private, Ben realized, replacing the phone. He saw that the bank of cloud had closed in behind them in a boomerang shape. A few fat raindrops hit the windshield with soft splats.

"Don't think we can outrun that storm," Ben said. "It's moving pretty fast."

"Wouldn't mind a good storm." Andrew spoke so softly Ben barely caught the words. "Blow the prison off me. I wouldn't mind that one bit."

He reached into his paper bag and pulled out a Marine Band harmonica.

"You still got that?" Ben asked. "Nobody kicked it to pieces?"

"Not this one. They liked it. You still play?"

"Yeah. Especially when I'm on a case and can't clear my mind. That, or paint."

"You got it with you?"

"Nah. Play something."

They fell into another short silence, but there was something in the moment Ben didn't want to lose.

"Andrew. You're out of there, buddy. It's over."

But the words sounded easy or insufficient or trivial, even in his own ears—so he added, "It'll be all right." He was that big brother again, with the big brother's brio or bravado or whatever it was.

Forever after, when Ben remembered this day, it was this moment and these words he'd recall. *It'll be all right.* He didn't say this day would destroy their dreams and alter their future. He didn't say that because he didn't know it—of course he didn't know it. So he promised it would be all right, and they sped north, toward the day.

"Play something," he urged again, and Andrew raised the harmonica to his lips. He blew softly, eyes closed, bending and stretching the notes, sliding them into a blues melody Ben didn't recognize. The sound blended with the roar of the engine as the Porsche hurtled along the I-road like a steel cocoon, a time capsule compressing ten years into three hours.

Ben glanced at the view framed in the rearview mirror. Nothing but agitated sky. No horizon, no road leading to prison.

Huntsville and the last decade swallowed up by distance and lurching cloud.

Andrew's music died away as the first serious raindrops slapped at the car. Then the storm surrounded them, slashing at the windows and the wipers, buffeting the Porsche as it sped north past vacant fields. Andrew lowered the window and braced himself, leaning his face into the driving wet, letting the wind tear noisily through the car, letting it tear through his hair, rain mixing with tears.

CHAPTER 7

So here's Sean Penn walking into the Cachet fuckin' Day Spa, Jimmy Snipes was thinking. *Come to see his lady. Looking good. Black suit, saffron accents. Yeah.*

He saw Dollie standing on a stool, Abner handing her some little gold boxes.

"So who," he asked, "wants to hop her cute ass off that stool and take a break?"

Abner warily shrugged into his doorman's coat and put on his cap.

"Not right now, Jimmy," Dollie said.

"Come on. Just down the street. Get a bite at the Ripe Olive."

"Ripe Olive," Zora said. "I'm going. Now."

"That's good, Zora," Dollie said.

Abner moved over to Dollie, and she put a hand on his shoulder and jumped down.

"Ab, can you take those empty boxes to the back room?"

He hesitated, and she nodded reassuringly.

"It's okay. Just take the boxes out, and you can come right back."

"Get Mr. Slaughter," she said under her breath as he passed.

"I don't want to walk down there, Jimmy. It's starting to rain," she said. "Or anywhere else, for that matter. So put it out of your mind, and we'll be just fine."

His face got ugly. "I thought we were just fine already."

She didn't respond, and he narrowed his eyes.

"You're dumping me."

"It's not a case of dumping, Jimmy. We've only had a few dates. Casual dates, if you'll recall."

"You're dumping me."

"Fine. Have it your way."

"Why?"

"Do I need a reason? I think I have the right to see you or not see you."

"And I have the right to know why."

"I disagree, but . . ." She lifted a shoulder. "I plan to discuss this only once. You were going to kick my dog. You crushed a cat's skull and laughed about it."

"Fuckin' dogs? Fuckin' cats? That's what we're talking about here?"

"I don't like mean people. You do mean things, so I don't like you. That's all I'm going to say."

Dollie went behind the counter. Get something between them. She didn't like the color of his complexion.

"Fuck you! I want the rest."

Their eyes met, hers like blue fire. "You have problems that I don't want—"

"Problems!"

He lunged at her, and she drew back, frightened.

"Problems! What problems, you lying bitch?"

The blue flame in her eyes turned to blue steel, but she said nothing.

"What problems?" he yelled.

"You're a hypochondriac. For just one thing. But that's no big deal."

"A hypochondriac? Why, because I own a thermometer?"

She sighed dramatically.

Jimmy looked around. There wasn't anyone in the reception area, but he could see people milling around in the lobby. *Fuck 'em. Here's Sean having a little lovers' quarrel. Stay cool. The greatest of ease.*

"You said that was no big deal."

Dollie sighed again.

"Don't make me hafta ask."

"Being mean is the main thing. But you believe things I don't believe. Silly things. Like people with allergies are superior, just because you have allergies. Like short people are superior. Like short men have made the greatest contributions to the world, just because you're short."

"What's this *about?* That's just a little historical *fact* that I happened to share with you because you're a short person! A short person like you should fuckin' appreciate that."

"I looked up short men on the Internet."

He eyed her suspiciously.

"And it's true," she went on, "that a lot of famous men have been short."

He was interested. "Like who?"

"I said *famous.* I didn't say great."

"And I said *like who?*"

"And I don't know if they made *great* contributions."

"Like *who.*"

"The point is, Jimmy, it doesn't matter whether you're short or tall. There are great short men and lousy tall men. And vice versa. Being great doesn't have anything to do with . . . it matters what you are inside—you can be great either way. Trouble is, you find meaning in everything, even stuff that doesn't matter, and apply it to yourself."

She sighed yet again to show how sick she was of the subject of Jimmy Snipes.

"Like when I told you that a study said blue was the favorite color of the insane. And you tossed all your blue hankies and ties and socks and shirts!" For emphasis, she slapped her hand down on the counter with a clash of bracelets. "As if that could make you sane."

"Like *who,* I said."

She threw up a palm in resignation. "Adolf Hitler, for one. His doctor said he was five feet seven. But another guy said Hitler was the same height as Joseph Stalin, and Stalin was only five feet six."

Jimmy saw where she was going, and an angry red flush started at his neck and moved upwards.

"Mussolini and Hirohito were five feet five or six," she went on. "And Khrushchev was only five feet three."

"Shut your mouth," he said through clenched teeth, grabbing her wrist.

She pulled away and returned his gaze, eyes steady. "The Marquis de Sade was five feet six, and Baby Face Nelson was even shorter. And you're tall next to Bonnie and Clyde—he was less than five feet seven, and she was only four feet ten."

He came around the counter, pulled her to him with an arm around her shoulders and with his free hand pinched her cheeks hard, pursing her lips.

"I told you to shut your mouth."

Her blue eyes filled, and she tried to speak, but his hold on her was too tight. When he relaxed his grip a little, she said, "Charles Manson is five feet five."

Fury flooded Jimmy's face, and he drew back a fist. But Dayton Slaughter was there, grabbing Jimmy's hand in mid-air, jerking him around and throwing him against the wall—into the racks of hair supplies and cosmetics, little gold boxes and brushes and jars and bottles and aerosol cans falling down all around him, bringing gawkers from the lobby and caped clients from behind the pink curtains to gape at him, mouths open and wet heads swathed in towels. They saw a small man in a black suit climbing out of a pile of cosmetics, face aflame, a wide swath of disheveled brown hair standing away from his scalp like a wing. His saffron tie and pocket silk matched the saffron socks that peeked above his shining Italian loafers, and his trouser creases were so sharp they looked set with a steamroller. His face still aflame, eyes on Dayton, he brushed at his jacket and reflexively raised slender fingers to comb back the swath of hair, but Dayton grabbed him by the sleeve, jerked him toward the door, almost carried him with one large hand, and shoved him into the lobby.

"Don't come in here again, you little bastard."

Jimmy looked at his suit coat. "You ripped my sleeve!"

"Don't touch her again."

"You ripped my sleeve, you sonsabitch."

"Get out of here while you can, or I'll rip off your whole silly suit and shove it up your ass. Along with your shiny new shoes."

"You sonsabitch. I live here."

"Not for long, you don't."

Jimmy repositioned his silk handkerchief in his breast pocket, flung a threatening backward glance at Dollie, and moved unsteadily to the Knowlton's marble entry. He brushed by the gawkers and by Abner, who held a brass-framed door in one hand and a big black umbrella in the other. Abner watched him walk under the red canvas of the canopy to the curb and called after him, "Want me to get your car, Mr. Jimmy?"

Jimmy didn't answer. He was trying to get around a large woman on the wet sidewalk—a woman of indeterminate age in a plaid scarf and an assemblage of ill-matched clothing, as if she'd dressed out of a clothes dryer. She placed herself in Jimmy's path and held out a flier that asked in big red letters, *Are you Doomed?*

"Excuse me, my boy," she asked with exaggerated courtesy, "but may I compliment you on your pretty yellow tie?"

"I ain't your boy, you creepy old bag. Get out the way."

"And yellow socks?"

"*Saffron* to you, looney tunes."

"Saffron!" Zora cried. "Hare Krishna! The name of the Su-preme! Also known as *Rama,* rhymes with *drama!* And that's all I can say about that. Allow me . . ." She placed an experimental fingertip on Jimmy's tie, her chin outthrust. He jerked and raised a palm. She didn't flinch; her doughy face loomed nearer, eyes squeezed to green slits. "Allow me to inquire if you have accepted Jesus Christ as your savior?"

"Yeah, sure," Jimmy said, sidling to get past her. "Now beat it."

"I can tell you're afraid," she said, laying a dirty hand on his sleeve. "Don't be afraid. I'm—"

"*What?* Get your hands off my suit!" It was almost a scream, making passersby stare at him yet again. He stepped back, splash-ing one shiny Italian loafer into a puddle and soaking his saffron sock. He withdrew his foot daintily, almost as a dance step, and he and the woman circled one another in a brief choreography under the red canopy before he cried, "Get the hell away, you crazy hag!"

"If I'm not in my alley," the woman announced, finger in the air, "I'll be on my sidewalk."

Abner hurried back through the glass doors and into the Ca-chet.

"Boy's gettin' all worked up out there with Zora, Dollie. I'd better bring her back in. Okay with you? Anyways, her umbrella's all tore up."

Dollie looked at Dayton, who paused, then nodded.

"Sure, Ab," he said. "Bring her on in."

CHAPTER 8

Friday, February 21

They arrived in Dallas beneath a low iron-colored sky and in heavy afternoon traffic worsened by brief bouts of rain. Andrew had been sitting back, eyes closed, trying to relax his taut muscles, but now he jerked himself erect and pulled the seatback forward. He watched intently as Ben exited Central Expressway at Fitzhugh and made several left turns to get to McKinney, which was one-way along this stretch. Ben pulled the Porsche onto a paved drive fronting a row of Colonial-style townhomes and pointed with his thumb.

"Number Twenty-Two, Andrew. I'm going to let you go in alone while I go park the car."

Andrew hesitated a second, eyes on Ben's profile, then got out and crossed in front of the Porsche, paper bag tucked under his arm. He brushed a hand at the trembling raindrops beading the car's hood, wiped a wet palm on his baggy pants, and headed for the townhome.

Nell waited in the doorway, her slender figure backlit by yellow light. She reached for him the instant he was near and hugged him close. He stood awkwardly within her embrace, one hand holding his paper bag and the other patting her on the back.

"How was the trip up?" she asked, her voice tremulous.

"We didn't see any bluebonnets."

She held him away to search his face and look into his eyes, her own bright with unshed tears.

"I can feel your ribs."

He stood at the sink in Nell's second-floor guest bath—a small and glittering room—and felt numb. From the second-floor living area, he heard the murmur of Nell's and Ben's voices. And drifting down from *his* quarters on the third-floor, he heard the strains of "O Patria Mia," one of the pieces on a CD of Verdi arias. Nell had shown him the suite she'd prepared for him, her arm in his, pointing out the state-of-the-art computer equipment and sound system and other electronic luxuries. He'd admired his new car. He'd chatted with his mother and brother, and munched on croissants and fruit and cheese and pâté. Dayton had called to say he'd see him soon and had something special to tell him.

And now he and Ben were leaving to get his driver's license. And to buy him some clothes that fit.

He took a deep breath. *Overload.*

He lathered his hands with a fragrant oval of amber-colored soap, rinsed in a flow of warm water from a shining brass spigot, and dried with a soft towel the color of whipped butter. Earlier this morning he'd washed in icy water, dried with rough brown paper, stood at a steel sink dull with scum next to an open toilet emanating the odor of waste and urine. As he had for more than thirty-six hundred mornings before.

Bracing his palms against the marble vanity, he leaned toward the mirror, his hazel eyes searching his own image. Who was he, then? An unexpected wave of weariness washed over him—weariness when he hadn't even begun, when he thought he would be clicking his heels and high-fiving.

When did things work the way you thought?

Yesterday, a fellow library trusty had placed a heavy hand on his shoulder and murmured, "Won't be the same without you, bro." And truth had placed a heavy hand on his other shoulder: While he was in here and learning to be, *here,* those he loved on the outside were learning to be, *there.* Without him.

He contemplated his unhealthy pallor in the sparkling mirror and thought how things seemed somehow faded in prison. He remembered being startled by Nell's and Ben's high coloring when they visited—ruddy-cheeked, vivid blue eyes. And Dayton in his perfectly tailored dark suits and snowy starched shirts, radiating a sense of purpose and energy even as he merely sat on the other side of the Plexiglas. Visitors from a world forbidden.

Andrew examined his jutting cheekbones, his straw-like hair. He decided that his overall aspect was as brittle as a locust shell, his hands raspy and freckled as a trout. He saw how his buttoned shirt gapped at the throat, making his neck look scrawny. He was not the person he remembered. He pulled himself up and squared his shoulders. He'd get some sun, some clothes that fit—maybe keep his mother from tearing up when she looked at him.

Giving his mirrored image a final, lingering glance, he stepped into the bright foyer on the second-floor landing. The tall oak clock he remembered from his childhood chimed twice. He moved to the clock and stared at its face, then laid a hand on its stout belly. It was like greeting an old friend. He moved to the opposite wall of the landing and to a large armoire, its doors open to reveal a lit interior and shelves filled with framed photos documenting Ben's and Andrew's infancy, boyhood, and college years.

Then Ben alone. No Andrew. For a decade.

On the adjacent wall hung a large American flag under Plexiglas. Andrew had grown up with that flag—the shroud for Benjamin Ryan's coffin, back from Vietnam. Below the flag was a fruitwood console that bore a single framed photo enlarged to graininess. It was a black-and-white shot of a student rally, circa late '60s, anti-war banners fluttering on the breeze. Two tall, slender young people stood in front, looking into the camera, long dark hair blowing across their faces—an unsmiling Nell Gallagher and Benjamin Ryan, leaning into each other, dark heads together, fingers extending peace signs.

Andrew had grown up with that photograph as well. There was no time in his life when it hadn't graced this particular console beneath that particular flag. He knew the young man and woman and their images in the same way he knew himself and his brother in their old school photos. He picked up the picture and brought the young people close—as he'd done many times privately when he was a child. He stared deeply into their eyes, two sets of bright blue eyes made black and unfathomable by the camera. They returned his gaze as they always had, somberly and frozen in time. And the shock of recognition Andrew felt seemed like . . . like coming home.

He returned the picture to the console and looked at the small brass plaque adorning the flag's frame:

Benjamin Andrew Ryan
February 12, 1947–May 5, 1970

He turned slowly to view the photo display in the armoire, the flag, the framed photograph of his mother and Benjamin Ryan . . . nothing of Andrew's own father. Growing up, Andrew had been only minimally curious. Besides, throughout his boyhood, he'd secretly pretended Dayt was his father. And he *was*—at least he might as well have been. And Nell never talked about his real father, so okay, there must be nothing to say.

But now . . . how bad could it be? How bad could *he* be? A one-night stand, some inappropriate liaison, married guy, whatever—Nell newly widowed, a young mother alone and unmarried, her baby's father killed in Vietnam. And beautiful! And rich!

Fuck it, he'd ask Dayton. Insist on some basic information. Not *who* his father was so much as *what* he was. That's all he needed to know.

"Pondering your place in the universe?" Nell stood in the doorway of her second-floor living area, shoulder against the casing.

"Exactly."

"You're absent from that little photo gallery for a while, Andrew. But that's where you belong."

She swept a hand at the armoire.

"I know I've said this a million times, but you didn't belong in prison. You were never one of them. You're one of us." Her voice quavered. "There are no pictures of you in prison jumpsuits because that's never going to be our truth. We'll have new pictures."

He realized she thought he was hurt by his ten-year absence from her photo display, and he almost smiled. Rather, the dry husk of the man he'd just examined in the bathroom mirror—that tired, lined, maimed man who'd done hard time—*that* man almost smiled.

"We'll have new pictures, Andrew," she went on, an appeal in her voice. "Pictures of you in your thirties and forties and fifties . . . With your wife and children. With my grandbabies."

Now he *did* smile. Nell the orphan, with her never-ending dream of *family*.

"Grandbabies! Ma. You might wait at least until my second day home to bring up babies."

She smiled back—and without a trace of guilt.

"Ben said I should prepare myself," Andrew added. "Says you don't let up for a second."

She sniffed. "Damned straight."

Both of them relaxed. It felt good.

"Actually, Ma, I *was* sort of pondering my place in the universe. But not in the way you think. Actually—"

He realized he was speaking carefully, falling back automatically into old patterns. Nell, nurturing and gentle as she was, could also be remote and uncommunicative. And she could withdraw in an instant if she thought you were trying to take her somewhere she didn't want to go. It was a trait Ben instinctively understood because it was a trait he shared. And Dayt? Andrew wasn't sure.

But he himself had learned long ago that the best way to navigate those particular shoals was to steer away.

"Actually?" she prompted, wearing a small smile of encouragement.

He waited a beat before answering. "I was wondering about my father."

Her smile froze.

"Ma. I just need to know—" He broke off, already sorry he'd spoken.

After a long silence, she seemed to find her own voice, but it was flat and cold. "What do you need to know, Andrew?"

"I need to know if . . . well, if he was a bad person. You know, what kind of genes I inherited."

She stood so still and looked so undone that he wished he could take back the words—whatever the truth, what did it matter *now?* Why had he brought this up, and on his first day? He'd ruined everything.

He patted her shoulder awkwardly.

"Never mind, Ma. Just never mind. We won't talk about it. It'll be fine."

Fuck it! He'd ask Dayton.

CHAPTER 9

Dayton crested a rise near the Trinity River and saw a mess on the other side of I-30. One car lay on its top and ambulance workers huddled at the driver's side. A red pickup with a demolished front end sat in the median. Glass and scraps of auto were strewn over the freeway amid emergency cones and flares. And, as far as the eye could see, stalled traffic.

Gawkers slowed him, but he still made decent time and the Jaguar was settling into the stretch leading to Arlington when his cell rang. Nell's voice was tight with suppressed excitement.

"Where are you?"

Flying past to his left was the Six Flags amusement park's enormous Titan roller coaster with its looming orange-and-turquoise spirals, lifts, and drops.

"On my way to Ben's."

"Oh crapola. I wanted to go with you. I've been to the florist, thought I could catch you. The boys are running errands."

"Our dinner reservations are for eight?"

"Yes." She made a snap decision. "I'll join you—I'll just hop on I-30. The boys might run over to Arlington, too."

"There was a tie-up near the Trinity."

"Where are you now?"

"Just passing Six Flags."

He maneuvered the Jaguar onto Fielder, traveled south, and turned into Aycliffe Court. Ben's place was at the top of a little rise on Aycliffe, a cul-de-sac not far from Rangers Ballpark. Dayton pulled into Ben's semicircular drive, which was mostly obscured by a stand of mature trees, their leaves almost black from a day of intermittent rain. He thought briefly about avoiding the dripping leaves by pulling around to Ben's garage, but that meant driving back onto the street to the corner and turning into the drive running behind the house and past the garage. Instead, he parked all the way around in the half-moon to leave room for Nell—and for the boys if they showed up—and got out of the car. He unloaded a couple of bags from the back seat—fancy gourmet stuff for a welcome basket that he hoped would gladden the heart of even an ex-con. Shifting his burden to one arm, he unlocked the iron gate to Ben's courtyard. It opened with a metallic rasp.

A cobblestone walk cut through the brick-walled courtyard to Ben's front entrance. Low-growing juniper flanked the walk, then a manicured hedge of glossy holly, then the arching branches of bridal wreath spirea, still weighted with rain. On one wall, a copper flat-panel fountain had oxidized to a green patina. Ben had forgotten to turn it off when he left for Huntsville that morning, and its falling waters seemed melancholy and redundant as Dayton passed through the courtyard.

He stepped into the sheltered entrance, found the key on his key ring and let himself into the hush of the closed house. It bore a faint scent of Ben's aftershave. The security system emitted its series of warning yelps, and Dayton punched in the code. From the direction of the master bedroom, he heard a small *thump*— Bood jumping off the bed—then the little dog's nails scrabbling on the hardwood floors.

"Boodles!" Dayton called. "Mr. Bood!"

Bood was on him in a frenzy of leaps and licks. Dayton set down his bags and knelt, stroking the animal's black curls and rubbing his sturdy little back. And off Bood tore down the hall, glancing back with a joyful grin. He was headed for his toy basket, Dayton knew, a large wicker basket overflowing with toys that Bood had greeted once and then ignored—the bear with the silken auburn hair, the soft aqua hippo, the long-legged monkey with striped stockings, all offering splendid grunts and growls, squeals and squeaks.

But the toy Bood truly loved was the ball. And not just any ball. He loved the little orange basketball with the voice box that gave off a cry like a wounded parrot. And here he came now—dreadlocks flopping, the orange ball squawking in his black muzzle. Dayton took his bags to the kitchen and set them on the granite island, then obediently tossed the ball down the hallway toward the living room, Bood scrambling to seize the ball between his teeth, drop it at Dayton's feet, and look up at him expectantly, tongue lolling

Dayton laughed.

"You and your ball. No. Go pee."

He led Bood to his doggy door, and Bood leapt through, obediently lifting his leg on a shrub. Then he rushed back to retrieve his ball and follow Dayton into the living room.

Dayton opened the armoire that held the sound system and pressed the power button on the CD player. With the first soft strains of Mahler's Fifth drifting from the speakers, he went back to the kitchen, snapped on the lights, and poured himself a modest glass of Dewar's Signature Blend. He took his time arranging his welcome basket and, Bood at his heels, wandered back into the living room to set it on a cocktail table.

Dayton loved visiting Ben's immaculate, ordered home. Nell once said that Ben's house and garden were like Ben himself: polished and orderly but contained and aloof, refusing to surrender secrets. Dayton didn't disagree. But he'd always had a soft spot for Nell's elder son. People gravitated to Andrew's warmth, but Dayton loved Ben for the same qualities of reflection and reserve he loved in Nell.

He stopped a minute to admire the room. Everything was as he remembered—spare and restrained, its creamy walls punctuated with accents of bold color, Ben's taste running to symmetrical design and modern furniture and art. Two pale, tailored sofas faced each other—perpendicular to the fireplace and flanked by Ben's favorite chair, a wide and deep bergère.

Dayton realized he was enjoying himself. Despite everything, he was enjoying himself—the scotch warming his middle, the music of Mahler's *Adagietto* swelling. He was flattered to see on the mantel the Modigliani bust he'd given Ben on his last birthday. Above it hung a large oil Dayton hadn't seen—an abstract in black, white, and gray, with splashes of Chinese red and yellow. He stepped closer and examined the canvas. He recognized the style. A mixture of textures: heavy knife work, and brush strokes by turns as delicate as Dali's and as robust and eccentric as Van Gogh's. A welter of razor-thin, diagonal black lines stretched from corner to corner—as if laid down with a plumb line. Ben's signature at lower right.

He walked down the hall to Ben's studio. He was always interested in Ben's works-in-progress, and as he expected, a canvas covered with a protective cloth leaned on the easel. It was a large canvas—not as large as Ben often worked, but large, twenty-four by thirty, Dayton guessed. He lifted the cloth and studied the unfinished painting. It was looser and more angular than much of Ben's work, a series of rectangles that Dayton saw on closer examination seemed to be doorways with differently colored doors opened to varying widths. And, hard right, one large door, firmly closed with an infinitely black slab—the door not taken, Dayton knew. He peered at the closed door and saw that its black, which seemed to drink up the light, wore daubs of deep brown and ultramarine, together lending depth and both warming and cooling the black.

The overall palette was different from Ben's usual choices. There was Ben's trademark Chinese red and sunlit yellow and sparkling white, but one partially open door was turquoise, a decided turquoise, too—nothing tentative about it. Interesting. It was a color Dayton knew Ben disliked—and disliked enough to try to explain. It was a marriage of color that was at once unsettlingly aggressive and retiring, he'd said, a marriage of the two least pleasing colors in the spectrum. Not that you could do without blue or green, but you could certainly do without turquoise.

Dayton, smiling, stood back and nodded approval.

Yet, even here in his art, Ben held something back. Nell was right. Was Ben a cop with a doctorate in Fine Arts, or an artist who split his talents in the pursuit of justice? To which did he give his hundred percent? With Nell, with Dayton himself, even with Andrew, he kept some central part of himself in reserve.

"You think I'm a dilettante?" Ben had asked him once.

Dayton had put a hand on his shoulder.

"Not yet," he'd said gently.

Dayton was in Ben's foyer unfurling a string of bright foil letters when he heard the iron rasp of the courtyard gate and footsteps on the cobblestones.

He looked at his watch, not quite five. She'd made good time.

Bood growled, and Dayt bent to stroke him.

"It's okay, buddy." He fondled the little dog's topknot of tangled curl. "It's Granny."

But Bood put his tail down and backed hard against Dayton's legs, watching the door.

CHAPTER 10

Ben pulled Andrew's Lexus into the left-turn lane just as a big black Chevy pickup lurched out of his cul-de-sac, careened through the intersection, and sped away. The driver slouched in the seat, head averted, eyes hidden behind mirrored sunglasses.

Malone. Unmistakably Malone.

"What the hell's with that guy," Andrew said. "He a neighbor? Or incognito?"

Ben shook his head but didn't say more. Aycliffe Court had only six residents and no reason for through-traffic. But this wasn't the first time Ben had seen Jacko's big truck cruising the cul-de-sac. He tamped down the little tempest of fury whipped up by Malone's juvenile behavior—he had more important things to think about right now. He pulled into Aycliffe Court and up the little rise to his half-moon drive.

"That Dayton's Jag?" Andrew asked.

"Great. We haven't missed him."

Ben led the way through the iron gate and into his courtyard, he and Andrew stepping inside to the sound of the fountain's cascading water and the soaring strings of Mascagni's *Cavalleria Rusticana*. The music drifted through Ben's front door, which stood a little ajar.

"Odd." Ben frowned, something triggering his cop's sixth sense, and stopped Andrew with a hand to his chest.

"Man, it's *Dayton*." Andrew tried to brush past, but Ben blocked him.

"Wait." Ben said, packing urgency into the word. "Dayt wouldn't leave the door like that. And where's Bood? He always—"

They stood a moment, listening, and Ben reached under his jacket and drew his Glock semiautomatic.

"*What*—" Andrew began.

"Stay here," Ben mouthed.

He slipped into the defused light of the foyer and waited until his eyes adjusted. The kitchen lights were on, but the rest of the house was shrouded in February gloom. The final strains of Mascagni faded, and the CD changer moved on to Callas singing an aria from *La Wally*. Ben took several silent strides to the living room.

Dayton's familiar figure lay slumped against a sofa, half-lying, half-sitting—Bood motionless beside him, his chin on Dayton's thigh. Hearing Ben's gasp, the little dog raised his head. He was so black he drank up the light, but Ben saw the shine of his eyes beneath his snarl of curl. He lay as wary and still as the day Ben had found him half-dead in a crack-house closet.

Ben felt Andrew behind him.

"My God! Dayt! Is he—"

Heart leaping, Ben was across the room in three bounds, squatting beside the body, touching Dayton's flesh. Warm. A small round wound in his right temple. Very little blood, at least from this side. Ben laid two fingertips on the side of Dayton's neck, over a carotid. He rose and, still without speaking, put up a cautionary hand to Andrew and moved swiftly through the brightly lit kitchen and up the stairs, Glock raised. Then he was back, Andrew still standing white-faced and frozen, staring at the dead man.

Ben returned to the body, scooped up Bood, and laid him in Andrew's arms.

"It's okay, buddy." He rubbed the animal's head. "Andrew. Hang onto Bood. Don't move or touch anything."

Ben crossed to the foyer closet and brought out a black leather bag, set it on the floor, extracted a pair of thin latex gloves, and smoothed them onto his hands. He went to the armoire and pressed the OFF button on the CD player. In the sudden hush, the only sounds were the rain's light patter and the fountain's soft plash. He switched on a table lamp and again squatted beside the body. Dayton's skin was blue-gray. Lips and nails pale. No lividity or rigor.

"Less than three hours," Ben said. "Could be less than half an hour."

A .22 caliber pistol lay in Dayton's lap. Clutched in his right hand was a string of red foil letters encrusted with gold and silver sparkles. Ben carefully poked a gloved finger at the letters. Party decorations. He realized that if he pulled the cord taut, the letters would spell *Welcome Home, Andrew.*

He leaned in to examine the bullet hole in Dayton's right temple. No exit wound. He extended an index finger and touched the rim of the wound.

"What . . ." Andrew's voice was choked.

"The wound has stippling or tattooing around it, but no burn rim, no soot."

"Tattooing is from gunpowder?"

"Gunpowder particles embedded in the skin. You can't wipe them off, like you can soot."

"What's the range?" Andrew asked.

"Six to eight inches."

"He do it himself?"

Ben looked up. Andrew's face was wet, and Ben felt tears spring to his own eyes.

"Suicides don't hold a gun away from their heads like that. They put it close or even touching the skin—leaves a burn rim around the bullet hole, sometimes a star-shaped wound from the explosion of gases between bone and skin."

He rose, knees creaking, and flipped open his cell phone.

"Besides," he added, "the wound's in Dayton's right temple."

He punched in a single digit on his speed dial.

"Dayton was left-handed," Andrew said, shifting Bood's weight to one arm and wiping his eyes with his free hand.

"You got it." Ben spoke into the phone and snapped it shut. "Pretty hard to fire a gun into your right temple with your left hand. They'll check his hands for gunpowder residue, but they won't find it."

He scowled.

"Can you find your way back to Ma's?"

"Sure."

"Then go."

"What? Leave a crime scene?"

Ben plucked at his lip, his expression torn. "Go. We got like five minutes."

Andrew stared at him.

"Andrew! You can't be mixed up in this! You just got out of prison. On parole."

"I was with *you*."

Ben tugged Bood into his own arms and urged Andrew back toward the courtyard. Then he stopped short.

"Shit! Ma!"

"Ah, Jesus . . ."

"I'll call her." Ben handed him the car keys. "Go to the end of the cul-de-sac and head for Fielder."

"I know the way."

"Fielder will take you to I-30."

"I know."

Go east on—"

"Goddammit, Ben!"

Ben handed him his cell phone.

"Turn this on. Punch number three for Ma if you—"

They heard a siren in the distance.

"Hurry!" Ben said. "Get clear of this neighborhood, then pull over. Get familiar with . . . whatever—wipers, blinkers, brights, dimmers. It's getting dark, and the roads are wet. Find the hazard lights in case you have to pull over on the I-road. And for God's sake, don't drive fast."

"Jesus Christ!"

"You always used to drive too fast."

"I used to do a lot of things."

Andrew headed for the door and turned around. "I don't like this."

But he kept moving. Turned around again.

"Your car's at Ma's."

"I'll say you dropped me. Go! Call my cell the minute you get to Ma's."

Andrew held up a hand, Ben's cell phone in it.

"Agghh, my home then. Or the station."

Andrew pocketed the phone and turned back to the living room.

"Wait just a second."

He stepped quickly to Dayton's body and knelt, laying his fingertips briefly against the dead man's cheek and bending to press his lips against Dayton's hand, careful not to disturb the spangles meant to welcome him home. Then he wordlessly brushed past Ben, his eyes wet, and headed into the courtyard. Ben followed, Bood cradled in his arms. He watched Andrew disappear through the iron gate, heard the gate rasp, then clink. Waited. Heard the Lexus start and saw its pale shape move out of the half-moon drive, make a competent sweep to the left, and head down the hill toward the end of the cul-de-sec.

"Lights," he whispered.

The Lexus' lights flicked on, the taillights like twin cigarette embers diminishing down the slope, the right one winking briefly before the car slipped beneath a streetlamp and disappeared around the corner.

Ben stood where he was, mindless of the drizzle, staring at nothing, fingers pressed against his head like a clairvoyant. He heard a second siren join the first. Then, with a ragged oath, he jerked into action—shifted Bood to one arm, thrust his hand into his pocket for his cell phone. But of course—he cursed again, dashed inside, set Bood on his feet in the kitchen, grabbed the landline phone, punched in his cell number.

"Pick up, Andrew, pick up," he breathed.

One ring, then a pleasant voice said his party was unavailable. He smashed his thumb on the OFF button, then ON, and tried again.

"We're sorry. The person you called is not—"

Goddammit! Andrew hadn't turned on the phone! Goddammit to hell! He slammed the phone into its base. Then he despairingly grabbed it up and tried again, disbelieving.

"Pick up, Andrew," he groaned.

Nothing.

What had he done? Police headed this way from the west and south, Andrew headed east to Dallas. What the fuck had he done! *Never lie!* If this job had taught him anything, it had taught him not to lie. The lie is always a snare, forcing you to create new lies to cover the first one. Unless, of course, you're guilty—then lie like hell, as every cop knows. Andrew the ex-con had been right, and he, chief of detectives, had been wrong. Dead wrong. Do it Ben's way, and Andrew would have no alibi. He'd have to lie. So would Nell. So would Ben. He'd boxed them all in.

Always a mistake to lie.

Standing at the fogged window above his kitchen sink, the one looking directly into the courtyard, Ben saw a pale shape slide into the half-moon drive, swoop past the iron gate and stop, its taillights just in view, then going dark. For a millisecond, Ben thought it was his fellow cops. But, no. They wouldn't answer a homicide call-out silently—or in a Lexus SC luxury coupe convertible.

He dashed into the courtyard and opened the gate. And Andrew came in—strolled in, actually, his hands in his pockets—and looked Ben in the eye.

"I just spent a bunch of time where I couldn't run even if I wanted to, Ben. So I'm all out of practice. I'm not running. And I'm not lying."

For a moment, Ben was almost overwhelmed with pride and gladness, his throat too tight to speak. Then he clapped his brother on the shoulder and managed a few strangled words.

"Ahh, Andrew. Ahh, thank God."

Yet another siren came up from the south to join the others—all of them screaming close now.

PART TWO

If that mockingbird don't sing,
Mama's gonna buy you a diamond ring.

CHAPTER 11

Ben dragged himself from a ragged and fitful sleep in the Arlington motel room the office had booked for him the night before. Like a man waking from a coma, he opened his eyes groggily, gradually becoming aware—weak light sifting through the narrow openings in the ugly vinyl-backed draperies, Bood snoring lightly beside him, flat on his back, paws in the air, exposing his fat black tummy. Ben had been dreaming about Dayton and Andrew and Nell . . . something he couldn't remember now.

What he could remember had been no dream. More like a nightmare. He raised his head from the pillow and peered at the digital clock on the nightstand. Twenty-four hours ago, he was filling his thermos with French roast, preparing to drive to Huntsville, to restore their lives. Instead . . . he also recalled how he'd almost screwed things up even worse and his own wash of pride and relief at Andrew's words.

I'm not running. And I'm not lying.

He knew exactly what those words meant. They meant Andrew had grown up. He was all done being the baby brother. Whether he needed protection or not, he didn't *want* it. And there wasn't a single thing Ben didn't understand about that.

He'd assumed the steepest learning curve after Andrew's parole would be Andrew's. Now he saw that it might be theirs, and that maybe the main thing they had to learn was to get out of the way.

He shifted his head on the pillow a bit, eyes stinging and temples pounding.

The night before. The worst of it was calling Nell and her silence at the end of the line—palpable shock, he'd heard it before. Still, he'd had to question her: *Tell me everything you know about Dayton's day, everything he did, everyone he talked to, every remark he made. Don't leave anything out.*

And her struggle to comply.

He'd spent most of the night waiting—for this or that person, for this or that procedure. It was almost eight hours into the investigation before he was free to leave. Except what he was free to leave was his own home. He'd packed a bag for himself and Bood—who understood when Ben stuffed a packet of doggy treats into the suitcase that he, Bood, was to be included. But he also seemed to sense somehow that joy would be inappropriate. So he'd contented himself with leaping onto the bed to oversee Ben's packing.

It was not until Ben was in the darkness of the motel room in the morning's wee hours that he allowed himself to mourn the man in the body bag, his strength and presence, his graveled voice rumbling on the periphery of Ben's childhood, his wide hand enclosing Ben's own small one. Life was a wash, Ben had thought, the words like a bitter aftertaste in his throat. Step forward, step back. A gain, a loss. Lose a father, gain a father—although he didn't remember Benjamin Ryan's death in Vietnam, *this* loss was real enough. Gain a brother, lose a father—the giant thumb of the uncaring cosmos tipping the weight on the universal scale. Shaking off the thought, he'd sunk onto the bed and let the tears slip through his fingers. Bood had appeared quietly at his side to stare gravely into his face and to press his warm little body close to Ben's thigh.

And, earlier, Chief Saenz out of town but on the phone long distance, not knowing the depth of Ben's relationship with Dayton but trying to find out. Asking the bare minimum: Why your house? What was this Dayton Slaughter doing there? What was your relationship? What do you know about him? Then asking for Kenechi Akundi, and Kenechi's quiet questions afterwards, scribbling in his notebook with his big black hand, onyx eyes steady on his subject—as Ben had seen him do many times, but the subject this time was Ben.

And Ram Ratzlaff, goddammit, his hawk nose sniffing. His manner deferential enough, but his notebook open, his eyes like a ferret's searching Ben's face, searching his home, examining, scouring, no corner neglected and no item left unnoted. Why your place, Ben? You have any ideas? Any bad blood we should know about? Notice anything missing? Anything out of the way? Ben scotched the temptation to say, "Yeah, come to think of it, I saw your buddy Malone tearing out of my cul-de-sac just before I found the body." He didn't say it. Hell of a thing to say. Anyway, he'd talk to Malone on his own. Or not. It wouldn't be the first time he'd planned to have a heart-to-heart with Malone and didn't. It was simply that he didn't relish the idea. He could see Malone pulling on his fake and practiced look of hurt: *Who, me?*

And Ben's colleagues observing Ben, too, as they moved through their work, their expressions guarded but revealing both suspicion and sympathy.

Ben was surprised and angry, then surprised and angry that he was surprised and angry. They were *cops,* for Christ's sake, schooled in objectivity, deep-seated and entrenched—and schooled as well to look hard at a victim's intimates. Yes, colleagues, but they had a job to do, and they were doing it.

And while they were doing it, the man who'd been like Ben and Andrew's father lay dead on the floor—through a night of photographers, forensic and evidence technicians, the medical examiner, the ambulance, formal statements. After five or six hours, Dayton—or what remained of him—was bundled onto a gurney and taken away in a body bag, and Andrew was free to leave. But he didn't leave, not then. Instead, he sidled up to Ben and asked, "Who could have done this? Why?"

His haunted, oddly hollow-eyed look dimly registered with Ben, and he realized how many hours had passed since they'd eaten at that seafood restaurant off I-45.

When Ben didn't answer, Andrew picked up Bood and slipped out the patio door to sit in the garden under the stars, the dog cuddling near, the night sky clear now and the air still and chill. Ben found him there later, Andrew's face buried in his hands, sobbing. Ben, dry-eyed himself but feeling the full weight of tragedy and loss, sat down and silently pulled Bood into his lap.

"I didn't even get to see him," Andrew whispered into his hands after a few minutes. "I mean when I was free."

Ben saw how that would hurt, and he laid his arm across his brother's shoulders. Bood shifted a little on Ben's lap and licked Andrew's hand.

"He had lots of plans for you, Andrew. For us. He was retiring. He and Ma were going to marry. He'd closed on the Knowlton He was happy."

But even as he spoke, Ben recalled something in Dayton's face—a gravity or sadness that hadn't been there before, a nameless tiredness or pallor.

"He was *happy,* Andrew," he said again, willing it to be so.

Andrew raised his head, the wet on his cheeks shining faintly in the moonlight. "I thought I'd paid."

"What do you mean?"

"An eye for an eye. I thought I'd paid."

"Ahh, God, Andrew, you can't think such a thing. You *have* paid. This has nothing to do with you."

"I killed someone."

"It was an accident! For Christ's sake, Andrew! You weren't even driving the car."

"I took a life. And now—"

Ben shook his head and swatted at the air.

"And now Dayt is killed—someone I loved. On my first day of freedom. It feels like—like the universe taking its due."

"Don't be crazy. We'll find out what went down here, Andrew. I promise you."

"Who, goddammit! Why?"

"I don't know. But we're going to find out." And he *would* find out, by God. He took a moment to swear it to himself. "And when we do, Andrew, I promise you it'll have nothing, *nothing,* to do with you."

Andrew sank his face into his hands again—but Ben, sitting with his arm over his shoulders, felt the tension drain from his body. And he remembered just such another time a decade ago, sitting on a holding-cell cot beside his brother and waiting for attorney Deke Boggs to call them back to court . . .

———————

Andrew had just finished another semester of perfect grades at Texas A&M. So, yeah, he and three buddies got drunk and stoned and tried to drive away with a brand new Ford Crown Victoria they'd found idling outside a College Station convenience store. There was no intent—just impulse. They were there, the car was there, and it was running. So they piled in and started to take off, Andrew in the front passenger seat.

Except the car's owner—one Browne Wilkins—ran from the store and grabbed at the handle of Andrew's door, grabbed at the handle and slipped, Andrew screaming *stop,* watching him fall and go under.

Wilkins died the next day. All four boys were charged with intoxication, manslaughter, and felony theft. Took a year for the trial to roll around. A year while Dayton, Nell, and Ben did what they could. Ben finished the final semester for his MA and delayed his doctoral studies. Nell spent more time in Brazos County than she did in Dallas, and Dayton cut fat checks to the Wilkins family every ninety days.

But nobody felt any better—a man had died.

Nell had begged Dayton to take the case, but as her executor and her sons' godfather, he had an intimate relationship with the defendant. And he was no criminal lawyer. Besides, a Yankee lawyer in Texas? Dayton believed what everybody said: Don't bring in lawyers from outside. These folks love their own. Get the best you can buy from the local pool. And the best was Deacon Boggs—wild white hair, sky-blue three-piece suit, cowboy boots curled at the toes, chewing an unlit cigar and hiding ice-blue eyes beneath the sweat-stained brim of a gray cowboy hat.

"What are y'all lookin' for?" Deke Boggs lopped a bony knee over the corner of his leather-topped desk and showed a lot of polished boot. His voice rasped like a rusty hinge. "I mean what would satisfy you, 'sides it not happenin' in the first place?"

Nell had stared at him wordlessly, face pale as death.

"A probated sentence," Dayton said, his tone firmly lawyer-to-lawyer.

"Won't happen. A local good ol' boy died, and some spoiled, big-city rich kids killed him." He silenced them with an upraised hand. "Hold on. I'm telling y'all how Brazos County folks will see it. Browne Wilkins had a family and grandbabies and now he's gone. If this were Dallas or Fort Worth or Austin, jury might have some sense. They'd see a good kid, never in trouble, caught in something foolish. And wouldn't ruin his life for him."

He stopped talking long enough to mouth his cigar from left to right and push a Kleenex box across the desk toward Nell.

"But this is country. Home of a university and all, but country. Say your boy's trial comes up in the summer, faculty folks out of town, and your jury a bunch of Bible-thumpers."

Ben was on the edge of his chair, mouth dry, and Deke Boggs answered his own unasked question.

"Meanest dang people in the world. Unless it's their own. You ain't noticed?"

He took a second to glare at Ben from under the brim of his hat, as if Ben himself were one of those mean dang people. Then he turned to Nell.

"Ma'am, you might could pop into the Ladies, get a private moment. I expect you want a good bawl, not those irritatin' little snuffles."

To Ben's surprise, Nell left the room.

"Y'all put yourself in the jury room," Deke resumed. "Least he's Texan. But Yankee stock. Least he's an Aggie. But not in the Corps. Least he's been workin' at his studies. But all A's, everything easy for him."

"Fucking shame to be smart," Ben said, his voice fierce.

"Especially in a state that ranks forty-eighth in education," Deke added, unperturbed. Paused a millisecond. "And bleedin'-heart rich."

"Meaning?" Ben said.

"Son, how long you been in Texas? You know you don't wanna look too smart, too lucky." Deke clumped to the floor and rose, came around his desk and parked a haunch on its corner. "Besides, they already made up their minds about your momma from what they heard on the news."

"Yeah. I've heard those reports."

"Yankee do-gooder—"

"Fucking shame to do some good."

Deke ignored Ben's interruption.

"Never heard nothin' about her church, though."

"Druid," Ben said.

Deke smiled.

"Roman Catholic," Dayton said.

Deke shuddered dramatically.

"*What*—" Ben began, and Dayton laid a gentle hand on his arm. Ben wasn't famous for his temper, because few people had seen it. But Dayton had.

"White-collar liberal who runs a welfare agency," Deke Boggs went on relentlessly. "Hands money to shiftless people too lazy to work. Never married but has two sons, both in college. Lives in a mansion. Drives a pricey foreign car."

Ben had leapt from his chair, towering over Deke Boggs as he sat on the edge of his desk.

Dayton rose.

"Ben," he said.

"Nell Gallagher," Ben enunciated clearly, as if explaining simple concepts to a dunce, "runs a *private* foundation that raises *private* money for poor children. And her so-called *mansion* cost less than half a million."

Deke pushed back his hat, revealing frosty eyes. Ben stared back, his own eyes the same black-fringed cobalt as Nell's, the same pilot-light flicker and flare. Fire meeting ice.

"And she drives a Toyota, for Christ's sake."

"Like I said." Deke's gaze was steady. "People round here like pickups and big ol' domestics. Like Browne Wilkins' brand new Crown Vic."

Dayton put a hand on Ben's arm again. "He's telling us what we're up against."

With desperation on his face, Ben dragged his hands through his unruly black hair and moved to the window of Deke's fifth-floor office. He stared down at the ugly parking lot, the sparse traffic, the monotonous landscape.

Dayton turned to Deke.

"A change of venue?"

The lawyer pondered, cigar clamped between nicotined front teeth.

"Be dramatic. But I don't see how."

"If we get a smart judge?"

Deke stashed the cigar in the ashtray and plucked at his lower lip.

"Smart judge," he said, as if it were an oxymoron. He wasn't smiling.

Ben turned to stare at the two solemn lawyers—rustic Texan, elegant Yankee. They in turn gazed at each other—some private, unspoken message passing between them—and Dayton shook his head and sagged in his chair.

"At least," Dayton said, "tell us it's true you're the best damned lawyer in Brazos County."

Deke had stood, readjusted the hat over his wild hair. "We're fixin' to find out."

Fifteen years. Time off, ten. Count your blessings, Deke had said—driver got twenty.

CHAPTER 12

Saturday morning, February 22

Nell is dancing with Benjamin Ryan amid whirling psychedelic lights, their bodies moving as one, Benjamin's thick black hair shorn into a coarse military burr that prickles her temple when he bends his head to hers. She watches his image come and go in the pulsing light, then it is gone, and she is alone, running blind down a steep stair, in danger. She realizes she has a weapon and closes both hands around it, marveling that it is so easy. Then a plume of pale sulfur-scented smoke emerges from the pistol barrel, accompanied by a small red flag bearing words Nell doesn't understand, but she pushes off the stair and that's easy, too, like pushing off the pool floor in the deep end. And she rises up and away without effort and feels herself growing larger and lighter until she's above the scene like an über figure in a Chagall painting. Then she sees Dayton below, shrinking and receding. And the thing in her hand rings and she sees it's not a weapon after all, but a telephone, and it rings and rings all the way down . . .

The phone on the nightstand at last jerked Nell awake, but she didn't reach for it. She lay as if bludgeoned, letting it ring, her brain fuzzed from the sleeping pill and disoriented by the dream, feeling the strangeness of a world without Dayton. The ringing stopped, and she lay staring at the ceiling in the sudden silence.

Gray light from the overcast morning filtered into the room at the edges of the closed draperies. Had the ringing awakened Andrew? She listened but heard only McKinney Avenue's morning traffic. No sound from the two floors above. She thought she smelled coffee, but then he would have had to grind the beans, and she hadn't heard the grinder, either.

She stared at the light rimming the draperies, behind her eyes the indelible image of the dance floor and its whirling psychedelic brilliance. And Benjamin. So easily conjured up by a dream, but decades and miles away—barely remembered in many ways. She banished the image, cursing herself for the loss and waste of her life, for a wish so modest and attainable for others but so large and elusive for her, for Nell the orphan. Family. It was all she ever wanted. And now Dayton, whom she'd kept at arm's length for nearly a lifetime and who gave shape and substance to her past because he was the only one who knew it, was gone too.

Loss and waste.

The phone rang again, startling her. She pushed a cold hand out of the blankets and picked it up, read the display, and pressed the talk button.

CHAPTER 13

Ben had called his mobile number first, hoping Andrew would pick up on the cell and he wouldn't have to bother his mother. His call went to the recording. So he hit Nell's speed dial number. It rang five times and went to voice mail.

"What the hell," he murmured, alarm mounting in his chest, and hit redial.

This time Nell picked up, her voice thick. "Benny."

"Scared me, Ma."

"Did you just call?"

"I did."

"Where are you?"

"In my office right now. Bood and I spent the night in an Arlington motel."

"Ugh. Why didn't you come over here?"

"It was really late. Make that early. Easier to just stay here. Andrew up?"

"I'm not sure. I think I smell coffee. Haven't heard anything, though—might be the sleeping pill."

"Ma, can Bood and I bunk over there for the time being? I won't be going home for a while." He paused. "If ever."

"Andrew might have gone to the Knowlton to talk with Tooley Deere," she said. He could tell she was crying and trying to suppress the sounds. "I told him Tooley was leaving and Dayt wanted him to manage the place. I didn't mention—"

"I'll see—I'm on my way to Dayt's. First I'll drop Bood at your place."

"Dayt's?"

"Search and seal."

"What? *You're* on this case?"

The red call light on his desk phone blinked, and he half-stood to look through his window on the squad room. Slydell Scroggins, the officer on the desk, pointed to his phone and mouthed the word *chief*. Ben shook his head and showed him a thumbs-down. Sly spoke into the mouthpiece on his headphone, and the blinking light on Ben's phone went dark.

"Ben?" Nell said. "*You're* on Dayton's case?"

"Not for long, probably."

"What does that mean?"

"It means Saenz is out of town. And it means it'll be touchy."

"Will he . . ." She sounded doubtful. "Is that wise, Ben?"

Ben shrugged. "Maybe not. Saenz doesn't realize how close Dayton was. If he did, he wouldn't let me near it. Far as he knows, Dayton was an acquaintance who happened to move to Texas."

"Follow policy, Ben. As you yourself are fond of saying, the rules are there for good reasons."

"Yeah. But this is *Dayt.* The fact that he was killed in my house is enough to keep me out right there. But Saenz wants to recognize some successes I've had lately . . . I have to work fast, though, get the jump on this before—"

"Before he gets back?"

He felt a flash of defensive anger at her tone.

"Don't tell me how to do my job, Ma."

To his surprise, she laughed. "I'm only reminding you of your own modus operandi, Ben. Not that I always agree with it. I prefer the golden mean: all virtues taken to extremes become faults."

"Yeah, I know. The dangerous progression. Steadfast becomes determined becomes dogged becomes mulish. So I've heard you say."

"And frankly, your fidelity to the *letter* of law—"

"I'm *police!*"

"And your ideas of justice are simplistic."

"Either you have the rule of law or you don't."

"You make my point for me."

"So sue me."

"Yes, so sue you. When you run out of argument, so sue you."

"Oh, ho." He gave a short, sardonic laugh. "I'm not out of argument, not by a long shot. I'm just trying to respect my mother—another convention you apparently despise. And for your information, my so-called excessive fidelity to the law made me send my brother away from a crime scene yesterday."

She silently digested that.

"Except he wouldn't go. But—"

"Good for both of you, I'd say." Her voice was tender. "Benny, I just want you to . . . to, oh, realize complexity. You're a black-and-white thinker in a world that isn't black and white."

"Mine is."

"Then . . ." She hesitated for a long moment. "Then God help us."

"Are you okay, Ma?"

"Of course I'm not okay."

"I mean . . . I mean besides not being okay, are you okay?"

"I'm okay. But let me just say this. You're emotionally involved in Dayton's death. But bulling your way through, you could get crosswise with Chief Saenz and your colleagues when you've worked so hard to . . . to dispel the spoiled rich-boy image."

Ben sighed.

"He *is* your chief."

"He is."

"And he's been in your corner so far."

"He has."

"But you're going to push anyway."

"I am."

She said nothing for a long while, but then announced abruptly, surprisingly, "Okay, fine. Actually, I hope you *do* investigate the case."

"*What?*" He snorted and looked toward the ceiling in astonishment.

"I said I hope you *do*—"

"I heard what you said. I just don't understand it. One minute you're—"

"I was just thinking. If you had the case, you could control the investigation."

"Yes? Yes? I guess I don't know what *control the investigation* means to you. But, yes, hell yes, I'd control the investigation."

He was suddenly intensely uncomfortable, but he didn't know why. Two lines on his phone began blinking.

"Ma. I've got to—"

The lights went dark.

"When will Dayt's body be released, Ben? I need to make plans."

"They'll release as soon as possible, Ma. But it'll be a while. Especially since Dayton wanted to be cremated. They won't—" He couldn't finish. The words were too stark. *They won't release until they're sure we won't inadvertently burn evidence with the body.*

"So what do you do next?" she asked.

"Interviews with principals. I've already pushed, as you say. Autopsy and ballistics report will be ready ASAP, and I've sent the ATF form, faxed it this morning."

"What form?"

"Form 4473."

She sighed in exasperation.

"The trace form," he said.

"What does that give you?"

"Involves rifling: the lands and grooves made by a bullet's trajectory as it moves down the barrel."

"What are these muddle-headed answers?" He heard her impatience. "I meant what kind of information does the trace give you?"

"Where the weapon was manufactured. When and where purchased. Name and address of the purchaser."

She was silent.

"Of the weapon."

"Yes."

"Ma. Are you sure you're okay?"

"Yes."

"Gotta go, Ma. But I'll join you and Andrew for dinner."

"Couldn't we do lunch, too? Have something here? You have time?"

He didn't have time, but he heard the need in her voice. "Sure."

"Ben. Dayton made a new will. Expressed the papers to his executor just yesterday morning. He willed the Knowlton Arms to Andrew. Left the bulk of his estate to me, and—"

"Wait! If you're going to mention my disposition in Dayton's will, don't. And you know, don't you, that whoever handles this, you're a prime suspect."

"Andrew? Is he a suspect, too?" Her voice was dry with accusation.

"Andrew was with me. He has an ironclad alibi, thanks to his excessive fidelity to the letter of the law."

"Oh crapola, Ben."

"Who's Dayt's executor?"

"Gabriel Gladstone. A partner in the Kalamazoo office."

"He needs to be notified ASAP. You want me to call him?"

"I'll do it. I have his home number."

"I'll need that number, too, Ma. Okay, then. Otherwise, we'll let all this stuff unroll as it will."

"Do you have to question me?" Nell asked.

"No. But someone will."

"I don't want to."

He laughed shortly. "Who does? You're a principal, Ma. And with the will—"

"Motive. I know—love, lust, loathing, and lucre. Please."

Tiredness wrung the patience from him. "Nobody's going to bother you today. If things go the way I think, the chief won't let me lead, but he might appoint Kenechi and assign me to his team, sort of a tacit . . . whatever. One way or the other, Ken probably will interview you. You like him."

"Can't you do it?"

"No. Look. If you weren't my mother—"

"But I *am* your mother," she said sharply. "That's why I said I hoped you'd be in control of the case."

A tingle began in his blood stream and worked its way to his fingertips.

"What did you do yesterday after we left?" he asked abruptly.

"Nothing. Stayed here."

"Talk to anybody? See anybody? Can anyone verify you were at home?"

"I was alone. I talked to Dayton on my cell about four, little after, maybe."

"Why your cell?"

She was quiet for a moment. "I was . . . I did go out, yes. To buy flowers. I wanted to catch Dayt before he left. But he was already on his way to Arlington."

"What time were you at the florist's?"

"About four."

"They know you. So they'd remember. How long were you there? What time did you leave? Did you go anywhere else afterward?"

He heard her swallow. "I thought you said Kenechi would do this."

"Anywhere else?"

"No. And this is the Ben I don't much like. An interrogator, barking questions."

"These questions have to be answered, Ma. Whoever asks them." His voice was hard. "And I gotta tell you—"

His phone lines were blinking again.

"Never mind," he said. "I've got to go."

His eyes fell on a pewter-framed photo on his desk, an old shot of him, Nell, and Andrew at a Springsteen concert at Reunion Arena, the teenaged brothers smiling for the camera, but Nell reaching out of the frame—for a toddler, Ben remembered, perched on a stranger's shoulders. His heart softened.

"Ma, you're not alone in this."

"Actually, I am."

She hung up, and Ben sat motionless, the receiver still in his hand, the slight tingle still creeping through his fingers. He recognized the feeling. It could come from a single word, a silence, a glance. But it spoke volumes. And even on the phone, he knew.

Nell was lying.

CHAPTER 14

The first thing Ben heard when he pushed through the Knowlton Arms' brass-trimmed doors was Cyndi Lauper's piped-in voice singing "Walk On By." He mounted the shallow steps into the lobby, which seemed even dimmer in the morning's half-light. Abner Zeeck had a foot on a marble bench and was pulling up the black socks that habitually wrinkled around his thin ankles. He looked at Ben, owl-eyed, and rushed toward him.

"Mr. Ben! Mornin'! I thought you was coming at eight."

"It's okay, Ab. I'll just sit there." He waved in the direction of a dove-colored velvet sofa facing an ornate table that ran almost the sofa's length.

Abner's thin cheeks were scrubbed pink and his lank brown hair damp enough from his morning shower to show the tracks of a comb, but Ben could still smell a slight tobacco funk as the doorman approached.

"You okay, sir? You surely musta not got much sleep last night, not to be up and around so early." Abner looked uncomfortable, and Ben knew he was searching for words. "Um, we all . . . Mr. Slaughter . . ."

Ben touched the gold-fringed epaulet buttressing Abner's bony shoulder. "It's okay, Ab."

"Well." He squared himself in his uniform and followed Ben onto the carpeted seating area of the lobby. "Everybody up early. Mr. Andrew's in there with Mr. Deere. He asked me to give you this, thought you might need it."

He reached into his pocket and handed over Ben's cell phone.

"Guess Mr. Andrew can't wait to get working."

Ben peered into Tooley Deere's office, saw Tooley and Andrew poring over a pile of ledgers. His eyes rested on his brother, whose color wasn't good. From convict to hotelier in twenty-four hours.

"How long has he been here?"

Abner thought. "Pert near an hour now."

"We need to talk to Tooley, but don't bother them right now." He turned on his phone, checked its juice, and sat, briefcase on his thighs, a yawn ballooning in his throat.

"Ab, I'm expecting some Dallas police. Let me know when they get here."

Ben had many DPD connections and was counting on their professional courtesy. But he'd already warned his team to defer to Dallas—he didn't have time to oil the troubled waters of territoriality.

"And some Arlington police will be here soon," he added, laying his head against the gray velvet and closing his eyes while the doorman bustled around him.

A blast of chilled wet air swept into the lobby and with it, Kenechi Akundi, Joseph Proudhorse, Hilda Cloy—and hard on their heels, the Dallas team. Ab hurried away to greet the newcomers, fussing at their perimeter as they crossed the marble entry.

Ben yawned again and watched them come. Kenechi leading, looking like a large Sidney Poitier, tossing back a few words in his clipped Nigerian accent. Following him, Joseph Proudhorse and

Hilda Cloy—Comanche brave and gay woman. Often called the odd couple, they had an instinctive understanding of each other and were the department's most successful team—silent, inscrutable, patient Proudhorse and mouthy, swaggering, impetuous Cloy. The smooth-skinned Proudhorse didn't share Hilda's cratered cheeks, a memorial to teenaged acne, but the two had the same body type— the squat stature and style, Ben thought, of pre-Columbian figures. Proudhorse had an aquiline nose, broad cheekbones, close-cropped hair the color and shine of coal, and a beardless face. Cloy had an aquiline nose, broad cheekbones, close-cropped hair the color and shine of coal, and only an occasional dark whisker on her upper lip. Together they traveled in a cloud of patchouli—Proudhorse's aftershave and, colleagues joked, Hilda's . . . aftershave.

Most striking about Joseph Proudhorse, Ben thought, was his intelligent but pained countenance. His heavy-lidded black eyes squinted at the world from beneath sparse brows, and his thin-lipped mouth pulled down at the corners to give him a look at once wounded and disdainful. Proudhorse seldom smiled—in fact a perpetual frown wrinkled his brow—but when he did, he showed a wide slash of white teeth made whiter by the contrast of his bright copper complexion. An hour of his glowering presence and smoldering black gaze had a profound effect in the interview room, and Chief Saenz often dispatched Joe Proudhorse to extract confessions from reluctant perps.

Ben closed his briefcase and stood, relieved to see Dallas had dispatched its own version of the odd couple—Bo Danke with his slab-like body, rumpled shirts, and nose like a bicycle seat, and Sal Smithers, a slight man, dapper as the toy groom on a wedding cake.

"We need the key to Dayton's suite, Ab," Ben said, after a flurry of handshakes.

Abner pivoted in mid-stride on the heel of his scuffed black oxford, wheeled behind the reception desk, and retrieved a ring bearing a key and a gold and red shield emblazoned with the scrolled numerals 601. He spoke a few words to the sallow-faced young man behind the desk, who'd been watching with interest, and returned to the little knot of detectives.

"A forensics team will be here, Ab," Ben said. "Bring them up. And nobody else—I repeat, *nobody*. We'll seal the sixth floor, and I don't want anyone up there, for any reason. Until further notice."

"I hear ya, sir."

"And we'll need to see Dollie Varnes when she gets in."

Abner hurried ahead to usher them into the elevator, punched the button, and nervously hummed in falsetto during the trip to the fifth floor. Shuttling them out of the elevator, he led them up the broad carpeted stair to the sixth-floor suite. All four detectives stopped short. Across the foyer, one of the ivory doors was ajar, and the small service elevator was open.

"What in *hell*—" Ben crossed the foyer with a stormy backward glance at Abner. "I expressly told Tooley to secure this area."

"I expect it's just Rosa, Mr. Ben," said Abner.

"I don't care who the hell it is. How'd she get in?"

Abner spread his hands palms up, not wanting to state the obvious: *with her key.*

"Um," he said and coughed into his fist.

"When I said secure the property, I meant—never mind, Ab, it's not your fault."

Bo Danke began unspooling yellow crime scene tape.

Abner frowned. "But it's not a crime scene, is it?"

"We're treating it as though it is, Abner."

Hilda Cloy disappeared into the apartment and returned with Rosa, a pock-faced little woman with bad teeth who pushed a cart loaded with cleaning equipment. The maid spoke too little English to know why she was being escorted from the apartment, but her veiled glance at the grim-faced detectives told her well enough that she *was* being escorted from the apartment, and that she was not to return. She jostled her cart onto the service elevator, seemingly without curiosity or resentment.

Kenechi watched her go and chuckled. "What's the Spanish for *whatever?*" He drew a little nearer, put a hand on Ben's arm. "Ben. I didn't have a chance to say . . . I can't think of anything but tired platitudes."

"Y'all okay now, Mr. Ben?" Abner inquired, searching Ben's face with his swamp-brown eyes. "I'll go wait for those other *po*-lice."

"Everything's fine, Ab," said Ben.

The doorman's expression cleared, and he headed down the stairs, the epaulets uneven on his bony shoulders and his butt no-where in the rump-sprung gray pants.

Ben pulled latex gloves from his pocket and snapped them on before entering Dayton's suite. He knew the place well. Still, on this day, without Dayton, the apartment seemed foreign and for-lorn. Rosa had been airing the suite—one tall window in the living room was open, its draperies drawn to the casing, a chill drifting from the wide-open pane.

Ben entered Dayton's book-lined office. He had come to think the most productive searches took place in office and bedroom—so he started there. Kenechi worked in the bedroom, Proudhorse and Hilda in kitchen and bath. Dayt's briefcase stood beside his swivel chair. Ben set it on the desk and opened it. It held only a few folders, most of them personal and pertaining to Dayt's re-tirement and benefits. The folders' contents looked jumbled, as if someone had hastily rifled through them and tossed them back. He put the briefcase aside.

The top of Dayt's large cherry desk was clear enough. The requisite lamp, phone, calendar. A silver pen in a holder. A pad of ivory paper engraved with a scrolled red *K*, another bearing the name David Dayton Slaughter, and below that: *Slaughter, Gold, Gladstone, & Dunne, Kalamazoo.* And contact numbers. He tore off a sheet with his gloved fingers and tucked it in the back of his notebook. A hemp-handled bag from Polly's Party Store, empty except for a fistful of white tissue paper, lay on the desktop. Ben remembered the foil letters in Dayton's right hand. He lifted the brown bag, revealing a dog-eared flier, its front taken up with large red print: *Are You DOOMED?* Beneath the flier was a pink message note from the front desk bearing only a date, time, and scrawled name: *M. J. Kildare.* Ben slipped the flier and pink message slip into a labeled evidence bag, wrote "M. J. Kildare" on another sheet from the pad, folded it, and stuck it in the back of his notebook.

The remaining item on the desktop was a silver-framed photo of a much-younger Nell and Dayton standing on wide steps fronting an official-looking building. Ben picked up the picture and studied it. The two had their arms draped over the stone shoulders of a statue—a goddess in Grecian robes, one shapely marble arm holding aloft the scales of justice. Dayton, with a malevolent grin, was pressing his thumb on one scale. Ben considered the photo, considered Dayton's godlike thumb tipping the balance on the universal scale, and remembered his own dark thoughts about the uncaring cosmos.

He opened the desk's shallow center drawer. Stationery, pens, sticky notes, stamps, paper clips, tape dispenser, stapler, scissors, a couple of membership cards, a passport, an expired Michigan driver's license. The deep drawers flanking the kneehole held hanging files. He riffled through the neatly labeled folders in the drawer on the left. Bills, receipts, cancelled checks. He flipped through a sheaf of cancelled checks and a thick medical folder holding invoices for a slew of tests, all of them recent. Frowning, he sat in Dayton's swivel chair and looked through the folder more carefully.

Hilda stuck her head in the door and yawned. "Anything, Boss?"

"Mmm." He didn't look up from the folder. "You?"

"Nope."

He laid the folder on the desktop and stared at nothing. Then he picked up the phone on the desk and punched in Nell's number.

She answered on the third ring, her voice tremulous.

"Dayt's name was on the phone display," she said. "Gave me a start."

"I'm on his desk phone."

"Andrew there? He left me a note."

"With Tooley Deere." He switched the phone to his left ear and picked up the folder. "Ma. I've been through Dayt's briefcase and don't see the Knowlton papers or Dayt's will—not even copies. Where are they, do you know?"

"They're here. We put them in the safe yesterday in case Andrew needed to see them. And Dayt expressed copies to Kalamazoo. You might also check the Knowlton's safe, but the originals are here."

Ben gave a little sigh of relief. "Good. Wanted to be sure nothing was missing. Dayt's briefcase looked sort of jumbled. There's something else. I'm looking at doctor statements—from an oncology clinic. For tests. But I don't see a result. Was something wrong with Dayton?"

She said nothing for a long moment. He gave her time, drawing a diamond-shaped doodle on the ivory pad and crosshatching it while he waited. Then he said, "Ma?"

"Pancreatic cancer. Terminal. He told me yesterday."

"And you didn't tell *me?*"

"When did I see you alone, Ben? I didn't want to greet Andrew with that news. Neither did Dayt."

"Yeah. I guess." His mobile rang. He tugged it out of his pocket, looked at the display, and punched it off.

"I called Gabriel Gladstone this morning," Nell said.

Ben was blank.

"Dayt's executor."

"Oh. What'd he say?"

"After he got over the shock, he said a lot. I could hardly bring myself to tell him, Ben. Gabe loved Dayt; well, they all did. They've been friends most of their lives. But main thing, Gabe will take control. Says as soon as he gets the administrative paperwork and filings finished, he'll fly down here for a reading of the will."

"Nice of him."

Nell was silent.

"Anything else right now, Ma?"

"Just that . . . I never knew Dayt to be afraid, Ben," Nell said. "But he was afraid. Not of dying, but of dying that way. Not that anyone wants a violent death. But we do hope for a quick one."

"His was quick."

She was silent for so long that he decided she wasn't going to answer. But at last she whispered, "Yes." And hung up.

He laid the folder aside and opened the desk's right-hand drawer. The first file, brand new, held copies of the Knowlton sale papers, a deal sealed just a day earlier. The others were Slaughter estate files, catalogued and up to date. Dayton's executor would have an easy time of it.

The last file in the right-hand drawer was unmarked and held only one object.

An unlabeled DVD.

CHAPTER 15

Ben turned the DVD in his hands several times, frowning, then stuck it in a clear plastic evidence bag and filled in the label. Kenechi appeared in the doorway.

"Forensics is here."

Ben and Kenechi took a final walk-round in Dayton's office. Emptied containers, opened decorative boxes, shook out books, examined the backs of the pictures hanging on the walls. Then they joined Bo Danke and Sal Smithers, who were watching forensics chief Karen Enid and her colleagues repeat what they'd done so painstakingly at Ben's the night before—dust for prints and collect trace evidence.

"Been up all night, Karen?" Ben asked.

She released a whiskey-and-cigarettes laugh. "I look it?"

Ben gave her a once-over. Slender. Polished walnut skin. Well-shaped head made shapelier by fraction-of-an-inch hair that curled flat against her scalp. Raffish purple eyeglasses. The best forensics expert Ben knew of.

"You look fine," he said. "Got anything so far?"

"Shitload of prints. Bagged the loose stuff, bathroom drinking glass, etcetera. Some good latents in the bathrooms, even some whole-hand. But they're about two feet from the floor."

Ben smiled. "Dwarves again."

"Maids. On their knees. Cleaning toilets, tubs, shower bottoms. Lots of great surfaces for prints in a bathroom: tile, Formica, porcelain, plastic, marble, mirror, enamel paint. Good latents. Even visibles sometimes. Unless the place has been wiped."

"And this hasn't been."

"No way."

"What about the Knowlton staff's prints?"

"Got 'em. One guy was cleaning the lobby and when he saw what was coming down, he dropped his vacuum and ran out the door and down the street."

"Illegal," Bo Danke put in.

Ben thought of Andrew. Would the Knowlton be left with a skeleton staff just when he needed them? He turned to Kenechi.

"Tell Tooley Deere to make it clear we're not Immigration and we're not interested in anyone's status with Immigration."

Kenechi spoke a few words into the house phone.

"Interrupt him," Ben heard Kenechi say.

A balding man in thick glasses and latex gloves was lifting prints from the ivory enameled door between office and living room. He smoothed a length of wide transparent tape over the dusted prints, taking care not to get bubbles under the tape, then stuck the tape and its images onto a white card for photographing.

"The visibles are dirt, maybe some grease," Karen said. "Eyeballing them, don't look like those on the flush handle and drinking glass."

Which would be Dayton's, Ben thought.

Karen examined the prints on the card through a magnifying glass.

"The usual Caucasian loops. But a couple of whorls—"

"Man?" Ben asked.

She shrugged. "Large woman?"

"Small man with large hands?"

Ben's cell phone rang again. He looked at the display, heart dropping, and put it to his ear.

"What are you doing, Ben?" There was a full head of steam behind Rolando Saenz's words. "And don't pull any King Cool stuff with me. Now's not the time."

"King Cool?"

"Don't give me that! You know damned well—well, let me just ask. Do you or don't you know you're not investigating a homicide that involves a friend and also happened in your own freaking house, for chrissakes!"

"I'm not?"

"Are you dancing with me, Ben?"

"Dancing?"

"Goddammit! You know you have a exasperating habit of answering a question with a question?"

"I do?" Hearing the chief's silence, he added, "Sorry."

"I suppose it's too much to hope that you dealt with the DPD," Saenz said, as though fearing the answer.

"I did. They're here. Bo Danke and Sal Smithers."

The chief didn't say anything, but the relief on the other end of the line was palpable.

"Whatever," he said, all the pressure going out of the word.

Ben heard someone talking in the background, Saenz answering in rapid-fire Spanish. He came back to Ben.

"I'll be back Monday. But for now, hand things over to Akundi."

For now.

"I mean it, Gallagher. You're off the case. And I'm not playin'. You know I'm right on this."

Ben slapped the phone closed.

"The chief?" asked Kenechi.

A phone trilled again, this time the house phone. Kenechi answered and turned to Ben.

"Want Tooley up here?"

"Let's go down."

Ben called to Proudhorse, who came over with Hilda Cloy in tow.

"I'm off the case," Ben said.

They gaped at him, open-mouthed and silent as a fish.

"What that means to you," Ben told Proudhorse and Hilda, "is that Ken's your command chief, as of now." He put his head back and blew some air at the ceiling. "What it means to me is that I have two days before I'm slapped in chains, and I'm going to continue what I've started. I want you to know that, but I also want the three of you out of it."

The others exchanged glances.

"How much can we get done in two days?" Kenechi asked.

CHAPTER 16

Andrew's head swam, and his nerve ends buzzed. Too much coffee—he wasn't used to it.

"Where's the john?" he asked Tooley Deere.

Tooley glanced at his watch and looked fretful.

"We still got a load of stuff to get through."

"A ten-minute break's all I need."

"Why *ten?* It's just a toilet break."

Andrew tossed back his head and laughed.

"Hey, man, I just got *out* of prison."

Tooley's face showed a series of mixed responses: surprise, guilt, relief. He tossed down his pen with a grin.

"Also," Andrew said. "I need to dash into the Cachet and make an appointment to get a haircut. My mother's orders. Which means top priority."

Abner, soldierly in his gray uniform, gold epaulets, and rump-sprung trousers rushed over to meet Andrew at Tooley's door and escort him through the lobby to the Cachet Day Spa. Close behind the doorman was a hulking woman in mismatched clothing who looked as if she'd spent the night in a bus station. A plastic bag was cradled in the crook of her arm. She extended a fistful of fliers toward Andrew with a fierce smile.

"I'm Romanian," she rasped, "defender of the faith."

"Not now, Zora," Abner said.

Andrew watched her draw back, the smile falling from her doughy face.

He held out his hand. "I'll take one."

She thrust the flier at him.

He read the question inscribed on the front, then looked at Zora.

"Am I doomed? What do you think?"

She gazed back at him with glass-green eyes. "Doomed rhymes with boomed . . . bloomed . . . zoomed."

"Loomed," Andrew said. "Roomed."

A scowl rumpled her broad gray face.

"Tombed. Varoomed," Andrew said.

"Stop!" Her voice sounded like pebbles grating on a tin roof.

Abner shushed her with an index finger to his lips.

"Whoa, sorry," Andrew said. "I thought she was a rhymer. I knew one of those in Huntsville."

"A rhymer." Abner smiled. "She is that. 'Cept she likes to play alone."

He motioned Andrew through the soft light of the Knowlton's lobby, past its curlicued tables flanking dusky gray velvet sofas and the red velvet banquette encircling a table that held tall calla lilies. In the far right corner of the lobby were Possum's Gifts & Books and a sign pointing the way to the Chez Dee restaurant.

Humming tunelessly, Abner pushed through the Cachet's glass doors, and they stepped into a potpourri of smells that confounded the nose: flowers, peppermint, eucalyptus, hairspray, something metallic and eye-stinging. The salon's reception room faced the street on the left, the red canvas canopy outside its plate glass window casting a rosy glow over the interior. To the right was a series of openings hung with flamingo pink curtains, and to the left waited a quartet of chairs, empty at the moment. Immediately ahead was a black marble counter, the wall behind lined with racks of beauty supplies packaged in gold. The shining counter was bare except for an appointment book, and a double frame holding photos of a little dog with a dark pushed-in muzzle and prominent black eyes, its thick auburn hair a silky aureole.

Abner pointed to someone sitting on the floor behind the counter.

"Dollie."

Andrew looked down at the dark gleaming top of Dollie Varnes' head, a zigzag part separating hair that looked as if it had been clear-coated. She was bent over an order book, running a blue fingernail down the columns, eyes five or six inches from the page. She looked up and the full force of her nearsighted gaze hit Andrew smack in the solar plexus. He'd never seen such eyes—large eyes with royal blue irises rimmed and centered with coal black and set in snowy white.

She scrambled up from behind the counter, tucking her book under her arm and brushing her palms together with a jangle of bracelets.

"Glad to meetcha," she said, and turned to lay the book on the counter. Her smile, even in profile, surprised Andrew—both the fact of it and its quality. It was a child's open smile, square white teeth, lips curled at the corners and accented by cheek dimples. He wanted to ask her if she knew she had a surprising smile.

"You're Andrew."

He cocked a brow.

"Mrs. Gallagher called."

Andrew looked blank.

"Mrs. Gallagher. Your mother."

"Yes. I remember."

"She wants you to have a proper styling. Hey, Zora."

Andrew looked around and saw that the large woman had followed them into the salon. Turning back to Dollie, he found her studying him. She came around the counter to walk a small circle around him, looking at his hair. Stopped in front of him. Met his eyes.

"You don't look anything like a criminal or convict."

Whatever was going on inside him froze.

Still considering Andrew's hair, Dollie reached out with a ringed hand to touch him. He recoiled, stepping back and upending a brass jug filled with dried flowers. Face flaming, she dropped her hand with a crash of bangles and awkwardly rubbed her palm on her skirt.

And continued to look at him with those blue, blue eyes.

"That was a dumb thing to say," she blurted.

Andrew bent to retrieve the spilled flowers, face expressionless.

"Um, why don't y'all . . ." Abner said, then lapsed into silence.

Dollie moved behind the counter and pulled the appointment book toward her.

"Dollie knows her stuff," Abner put in. "You can tell by her hair." He glanced at Dollie's lacquered head. "And nails. And . . ." He gestured vaguely, "makeup and clothes. You know."

Andrew, blinded by her smile, hadn't noticed her hair or nails or makeup or clothes. But now he did. Glittering deep blue talons. Hair a glossy boy-cut with longer sidepieces, a raffish swirl of polished black hair pulled from her crown and plastered over one bright blue eye, secured with a jeweled hairpin. High contrast makeup: pale skin, black eyeliner and mascara, magenta lip-gloss, no blusher. Snug magenta tee over small breasts. Tiny skirt striped horizontally in magenta and mustard, impossibly high yellow shoes with platform soles.

He needed a minute to take it all in, and she watched him do it.

"Nice socks," he said. She wore burgundy anklets with the tall yellow shoes.

On came that high-wattage smile, and in his mind, Andrew fell to his knees.

"And nice legs," he added.

"Oh, come on," she said. "They're skinny."

"I haven't seen real legs for a while. At least not a woman's. How tall are you without those shoes? Four feet?"

"Four o'clock. No!" said Zora.

"No, not yet, Zora," Abner said, turning back to speak to Andrew. "Zora's—"

But Andrew was staring after Dollie, who'd made a back-in-a-minute gesture and stalked away toward one of the pink-curtained doorways, her color high. He watched her careful, clunky movements—knees flexed, legs thin as wicks, a little distance apart. He watched her thrust the curtain aside with a clank of bracelet and disappear, and wished he knew her well enough to ask . . . *You know Olive Oyl, Popeye's goil? You have her walk.*

"Should I go get your fine new car for you, Mister Andrew?" Abner asked.

Andrew was still staring at the pink curtains. "Sorry?"

"I was wondering if I should go get that fine new Lexus for you."

"Ah, no, no, Abner. I have to get back to Tooley Deere. I just needed to make an appointment." He reflected. "Which I guess I didn't do."

"Oh."

"No. That's okay. I'll do it later."

As he stepped into the lobby, he saw something glinting on the polished marble floor. He bent to pick it up, a silver ring holding two keys and a small initialed disc. He'd barely had time to make out the *M* or *W* engraved on the disc when a horse-faced woman in green snatched it from his hand.

"Those are my keys," she announced.

"Fine," Andrew shrugged. "You keep them on the floor?"

The door had closed behind Andrew when Dollie came back through the pink curtains.

"He left? Would you tell him he can come any time this afternoon? I've cleared my calendar. I decided to do his hair myself."

"Aw, Dollie," Abner said, brushing an invisible speck from his sleeve. "Why'd you have to say that? To Mr. . . . er, Andrew. That he didn't look like a criminal or ex-con."

"That was a mistake, wasn't it, Ab. A bad mistake."

"I reckon."

Dollie put her elbows on the marble countertop, rested her chin on her hands, and stared out the window, the rosy light from the red canopy casting a glow on her pale face.

"Must have hurt his feelings, the way he acted."

Abner grunted an assent. "Surely musta."

"Did you see him jump when I went to touch his hair?"

"He been in a mean place."

She nodded, her expression grave. "You know what I *meant*, Ab? I meant that he looked nice. Neat and nice. And handsome."

"Wudn't how it sounded." Abner muttered something she didn't catch, adjusted his hat and tugged at the door.

Dollie watched the traffic in the gray drizzle. She was thinking, *Good thing his hair has grown out a little. Guess you don't get a real good styling in the . . . in the Big House.*

CHAPTER 17

Ben drew Kenechi, Joe Proudhorse, and Hilda Cloy off into a corner of Dayton's living room for a powwow.

"Are you sure of this?"

"We're sure," Kenechi said, speaking for all of them. Proudhorse's and Hilda's set faces confirmed his words.

"It might mean trouble for you with the chief. I suppose I could say I hadn't told you, but then you'd have to back me up, and we'd all be lying."

To his relief, they shook their heads.

"We're not lying," Kenechi said.

"So," Ben said. "Two days." He opened his notebook. "Right now, we've got half a dozen majors to talk to for background. Plus a handful of the Knowlton's employees."

He ticked them off. "Knowlton manager Tooley Deere. Dollie Varnes, manager of the Cachet Day Spa. Sylva Kaye—she owns the Cachet. Maisie Delacourt—owned the Knowlton Arms until yesterday, when Dayton Slaughter bought it. Plus, Dayton's law partners in Kalamazoo: Gold, Gladstone, and Dunne."

He handed the folded sheet from Dayton's ivory memo pad to Kenechi, who stuck it into his own notebook.

"The partners aren't priority, but for phone work if we get a little down time. Let's see if there's someone there today. Probably have to keep till Monday, though." He hesitated. "Then there's . . . my mother. And me. Andrew's been . . . out of pocket for ten years. Yesterday was his first day home, and he was with me the whole time. I'd like to leave him out of this."

Kenechi asked, "Dayton's family?"

"Dayton was an only child, and his parents died when he was in his early twenties. We were his—" His voice caught, and he struggled to bring it back under control. "When I talked to Ma on the phone last night, she gave me some names for the bad blood brigade. A Knowlton resident named Jimmy Snipes. Third floor. He and Dayton scuffled yesterday. Ditto Karl Novak."

"The Mississippi preacher?"

"That television evangelist? Nah, his son. Novak the younger is a builder, developer, something. He and Dayton got into it yesterday. Over this property, the Knowlton. Novak wanted it, and Dayton got it. And Sylva Kaye, who may turn out to be more than background. Ma said once that Sylva holds grudges and that she had one against Dayton. Don't know why. We'll see what Ma can add to what she's already said. I didn't want to press her too much last night."

Frowning, he flipped through a few pages of his notebook.

"Dayton was killed at my place. Why? Did the killer want him or me? Or was he trying to implicate me? I do have an enemy here and there."

Kenechi and Proudhorse continued to write in their notebooks, but Hilda looked up with a small smile.

Ben tapped his notebook. "The autopsy and ballistics are being expedited, and I've faxed the ATF. It's Saturday, but Karen Enid will stay with the prints till she gets something. Could be today, depending."

"Let's split up for the interviews." Kenechi suggested.

"Alone?" Ben hesitated. "Not protocol."

Kenechi tossed back his big head and broke into a soprano laugh, Hilda and Joe grinning along.

"Right," Ben said. "I guess we've already dispensed with the protocol. So I'll take Dollie Varnes. Ken, you take Tooley Deere. Whoever's done first will move to Jimmy Snipes. They're all on the premises. Ken and I will see Karl Novak together—he's the kind of guy you talk to with a witness present. Joe, Sylva Kaye. And Hilda, Maisie Delacourt."

He tore a couple of pages from his notebook, scribbled on them, and handed them to the partners.

"Neither place is far, and it's early enough on a Saturday— they'll probably be home. Let's reconvene at noon, see what— wait. Let's reconvene at Ma's, for lunch. We could use the sit-down for a briefing. It'll be good for Ma, too. I'm worried about her. She's alone and pretty ragged."

Hilda smacked her lips. "Omigod. Lunch chez Nell."

Bo Danke and Sal Smithers agreed to keep an eye on the sixth-floor operation, and Ben and the others pocketed their notebooks and headed for the lobby, in a hurry now, leaving the forensics folks busy with their ostrich-feather brushes and variously colored powders.

In the lobby, the Cyndi Lauper CD was playing again. "Money Changes Everything," she sang.

———————————

Ben peered into Tooley Deere's office, saw Andrew and Tooley hard at work.

"Abner, give us a holler when they take a break. Kenechi needs to talk to Tooley."

"I can check with Mr. Deere," the doorman said, lifting his knuckles to the door.

"No, leave it. For now, Kenechi and I will be with Dollie Varnes."

Abner hustled to usher the detectives into the perfumed air and fluorescent brightness of the Cachet, where Dollie stood at the window in the rouged reflection of the awning, her back to them, watching the traffic move down Houston Street in the gray morning.

She turned to Ben and said, apropos of nothing, "I just met your brother."

"Hang on, Ab," Ben said, pulling out his notebook. "Before you go. Did you hear the commotion between Dayton Slaughter and Karl Novak yesterday?"

"Seems like we had one commotion after another yesterday morning, Mr. Ben."

"What happened?"

"Delivery guy brought an express packet for Mr. Slaughter, some papers he had to sign, and I was at the elevator when Mr. Novak came stormin' out, his face bloody and red as hellfire."

"Did he say anything?"

"He wudn't talkin' to nobody—least nothin' nobody wanted to hear. I said, *Mornin', Mr. Novak. Want me to get your car?* And he said . . . well, that's the part I can't say, but it had a load of *F*-words in it, and when Zora said something to him, he told her to get lost and called her an ol' . . . well, the *K*-word."

Dollie, listening by the window, giggled.

"C-word, Abby," she said.

"Oh. Huh. Well, I wudn't sure how to spell it. Seemed like maybe a German word."

"Did Mr. Slaughter say what the papers were?" Ben asked.

"No, just signed them and filled out a new label. And tole me to get them off in the express right away."

"To whoever sent them?"

"Yessir."

"Did you happen to notice who that was, Ab?"

"Can't rightly say I did." He chewed his lip. "A law firm, though."

"Slaughter, Gold, Gladstone, and Dunne?"

He brightened. "Yessir! That's what it was, sure enough."

"In Kalamazoo?"

"Yessir! That's the town, right enough." He put on an uncharacteristic impish expression and said to Dollie behind his hand, "Another one of those dang *K*-words."

CHAPTER 18

Dollie led Ben and Kenechi to her small office—through the pink curtains and past the shampoo room's inner sanctum to a white-painted louvered door. Ben looked around the shampoo room with interest. As vain as he sometimes knew himself to be, he'd never visited a professional stylist. He patronized a narrow barbershop sandwiched between a shoe repair and a leather goods store a five-minute drive from his Arlington home. That's where Sammy Nazario cut the hair of walk-ins. Nazario was a barrel-chested man with a Roman nose, coffee-colored stains around his black eyes, and white hair as impeccable as his starched barber's coat. He had one barber chair, one sink, and he worked alone.

The Cachet wasn't large, but Ben counted five black leather recliners at five black sinks, at the moment occupied by two women and one man, all supine, attendants briskly massaging and hosing their wet heads. A third woman in round spectacles and a hairnet sat beneath the raised and silent dome of an old-fashioned hair dryer, rectangular patches of black dye laid on her brows.

Ben checked her out and hid his smile. Add a mustache and cigar and you got Groucho Marx.

Dollie's tiny windowless office was as unlike the Cachet as it was like Dollie, Ben thought. Her desk consisted of two black lacquered chests joined by a smoked glass top. Besides lamps and telephone, only four items occupied the desk's glass surface: a Mac laptop computer in an aluminum case, a calendar, a white miniature orchid in a silver cup, and an ebony-framed photograph of her auburn-haired pup. The floor was painted and varnished concrete the color of steel, a loopy white rug beneath the desk. Three large prints, meticulously matted, hung on the off-white walls.

Ben crossed to the nearest print. Matisse. Raucous color sprawled over black on the right. In the painting's lower left quadrant, ungainly mustard-colored fruit posed on a pink and orange table beside a garish curtain of black, scarlet, green, and yellow.

He moved to the other two prints.

"Braque and Klee," Dollie said, mispronouncing *Klee* to rhyme with *key*. "From the Phillips Collection."

"We have the same taste in art," Ben said.

"Did you ever go to the Phillips in DC?"

"Many times."

"Did Andrew?"

Ben cocked his head at the question.

"Your brother."

"Yes. I remember."

She blushed. "Andrew made the same joke."

Ben waited for further explanation, but she said, "Did he like the Phillips? Andrew? Does he like art?"

"Yes, to all that."

She looked pleased, her eyes deep blue pools in the subdued light.

"I have a Kandinsky I think you would like," Ben said.

"A *real* Kandinsky?"

Ben nodded.

"Someday, if I get rich," she said. "I mean *when* I get rich—I'm trying to think positive—I'm going to have real art."

"What you have here is real art, Dollie."

"I guess I mean original." She fixed her gaze on Ben. "Could I see the Kandinsky some time?"

"My place is off-limits right now, but sure. Later . . . Andrew could take you over. He'll be right here at the Knowlton."

"Mr. Slaughter told me your brother's going to be the new manager."

"The *owner,* now."

Her smile started out like sunrise, then dimmed. "Poor Mr. Slaughter."

Ben and Kenechi sat at the chairs fronting Dollie's desk, and Ben leaned forward to pick up the photo framed in ebony.

"Name's Snazzy," Dollie said. "You like dogs?"

He nodded.

"Does Andrew?"

Amused, he nodded again.

"You have a dog?

Another nod.

"What's his name?"

"Bood."

"Boob?"

Ben laughed. "That too, but don't tell him I said so. Bood— cross between a bear and a poodle."

"The Pekingese is the ancient imperial dog of China. Supposedly the offspring of a lion and a marmoset, did you know?"

Ben returned the photo to the desktop, and Dollie picked it up, pursed her magenta lips, and blew at a speck of dust.

"I got him because I heard Pekes were one-person dogs and I'm one person."

"A lion and a *marmoset?*" Kenechi asked.

"A monkey," Ben said, and Kenechi showed him a sly grin that headlined: *Texan Explains 'Monkey' to African.*

"A marmoset and a lion." Dollie said. " 'Course that's just legend. Rumor. Smart as a monkey and brave as a lion. And Snazzy would fight like a lion to protect me, I know."

The detectives opened their notebooks, and her smile fell away.

"Dollie," Ben began, "we know about the bad blood between Dayton and Karl Novak, as you just heard, and between Dayton and Jimmy Snipes. But we want to hear about it from you as well. And we want you to tell us of any problems you know of that Dayton had with anyone else."

Dollie opened her mouth and closed it.

They waited.

"Well, it's nothing, really."

"The smallest thing can be something, Dollie," Ben said.

"This isn't that sort of small thing."

"Let us judge."

"Sylva Kaye."

"Your boss?"

She nodded. "The owner of this salon and one like it in Fort Worth."

"You needn't be uneasy, Dollie. It stays with us if it doesn't belong to the case."

"Well. Sylva had some trouble with Mr. Slaughter. First, she— she came on to him. I saw it. He was sitting right there in that chair. And she was sitting there," she pointed to Kenechi. "And apparently he'd found out—"

"Wait." Ben was watching his partner write. "Describe what happened when she, as you say, came on to him."

"The deal is, she's had this great big crush on Mr. Slaughter for a long, long time. Not that he ever paid her any attention. Till that day."

She took a little breath.

"She put her hand on his . . . well, thigh. But pretty high. And left it there. God." She blushed. "Mr. Slaughter just brushed it off. And she puts it back! And he brushes it off again. Then she goes, *It can get lonely in a new town, Dayton*. And he goes, *I'm not in your market, Miss Kaye.* And Sylva—well, you don't know her, but she has a temper and gets her back up."

"And?"

"And she said—in this scary voice, soft but scary, you know what I mean?"

Ben nodded.

"She said, pretty much in his face, *And what market might that be?* And Mr. Slaughter said she knew damn well what market he meant. Then he said he was going to talk to her about it anyway. But . . ."

"But?" Kenechi prompted.

"But something like he planned to check out her other services but only because he didn't want the Knowlton connected to certain things."

"A second ago, you said Dayton had found out something. Did you or do you know what he found out, or what it involved?" Ben asked.

"No."

Kenechi's fathomless black eyes met Ben's. *Not telling all she knows.* Both detectives looked at her until she began twisting the rings on her fingers.

"From here on, it's just rumor," she said. "Hearsay, whatever."

"Okay, lions and marmosets then," Ben said, and she dimpled.

"Sometimes men call here, business travelers, whatever, and they want to talk to Sylva Kaye. Sometimes they talk about needing an escort." She riffled the pages on her calendar. "Maybe it's more than that, and Mr. Slaughter was, well, telling her he knew and didn't like it. Anyway, after he left, she was in a rage, got on the phone and shouted, and came out to reception where I was then and shouted some more."

"Like?"

"Like for me to keep my mouth shut about that little scene. And like if he thinks he's going to brush her off, if he thinks he's going to oust her from the Knowlton after all these years blah blah blah." She hesitated. "Then she said, *That asshole's going to get himself hurt.*"

Kenechi looked up from his notes. "Those were her words?"

"Those were her *exact* words."

"Do you know who she called?"

"I don't." She looked uneasy. "She has guns."

"Why do you say that?'

"I've seen them. In her purse. She goes to get a lipstick or a cough drop or a tissue, and she has to take out a bunch of stuff—she has big purses. So she pulls out keys and wallet and address book and notebook and pens and nail polish and pills and cosmetic bag and perfume and—"

"Yeah. Okay."

"And a gun . . . Somewhere in there, she pulls out a gun. She practices at a shooting range. Brags about being a good shot."

"Do you know what kind—no, just tell us what you've heard her say about guns. In your own words."

"In my own words. Well, yeah, that's what I've been using."

She fell silent, examining the top of Ben's head as he bent to his notebook and wrote something. He looked up, meeting her gaze.

"You have stubborn hair," she said.

"Excuse me?"

"I know your kind of hair. But it's nice. Styled nice, I mean. Who does it?"

Would you believe Sammy Nazario, in his one-chair barbershop?

"What can you tell us about Karl Novak, Dollie?" he asked.

"Oh. Yeah. Well, I don't know him. Or anything about him. Just that he wanted to buy the Knowlton, but everybody knew that. I didn't even know about what Ab just told you. But I saw him here yesterday afternoon."

"Novak?"

"Yeah."

"You mean in the morning?"

"No. Afternoon."

"Here in the Knowlton?"

"I guess. I mean—I saw him go past the window and into the lobby. At least I think he went into the lobby. Anyway, past the window for sure."

"On foot? What time was this?"

"Four? Yeah, four. Or so. Maybe a little earlier. How I know is Zora came in right after that to pass out her leaflets. She does that at four. You can set your watch by her."

She examined her rings and sighed.

"Poor Mr. Slaughter," she said again.

"Why do you say that?"

"He had a bad morning."

"Yes?"

"Jimmy Snipes came in here and got rough with me, and Mr. Slaughter threw him into the street—"

"Let's hear about Jimmy Snipes."

She took a deep breath, thought a second, and told them everything, Ben listening, Kenechi writing.

"Another thing," she said when she'd finished, "Jimmy had a gun, too. At least I think it was a gun. All I saw was the handle. He bragged about it, then had it with him when he came down here to the Cachet once. Stuck in the waistband of his trousers. Showing it off, letting his jacket fall open like it was an accident."

Kenechi stopped writing and looked at her. "What did it look like?"

She shook her head. "Like a gun. I don't know anything about guns. If it *was* a gun. For all I know, it was a toy. Be just like Jimmy, him and his dream world."

"Meaning?" Ben asked.

"Ahhh," Dollie waved a dismissive hand, bracelets clashing. "Jimmy Snipes is always pretending. Or . . ." She thought. "I don't know. Imagining. He wants to be special. But I don't think he knows the difference between good-special and bad-special. You'll be talking to him, right?"

"Yes."

"When you talk to him, you'll see what I mean."

Ben looked at her.

"He has this sicko relationship with his mother. He used a word . . . what is it when some small thing lives on a big thing, but the big thing needs the small thing, too?"

"Symbiosis," Kenechi said.

"Yeah. That's the word. Well, here's what he said, *We've had our teeth in one another's throats so long that if we ever let go, we'd both bleed to death.*"

Kenechi was rapidly writing in his notebook, and Ben waited until he finished. Then he said, "We've been told that Dayton said he got into it with several people at the Knowlton yesterday, that everyone was 'spoiling for a fight.' Can you add anything to that, or to anything you've told us?"

Again, that small hesitation. The detectives waited. Then Dollie shrugged.

"Well, this really isn't anything. I know that for a fact. And I don't want to get anyone in trouble when it's not anything."

The detectives waited.

"You know Zora Sanda."

"A street woman who hangs around here."

"Yes. Well—and this is *nothing*—she got mad at Mr. Slaughter yesterday and shouted some threats at him. The shop was full, so people heard her. "

"Threats. Like what?"

"Actually, that she was going to smite him. The only reason I'm telling you is you might hear it from someone else, and it's *nothing*."

"What set her off?"

"Mr. Slaughter said she wasn't to pass out her religious stuff in the lobby anymore. He told me to tell her so in no uncertain terms. But he also said he understood about her and everything, and that she could come into the Cachet, even sit in the lobby as long as she didn't bother others or pass out that religious stuff. So I had to tell her."

"And she didn't like that."

"No way. Zora can have like little tantrums from time to time. They don't mean anything. She would never hurt anyone. Anyway, a gun? She'd never have anything like a gun."

"I think smiting involves the jawbone of an ass."

She dimpled. "She doesn't have one of those, either."

CHAPTER 19

A thick woman opened the door. She had a maroon wool coat over one fleshy arm and wore transparent vinyl rain boots over her oxfords. Her torso was soft under her sand-colored dress, flesh puffing like rising dough above and below a tight brown plastic belt.

"Mrs. Snipes?" Ben asked. Drifting past his nostrils were the apartment's merged smells of fried food and Lily of the Valley cologne.

She pursed thin lips. "Who wants to know?"

Ben stepped just across the threshold and showed her his badge. The room beyond was in half-light, despite the draperies being drawn back from the windows. She took his badge with blunt fingers and examined it at length, hazel eyes narrowing, handed it back to him.

"I see you're ready to go out. I'll detain you only a moment," Ben said.

She studied him through her lenses. "Actually, you're not going to detain me at all."

Ben imagined himself jousting in the doorway with this pugnacious woman and felt a flash of amusement.

"We can talk here, or we can talk at the station," he told her, "but talk we will."

She tossed her dusty-looking curls and showed him a faux smile full of dead-looking teeth. "What do you want?"

"I'm investigating a murder, and I'd like to speak to your son. But first, where were you yesterday afternoon and evening?"

As soon as the question was out of his mouth, he recognized it as an effort to ruffle the smug composure of a woman who wasn't a suspect. He felt a tiny spike of shame. It was only a small abuse of authority, but still the kind of thing he despised.

It didn't work, in any event. She was neither ruffled nor intimidated. Her eyes sharpened and an unreadable spark seemed to glance off the amber rim of her spectacles.

"My son? What do you want with my son?"

"Let me repeat," he said, still ashamed but now committed, "we need to know where you were yesterday afternoon and evening."

"Right here." She swept a square hand behind her. Ben looked around and thought that with her own pallid hair and complexion and dress, she could almost vanish in this pale room.

Smile if you're in here!

"Alone?" he asked.

"Yes."

"Did you talk to anyone during that time?"

"No."

"Did you see anyone during that time?"

"Or more to the point, did anyone see *me* during that time."

"Either way."

"No."

"No one at all?"

"No."

"You didn't go to dinner?"

"I had a bite here."

"At Chez Dee?"

She snorted. "At those prices?"

"Did you call somewhere for take-out?"

"No. I brought something in earlier. From the Ripe Olive."

"Earlier than what?"

"Earlier than the period you're interested in."

"What period is that?"

"Yesterday afternoon and evening. According to you."

"What did you bring in?"

"Oh! You're the food police. Why didn't you say so?" She took a step toward him with an outstretched hand. For an odd moment, he thought she was about to grab him, and he pulled back involuntarily. But she merely jerked the door closed behind him, then stood back and looked at him with a mean little scrap of smile— as though she knew his sham questions for what they were and wasn't letting him off the hook.

Ben almost smiled. *Big bad policeman fails to rattle little fat woman.* In his mind's eye, he saw her raise an index finger and draw an invisible stroke on the air. *Mrs. Snipes: one.*

Served him right.

He took out his notebook and uncapped his pen.

"Let's leave last night's menu for another time, Mrs. Snipes. I have just one more question. Where was your son during this time?"

"Whyn't you ask him?"

"Is he here?"

"No."

"Then I'll ask you. Where was your son yesterday afternoon and evening while you were here, as you say, alone?"

Her bosom, full as the breast of a partridge, rose and fell, and she examined her square nails.

"One more time," Ben said. "Where was your son Friday afternoon and evening?"

She gazed at him with golden eyes. "My son . . ."

"Yes?"

She shrugged.

"Is that question too hard for you? Let's start easy. Is Jimmy Snipes your son? Does he live here?"

"He is. He does. He—" She stopped.

"You were going to say?" he asked.

"I wasn't going to say anything. You can do your own work."

She withdrew into the room and yelled toward a closed door. "James!"

In a moment, the door opened and Jimmy Snipes appeared in the opening buttoning his cuffs. He looked natty in a starched white shirt, chartreuse tie, and belted black trousers, but his lean face wore a sour look.

"Detective," his mother said, indicating Ben with a toss of the head, and fitted a large handbag over the arm that held the maroon coat.

Jimmy Snipes raised his brow, and Ben his badge.

"I need to ask you a few questions, Mr. Snipes."

"Like?"

"Like where you were yesterday afternoon and evening?"

Ben saw something come into Jimmy's eyes.

"Dayton Slaughter. Right?"

"What do you know about it, Jimmy?"

"I know what the whole building knows. That he was shot. Killed."

"How did you hear about it?"

"Um . . ."

He sat on the beige sofa, then jumped up with a rebellious glance at his mother and turned on the lamps at either end. He plopped down again, placed a shining black loafer on the coffee table and, with another unreadable glance toward his mother, nudged the figurine on the tabletop with his toe of his shoe. When she ignored him, he bent and smoothed a chartreuse sock.

"Man told me at the newsstand."

His mother turned at the door. "Murder, eh, Jimbo? Now you've done it."

A look of dark animosity came over Jimmy's face.

"Toodles, Miz Snipes," he said, without looking her way.

"Let's talk, Jimmy," Ben said as the door banged shut behind her.

The animosity drained from Snipes' face and left it, Ben thought, looking empty, even bereft. As Ben watched, he brought up his hand to comb back his forelock with four fingers, his gaze veering to Ben, veering away. Then he jumped up, went to the window, and looked down at the street, gnawing on an already thoroughly chewed thumbnail.

"What was your name again?" he asked, back still to Ben.

"Gallagher."

"So Gallagher. Go fuck yourself."

Inherited his mother's gene for geniality, thought Ben.

Jimmy started at a knock on the door, then gave off a burble of soprano laughter.

"Whah, ah do declare, heah's Miz Moneypenny back evah so soon."

But it was Kenechi who loomed in the doorway, finished with Tooley Deere and now badging Jimmy, following him to the sofa and sitting down beside him.

"King Kong," Jimmy announced, eyeing Kenechi. "Or Darth Vader."

Ben said, "Jimmy. Where were you yesterday afternoon and evening?"

"Where am I any afternoon and evening?"

"I asked first."

"Living large, Sherlock, any afternoon, any evening. The daring young man."

"Yeah." Ben sighed. He saw what Dollie meant.

Jimmy's face reddened at Ben's sigh.

"What do you know about it, you big bastard, another big tall bastard like Big Boy Slaughter. And look where it got him."

"Where'd it get him, Jimmy?"

Jimmy gave him a hard stare. "I was at the doctor's, since you ask so nice."

"If that's the case, why didn't you say so?"

"I thought it was my business."

"We're investigating a murder."

Jimmy waved that away.

"Who was this doctor?"

"An MD kind of doctor, whaddya think, a pee aitch fuckin' dee?"

"What's this doctor's name?"

"Lessee. Dr. Strudel, I think." He chewed his lip. "No, Dr. Schmaltz. No. Schnitzel. Wait!"

He held up a hand as if warding Ben off.

"It was Schwartzkopf. Which in German means *blackhead*. Good name for a dermatologist, hee hee."

He caught Ben's expression and changed tack.

"His name was Schwartz. Internist. Fourth floor, a medical building on Gaston."

Ben took his notebook over to the desk and picked up the telephone book, leafed through it.

"You had an appointment?"

Jimmy rolled his eyes.

"Maybe I should ask you something more challenging. What time was your appointment?"

"He worked me in, after his others. I went there at three and saw him at like four, little after."

"You went an hour early?"

Ben copied something from the phone book into his notebook and turned to Jimmy.

"Why did you go to the doctor?"

Jimmy studied Ben a moment, then gave a small, derisive laugh.

"And why aren't you writing in your wee brown notebook? Jimmy's little four o'clock with Dr. Schwartz screwing up your detection?"

He held up an imaginary notebook, wrote on it with a slender index finger.

"James T. Snipes," he said, screwing up his face. "His Unbreakable Alibi. Also known as: *Well, Shit.*"

Kenechi gave Jimmy a long look with eyes black as oil.

"What time did you leave the doctor's office?" he asked.

Jimmy turned on the sofa to face Kenechi.

"Oh, you speak, Mr. Kong?" He slapped his hand across his forehead. "Oh my God, it's my long-lost father!"

He did a brief breath-rattling Darth Vader impression before saying, "Four thirty, like that. I don't know. Check with Dr. Schnoodle."

"We'll do that." Ben said. "One last question. You have a gun?"

For the first time, Jimmy looked wary.

"Uh uh."

"Was that a no?"

"Yes."

"You don't have a gun?"

"Yes. I mean no."

Ben stood, looking at Jimmy so long that Jimmy dropped his eyes and fiddled with a hangnail.

In the corridor, Ben looked at his watch.

"Let's go ahead and leave for Ma's," he said to Kenechi. "We'll stop at Novak's on the way."

He tore a page from his notebook and handed it to Kenechi.

"We'll check in with this Dr. Schwartz. But either way, we need a search warrant soon as possible. I didn't pursue the gun question because he was getting spooked. I don't want him to get rid of it if he hasn't already. And we need a tail, twenty-four seven. Beginning now. No way I can manage that, though, being—as they say—off the case."

"I'll put that together. But if Snipes is at the doctor's at four—"

"If he's out of there by a little after four, there's leeway. Ruben Naldo's back in town but has some vacation time left, might want the work."

"I could get Naldo and Ramsey Ratzlaff."

"Naldo and Foncell Pratt would work better."

Kenechi gave him one of his oblique glances. "Pratt? Why not Ram? Used to be Naldo's partner. Also, Ram said he'd like to work the case."

"I bet he did." Ben waited a couple of beats. "It's your case, Ken."

Kenechi studied Ben with those obsidian eyes. "Pratt and Naldo then."

CHAPTER 20

Andrew found Dollie Varnes squaring up a pile of magazines on a chrome table and sashaying a little to the piped-in music.

"Thanks for working me in," he said. "Guess I'm a bit early."

"You're fine." She gave him one of those smiles. "I just need to straighten up here and get someone to take the desk."

He stood at the marble counter and watched. Gone were the magenta tee, the striped skirt, the yellow shoes. Now, she clomped about the reception room in black leather boots with four-inch platforms and wide Velcro-backed ankle straps. Her dress was fuchsia crepe with a peplum, a snug ankle-length skirt with a deep slit, and an Oriental symbol emblazoned in gold sequins across the breast. Each wrist held half a dozen bangles.

"You changed clothes."

She looked pleased. "You noticed."

"Who wouldn't?"

She waved in the direction of the little boxes she'd been shelving.

"One of my chemicals had a loose cap. Spilled on my skirt. A bonus of living where you work, though. Better yet, living in a hotel where you work!" She fidgeted. "I guess you're going to be landlord, with Mr. Slaughter—"

She blinked and dropped her eyes.

"That's some dress," Andrew said. "Like something from the '40s."

"It's vintage. You like it?"

"It's . . . interesting."

She smiled broadly.

"It's from World War Two. My favorite."

"Your favorite war?"

She laughed, a sound that brought to Andrew's mind the word guffaw. He moved closer and touched the ruffle that went from her waist to her hips and covered part of the long, slim skirt beneath.

"What's this?"

She didn't pull away when he touched her.

"It's a peplum," she said. "Very big in the '40s. What'd you think it was?"

"I thought your skirt broke off and another one grew beneath it."

"Hahhhah." She clapped her hands, bracelets jangling. "Like a new fingernail beneath a fake nail. I've seen a few of those!" She fingered the bodice of her dress. "They said at the shop that this symbol was Chinese, but I found out it's Japanese. Maybe the dress wouldn't have sold if people thought it was Japanese. I mean back then."

When Andrew didn't say anything, she added, "The Japanese were our enemies."

Andrew looked at the dress. "I can tell."

She narrowed her eyes at him for a second, and then touched her sequined breast.

"Do you know what this means?"

"That symbol? Yes."

She drew back, surprised. "You do?"

"Yes. But go ahead and tell me."

"It's Japanese for happiness."

"Oh."

"What did you think it meant?"

"I thought it meant ugly dress."

She broke off her laugh even as it began.

"Are you being mean? Getting even with me for before? Because if you are—"

"No. Believe me."

"Because if you are—one, I didn't mean it the way it sounded, and two . . . ugly dress. Hahhhah."

"I was joking—but maybe my jokes were mean. I haven't been around girls for a long time. I won't do that anymore, Dollie."

She sent him a glance from beneath thick black lashes.

"We going to have an anymore?"

He looked at her standing at the window in her fuschia dress, the sunlight stained red, too, through the filter of the red canopy, and thought everything about her shone—her hair, her eyes, her sequins.

"Oh God, I hope so," he said, surprising himself with his intensity.

A fireplug of a woman adrift in a fog of Lily of the Valley cologne thrust herself between them, invading Andrew's space enough to make him move, slapped a crumpled ticket and credit card on the counter, and leaned forward, elbows outthrust, exuding cranky impatience. Andrew noticed her blunted fingers and the short, spatulate nails, freshly lacquered a muddy shade the color of earth.

He studied the woman while Dollie rang up the sale and fussed with the credit card. She'd shoved her broad, high hips against the counter, and her large breasts lay upon the marble top in one overstuffed prominence. Her meaty forearms, folded on the counter, were hairless and freckled. Frizzy curls of ash blonde framed her sallow moonface, and skimpy lashes almost disappeared in the flesh above her eyes, giving her a denuded look. She wore spectacles with amber frames, and from the side, in the slanting sunlight, her eyes looked more golden than hazel.

Like a goat's eyes, Andrew thought.

She retrieved her credit card with an aggrieved air and stuck it into her handbag.

"Did you give me my discount?" she asked Dollie.

"Yes, ma'am!"

Andrew's glance followed the woman's broad back as she moved through the brass-framed doors. Though her transparent rainboots, he could see that her calves were thick but her ankles slender, her feet small and prim. She moved into the lobby and motioned Abner to get her car.

"Thank you, Mrs. Snipes," Dollie sang after her.

As they watched, the woman shrugged into a maroon coat and plopped on her head a feathered, dun-colored hat so flattened that it resembled a pigeon put through a wringer. She lumbered out of the building toward a gray Cadillac, plucking the keys from Abner's hand on the way.

"She stiffed him," Dollie said. "She didn't tip the folks in here, either."

"What was she in here for?"

"Her nails."

"No kidding. Who did them—the gardener?"

CHAPTER 21

The bronze elevator doors slid open silently on the top floor of Karl Novak's Turtle Creek high-rise, and Ben and Kenechi stepped out onto thick velvet-pile carpeting the color and sheen of platinum. They strode down the corridor to Novak's apartment, pressed the bell, and heard footsteps from within.

The door swung open.

Novak wasn't going to let them in at first; you could see him toying with the notion. Then he held the door wide with one hand and motioned them in with the other, a heavy paw adorned with gold rings, the wrist encircled with a bracelet of gold and rawhide. Passing, Ben caught a whiff of bourbon and stifled the impulse to check the time.

"We'll go into the den." Novak's voice was thin and high and edged with a cigar rasp.

"Den" was the right word, Ben thought, recalling Nell's description of Novak: *a bear with furniture.* Ice blue silk draperies presented an incongruous backdrop to the rest of the room. Kenechi, eyeing the African safari heads, monkey-base lamps, leopard-skin seats, and glass-eyed lion rug, muttered under his breath, *Just like home.*

Karl's suite was cold, even frigid, but he was sweating, his open-necked black silk shirt damp at back and armpit. He went to the bar, poured a couple of fingers of bourbon into a squat glass and raised it toward the detectives.

"On duty, I take it?"

He did not offer them anything nonalcoholic nor invite them to sit. They sat nonetheless, Ben on leopard and Kenechi on oxblood leather off to the side.

"How's your lovely momma, Ben?" Karl asked.

Ben opened his notebook and gazed at Karl's fleshy face, thinking—as he had before—that the two halves of Novak's face didn't match: mouth up on the right side, down on the left; right eye normal, left squinted. His hair was the dirty yellow of a bad dye job. His bruised and swollen nose shone with an oily gleam, its perpetually flared nostrils reminiscent of a panicked horse.

"Nell's one fine lady," Karl continued, "trying to put together something for them poor little poor kids, bless their hearts. My daddy—he was a Southern Baptist minister, you know, deceased— he would have put his shoulder behind that."

"Let's talk about your relationship with Dayton Slaughter, Karl."

Karl's eyes flared, and he twisted his lips into an almost-smile. Ben thought his pale irises matched the icy draperies.

"We don't—didn't—have what you call a relationship. We had business interests in common, that's all."

"You know he was killed yesterday."

"I heard, yes."

"Tell us about those business interests."

Karl sat on the other leopard-skin seat, his back to Kenechi, and rested a heavy ankle on his knee.

"Can we make this short, Ben?" he said, offering another rictus-like smile, this one intended to be ingratiating. "I have an appointment."

Kenechi reached into his pocket, took out a notebook and pen, and asked, "What happened yesterday with Dayton Slaughter, Mr. Novak?"

Karl turned and shot a surprised glance in Kenechi's direction, but instead of answering, he bent and rubbed a finger over an invisible smudge on his tasseled loafers. When he sat back, his face was reddened either with the exertion of bending forward or the outrage of being questioned by a black man. He swung his eyes toward Kenechi in a stare meant to scorch.

"I was born in Biloxi in nineteen hundred and fifty-six, boy, and in Biloxi—"

"Karl." Ben didn't let him finish. "What happened yesterday with Dayton Slaughter?"

"We had a little bidness is all. Like I said."

"What sort of business?'

"A property sale."

"Which didn't go your way, I understand."

Karl didn't speak for a moment. Then he said—irrelevantly, Ben thought, "I'm nigh on sick to death of this."

"Of what?"

"You carpetbaggers. Meddlin'."

"What are we talking about exactly?"

"About Slaughter, of course." He paused meaningfully. "And rich Yankees like him. Comin' down here to snap up properties at fire-sale prices."

"Is that your version? Fact is, Dayton's bid far exceeded yours."

Ben longed to ask who, exactly, was the carpetbagger—and to remind Novak that he, Ben, had spent his life in Texas, while Novak, a latecomer from Mississippi, was known for making lowball offers to down-on-their-luck property owners. But he recognized his response for the pissing contest it was and held his tongue.

Karl finally turned his glacial eyes toward Ben. "We're not doing this."

"We need to hear about yesterday. We can hear about it here or at the station."

"We both bid on the same property, Ben. Bidness. Happens all the time. You don't kill because of a busted deal."

Kenechi looked around the room. "Why *do* you kill?"

Karl ignored him, but the ruddiness of his complexion deepened.

Ben kept his voice pleasant. "Nasty cut above your nose."

Karl gingerly fingered the laceration, the blue knot, but said nothing.

"How did you get it?"

Karl rose and moved behind a dark and heavy desk in the corner, shifted some papers. "Are you about through here, Gallagher? As I said—"

"How did you get it?"

"As I said, we're not doing this."

"How'd you get the cut?"

"Ran into something."

"What?"

"Does it matter?"

"Might. We hear you got it running into Dayton Slaughter. You have any occasion to go to Arlington yesterday?"

Karl worked his lips, but no sound emerged, and he shifted his gaze from Ben's.

"Where were you yesterday?" Ben persisted. "Afternoon and evening. We want to know everything about yesterday. Walk us through it."

Karl's face reddened again, but his lips looked pinched and white.

"I'm not walking you through fucking anything, Gallagher." He picked up a cordless phone lying on an ottoman and hit a number. "I'm calling my lawyer."

"As I just said, you can answer our questions here and now or downtown and later—with or without your lawyer," Ben said in the same pleasant voice.

"Hang on, Jenk," Novak said into the receiver. He turned to Ben.

"Yesterday afternoon and evening, I was either here or at my office downtown."

Ben wrote in his notebook. "Anyone who can verify that?"

Karl was looking at Ben's notebook as though it had sprung to life. He poked himself in the chest with a thick thumb. "I can verify it."

"Anyone else? Because you were seen—"

Ben looked up just in time to put out a hand and neatly catch the telephone Karl threw at him. He put the phone to his ear, said, "Hang on, Jenk," and placed the phone and the waiting Jenk beside a monkey lamp.

"Because you were seen around four," Ben continued, "and it wasn't in your office."

"I was either here or downtown. Part of that time I was with Sylva Kaye. But you can talk to my—" He broke off, watching Ben, who had his own phone out, punching in a number, waiting.

"Proudhorse? Where are you?" Ben's eyes on Karl's were calm and steady. "Great. Novak says he spent some time with her yesterday. Without tipping her that he says so, see if you can get that confirmed. If she says yes, pin down exact time and place."

Ben pocketed his phone and gathered up notebook and pen, Kenechi rising.

Taking their time.

"We'll have to get back to you, Karl."

"Do that." The response sounded strangled, Karl's face now an even deeper and more dangerous-looking burgundy.

Outside the door, Kenechi held up his blank notebook. "That went well."

"God, Karl Novak," Ben said. "I don't know what makes him that way."

"I do," said Kenechi. "Tribal warfare."

CHAPTER 22

ndrew sat in Dollie's black leather salon chair wearing a capacious gray nylon cape and that curious docile, naked air that afflicts men sitting swaddled in salon chairs. A lyric resounded in Andrew's head as Dollie spritzed his hair with something that smelled like peppermint, and dried and combed and fluffed and snipped, weaving her long blue nails through his hair with an expert delicacy.

The lyric. What was it from?

If they could see me now . . .

He hummed it aloud, and then stopped long enough to ask, "What's that stuff?"

"A styling mist."

"I like the way it smells."

He'd liked the way she smelled, too, bending over him and the shampoo basin, for a moment replacing the Cachet's pungent scents with her own soapy aroma. He'd felt the heat of her body, the light touch of her small, firm breasts as she brushed against him, the jet of warm water massaging his scalp. Eyes closed, he'd smiled with something close to delirium—nothing had ever felt more intimate, nor more welcome!

If they could see me now . . .

Andrew pointed to the framed photo on the vanity facing him.

"That your dog?"

"Snazzy. When he was a puppy. He's six now. Can't believe it. I've had him since I was seventeen."

Andrew did the math, wondering if he seemed as old as he felt to this odd girl.

"Snaz is the best thing in my life," she said. "Except college."

"College?"

"Night school. Taking it slow. I did two years of beauty school, but no college. Business administration, ugh. But I can use it right here. I manage this place for Sylva Kaye."

"That's pretty good. At your age."

"Oh, from your lofty thirty-plus years."

"How do you know that?"

"Um . . . Mr. Slaughter. He mentioned you'd had a birthday February twelfth but that you'd all celebrate it together when you got home. I thought—"

He tensed, his throat tightening, at the mention of Dayt's name, and Dollie's hands went motionless on his head for a moment.

"I'm really sorry about Mr. Slaughter," she said, looking at him in the mirror.

He nodded.

"Anyway, I thought it would be sad to have a birthday in . . . in the Big House."

She caught his expression in the mirror.

"What's funny?"

"Big House. You been watching old movies?"

"I *did* get that from an old movie. A movie called—"

"'Big House.' Right?"

"They don't call prison the Big House anymore? Shoot."

"Some do. The inmates not so much. But why *shoot?*"

"I like the way it sounds." She assumed a rough voice and a gunfighter stance. "I tell ya I ain't goin' back to the Big House!"

He laughed, and she grinned back in the mirror. "Better than the clink or pokey or slammer. Or hoosegow or cooler."

"Or can or joint or jug." He thought for a second. "Or stir, pen, lockup, chill, cage, yard, icehouse, inside, freezer . . ."

"You musta spent your time in the Big House reading the thesaurus."

They'd skated past the rough patch of Dayton's death, and Andrew was relieved.

"So if you don't like your business classes, what classes do you like?"

"You'll probably laugh, but . . . philosophy."

"Putting your Horace before Descartes."

"Hahhhah." She resumed with her scissors, her fingers a caress as they moved through the hair at the nape of his neck. "And I like my biology class."

It had been so long since he'd been touched by a woman.

"I saw something this morning." She put down the scissors, clunked to the window in her black boots, and scanned the sill. Then, making pincers of her blue talons, she grasped something, dropped it into her palm, and moved toward him, holding out a fist.

"Something I learned." She swiveled his chair so he faced her and opened her hand. He saw a tiny silver ball on her palm.

"Sow bug," he said. "Rolls up in little balls like that. Cute. Suited up in hinged armor."

"So it's a bug?"

"Something tells me it's not."

"Sow bug or pill bug or roly-poly. It has lots of names. And this little suit of hinged armor is really—"

He realized that the intense blue of her eyes was the same as Nell's and Ben's.

"—is really a *flattened elliptical body,*" she quoted, "*capable of being rolled into a ball.*"

Andrew licked his index finger and touched Dollie's arm. *Sssst.*

"But here's the best part. It isn't a bug. It's a terrestrial isopod crustacean."

"A crustacean. Like shrimp? Crayfish?"

She turned his chair back to the mirror. "By the time I get my degree, I'll be as smart as you."

"Get thee to Huntsville."

She met his eyes in the mirror. "I think it speaks well of you, Mr. Gallagher, that you finished your education."

"Call me Andrew," he said.

She fluffed his hair this way and that. "You have great hair. Nice body, a little wave. Good thing you didn't get your brother's hair. His kind of hair is hard to tame."

"The luck of the draw. We don't have exactly the same gene pool—I think Ben got his dad's hair."

"Andrew? Earlier, when I put my hand out to touch your head, you—"

"I recoiled."

"I was going to say flinched. But, yeah, recoiled. That's a better word."

What could he say to this girl with the electric eyes and magenta mouth, whose world was a beauty salon and night classes?

She took both hands from his head for a moment and looked at him mournfully in the mirror.

"Did they hurt you in there, Andrew?"

The directness of the question startled him and, without warning, his throat tightened. But her hands were on his head again, gentle.

"In the Big House, you mean? Sometimes they tried to," he said, with as much honesty he could muster, "and sometimes they did."

CHAPTER 22

Ben and Kenechi left Karl Novak's high-rise, turned onto Turtle Creek Boulevard, and worked their way toward McKinney. There was a break in the rain, but the wind had picked up, the sky a gray canvas scrawled over with dingy clouds.

They pulled into Nell's drive behind Proudhorse and Hilda, who in turn had pulled in behind Andrew. Ben, seeing his brother emerge from the Lexus burdened with bags and boxes, trotted over and grabbed a couple of the parcels.

"New threads, eh? Hey, your hair looks great. Ma will love it."

Andrew drew closer. "Does Ma have plans for tonight?"

Ben laughed.

"What," Andrew said.

"You have a date."

"I do."

"With Dollie Varnes."

Andrew stared at him.

"Elementary, my dear Watson. She's the only woman you've been near except Ma. And Zora the bag lady." He waved in Hilda Cloy's direction. "And now Hilda the lesbian."

"I'm not taking Dollie out because she's the only game in town."

"No. I didn't mean that," Ben said quickly. "And I wouldn't think of her like that, either. And you obviously made an impression on her."

"I did?"

"She used our interview this morning to interrogate me—about you."

Nell opened the door, warmth and the fragrance of garlic wafting to meet her guests. She directed the others to a table near the balcony window while Ben and Andrew climbed another flight to dump the parcels.

"What'd you buy?" Ben asked.

"Whatever wasn't a jumpsuit."

Downstairs, Ben followed Nell into the kitchen.

"Ma, did Dayton still carry that gold money clip with him all the time?"

She nodded. "Why?"

"It wasn't on his body. Neither was his Rolex. Or his car keys."

She thought a second. "He probably would have laid the keys on your console table when he came in."

He shook his head. "We looked everywhere."

"He had your house key too, Ben."

"Huh." He considered. "Well, let's not worry about that right now."

They sat down to antipasto, followed by roast chicken cozied up to capellini smothered in cream and Gorgonzola and studded with bits of olive and parsley. Hot garlic bread nestled beneath a stiff white napkin, and the wine glasses held a chilled Verdelet Blanc. Club soda with lime for Andrew.

"Omigod," Hilda said.

Ben watched Nell with concern as she served her guests. He thought she looked exhausted—even ashen. The fragile skin around her eyes seemed bruised, and her fork trembled in her grasp.

Her eyes met his and, swallowing hard, she asked, "What's with the case?"

The question was one she'd asked many times about other cases—and one that he'd answered many times. Now, he froze and looked away.

"Best not to discuss it right now," he said. Nell rose abruptly, her napkin falling from her lap.

"You can trust me, Ben," Andrew said.

Ben saw the shadow of hurt in his brother's hazel eyes, and Nell wheeled on Ben, her glance dark with fury, but she only bent to pick up her napkin and toss it over her chair back.

Ben felt tension build around the table. *Christ!*

"Of course we can, Andrew. It's not that. It's—"

It's *what?* It's *Ma* I don't trust?

Nell left the room—no, *marched* from the room, her back stiff and straight. There would be trouble later, Ben thought. Meantime, the table waited. Andrew waited.

"I just meant the specifics aren't solid yet," he said lamely. And saw in the other detectives' expressions what they were thinking: we're here for a briefing; that means we're here to pool specifics. He tried to fix it by adding, "Right now, we're waiting on the ATF and Karen Enid."

"Are fingerprints all filed in one place?" Andrew asked.

"In a computerized data bank. FBI maintains it. This is down your alley, Andrew. You can get search results within two hours for criminal submissions and in a day for civil. Twenty-four seven, three hundred and sixty-five days a year. You submit electronically and the search is automated. That's how we could hear from Karen as early as today. Meantime, interviews."

"What do you look for in interviews?" asked Andrew. "Non-verbal cues, that sort of thing?"

Ben grunted. "What would you look for if you thought some-one was hiding something?"

Andrew mused. "Skirts or evades. Won't meet your eyes."

"Eye contact is a biggie," Ben agreed. "But you can be mis-led. Especially with the pathological: Bundy didn't have a hard time meeting anyone's eyes. Or an aggressive or confident suspect might deliberately meet your gaze beat for beat."

"As a challenge."

Ben nodded. "Or say someone who has seemed unengaged suddenly looks at you while you're talking. May mean special knowledge or interest in whatever you're saying at the moment."

"But people from some Asian cultures might not meet your eyes," Andrew said. "Not because they're guilty, but to show def-erence. To avoid seeming aggressive."

Kenechi nodded. "Cultural differences."

"You'd make a good detective," Ben said.

"Hire me."

There was laughter around the table, and Nell reentered, car-rying a water pitcher.

"What about the physical stuff you can't help?" Andrew asked. "Autonomic nervous system stuff? You turn color. Or keep swallowing. Or your hands shake."

Ben thought of his mother, who was moving around the table refilling glasses. She returned his glance with an unreadable one of her own before returning to the kitchen. Ben heard the buzz of the coffee grinder.

"Some things are intuitive," Kenechi put in. "You don't have to be a detective to see biology at work and understand it on a basic level. You know when someone's literally sweating it out. Racing heart, clammy hands, dry mouth. Yawning or sighing, showing difficulty in breathing. Blanched or flushed complexion. Nausea.

"Some people can do a fair job of controlling biology," he added. "But that's rare. The interesting thing is the more intel-ligent and 'normal' you are, the more reliable and predictable the behavior."

"I read something about analyzing the suspect's narrative," Andrew said.

"Ken's specialty," Ben said.

Nell brought in coffee and sat down. Ben stole another glance at her. Avoiding his eyes, she fiddled with her spoon and seemed detached and distracted.

"The narrative of the innocent," Kenechi said, "is usually emphatic. Specific. Concise. Whether written or spoken. The guilty say too much, or not enough. Answer too quickly or take too long. Recount trivia in detail, but say they can't remember big things. Hedge or delay—cough, ask you to repeat the question. Change nouns, pronouns, maybe tense."

Ben said, "A guy shot his wife. Accidentally, he said. Ken noticed that in his written account, the shooter referred to the victim before the shooting as *my wife,* or *Maggie.* During and after the shooting, he referred to her as *Margaret.*"

"So?"

"We learned he never called her Margaret. So he was disclaiming the act," Kenechi said. "Distancing himself from it and from the victim. Depersonalizing her. The effect: it wasn't his wife or Maggie, but someone named Margaret. There had to be a reason he referred to her as *Margaret* when describing her death. And that reason was that he'd murdered her. Distancing himself was the only way he felt he could talk about it and hide his guilt.

"The guilty also avoid harsh or realistic terms—*kill, rape, steal,*" Kenechi said. "They say: 'I didn't hurt anyone, didn't take anything.' While the innocent say emphatically: 'I didn't steal! I'm not a thief!' "

Andrew nodded. "In the joint—they're all innocent there, you know—guys would say, 'I never touched that girl.' And we'd go, 'Yeah, right.' But there was a guy who'd get in your face and yell, 'I never fucking raped anyone, let alone a child!' You know what? We believed him. And I'll be damned if DNA evidence didn't get him out."

"It's hard to feign outrage," Ben said. "But the guilty still try. You wanna say, *Try an acting class, buddy.*"

"Main thing," Kenechi added, "is that what folks say and how they say it can reveal way more than they intended."

"Jesus Christ," Nell muttered. "Remind me never to talk to you fuzz again."

"You okay, Ma?" Ben asked.

"I'm fine." But she didn't look fine. She looked sick and sour, and gray as a sidewalk.

CHAPTER 24

"I'm going to get flowers for Dollie, for tonight," Andrew said after lunch. "Any suggestions?"

"She had a white orchid in a silver cup in her office," Ben said.

After Andrew left, the four detectives milled around Nell's foyer. Ben wanted to check out the DVD he'd found in Dayton's desk drawer, and Kenechi decided to hitch a ride back to the office with Hilda and Proudhorse. Ben's mobile rang

"Those unidentified prints in Slaughter's apartment," Karen Enid said.

"Tell me."

"Woman named Zora Sanda."

"Zora?" Ben blinked, and the others stopped talking and started listening. "Shit. Really?"

"You know her?"

"Street woman. Hangs around the Knowlton, passes out religious literature."

"Short rap sheet. Picked up for vagrancy's about all. But she was questioned after a homeless guy was knifed under the Elm Street viaduct. They charged another homeless guy."

"I saw one of her fliers on Dayton's desk this morning, under a party store bag that he left there yesterday afternoon. There was a receipt in the bag, timed and dated. That flier was *under* the bag, but it had to be put there recently—Dayton kept that desktop clear so Rosa could dust."

He thought a second. The dangers of assumption.

"I assumed Dayton left the flier there."

"Maybe he did," Karen said.

"And maybe *she* did. We talking about the latents and invisibles on the bathroom door casing and the nightstand?"

"Right. Our other matches so far are Slaughter and staff. Two nice unidentifieds, though."

"You'll keep working on it?"

"You bet."

Ben put down the phone and envisioned Zora, her square gray face and mop-strand hair. "Dammit to hell."

How'd she get into Dayton's suite? And, more important, why? He couldn't imagine questioning her. Rather, he *could* imagine it.

"Dammit to hell," he said again. "Who wants to interview Zora Sanda?"

Nobody said anything, so Proudhorse offered.

Ben thought of Proudhorse's pained Comanche gaze meeting Zora's crazed green glint, the wrinkles on his copper brow deepening further into stoic gloom as she turned his words into rhyme. No way. Not that it required finesse, but . . . Besides, he needed both Proudhorse and Hilda. He turned to Kenechi.

"Ken, did you say Ramsey Ratzlaff wanted in on this case?"

Upstairs in Andrew's sitting room, Ben took the DVD from his briefcase, opened the armoire that held the entertainment center, and pushed the DVD into the player.

Remote in hand, he sat down and pressed PLAY.

The screen lightened and ran through a few gray frames before settling on the grainy image of a slender and abnormally big-breasted blonde and a slender and abnormally big-breasted brunette. Both were leggy, tanned, bikini-waxed, and nude. Aside from hair color, they looked drawn from the same template: long hair, long nails painted shell pink, swollen lips painted shell pink, daintily tattooed at shoulder and ankle—one girl with what Ben thought he recognized as zodiac symbols, and the other with arrow-pierced hearts. They lay or half-sat in a tumble of burgundy velvet bedcover, stroking and rubbing, lips *almost* touching, the better for the camera to record their writhing tongues. Main thing, Ben thought, they made an inordinate amount of noise—pain or ecstasy, he couldn't tell.

Suddenly, a rounded pair of masculine buns appeared in close-up. The camera pulled back, revealing a muscular, tanned, naked man with lank blonde hair. He was also tattooed, but not so daintily—crossed broadswords on his forearm and a likeness of Spider-Man's mask on his shoulder. He moved sinuously, or what passed for sinuously, toward the women and said in a baritone:

"Hello, girls."

"Oh wow," Ben said.

In unison, the women looked up at Mr. Buns and then down at his engorged penis, now turned toward the camera—and clearly a major player—and exhibited something resembling surprise. That is, two identical sets of waxed brows lifted a quarter of an inch. Two identical sets of shell pink lips opened slightly. Or, if not surprise, Ben reflected, maybe alarm, puzzlement, dismay, gas.

Abruptly abandoning the reaction, whatever it was, the matched set on the bed focused on Mr. Buns' penis and began making twin noises.

Suddenly the camera lurched and swung a little to the right, and for a split second Ben saw a fully clothed man—rather, a man's fully clothed lower body and a left hand and forearm. He wore navy slacks, and his shirt—what Ben could see of it—was a splashy pattern of tropical flowers in navy and turquoise. On his left wrist hung a bracelet of gold chain braided with strands of rawhide. The camera righted itself and returned to the threesome on the bed, now a mélange of arms and legs and grunts and oohs and aahs.

Andrew came in, carrying a white orchid in a silver container. Ben looked at the flower and smiled.

"Well, I know she'll like it," Andrew said.

"Come watch this with me." Ben said. "It's a porn production. If *production* is the right word."

"I thought you were working."

"This is work. Come have a look. I just saw something interesting. You can help me get a fix on it."

Ben ran the DVD back a little and pressed PLAY. The naked women were alone on the bed again.

Andrew watched. "Good plot."

"Strong characterization and dialogue, too. Watch this scene where—here it comes—the dialogue really gets snappy."

Mr. Buns repeated his sinuous movements and said, "Hello, girls."

Andrew laughed. "Oh wow."

"That's exactly what I said." Ben jumped up and moved closer to the monitor. "Here, right here, watch this, off to the right." The camera lurched dutifully, showed the guy in the tropical shirt. Ben hit PAUSE and searched the screen.

"What are you looking for?"

"Anything."

"Guy's wearing navy pants, loud shirt, complicated watch or bracelet of gold and twisted—what is that, rawhide?"

"Yeah. I saw that bracelet, or one like it, just a few hours ago. On Karl Novak's wrist."

Ben ran the player back a second and let the camera lurch again, paused it, nodded.

"Where'd you get the DVD?"

Ben didn't know how Dayton had come by the DVD, but his possession of it and his secreting it away in his desk showed he was concerned with Karl Novak's activities—and maybe, based on what Dollie Varnes had said, with Sylva Kaye's. Ben knew full well how Dayton operated. He played his cards close to his vest and never betrayed his hand. He was patient, wily, and capable of laying and executing long-range plans—part of what made him such a skilled advocate, as well as such a formidable adversary. Ben just wished he knew what Dayton knew—and what his plan had been.

He looked at Andrew for a couple of long beats. "Don't ask."

CHAPTER 25

A ndrew pulled over in front of the Knowlton, and Abner Zeeck hurried under the canopy to the driver's side of the Lexus. He'd barely opened Andrew's door when he slammed it shut again, flattening himself against the car as a city bus swooshed by.

Close, too close.

"Christ! You okay?" Andrew asked, getting out.

"I surely am," Abner said, his voice weak. "Them dang city buses go too dang fast through here."

"Guess you better park it, Ab. I have a seven o'clock date with Dollie Varnes, but I'm way early."

Abner looked pleased. "You can sit in the lobby, Mr. Andrew. I'll be in there directly to see if you need anything."

Andrew headed inside the Knowlton, reflecting that he'd spent most of his life being late. When had that changed? In Huntsville, where he had no choice and nowhere to go, anyway?

He rang the bell of Dollie's fifth-floor apartment at seven on the nose and heard a scrabble of dog claws on the other side of the door. Dollie admitted him into a small foyer and led him to the living room. He looked around. Muted, considering Dollie's colorful wardrobe.

"Nice," he said.

"It's one of the smaller apartments, but it's just right for us," she said, nuzzling the little red Peke in her arms. She wore a long-sleeved purple knit dress with a skirt that exposed her bony knees. Her varnished hair was partly in a topknot and partly in two long, loose strands that curved like Saracen blades on either side of her face. She'd impaled the knot atop her head with two crisscrossed, bejeweled dowels. Around her neck, she'd knotted a man's wide tie splashed with purple and orange.

Andrew smiled. "Vintage?"

He'd meant the tie. But she smoothed her skirt and made a circle so he could view the dress from all angles . . . put out a foot so he could admire her purple suede platform pumps.

"You know that during the second world war," she said, "women couldn't get silk stockings, so they wore leg make-up and drew a line down the backs of their legs with black eyebrow pencil?"

"Why would they do that?"

"For seams! Pretend stockings. They couldn't get silk. We needed silk for parachutes and stuff. I guess we didn't have nylon yet."

"Huh."

She set the dog down and reached into a closet to retrieve her coat, an unfortunate tent shape in a shaggy red horse-blanket plaid. Andrew stole a glance at the backs of Dollie's Olive Oyl legs and was relieved to find no penciled lines.

"What do you think of this coat?" She asked.

"Um . . ."

"I can't decide. I think it's a love-it-or-hate-it deal."

"I'm not sure, either."

They rode the elevator downstairs, where Abner stood at the door, smiling broadly. He hustled outside, brought the car around, and escorted Dollie to the passenger side, singing something falsetto under his breath.

"Geezy peezy, a Lexus SC convertible hardtop," Dollie said, stroking the pale leather. "I looked it up when Ab told me your mother got you one. Something like seventy thousand smackaroos. I thought, what a car for somebody just . . ."

She trailed off.

"For somebody just out of the Big House. I thought we decided that would be our preferred term."

She was busy touching every surface and button and knob she could reach. "This is the most fabulous car I ever saw. I could almost cry about it, but in *Gatsby* this shallow character Daisy cries over a pile of silk shirts, so . . . here we are talking about silk again."

"But not crying about it."

"That's because we're not shallow."

"My mother had a T-shirt that read *I am deeply superficial*—think that was an Andy Warhol quote. Used to be in a trunk of old clothes she had.

He felt her eyes on him. "Does she still have it?"

"The shirt?"

"The trunk."

"Probably."

"Oh man. I'd sure like to go through that trunk," she mused. "In twenty seconds, the aluminum top lowers into the trunk."

Andrew glanced at her in bewilderment, and she burst out laughing.

"No, I meant the trunk of this *car*. In twenty seconds, the aluminum top lowers into the trunk."

"You *did* look it up."

"Can we put the top down?"

"In February? Be my guest."

"Just to see if it works, I mean." She pressed the button. The top disappeared and the damp wind pushed her lacquered hair back and up in one great sheet, bejeweled dowels and all, the curved sidepieces like twin sabers winging from her temples. She patted the stiff arcs.

"You're laughing at my hair."

"Looks like Vampira. Or a weapon in a double-oh-seven movie. Decapitate the bad guys."

She let out a whoop of laughter, and Andrew's heart warmed.

"We can put the top up now. So my hair won't be like this permanently." She looked at him. "I want to tell you something. Something nobody knows—about Mr. Slaughter."

She turned in the seat to see him better.

"I had a clunker car, all I could afford right out of beauty school. He saw me pulling into the parking lot one morning and later came into the shop and said move into the Knowlton. He was already planning to buy the Knowlton, I guess—taking a big interest in it. Said one of the smaller suites on the fifth floor was nearly finished, and he'd arranged a big discount on the rent with Maisie Delacourt. So I could move in there and get myself a decent car."

"And you said?"

"I was flabbergasted. Said I didn't know how I could do that. I also didn't see how he could get Mrs. Delacourt to give me a discount."

"What'd he say? It was a business decision? That he planned to buy the Knowlton and it represented the place well if employees seemed prosperous and well treated? That this fifth-floor suite was less desirable than the others, and it was a good deal for the Knowlton to have it rented long-term? That you could pay full rent when you'd saved enough for the car?"

She stared at him.

"That's exactly what he said. Anyway, that's how I ended up with a new car and a nice apartment downtown."

He pulled into a narrow drive that led to a squat red building well back from the street.

"Nong Khai!" she said. "Yay! I love Thai food."

He pointed at the long, jeweled dowels crisscrossed in her top-knot.

"And you even brought your own chopsticks."

The waiter brought spring rolls with peanut sauce, and green chicken curry, and prawns with garlic, and backed away bowing like a flower in a breeze.

Dollie pointed at Andrew's club soda and lime.

"You don't drink at all?"

"Not for five years. One of the terms of my parole."

"Does it bother you if—"

"Nope. Remember, I've been dry for ten years."

She looked at him curiously. "Was it a problem before that?"

"Only on one particular night. And then it was a very big problem. But I don't want—let's talk about you, Dollie. Starting with your birth."

Her open expression closed and showed a scrap of defiance.

"None of that's interesting."

"It would interest me."

"Fine. Let's start with *your* birth."

"I see what you mean. Invasive."

She looked at her hands.

"Okay," he said. "But I *was* interested."

She brought her eyes up to meet his.

"I'm twenty-three," she said. "Born in Louisiana, December eighteenth. Sagittarius, on the cusp with Capricorn." She paused. "Everything?"

"That would be nice."

"Illegitimate. Orphanage. Foster homes."

"My mother was an orphan," Andrew said. "She was a ward of the state for five years and lived places where people were paid to care for her. Glorified foster homes, I guess. She doesn't like to talk about it. I can't imagine being in an orphanage." He dipped a spring roll in peanut sauce. "Or maybe I can. Maybe it's like being in Huntsville."

"It's pretty basic. You just long to be *adopted*. To be wanted and loved. Especially as you get older and understand it's not going to happen." She sipped at her wine thoughtfully. "A woman brought her little daughter into the shop the other day. The daughter was going to be the flower girl at a big family wedding. I piled her hair into curls and wound white satin ribbons through them."

Andrew listened.

"When they left, the mother buttoned the little girl into her coat, a little red plaid coat." She patted the shaggy plaid coat folded beside her on the booth. "Kind of like mine. Maybe that's why I got it. And the mother put her face close to her little girl's. They both had dark, dark hair and blue, blue eyes, and the mother kissed her on the cheek and whispered, *You are so lovely.*

Andrew nodded.

"I thought, *I could be from that family.* We have the same coloring. I could be related to that little girl's mother. Or "

Her eyes filled.

"Or you could be that little girl," Andrew finished.

"The nuns said my blood mother wanted me to be raised a Catholic. I graduated from St. Anne's School for Girls in 1998. Went to beauty school. And here I am. End of story. Sorry you asked?"

"No."

"What are you thinking?" she asked.

"That we all need to belong. I saw it even in prison, how newcomers horrified at the prison population and its behavior eventually came to . . . if not embrace, at least partake."

"Did you?"

"No. Thanks entirely to my family and Dayton. They stayed close. I never felt unconnected. And I stayed busy with stuff that had nothing to do with what the other inmates did. Books, school, the library, computers. I was a trusty." He refilled her glass. "I was also thinking about a metaphor. About the prison that contains us and the prison we contain."

He saw that flash of defiance again. "We make our own prisons?"

"I'm not saying that. You were an orphan. And that's a sort of prison. But you were also a child. You didn't make the choices that made you an orphan."

She was in profile, looking down, pensive, a fringe of lash lying on her pale cheekbone. He traced a finger down the plane of her cheek.

She turned to him full face, eyes calm. "But I'm grown up now. And so are you."

It was astonishing, the immediate flare of warmth he felt for her, and before he could check himself, he leaned toward her and pressed her hand to his lips. It felt small and soft and smelled of flowers, a scent he almost recognized.

Later, outside Dollie's door, warmed by the evening and the conversation, Andrew pulled her close, and she threw her arms around him. They held on tightly for a second, then let their lips meet. Again. And once again, lips parted and tongues touching. Afire, they lost themselves in a kiss so long and deep they came out of it dazed.

"I need to trust you," she whispered at his ear.

Hands on her shoulders, he drew his head back to meet her eyes.

"And I need to be trusted."

CHAPTER 26

Ben and Kenechi found Joe Proudhorse and Hilda Cloy sitting over the remnants of dinner at the Knowlton's Chez Dee, a wine glass in Hilda's little fist and a Dr Pepper in Proudhorse's large one.

"Sorry about your Saturday night," Ben said, pulling out a chair to sit down.

"Hey," Hilda said, passing her hand like a benediction over the white-clothed tabletop. "Who's complaining? We should have all our debriefings over dinner."

A waiter approached to bus the table, and Ben spied the spent carcass of a lobster on one of the departing plates.

"At least you're eating well."

"And expensing it," Proudhorse said.

"Ben and I had a burger at the Ripe Olive," Kenechi said.

Nothing changed in Proudhorse's somber expression.

"Good burgers. Bad decision."

Hilda smirked. "Would you gentlemen care to join us for dessert?" she asked.

They ordered chocolate cheesecake with raspberries, and Ben pulled out his notebook.

"Okay, let's have an overview, Ken."

Kenechi consulted his notebook, counting with the nib of his fountain pen.

"We've interviewed seven people: Dollie Varnes, Tooley Deere, Sylva Kaye, Maisie Delacourt, Jimmy Snipes, Karl Novak—"

"Zora Sanda?"

"Ramsey Ratzlaff talked to her this afternoon."

Ben shook his head and smiled at the thought of it.

"He's tied up tonight but will report on Monday morning. Unless we want to hear from him tomorrow, Ben?"

"Monday's fine."

"From what I understand, the interview didn't yield anything."

"I can imagine."

"So," Kenechi said, taking a deep breath. "Among these six, from what we know now, three had motive, means, and opportunity."

The waiter showed up with the cheesecake, rearranged the flatware and tabletop to his liking, and bowed away. Ben busied himself with his dessert briefly, then pushed away the plate and brought his wineglass near.

"Okay. We've talked to seven people all told. Two are not under suspicion: Dollie Varnes and Tooley Deere. One has no motive and a confirmed alibi: Maisie Delacourt. Two have motives and unconfirmed alibis: Sylva Kaye and Karl Novak. Another has a motive and a sort of alibi: Jimmy Snipes. And a wild card: Zora Sanda."

"Point being, if you're screwy," Kenechi continued, "you don't need a motive. But there's a problem with opportunity and means."

"Speaking of means," Ben added. "Three of the seven have guns and know how to use them—as it happens, the same three who have motives and unconfirmed alibis. Sylva Kaye, Karl Novak, and Jimmy Snipes."

"Neat," said Hilda.

Kenechi took over again. "Hilda, let's start with Maisie Delacourt."

"Nothing there," Hilda said. "She knew surprisingly little about Slaughter for having done a major business deal with him. Except that he was, as she put it, a *really really really* nice guy. She was at her Spa Friday afternoon from three till five-thirty. They have a computer sign-in deal, timed and dated."

Hilda studied her notes.

"She said she worked out from three to four, was on the tanning bed for twenty minutes, and had a Swedish massage from four-thirty to five-thirty. And her maid says she got home around six."

"Do they have to sign out, too?" Ben asked.

"No."

"Did you verify the four-thirty to five-thirty massage?"

"Not yet."

"Do that," Ben said. "If it checks out, we'll scratch Delacourt."

"Sylva Kaye?" Kenechi asked.

Joe Proudhorse leaned forward, elbows on the table, stormy brow creased.

"Something wrong, don't know what. Nervous as hell. Furtive and hostile."

Ben flipped back in his notebook.

"Dollie Varnes said Sylva put the make on Dayton, and he turned her down. Something else cooking there, though." He read from his notebook: "Sylva said, *That asshole's going to get himself hurt.* That may be haunting her. Alibi?"

"Nada. Says she had a Friday night bash and was home napping three to six."

"See if you can tack that down," Ben said. "And let's talk to her again. With a little of your famous pressure, Joe. She may be involved in a so-called escort service. Maybe porn films. That could explain her behavior, too. Lean on her. Get her to understand we're interested in homicide, not sex, legal or otherwise."

He doodled a rectangle on his notebook, filled it with little stars.

"You ask her about guns, Joe?"

"She acknowledged the shooting range. Wouldn't discuss the kinds of guns she does or doesn't own. That's when she started hollering lawyer."

Ben wrote something. "You're up, Ken."

"Karl Novak," Kenechi said, his chair creaking as he leaned back and clasped his big hands behind his head. "A piece of work. Like Sylva Kaye, Novak had motive, means, and opportunity. And there was bad blood between Novak and Dayton Slaughter. They got into it Friday morning. No confirmable alibi. He owns and shoots guns, has a menagerie on his wall. Hostile."

He looked at the other detectives with a hint of amusement.

"He threw us out. And before that, he literally tossed his lawyer at Ben—in the form of a telephone."

Hilda looked up from her notes. "Ben catch the lawyer?"

"With one hand."

Hilda saluted Ben with a forkful of cheesecake.

"Tooley Deere?" Ben put in.

"Nothing there," Kenechi said. "But we didn't expect anything. Slaughter was taking over the Knowlton, getting a new manager, but that's because Tooley had already resigned. Took another job. The most interesting thing Deere said concerned Jimmy Snipes. Said he was a wannabe who didn't know who he wanted to be."

"Smart-ass," Ben said. "Okay. My turn, best for last. Snipes had motive and means, but only narrow opportunity. Dayton Slaughter tossed him into the street Friday morning because he was manhandling Dollie Varnes. It's also clear that Dayton wanted the Snipes family out of the Knowlton—Tooley Deere said he was thinking about breaking the lease. For whatever that's worth."

"They been at the Knowlton long? You know when the lease runs out?"

Ben shook his head. "Anyway, Snipes says he left his doctor's office at four-thirty Friday. His doctor says he can't remember; it could have been earlier. It would be tight at best, especially with rush-hour traffic on I-30, but he could possibly get to Arlington by the estimated time of death."

Hilda looked dubious. "The ETD is five-ish? From Dallas to northwest Arlington in Friday afternoon traffic in less than an hour? Anyone check the traffic reports for accidents or slowdowns?"

Ben looked at Kenechi, who said, "An accident in the eastbound lane a little before four. Gawkers going west, but nothing major in that direction. It was cleared up by five or so."

Ben closed his notebook. "Anything else?"

They closed their notebooks, too, and waited.

"I have one other thing. It's hanging fire, but FYI."

He told them about the DVD.

"Where do you think Dayton Slaughter got it?" Proudhorse asked.

"Dunno. But I think it's what Dollie was talking about when she said Dayton had found out something about Sylva Kaye."

"The bracelet you said the guy on the DVD was wearing," Kenechi said. "We saw one like that this morning. On Novak's wrist."

Ben nodded. "Okay, salvage what you can of your weekend. I'll call you tomorrow if there's any reason, but I think I can leave you alone till Monday morning. And who knows what's going to happen Monday morning." He felt a sudden, sobering chill. "I guess I don't have to tell you what a good job you did, or how much I appreciate it."

"Aw, go ahead," Hilda said.

CHAPTER 27

Dollie had barely waved Andrew down the hall and lain back among her tumbled bedclothes when a rapid-fire knock told her Andrew was back. She tossed the blankets aside and ran to the door, snatching it open.

For Jimmy, he looked a little slept in, white shirt disheveled, collar loose, black suit coat slung over his right shoulder. But his intense chartreuse tie, pocket silk, and socks were as robust as when he'd put them on that morning. He leaned his left forearm on the door casing, casual, a thumb against his forehead, a wing of hair drooping over one delicate brow.

Snazzy growled, and Dollie bent to pick him up.

"I thought for a while there," Jimmy said, "that your ex-con was going to stay the night."

"What are you doing here, Jimmy?" Dollie asked, her color mounting. "Spying on me?"

He brushed past her and strode into the bedroom. She followed, apprehensive, Snazzy in her arms, and watched as Jimmy took in the rumpled bed and moved to the window, which she opened at bedtime as a defense against the stuffiness of the building's steam heat—especially given Northeast Texas' usually mild winters.

Jimmy stood with his back to her.

"I asked you—what are you doing here?" she repeated.

He was silent at the window for a second, then said, "I want to know what you told those dicks and, for the last time, I want to know why you won't see me again. Because that old creep in the glasses roughed me up a little?"

He turned to look at her, clasping his hands beneath his chin, fluttering his lashes and saying in falsetto, "My hero!"

Dollie shifted Snazzy to her other arm, the dog never taking his eyes off Jimmy.

"We've already had this conversation, Jimmy."

"Well, that bully bastard got his, didn't he?"

"Mr. Slaughter was a wonderful man, but you don't feel a moment's sympathy. That's something you don't know about. Just like that poor kitty. It's the sort of thing you would do, isn't it, Jimmy. Sneak around. Shoot someone."

She brushed past him to close the window, but he stopped it with his palm and opened it wider.

"I didn't happen to have a vise with me," he said.

Dollie was closer to him now than she wanted to be, and she averted her eyes, buried her face in Snazzy's auburn fur.

He took a lock of her black hair between his thumb and index finger, tugged a little, harder than was comfortable. She didn't move.

"You love that stupid mutt, dontcha?" he said.

Her eyes grew wary.

"You love that stupid mutt more than anything, dontcha."

His eyes slid toward her, then to the open window.

"Jimmy," she whispered.

He seized Snazzy by the auburn ruff at his neck and yanked him out of her arms. The little dog yelped, no, *screamed*, his voice going right to the top of the register.

"Jimmy Jimmy no no no Jimmy no!" Dollie screamed, along with the dog.

Jimmy held the squirming little bundle out the window, looking back at Dollie, who stared, dry lips moving *please please please* but making no sound.

He said, "All I have to do is open my hand," and watched as Dollie's eyes widened and rolled away. She sighed softly and slid down the wall, falling sideways with a bump, right at his feet.

"Jesus Christ."

He moved back and dropped Snazzy beside her, looking at her on the floor in her fuzzy pink robe.

"Jesus, out like a light—I mean over a fuckin' yappy little bug-eyed dog."

He reached toward her. Snazzy braced himself beside her and growled, his hair high on his back and grizzled lips pulled back over crooked little teeth.

Jimmy snorted. "Whee, lookee here, Snazzy Razzy standin' his ground."

He put out another tentative hand, and the dog snapped at it.

"Shee-it. Well, believe me, Razoo, shut your fuckin' mouth. Just gonna close the window so's you and Miz Varnes can have a nice nap."

He gave the window a push, grabbed his jacket, examined himself in the mirror, and strode from the room, slamming the door.

Snazzy licked Dollie's face with a long pink tongue, and Dollie's lashes fluttered. Seeing the little dog, she held out her arms, and Snazzy settled into her embrace.

"Oh Snaz," she whispered. "Darlin' doggie."

As she held the little warm body close, a fierce rage bloomed in her chest, large and hot and heavy. Big mistake, Jimmy Thatcher Snipes, she thought. Big, big mistake.

CHAPTER 28

I t was almost eight on Sunday morning when Ben pushed back the blankets and crossed the room to look out over Nell's backyard. Almost eight and the sky still dark. A blustery front had moved in during the night, pushing a warm wet wind before it and driving the temperature up twenty degrees. A hard rain had wakened Ben around three, and he'd lain sleepless for an hour, listening to the drops slapping the skylight and his brother's steady breathing in the other bed.

He unlatched the window and let the moist breeze flow in. Cool but not frigid. The streetlamps were still on, and with their help, Ben saw that the rain had battered Nell's tulip tree, which had bloomed early. Its new blossoms lay on the lawn in sodden pink and white ruins.

Andrew's bed was empty now and the house quiet. Ben dimly remembered the phone ringing and Andrew answering in a near-whisper. What time was that? He closed the window and turned on the lamp beside his bed.

Several photos had been arranged atop the nightstand, accompanied by a note in Andrew's large round hand: *You were right. Novak is Video Man.*

He picked up the photos, apparently shot with Andrew's new digital camera and printed from his new computer setup. The first was of a shirt, a splash of tropical flowers in navy and turquoise, spread out on a pale marble surface Ben didn't recognize. The next was of a man's bracelet, a thick twist of gold chain and rawhide leather, laid out on the same surface, maybe a bathroom counter.

"Oh shit. Impulsive! Unthinking! I'd hoped he'd grown out of that!"

Ben sat on the edge of the bed, the prints dangling from his fingers, examined them again, jumped up and tore downstairs in his pajamas, where he found Nell, coffee cup in hand and still in her robe.

"It's so dark," she said. "Want some coffee? What's the matter?"

"Where's Andrew?"

"Is that rain? God. Endless."

"Ma. Where's Andrew?'

"He came in late and left early this morning. I heard him go, but I took a sleeping pill and couldn't get awake. I've been up half an hour or so."

She looked at him, eyes dark.

"I'm worried, Ben. What is it? Is it this girl? I understand, but I'd hate to see him get seriously involved when he's only been home for—"

Ben pivoted and flew upstairs, threw on some sweats without showering, splashed cold water on his stubbled cheeks, stuck his bare feet into a pair of loafers on the closet floor, shrugged into his leather bomber jacket, and headed for the ground floor, wallet in one hand and car keys in the other.

As he rounded the second landing, Nell called, "Ben! What's going on?"

Already at the front door, he yelled back, "Don't ask!"

A wall of water met him head on as he dashed to the car.

It took him just ten minutes to get to the Knowlton, where he pulled around to the back and parked in the lot behind the building. He sloshed through the rain and through the back entrance of the lobby, past Possum's bookstore and the sign pointing to Chez Dee, toward the elevator standing open.

And stopped cold.

Joe Proudhorse was in the lobby, sitting in one of the plush gray chairs reading a newspaper. He was situated with a clear line of vision to the guest elevator and stairwell as well as to the two service elevators. He looked up from his newspaper when he saw Ben.

It was hard to tell which man was more surprised.

"What are you doing here?" Ben asked.

"Watching for Snipes."

"What? Where are Pratt and Naldo?"

"They . . . what are *you* doing here?'

"I'm . . .where's Hilda?"

"Went down the street to get coffee. Kitchen wasn't open yet.

"You've been here all night? Christ." Ben ran his hands distractedly through his hair. "Did you see my brother?"

"I did." Proudhorse nodded toward the elevator. "He went up to the fifth floor. What's going on? Everything okay?"

"Yes. I mean no. Joe, I'm sorry about the all-nighter. I never intended . . ." He laid a hand on Proudhorse's shoulder. "Soon as Hilda gets back, the two of you go home, get some sleep."

"What about Snipes?"

"Forget Snipes for now. I'll take care of him," Ben said firmly. "Go home. That's an order. Right now I have some business with my brother."

Proudhorse nodded and sat back down, stifling both a yawn and his curiosity.

Ben stepped into the elevator and pushed the button for the fifth floor.

Dollie answered the bell without saying anything and returned to her seat on the sofa next to Andrew. Ben took in the scene: their eyes intent on each other for a second, her fingers clamped on his wrist—something going on. She wore a fuzzy pink robe and a look Ben didn't understand. Then she rose, said something about getting dressed, and moved down the hall to her bedroom, not meeting his gaze as she passed. She wore no makeup, and he thought she looked pale and vulnerable.

"Let's talk," Ben said, getting a slow nod from his brother. "Well? Do I have to ask? What'd you do?"

"I got you proof."

"How?" He didn't need to ask, but he needed to hear.

Andrew shrugged.

"You broke into Novak's. Jesus Christ, you broke in. Are you fucking crazy? Are you fucking out of your mind?"

He uttered the last two questions in a muted scream, not wanting to alarm Dollie.

Andrew looked unperturbed. "You said you didn't have much time. You said you thought your chief would take you off the case. I wanted to help."

"Who saw you?"

"Nobody but the security guy, and to him I was a guy delivering a white orchid."

"Don't tell me. I don't want to know. Will Novak know anyone was there?"

"No way. If there's one thing you learn in Huntsville, it's B&E."

"Oh Jesus." Ben sandwiched his head between two palms. "Fucking crazy."

"The guy in the video is Novak. And he's got some sort of porn thing going with Sylva Kaye."

Ben released his head. "What?"

"She called while I was in there. Machine picked it up. She spoke in a loose sort of code, if you know what I mean, but it was obvious. I can tell you about it."

Ben groaned and went back to holding his head.

"In the first place, you're an ex-con on parole. How could you take such a chance with your life? With ours?"

Andrew made a dismissive gesture.

"I don't think you get it, Andrew."

"I get it."

"I know you've spent a long time where—" He threw up a hand, unable to finish. "In the second place, we can't even use those pictures."

"Novak doesn't know that."

"Are you shitting me? Of course he knows it!"

"At the very least, you now have proof of something you only suspected."

"Proof I can't use."

"But proof to know."

Ben shook his head. "Promise me, Andrew. Never never never do anything like that again."

"Fine."

"No, think it over. Then promise. Never never never."

"Gotcha."

"You've got to be so clean that you squeak."

Andrew looked at him and nodded.

"Never again. Promise."

Andrew saluted.

Ben sighed.

"Now. Let's turn the page. What's going on here?"

Andrew was quiet.

"What's up, Andrew?"

"She doesn't . . ." He fell silent. "She doesn't want me to say anything."

"Something I need to know?"

"Not really."

"Something involving you?"

"Sort of."

"Then I need to know."

"Something that happened."

"Between you and her?"

"Huh? No. What would that be?"

"C'mon, Andrew."

"Fucking Jimmy Snipes."

"Yeah?" Ben waited. "*Yeah?*"

"He held her little dog, Snazzy, you know, out the window, threatened to drop him. Out the window. Five floors."

Ben had a hard time grasping it. "Her dog."

"Yeah! That little dog you saw in the photos. He held it out the window."

Ben pursed his lips and blew, thinking of Bood. "When did this happen?"

"Last night after I left."

"She was the one who called you this morning?"

Andrew nodded.

"He's a psychopath."

"She's afraid of him."

"Sure."

"Afraid he'll hurt her dog. She loves that dog."

Ben waited, knowing there was more.

"She wants a gun." Andrew shot him a sideways glance. "She wants me to get her a gun."

Ben turned to his brother. "And you said?"

"That's when you came. But that's what she's asking me to do."

"You're not getting her a gun, Andrew."

"Nope. But I *am* going to kick the shit out of that little creep."

"Like hell." He gave Andrew his hardest look, but Andrew's look was harder.

"Another thing I learned in Huntsville, Ben," Andrew said, "was about animals like Jimmy Snipes. Only one way to handle them—you keep murmuring *nice boy* while you fill up your hands with stones."

He rose to his feet. Ben grabbed his arm, but he shook him off and was out the door and into the stairwell, Ben surprised at how strong he was, heading down the stairs three at time, Ben right after him.

"Andrew!" Dollie's voice followed them down the stairwell. Ben glanced up and glimpsed her, improbably dressed now in something that looked like white feathers, leaning over the banister. Then Andrew was out through the third-floor door.

They scuffled in the hall, Andrew managing to bang on Jimmy Snipes' door with one fist while he held Ben back with the other, Ben again amazed at his brother's strength. Then Jimmy was in the doorway, scowling at the noise, dressed to go out, flashes of burnt orange accenting his black suit.

"You Jimmy Snipes?" Andrew shoved Ben back with all his might, breathing hard.

"Who wants to know?"

Andrew strode into the apartment, past Jimmy, crossing to the window and opening it wide. He turned back to Jimmy.

"You held a little dog out the window?" Andrew said. "Threatened to drop it?"

Jimmy looked at Andrew in alarm. Then Andrew had him, one hand curled over the back of his collar, the other looped through the back of his belt. Carried him to the window and put him out, held him parallel to the ground, one fist at the scruff of his neck and the other at his belt, Andrew's knees flexed and feet braced against the baseboard, Jimmy's eyes like saucers and not moving a muscle or making a sound.

"No!" Ben cried, but then fell silent, only a yard away but too far away to grab Jimmy, thinking, *Jesus, Jesus . . .*

"You held a little dog out the window, Jimmy?" Andrew repeated. "What was that line again? All I have to do is open my hand?"

Jimmy looked down, then up, his face the color of putty.

"That what she said?" he gasped. "I wasn't—I wasn't going to drop him. I was . . . she's—"

"All I have to do is open my hand," Andrew reminded him.

After Jimmy's first involuntary convulsion—as if he were trying to roll into a fetus position—he was motionless, hanging with his back to the rain, sharp knees bent, sharp toes and sharp nose pointed toward earth. His arms and fingers were spread a little, ready to grab anything that wasn't a handful of air.

Like so, he hung for a second, terror in his eyes. Andrew didn't throw Jimmy; he simply opened his hands. Ben's explosive *No!* behind him, Ben halfway out the window, reaching. Jimmy falling, burnt orange handkerchief lightly trailing, burnt orange tie a fluttering banner. Even from the third floor, they could hear the muffled *whump!* of Jimmy's body striking.

"Christ!" Ben shouted, ducking back from the open window and running toward the door. "Jesus Christ! He hit the canopy!"

CHAPTER 29

The daring young man.

Jimmy hit the belly of the stretched canvas hard, square on his butt, and bounced as if on a trampoline—straight up. He straightened out and plunged straight down, a little too hard but on his feet, burnt orange ankles buckling a bit, correcting on the next bounce, coming down knees flexed, sliding a few feet down the wet canopy, grabbing one of the poles supporting the canopy and half-falling, half-leaping onto the sidewalk, unstable but on his feet.

And almost crashed into Abner, putting someone into a checkered and moving back from the curb.

"Good God a'mighty!" breathed Abner, eyes widening. Jimmy wet front and back, smoothing his hair and tugging here and there at his black suit and burnt orange tie.

"Where'd you come from? You fall off the canopy?"

Dazed, Jimmy stepped off the curb to retrieve his square of orange silk, afloat in the gutter. Ben and Andrew rushed panting through the big glass doors, Dollie not far behind, wearing a long white feathered boa, Snazzy in her arms.

They made a frozen tableau under the canopy, as all hell broke loose. Lights from a city bus caught Jimmy full in the face as he straightened, paralyzed, cheeks and hair wet with rain, fingers ready to poke the wet silk into his breast pocket. Horn blaring, the bus braked and slid sideways on the slick pavement toward him as he stood transfixed, the bus nearly on him, everyone on the street transfixed. Except Andrew, who hurtled beneath the canopy and scooped Jimmy Snipes out of the gutter and the two of them sprawled on the sidewalk as the bus sped past and careened into parked cars.

"God a'mighty," cried Abner. "Boy's gittin killed right and left out here."

He hurried to Andrew and Jimmy, who were picking themselves out of a puddle and eyeing each other, Andrew breathing hard, Jimmy trying not to look wobbly.

Dollie was at Andrew's side in a flash of white feathers, damp hair shining blue-black, blue eyes awash in tears.

"Jimmy Snipes," she cried, Snazzy backing her up by pulling his lips away from his teeth. "Don't you dare ever come near me again."

Hilda, carrying a cardboard holder that held two giant Styrofoam cups, pushed through the cluster of onlookers and stared at the gathering with eyes red-rimmed from lack of sleep. She approached Ben and touched his elbow.

"Ben. What's going on? Why y'all . . ."

"Everything's okay, Hilda. Bus accident. Go home."

She took in the scene.

"Where's Joe? Why are *you* here? What's Snipes doing out here? Why's he all wet? He get hit by that bus?"

"Everything's okay," Ben repeated. "Joe's inside, and I'll tell you what I told him: Go home and get some sleep. That's an order."

She studied him a millisecond. "Did Snipes get past Joe?"

"No, no. C'mon, kiddo. You and Joe did a great job."

"But—"

"Snipes went out the window."

"He *what?*"

"I'll tell you about it later."

Hearing his own words, he said to himself: *As if!*

"All righty," Hilda said. "See you tomorrow then."

She cast another long look at Jimmy Snipes as she headed for the Knowlton entrance.

Jimmy was backing away from Dollie, backing beneath the canopy and toward the door, feeling sick, legs feeling funny, thinking, *Shit, I coulda been killed.* He picked up the errant orange hankie, gave it a brisk shake and planted it in his breast pocket, real calm-like.

"And Andrew just saved your life," Dollie sobbed. "Don't you forget it! You owe him."

Jimmy raised his narrow palm.

"We're quits, call it a draw," he said, showing a good curl of lip—let them wonder later what that meant—and walked away, tossing back a dismissive wave, drained but shoulders back hard, thinking: *Push my wet hair back a bit, the RFK move. This deal right here, this whole deal, is something to think about. What it means. Later, when I get myself together. Figure out what it means to be tossed out the window and walk away. Tossed out the fuckin' window. Fly through the fuckin' air for three stories. And fuckin' walk away.*

With the greatest of ease.

Yeah.

CHAPTER 30

N ell and Andrew were glumly nursing drinks between dracaena palms when Ben arrived at Chez Dee Sunday night. He ordered a Pinot and looked at Andrew's glass.

"What are you drinking?" he asked

Andrew gave him a *screw you* look, and Ben realized he thought he was being monitored. Ben didn't blame him—but it wasn't the way he meant it.

"Club soda," Nell said.

"This doesn't promise to be the happiest birthday celebration ever," Ben said.

"Let's perk up. Dayt would want it to be joyful. It was his idea to wait and celebrate your birthday tonight, Andrew. Let's do this for him."

"Maybe the Knowlton wasn't a good choice," Andrew said. "I wanted to see what the restaurant was like. Since I'm going to be . . ."

"It *was* a good choice. Dayt loved this place."

The room was small and its tables bistro-close, but its off-white color scheme and murals of Parisian street scenes gave it dimension, and Edith Piaf sang lustily from the speakers.

"Did you know Piaf was Italian?" Andrew asked, apropos of nothing.

Nell and Ben looked at him.

"It's true. Piaf's ma was an Italian street singer. Turned tricks on the side. Her pa was an Italian street performer, too—an acrobat. La Piaf was born on the street. Literally. With gendarmes in attendance. True."

Ben rolled his eyes, and Nell laughed.

"Where do you get this trivia?"

"I don't call it trivia—I call it knowledge." Andrew sang, *Non, je ne regrette rien,* under his breath. "Courtesy of Huntsville prison library."

Ben looked at him, heart lifting. For a decade, when he'd thought of his brother, he'd thought of a sad convict in chains and jumpsuit, surrounded by bars and locks and losers. But now . . . it wasn't that Andrew was exactly the same, that there were no changes. There were. But Andrew *was* still Andrew.

Nell showed her empty bourbon glass to the waiter, who hustled away. Andrew caught Ben's eye, pointed to Nell's empty glass, and held up three fingers. And when the waiter returned with a fresh glass, Nell pointed to a Chilean red on the wine list.

"I'll have that with my meal."

"Me, too," Ben said.

"Yeah, let's the two of you get hammered," Andrew said. "Don't mind me."

"I've discovered," said Nell, "that alcohol taken in sufficient quantities produces all the effects of drunkenness."

"Oscar Wilde," Andrew said.

She saluted him with her glass, then raised it in a toast.

"Here's to our darling Dayt. I miss him already. I will miss him forever."

They clinked, sipped.

She raised her glass again.

"And here's to our darling Andrew. We've skipped a few birthdays, so let's make this one count."

They clinked and sipped again.

"And," she announced, "here's to other February twelfth birthday boys. Abraham Lincoln. Charles Darwin. And Benjamin Andrew Ryan."

"Wait," Andrew said. "Ben's dad and I had the same birthday?"

"You knew that. It's on that little brass plaque beneath Benjamin's flag. You've seen it a thousand—" She stopped mid-sentence, staring over Ben's shoulder, her reaction so pronounced that Ben looked behind him. He saw only a horse-faced woman in luminous green making her way toward the exit.

"Something wrong, Ma?" he asked.

She waved the question away, as another waiter appeared to take their food order—a swarthy unsmiling man with hooded eyes and no small talk. Ben ordered for all of them: wild mushrooms, shrimp mousse, smoked trout with chervil butter, and grilled salmon with red onions.

"Glad the entrées are in English as well as French. I ordered Rognons à la Brochette once. Lamb kidneys on a skewer."

Nell laughed. She wore a sweater Ben hadn't seen—steel gray, a tiny gold flower pinned near her shoulder. She seemed ambiguous in the candlelight, her eyes as smoky and muted as her outfit.

"You look pretty, Ma," Ben said.

"I was going through the trunk in the attic." She plucked at her sleeve. "This sweater is older than you, Ben. Nine months older."

"Huh."

"Your father gave it to me for Christmas, 1968." She touched the little gold flower pinned to her shoulder. "He gave me this, too."

"Huh," Ben said again.

"His number came up while we were still students at Western Michigan University—he was a senior and would be leaving for Vietnam as soon as he graduated. He hated the war, but two of his closest friends had been killed, and he'd decided that if his number came up, he would go. For them, for the country. He said the war was winding down anyway, and he wouldn't be gone long. He promised."

This was more than she'd ever said about those days, and her sons were intent on her words—which were, Ben realized without surprise, a little slurred. What the hell. It was a tough time for all of them. But especially for her.

"Nixon pledged to end the war, but when he became president, he extended it. The protests were out of hand, but the bombing in Cambodia went on for four more years. Half a million tons."

"The more things change," Ben said.

"By Benjamin's graduation, more than thirty-three thousand American soldiers had died. For nothing." The candlelight flickered in her eyes. "That Christmas Eve, in 1969, we went to a dance in Kalamazoo. Ben had the band play 'Someday We'll Be Together.' He promised, and I believed it."

"I don't know that song," Andrew said.

She smiled. "No, probably not. The Supremes. Ever heard of them?"

The waiter hovered, pouring wine, refreshing Andrew's soda.

"In April, Vietnamese troops pushed through Cambodia toward Vietcong bases, and our forces followed. I didn't know it then, but Benjamin was among them. That operation lasted two months and killed ten thousand. But most of the Vietcong fled over the Mekong."

Her voice wavered, and Ben knew she was reliving a watershed moment, a moment after which nothing would be the same again. He'd seen the same trembling intensity in victims and survivors, other people who'd lost something precious to violence. He'd always wondered if such a wound became strength one day.

"Benjamin Ryan," Nell said. "Killed the fifth of May, 1970, and I didn't even know. I was five months pregnant. We were both alone and wanted lots of babies. It's odd—all I ever really wanted was family, but I seem to gravitate to people like me. People alone, solitary people. Maybe I identify."

"You weren't entirely alone," Ben said. "I mean after your parents' auto accident. You had Grandma Casey."

"Gran was already in her late sixties then. I was nine. And she was . . . oh, austere. I asked her once if she loved me, and she said, *Don't be absurd.* I never knew if that meant, *Of course I do,* or *Of course I don't.*"

"You were thirteen when she died?"

Nell nodded. "That's when I became a ward of the state."

"But you had relatives in Ireland," Andrew said. "What about your great-aunt Fiona? She loved you enough to leave you all her money."

She put her hand over his.

"The authorities let me have some say in my future. In five years I would be an adult, and I didn't want to go to a country I'd never known. And Fiona hadn't left her estate directly to me—she left it to Gran, her only sister. That's how I inherited. I was the sole survivor per stirpes, meaning only the heir's bloodline inherits. In any case, most of the Casey family's children died young."

"Were all those relatives—the Caseys and the Gallaghers—tall and dark-haired like you and Ben?" Andrew asked.

She shook her head. "Some had reddish or red-gold hair. Like yours."

"I'm a throwback."

She patted his hand. "Not much of one. Most of the Caseys had your build and coloring. Ben and I might be the anomalies."

"But Benjamin Ryan added his genes to Ben's mix."

"True." She turned the stem of her glass, watching the wine glint in the transient candlelight. "Did I ever tell you that your great-aunts and uncles were named after Irish saints and in the order of the alphabet?"

"You never told us *anything*," Andrew said.

"That's not true." She gazed at Ben defensively, as if for corroboration.

"It's perfectly true," he said.

"Well, crapola! It most certainly is not. What *happened*," she said with emphasis, as if this were the hundredth time she'd said it, "was that when Gran realized her first-born's initials were ABC—Ana Brígh Casey, my mother—she decided to follow through with the rest of the alphabet. With the first and middle names, I mean. *CD, EF, GH,* and so forth."

"You'd need thirteen children to get through the whole alphabet." Ben said. "That's a reach. Even for a Roman Catholic."

"A reach that exceeded her grasp. The best she could do was four."

"What were their names?" Andrew asked.

"Oh, hardly the top ten. Colm Declan. Evin Fergus. Gobnait Hugh."

Andrew grinned. "No surprise they ended up saints, with names like that."

White-jacketed waiters appeared, bearing silver-domed plates.

"Once more," Nell said, raising her glass. "Happy birthday to darling Andrew."

"And Benjamin Ryan," Ben said.

"And Abraham Lincoln," Andrew said.

"And Charles Darwin," Nell said.

They clinked.

CHAPTER 31

Monday morning, February 24

It was still dark at five-thirty Monday morning when Ben got to the office. He nodded at the officer sitting bleary-eyed at the front desk, passed through the metal detector, took the elevator to the third floor, skirted the large patrol briefing room with its subdued light and cubicles, let himself into the break room, and plopped a donut box on a table. He had time to fill the coffee maker with water, dump some Starbuck's into the filter, and hit the ON button before Hilda and Proudhorse arrived, straight from their surveillance of Jimmy Snipes.

"Sorry about the all-nighters," Ben told them. "I didn't know Pratt and Naldo were on another job. You shouldn't have done that."

He'd called them at midnight, after talking to Kenechi, and told them to go home, but they'd waved him off.

Hilda yawned at the gurgling coffee maker.

"We had to work off our gourmet weekend, anyway."

Ben set up shop in one of the smaller conference rooms. Hilda went off to wash her stubby little hands, and in came Kenechi, smelling good, dapper in black leather jacket and stiff white shirt with a banded collar. Ben pushed the donuts across the table, opened his notebook, and looked around.

"Okay, let's do it. Kenechi?"

They heard a light knock at the door, and Ramsey Ratzlaff came into the room. He was carrying a handful of dog-eared fliers that asked in red letters if you were doomed. Hilda grinned at Proudhorse, and Ben raised a brow.

"Passing out religious literature, Ram?"

He glanced at the fliers in his hand, hawk nose looking pinched.

"Well, whatcha gonna do?" He put the fliers in the center of the table. "I came in to write up Zora Sanda, and here y'all are."

"You got anything?"

"Naw," Ramsey said, opening his notebook and showing them a few scrawls. "Nothing there. Least no motive far's I can tell. She's a nice enough lady. Kinda screwy's all."

Nice enough lady. All four detectives thought that over, and Ramsey looked uncomfortable.

"Trouble with those born-again types," he said gruffly, "is they're worse the second time around."

Ben eyed Ram for a second, then roused himself.

"You find out what she was doing in Dayton's and how she got in?"

"She went up there to leave one of those," he pointed to the fliers. "Slaughter pissed her off because he wouldn't accept it earlier. But when she got up there, the maid—" He flipped a couple of pages in his notebook. "The maid, Rosa, was cleaning, and the door was open. She—"

"Did you talk to Rosa?" Ben interrupted.

"Yup. Doesn't know anything about it."

Ben thought of the acquiescent little woman.

"Maybe, maybe not."

"Zora says the maid was cleaning the kitchen, and she didn't go in there. Says she left the flier on the desk in the office. Finally, though, she admitted that she also went into the bedroom and bathroom. Just to look. Because it was pretty, she said."

"You believed her?" Hilda asked, her eyes narrowing.

"I did." He looked around the table uneasily. "But if—"

"What?" Ben prompted.

"Well, just that if that woman . . . acts suspicious, it's because she's afraid. Afraid of police. She was afraid of me. You hate to see that. Woman like that. Nowhere to go. She's been picked up and put in jail. You hate to see that."

Ben studied him a second longer before turning his attention to the others.

"Okay, so where are we?"

Ramsey, who had not taken a chair, turned to leave, and Ben said, "You don't have to leave, Ram."

He stood awkwardly in the doorway.

"Stay if you have time," Kenechi added. "We could use your input."

Ramsey hastened to a chair and sat, an earnest scowl on his narrow face, and Kenechi briefly reviewed the weekend.

"Let's hear about your surveillance of Jimmy Snipes," Ben said to Proudhorse and Hilda.

The two detectives exchanged glances.

"Main thing to say is *Christ almighty!*" Hilda said.

"Can you elucidate?" Ben asked.

Proudhorse shrugged his heavy shoulders and looked as if he had a stomachache.

"Mostly, he goes to doctors. Saturday afternoon, for example, he spent ninety minutes in some doctor's office on Gaston. Don't know how he got him to come in on a Saturday. A doctor—"

He checked his notes.

"Schnoodle," guessed Ben. "Or Schnitzel."

Proudhorse gave him a pained look. "Schwartz. After that, Snipes went to Baylor Hospital, waited around for a couple hours, got some X-rays."

"Then Saturday night," Hilda added, "he skulked around the Knowlton. Spent most of that time up on the fifth floor, cruising past Dollie Varnes' place. Stalking, looked like to me. You think, Joe?"

Proudhorse nodded. Ben tensed, but kept his face unreadable.

"Then yesterday," Hilda continued, "he went to emergency, got some X-rays."

Ben relaxed. Bless Joe Proudhorse. Bless Hilda Cloy.

"Thought you said he got X-rays Saturday."

Hilda sat back and crossed her arms. "Like we said."

Ben dropped his head and made a snoring noise. "He must do something else."

"Not on our watch," Hilda said. "If he manages to spend the whole weekend at the doctor's or the hospital, what must he do on weekdays?"

"Here's the picture," Proudhorse said. "Sleeps, eats, gets spiffed up in black suits and Day-Glo socks—"

"What does this guy live on?" asked Ramsey.

"On Mama," Hilda said. "Anyway, hops in his Infiniti, sees his doctor or goes to the hospital, comes back to the Knowlton, sleeps, eats, gets spiffed up in Day-Glo, goes to the doctor or to the hospital—"

Ben held up a hand. "Okay. I gather you'd like to get off this detail. If Pratt and Naldo—" He saw Ratzlaff's expression, "or Ramsey can't take over, let's hang it up for now."

Proudhorse's expression betrayed nothing beyond his habitual solemnity, but his black eyes turned slowly to Hilda Cloy, who smiled.

"Many more hours in a closed car," she said, "and Joe would have asked me to marry him."

"Hope it works out," Ben said.

"Good luck with the family," offered Kenechi, with the air of One Who Knows.

The others grinned, considering blonde, blue-eyed Grace Akundi and her unforgiving, race-conscious family.

"Hey, my Okie bigots, you mean, dude?" Hilda asked. "My family only *suspects* I'm what they call a homo, and they'd be ecstatic if I married a *man*. Any man. Any color."

Proudhorse showed them one of his rare smiles. "I like it when one deep prejudice gets overthrown by an even deeper one."

Hilda laughed. "By the way, you hear about the married couple so liberal they tried to adopt a gay baby?"

Ben looked at his watch. Six-thirty. The open slats of the Venetian blinds showed gray slices of dawn, and they could hear the station, never fully asleep, beginning to waken.

"Okay, let's recap and decide where we go from here. I might be tossed off—"

They all noticed Chief Saenz peering through the door glass at the same time. He gave them one of his hard brown stares and stepped into the room.

"Gallagher. Akundi. Proudhorse. Cloy. And Ram? Going to the dark side?"

Ramsey rose and looked uncertain. Saenz turned to the others.

"I want to visit with the four of you. But first, Gallagher, I want to talk with you. Alone. In my office."

He went out and closed the door, then opened it again.

"Now."

CHAPTER 32

Ben was off the case. No matter what he said, Ben couldn't shake Rolando Saenz. He tried every way he knew to lessen the chief's apprehensions. But after thirty minutes of discussion, they were back where they'd started: Ben was too close to it. Saenz would give it to Akundi, and Akundi could put together the team he wanted—except for Ben.

Ben knew the pressures the chief was under, he also knew Saenz would give what he could. But Ben's exposing Jack Malone as a dirty cop—the Malone mess, as they called it downtown—far from reassuring his bosses, had made them uneasy. They didn't like not knowing who leaked the mess to the press, and they liked even less the "Cracko Jacko" headlines. Ben was sure Saenz knew he wasn't the leak; he was less sure if downtown knew it. He figured the word was he wasn't a team player. He'd never ventured into that territory with Saenz, but now . . .

"Chief, I know you've had to walk on eggshells since Malone, but—"

"I don't mind walking on eggshells. Those eggs are already broken. It's the unbroken eggs I'm trying not to step on."

Saenz's voice was thin and boyish, and his Mexican accent was easy to imitate because he dropped *g*'s and doubled negatives—

traits that amplified when he became excited. The staff members teased, but they liked and respected Saenz as a chief who would take their side in almost any issue.

"Two weeks," Ben said.

Saenz shook his head, and Ben felt his impatience.

"Give me two weeks. Give me the case and my team. If I haven't done anything significant with it by then, I'll walk away without a word."

"I came in here, Ben, because we needed to talk. But why are we having this particular conversation? Why am I even telling you this? Policy is policy. Rules are rules."

Ben almost laughed. Damned if you do and . . .

"I follow the rules," he said. "The whole Malone thing happened because I follow rules. But I don't want to go along to get along, and I also don't want to be made to feel like a grade-school tattler. Remember, I didn't come to you. And I didn't go downtown. I went to Jack. And I didn't leak, and you know it."

Saenz stared at his desktop for a millisecond. Ben knew the chief was trying for restraint, and that he'd lose—Ben had seen that mini-struggle plenty of times.

"You should have gone through channels, Ben! That's what they're there for. But you can't let go, you have to control it, take things in your own hands. Now you have an enemy."

"You think he wouldn't have—"

"Suspected, yes. But not *known*. Now you have to watch your back. Didn't you want to rub his nose in it? Just a little?"

He lowered his voice a little, looked at Ben intently.

"Never wrestle with a pig, Ben."

"I know. You both get dirty, and the pig likes it."

"You think he doesn't have plans for you? Someone going to find a little bag of something? In your trunk? A closet? Someone going to find your throw-down?"

Ben knew what Saenz wasn't saying and his blood chilled. *Someone going to get killed in your living room?*

The chief fingered a folded note tucked into the leather corner of his desktop blotter and, after a moment's reflection, handed it to Ben.

Ben opened it, studied it, then handed it back.

The chief read the intransigence in his face and whispered, *Ay yi yi,* to himself.

"All I'm saying," Ben went on, "is for this once, could we set policy aside? Just for two weeks."

"And all I'm saying is you should step aside, make my life easier."

Ben almost smiled—that was *so* Saenz.

"Maybe. Still, I head your investigation team, and haven't I done a good job?"

"The best. It's not down to that. Tell me why you want the case."

Ben sensed a trap, but he didn't know what kind. He needed a safe answer, a way to avoid saying, *Dayton Slaughter was like my father.* That would play a card right into the chief's hand.

"I'm a cop," he said finally.

Saenz raised a brow.

"I want to solve this case."

"Why?"

"I would feel . . ."

Saenz was squinting at him, measuring. I want to control it, Ben wanted to say. But that was a trap, too, even if true. Especially if true. He felt squeezed. He didn't like dancing to this tune. And he'd be damned if he'd say anything more.

"It's a personal challenge, goddammit!" he blurted, surprising himself.

The chief nodded, his velvety brown eyes steady on Ben. And Ben, feeling manipulated and misrepresented, realized he had been forced past obvious and acceptable answers to less obvious and less acceptable ones. He pushed his anger aside.

"Chief, I'm asking for two weeks. My team worked all week-end. So did I. We have a good start. A damned good start. Don't throw that away."

The chief steepled his fingers beneath his chin. "So you worked on the case for a weekend, got a good start. Why can't that be enough?"

"I'm the superior officer. Would it be enough for you?"

Ben knew he'd scored: Saenz understood being ambitious and status-conscious.

"Ben, it's my feet that are going to be held to the fire. And it's not just downtown. Part of the problem is out there."

He tipped his dark head in the direction of the patrol room.

Ben looked at him.

"It's not just Malone with them. It could make things worse for you if it looked like you were getting a privilege. They already resent you for a lucky son of a gun. And then to have talent, too, to be younger and smarter than they are . . . I'm not saying you deserve it, Ben. You don't. But the idea is there. And Malone mat-ters. You might not be the kind who—you might not always have their backs."

"Oh yeah?"

Adrenalin got Ben to the door in two steps and he jerked it open, saw a roomful of eyes shift away. He spoke in a voice so rich with fury that even he didn't recognize it.

"I might not have your backs? I don't give a goddamn what you think about my trust fund, my mother, my doctorate, or the fact that my brother's an ex-con. The truth is—"

Somewhere in his mind, Ben didn't believe he was having this tantrum, but having lost control, he found he couldn't stop. "The truth is that not even a dirty cop need fear when I'm behind him. I'll cover his ass. But out of the field, a dirty cop? Hell no."

He met as many eyes as he could bear, dimly aware of Kenechi's level black gaze and Proudhorse's and Hilda's astonish-ment. And Ramsey Ratzlaff looking at him somberly. Ben thought of the unsigned note tucked into the chief's blotter. An act of malice, undeniably. And, also undeniably, from a colleague.

Ask Gallagher how much he'll inherit from Dayton Slaughter.

He let his glance linger on Ramsey.

"So sue me." He turned back to Saenz. "We through here?"

"Not quite." The chief waved him back inside. "Feel better now?"

Ben didn't say anything. He was breathing hard and still angry.

"That's not you, Ben," Saenz said. "I'm just going to forget it. Mighta been building for a while. You need some rest, you've had a bad couple of days."

Ben felt shame blooming in his chest over his loss of control, and for some reason, the chief's sympathy made him even more embarrassed and angry. He shoved the door closed with such force that it rattled on its hinges and a framed picture of Chief Rolando Saenz getting a cockamamie award from the cockamamie mayor slipped from its hook and crashed to the floor. The chief eyed it for a millisecond then turned a noncommittal gaze on Ben.

"We through here?" Ben repeated.

The chief's dark eyes stayed calm. Actually, a hell of a guy, Ben thought, wanting now to repent his outburst but not knowing how, when Saenz said, "One week."

Ben gaped at him.

"You and your team have one week from today to work this case. But Ken Akundi leads. He's the primary. You're secondary. And I want to be in the loop. Constantly. Whatever's going on, I need to know it."

Saenz looked at him hard. "You got that?"

Ben walked to his own office under every eye in the patrol room and sat behind his black steel desk. His phone rang immediately,

"What," Kenechi said.

"We've got one week and you're leading."

"What?"

"One week from today."

Through the glass that separated his office from the patrol room, Ben watched Kenechi come around in his swivel chair and stare at him.

"One week."

"Yes."

"And then?"

"Then, best case, you're on and I'm off."

"Worst case?"

"Same thing, I'm still off. So—"

Kenechi had already hung up, was already on his feet, shrugging into his smoky gray suit jacket, giving his cuffs a pull, gathering up folders, notebook, murder book. Unlike the rest of the staff, he never walked around in his shirtsleeves—even if his destination was only Ben's office.

Ben put down the phone, rose, and stepped out the door, down the corridor and across the silent, watchful squad room toward the break room. He poured coffee into a couple of mugs—one for him and one for Kenechi—and retraced his steps "*Doctor* Gallagher," said Hilda as he passed her cubicle. "Shoot, you're even cooler than I thought. For a guy, I mean."

There was relieved laughter around them, and Ben felt his own tension recede.

They had a week.

CHAPTER 33

Ben set the coffee mugs on his orderly desktop and sat opposite Kenechi, who pulled up to the desk and opened the murder book.

"Ramsey," Ben said. "I thought he'd want to line Zora Sanda up in his pickup lights and mow her down with the automatic weaponry he calls sporting equipment. Instead, he says she's a nice enough lady. Anyone but him."

"Why anyone but him? He's a good cop," Kenechi said, eyeing him.

"Call it my sixth sense."

"Your sixth sense. Even a guy like you, Ben, who's right ninety percent of the time, is still ten percent wrong. Enough to worry about a little, enough not to be always so sure. Besides that, who's completely bad?"

"Lucifer? Hitler? Ramsey Ratzlaff?"

Kenechi touched the purple scar on his cheek.

"The man who did this also saved my life."

Ben looked at the scar that ran obliquely over Kenechi's cheekbone from below his left eye almost to his nostril, a deep violet stroke in the polished ebony of Kenechi's complexion. "He was Ibo?"

"Igbo, part of the Ibo group. They crossed the Niger to attack Lagos."

"You lived in Lagos?"

"Nearby. The Igbo rampaged through the villages, slaughtering whoever crossed their paths."

"So this Igbo slices you with a machete, then saves your life? Great symmetry."

My brother tosses a guy out a window, then saves him from a speeding bus.

"He was older than the others. Maybe he hadn't learned to kill children."

He clasped his big black hands on the desktop in front of him.

"He . . . cut me. And my uncle and I saw he couldn't strike again. So he saved us, hid us."

"Your uncle—"

"Was also a child. A year older than I."

"How old were you?"

"Eleven."

Ben shook his head, not knowing what to say.

"I was eight when war began and a thousand when it was over. But I learned important things."

"Like?"

Kenechi took a deep breath and let it go.

"That nobody's completely bad?" Ben said.

"Or completely good. Some are very good, of course. And some very bad. We need the rule of law because of the very bad."

He reflected, tapping his fountain pen on the desktop.

"Africans have a saying: when elephants fight, it's the grass that suffers. What I learned was that when elephants fight, we need the rule of law. To save the grass."

Proudhorse put his head in the door, his smooth black hair shining like blue steel under the fluorescent lights.

"We've got our trace. Registered in Michigan, to a William Longstreet Smollett."

"Whoa," Ben said, fingertips prickling. "Kalamazoo?"

"You got it. Purchased there anyway."

Kenechi whistled. "Looks like Slaughter knew the shooter."

Their relief was palpable. The murder among strangers was the murder least likely to be solved.

"Maybe we caught another lucky one," Ben said. Was this the early break that could make an early end to the case?

"The report is coming in now," Proudhorse said. "Hilda's collecting it."

Ben picked up the phone, turned to Kenechi. "Can you check on flights?"

Kenechi rose and was back before Ben got off the phone with the Kalamazoo police.

"We can get a flight out at noon," Kenechi said when Ben finished his call. "Into O'Hare at 2:20. An Eagle flight for Kalamazoo leaves forty-five minutes later, pretty tight connections for O'Hare. And we lose an hour, so that flight gets into Kalamazoo around five. If we miss it, the next one gets us in after eight."

"Book that noon flight, Ken. All I need to do is get my roll-on and a change of clothes. Can you make it?"

"I can."

"I need to talk to the chief and call Ma and Andrew. Then I'm outta here."

———

Andrew picked up on the third ring. Ben heard voices in the background.

"Andrew. What's happening?"

"Dollie and I are with Ma. Dollie found out Ma had a trunkful of vintage clothes."

"Andrew, listen, I've got to go out of town for a couple of days. Will everything be okay here?"

"Huh? Sure. When?"

"Today, a noon flight. We got the ATF report on the trace. The guy it's registered to bought the gun in Kalamazoo. Dayton may have known him."

"You talk to the Kalamazoo police?"

"Contact is a Lieutenant Smolovick. He's been out of town but returns today and will check it out. One way or the other, I'm going."

"Want me to drop you at the airport or anything?"

"No. But I need to know things are going to be okay here while I'm gone."

Andrew lowered his voice, and Ben could tell he was speaking directly into the receiver.

"I've been thinking about yesterday, Ben. Couldn't talk about it last night at the restaurant, with Ma there. But I've been mulling it over. A lot."

Ben heard Dollie and Nell talking in the background. "When you were taking those classes in the stir—"

"I like to think of it as the Big House," Andrew said, a grin in his voice.

"Whatever. Anyway, didn't they have a course on impulse control?"

"They did."

"Too bad you didn't take it." Thinking, *I'm a fine one to talk.*

"I did. It was one of the biggies. That and anger management."

I could use that, too, Ben thought, but said, "I won't ask what grade you got."

"Pass/Fail."

"Bet they weren't failing a lot of mean guys who'd signed up for both impulse control *and* anger management."

Andrew laughed.

"Main thing, Andrew," Ben said, serious again. "*Main* thing—and here's some advice the chief just gave me, so it may be a family trait—don't take things into your own hands."

The line went a little muffled, and Ben knew Andrew had cupped the receiver. "I spent ten years accumulating that . . . whatever it was, Ben. It's spent."

"Hope so."

"Ben? The split second I let go of him, I thought, *Here goes the rest of my life. Down the drain.* But it was too late."

"I know what you mean."

"Tell you the truth, I almost jumped out after him."

"Me, too."

"But it wasn't too late. Dumb luck got me into trouble a long time ago, and dumb luck got me out of trouble yesterday."

"You called in a chit."

"So now I owe one?"

"I think it's a wash."

Ben saw Hilda outside his window, waving a sheet of paper at him.

"Gotta go, Andrew. Will you put Ma on?"

"You're going where?" Nell asked.

"We got the report on the trace, Ma. The gun that killed Dayton was registered to a William Smollett." He looked at the paper in his hand. "Purchased from Sharpshooter Gun Shop in Kalamazoo on July 10, 1969. At the time, Smollett lived in an apartment house at 1160 Undermain in Winnesaka, a village outside Kalamazoo. I'm guessing Dayton knew him. Birth date 1940—Dayton's age."

She was silent.

"Your old stamping grounds, too, Ma. Dayton ever mention a William Smollett to you?"

Nell didn't answer.

"You there?"

"Jesus God," he heard her whisper.

"What's wrong, Ma?"

"Jesus God," she repeated.

"Ma? What's going on? You know him?"

Nothing.

"Ma! You know this Smollett? What do you know about him? Talk to me."

Another long silence. *What the hell.*

"No. Nothing," she said.

"My ass. You know that name."

"No. Ben."

"Or you know something. Don't do this, Ma."

She said something, but her voice was muffled.

"What did you say?"

He heard a rustling, and her tone went flat and deliberate. "Ben. I can't discuss this now."

Hilda Cloy came into Ben's office and laid a faxed sheet in front of him. Ben told Nell to hang on and raised his brows at Hilda.

"From Kalamazoo. The tenants at 1160 Undermain. In Winnesaka," she said. "When William Smollett lived there."

"Oh?" Ben's eyes ran over the names. By some wild chance . . .

"He's not still there, is he?"

"No. He—"

"Ben?" Nell's voice came through the receiver, louder, but still indistinct.

Ben picked up the phone. "Hang on a minute, Ma."

Hilda laid a paper-clipped sheaf of papers in front of him. He put his hand over the receiver and looked up at her.

"Smollett's dead," she said. "Shot to death March 17, 1971, on the stairs of the Undermain apartment building."

"Huh."

"With a twenty-two caliber handgun. It's all there."

She moved into the corridor, leaving Ben's door open behind her.

Ben looked at the list. Five apartments. Apartment one: Gene and Marta Sypinski. Two: Eleanor Ryan. Three: William and Molly Smollett. Four: Manning Boyle. Five: Otto Sonigson.

At first it didn't register. But his eyes swung back to apartment two. Even then, distracted by his mother's voice, the name didn't click. And when it clicked, it didn't equate. He stood abruptly, the words swimming before his eyes.

"What the hell," he breathed, a cold wave rushing through his blood.

"When was Smollett killed?" he called after Hilda.

She came back and put her head in the door. "March 17, 1971. Like I said."

"Ben!" Nell said. "Goddammit!"

"Just a minute, Ma."

He laid the phone on his desk and lowered himself to his chair with his right hand, staring at the paper in his left. A close-contact wound beneath the victim's chin, bullet hole and burn rim, no exit wound. Made with a .22 caliber bullet—same kind of weapon and wound that killed Dayton. A .22 doesn't have the velocity to penetrate the skull twice, entry and exit. So it ricochets around inside the cranium, causing massive hemorrhage. Smollett was right-handed and had gunpowder residue on that hand—indicating that he fired the gun. Consistent with the victim's weapon being turned on the victim in a struggle. No weapon at the scene. A flurry of activity and interviews, but no real suspects. The case was reopened briefly by a cold-case team in the mid-'70s, but that effort likewise yielded nothing.

"Ben?"

His name sounded faintly from the receiver, and he picked up the phone.

"Ma. Sorry. I'm going to have to get back to you."

A moment ago, he was energized and excited. Now he sat limp, the report dangling in his hand, his elation spent, his belief in his good luck drained.

"But . . ." she began.

He laid the receiver softly in its cradle.

In the quiet of his closed home on Aycliffe Court, its entries blocked with their flimsy barriers of crime-scene tape, Ben hurriedly tossed clothing and toiletries into his roll-on, then stepped into his studio and lifted the dry and stiffened cloth protecting the unfinished painting on the easel. Its scrupulous design, perfectly executed rectangles, and wide-open, flatly painted background now seemed Daliesque. He let his gaze rest on the heavily painted turquoise door in one rectangle. The color was that unpleasant blend of boldness and blandness he hated. He loved most color— in its place and context. But not turquoise. He didn't even like the affected way some people pronounced it: *turkwahz*. Please. Why had he chosen it? He couldn't remember. Another failed attempt to be open-minded?

Most of the paint on the canvas was dry except for the impasto laid on with his palette knife. Staring at the work, it seemed to Ben to have been painted by another man. A man he had been, more innocent, more hopeful, less aware, and less wary. And he knew Dayton's death would bifurcate his life, as only one other event had done—Andrew's arrest and incarceration. Now, and for the time remaining to him, events would be catalogued in his memory as before or after Dayton's death, as they were catalogued as before or after Andrew's imprisonment. He also knew, gazing at the painting with a certain loss and sense of mourning, that he would never touch or retouch it again. It was of another era, finished, through. But he would never discard it. It was a tangible marker, a memorial. He stared at the unfinished work a moment longer, then he selected a fat-bristled brush from the jar on his paint stand and uncapped an almost-spent tube of titanium white. He squeezed a heavy blob onto his palette, added a small splash of paint thinner, worked the bristles through the paint, and drew a short, thick downstroke, then a diagonal upstroke—like a large check mark—across the painting's face. He stepped to the sink to rinse and soap the bristles, swab them in the palm of his hand, rinse them again, and shake away the moisture. Restoring the brush to its jar, he gazed at the painting a final moment, replaced its protective cloth, and left his home on Aycliffe Court for the airport, and for a cold case in Michigan.

PART THREE

And if that diamond ring turns brass,
Mama's gonna buy you a lookin' glass.

CHAPTER 34

Ben and Kenechi changed planes at O'Hare, leaving their uncomfortable coach seats in the Boeing MD-80 for even more uncomfortable seats in a diminutive fifty-seater. The plane from Dallas had been so crowded there was no room in the overhead bins for Ben's carryon. He'd shoved the bag under the seat in front of him and sat for the next two and a quarter hours with his feet cramped into the remaining narrow space and his long legs bent sharply. Now his legs felt tense and jittery, his back and neck stiff. He lolled his head side to side and was relieved when a boarding attendant pulled him out of the boarding queue to say his bag was too large for the overhead bins and they'd stow it below.

Kenechi strode on unhindered and was in seat 8B beneath a cone of reading light when Ben entered the cabin. He grinned as Ben passed and said, "Welcome to Lilliput."

"Hope Gulliver is booked on another flight," Ben muttered.

He jammed his leather bomber jacket into an overhead and sank into 11B. The window seat beside him was empty, but down the aisle strode Gulliver, stomach leading, a nice rhythm to his movements. Not 11A, Ben begged silently. The big man stopped, eyeing his boarding pass, then the empty seat to Ben's left.

"Wouldn't you as soon slip over there, nice window seat?" the man wheezed, hoisting a bag into an overhead bin. Ben pictured himself plastered to the fuselage for the forty-minute flight to Kalamazoo and leapt to his feet.

Gulliver pressed past him, exhaling, his girth almost taking Ben with him. Ben waited while the man heaved to and fro in the miniature seat (for so it seemed now) and then pulled the seatbelt over his belly with an oath. Ben sat carefully, fastened his own belt and sought a square inch on the armrest where he might place an elbow.

"Snowing hard now," his seatmate rasped. "Wonder if they're gonna de-ice this baby." Then, looking around, "What kind of crappy plane is this anyway?"

Ben said nothing. He guessed it wasn't a question. He put his head back, closed his eyes, and tried to ignore the commotion beside him—which was, after all, just his seatmate breathing. Through half-closed lids, he regarded him. He'd pulled a brochure from the seat pocket and was examining a sketch of the aircraft's interior.

"CRJ200," he announced. "Canuck flying machine."

Ben fought the impulse to open his eyes. If he had to spend the better part of an hour engulfed in another man's being, he'd be damned if he'd endure a chat fest, too.

The flight attendant, a guy named Jerry, showed the passengers how to fasten the seatbelt and breathe normally should the mask fall from its overhead compartment. Ben opened his right eye slightly to observe Jerry through his lashes, noticing that the flight attendant's left brow was higher than the other, giving him a rakish look incongruous with his spiel.

"In case of an emergency," Jerry said, his wicked brow commenting, *Heh, heh.*

"One time," remembered Gulliver, maybe noticing Ben's lashes twitch, "I was sitting in the back of a dinky little plane like this, and they asked me to go forward a few rows to balance the load. Couldn't believe it."

No? Ben felt his own brow shoot up. The intercom sputtered, and the voice from the cockpit said they'd lose an hour between Chicago and Kalamazoo time zones and that the current temperature in Kalamazoo was twenty-four degrees Fahrenheit, windy and snowing, with a high of thirty-one expected tomorrow.

When Ben had gone home to pack, he ducked beneath the yellow crime scene tape, unlocked his door with dread, and deliberately looked away from the living room, where Dayton's body had lain. The cleaners had not yet come to work their magic. But when they'd come and gone, and he'd had the carpet ripped up and replaced, would he still see that image in his mind's eye? Some images are indelible, he knew, and he wondered if he'd ever be comfortable in his home again. Even with the old carpeting gone, would he avoid stepping on that place where Dayton died, as if it were a grave? There were so many felt but unseen lines in life. Would he be as conscious of stepping over invisible lines in his home as he was in his world?

He'd dressed and packed fast and light—pale gray silk knit slipover and black wool pants and blazer, both of which he wore, and in his roll-on, a red tee and a charcoal cashmere V-neck for layering, toiletries, boxer-short pajamas, socks, underwear. He'd remembered to shove a pair of fleece-lined gloves into a pocket of his bomber jacket.

The fasten seatbelts light went off, and Kenechi rose, stooping to fit his height in the little plane, passing row eleven on his way to the john. He saluted Gulliver with an ebony hand, nodded at Ben, and let his hand drift down over his mouth to cover his smirk.

The little plane swung hard to the left, and Ben woke with a start, surprised that he'd slept. He checked his watch and advanced its time an hour. They would land soon. The passengers were quiet, mostly napping, reading lights dark. But the plane's motors were loud, and the flight was punctuated with little drifts to the side and occasional bumps. Ben sat leaning toward the aisle, but felt crushed and over-warm, and wondered if they were still above the shadowy waters of Lake Michigan. Through the small window next to Gulliver, he saw only a swirling winter mist, opaque and ambiguous. He imagined the waves below moving like white feathers toward their beaches, sea and sky blurred at the horizon in a shimmer of winter gray. He looked at his watch again. No, surely land by now. He revised the picture in his head: a frozen landscape, frosted with snow, neatly platted and starkly immaculate, its dormant fields carved into squares, etched with stands of leafless trees and limned with meandering rivers of satin ribbon. A Breughel landscape without the people.

He turned on his overhead light, reviewed his notes, reconsidered the interviews with Varnes, Snipes, Novak, and Kaye. Jimmy Snipes was a loose cannon, but could he have left Schnoodle's waiting room, driven to Arlington, shot Dayton, and returned to the doctor's office before the nurse called his name? Maybe. Or could he have an accomplice? Ben thought not; Jimmy Snipes was a loner. Not so Karl Novak, who'd have any number of bad actors to call on. Novak had manufactured his alibi. Why? And Sylva Kaye. A tough nut, but she was scared and hiding something. Was it only her "escort" business?

What wasn't he seeing? Ben asked himself. He had only these interviews to go on right now. He'd know more when Proudhorse and Hilda had finished investigating. And it was early days, yes, but early days were all he had. One week.

Right now, they had to follow the weapon.

And Nell. What in hell was that about? She was there, in the same apartment building where Smollett was killed. Something wrong there, and it made him feel sick. They'd talk when he got back, whether she wanted to or not. And whether he wanted to or not.

He took some loose paper from his notebook's back pocket and saw his note about the pink message slip on Dayton's desk. M. J. Kildare. He'd meant to ask the Knowlton's front desk about M. J. Kildare and had forgotten. Abner Zeeck had mentioned that a woman in green had been at the Knowlton looking for Dayton. And Andrew, hearing that, had said a horse-faced woman in neon green had snatched a key ring he'd found on the floor—a ring also holding a silver disc bearing the initial W or M. Then there was Nell's reaction to a woman in green at Chez Dee Sunday night. Ben tapped the folded note in his palm, looking morose. What else had he forgotten?

The plane dipped suddenly, sending a thrill through his middle and causing the other passengers to stir. The pilot banked, tilting to the left, and the clouds thinned suddenly. At that angle, as though the ground had rushed up to meet them, Ben saw the concrete canyons and rooftop geometrics of a city below, not so much buried in snow as lit and adorned and defined by it.

CHAPTER 35

"**Y**ou staying in Kalamazoo?" Detective Smolovick asked on the phone.

"Winnesaka. The Ceylon Inn."

"An old mansion, bricks painted yellow, three floors, like that?"

"Yeah. Sounds like a theme place," Ben said. "But not an elephant in sight."

Smolovick laughed, a sound like a wasp caught between screen and glass.

"Sail on in. Play on words."

Ben snorted.

"B&B," Smolovick continued. "You like those?"

"I thought it would be closer to the calls we have to make."

"None of the distances are that great."

Ben thought again that John Smolovick's voice sounded like a fuzzed-up boy's voice. Wayne Newton with COPD.

"Can we talk in the morning?" he asked.

"What about tonight," Smolovick suggested. "How about dinner, some drinks?"

"My partner's with me. We can meet you somewhere."

Ben looked out the window. The snow drifted downward beneath the streetlights and turned to gray slush on the salted roads.

"I just got in myself and could use a real dinner. I'll swing by and pick you up."

"I can drive my rental," Ben said, careful not to say he'd *rather* drive. When he'd said that on Sunday night, both Nell and Andrew had sighed. And Nell had said firmly, "Andrew's driving, and you can be a passenger for a change."

"I'll swing by," Smolovick repeated, his voice as firm as Nell's had been. "Honda Accord. Seven."

At ten to seven, Ben was at the front entrance. Kenechi came down just as a silver Honda with smoked windows swept into the sheltered drive and lurched to a stop directly in front of them. The driver opened his door and stood to look over the car's roof.

"Gallagher?"

Ben grinned at Kenechi. "Hey. It's Gulliver."

Ben settled in front, Kenechi in the rear, and Smolovick turned to greet them.

"No shit," he said in his cottony rasp, setting the car in motion before Ben closed the door. "The guys from the plane."

"If we'd known, we could've talked there," said Ben.

Smolovick deftly pulled the car into the boulevard traffic, gunned it and—eye on the rearview mirror—moved rapidly left three lanes, made a tight U, and headed back in the direction he'd come.

"You weren't in the mood to talk," he said.

And was rewarded by Kenechi's rare laugh, high-pitched and hearty.

"Toni's is up here in a shopping strip. Popular neighborhood place," Smolovick said. "It's a weeknight, so they probably won't be that crowded. Italian food, but the family that runs it is Albanian. Go figure."

He flicked his eyes toward the rearview mirror and moved into the passing lane.

"The lady that runs the place, everybody calls Mama. Must have a name, but I never heard it."

"How far is it?" Ben asked.

"Three, four miles down I-94." He poked a thumb over his shoulder. "Town back there called Texas Corners."

"Huh," Ben said.

"South of that, village called Schoolcraft. The Underground Railroad stopped there. The house used for the runaway slaves is still standing."

"I read about that," Kenechi said from the backseat.

"Schoolcraft is also famous because James Fenimore Cooper wrote about it."

"Leatherstocking," Kenechi put in. "Natty Bumppo. Chingach-gook."

Ben turned to gaze at his partner sitting large and placid in the backseat.

"Also a town near here called Climax," Smolovick said.

"Texas has a nice match for that—town called Bangs," Kenechi said. "And another town, Gun Barrel City."

Smolovick grunted appreciatively.

"Also Needmore. Oatmeal. Muleshoe. And north of Houston, a town called Cut and Shoot."

Ben turned in his seat to gaze at Kenechi again.

Smolovick spun the wheel clockwise and lurched into a parking area fronting a nondescript shopping strip, rocked to a stop on the salted blacktop, withdrew the ignition key, set his hand brake, and got out of the car—all in several economical movements. He was already yards ahead, head back, walking as if to a compelling inner rhythm, when Ben and Kenechi extricated themselves from their seatbelts and hauled themselves out of the Honda.

"I hate all these clothes," Ben said, slapping at himself. "You learn about Leatherstocking in Africa? Natty Bumppo? Chingach-gook?"

"What I learned in Africa was how to read."

They hurried after Smolovick, who'd aimed himself toward a glass front sandwiched between a bakery and a crafts shop, a red neon sign in the window lighting only *Ton*. Ben pondered Smolovick's broad back, mentally placing his and Kenechi's bodies into the large man's form and finding they almost fit. As Smolovick reached the door, it swung outward, and a young woman appeared, leading with her shoulder. Smolovick executed a surprisingly dainty pirouette and swung the door wide for the woman, who balanced a large, fragrant, greasy paper bag on her palms.

Smolovick sniffed and fluttered his fingers at his nose. "Be still my heart."

The woman smiled and met Ben's eyes as she passed.

"He means the food," Ben said.

"I guessed," she said.

Entering Toni's, they were met by a wave of warmth and garlic.

"Hey, doll," said a short, big-hipped woman with heavily penciled brows and hair the color of a rusty nail. She grabbed three menus, led them to a table in the room's center, and busied herself with corkscrew and wine glasses as heavy as Mason jars. Ben and Kenechi looked around. Toni's was an overheated warehouse of a room with square wooden posts supporting a low acoustic-tile ceiling. The tables were topped with beige-flecked Formica, the seats simple wooden chairs that scraped the dun-colored vinyl floor in a ceaseless abrasion of sound as diners sat, shifted, rose.

The three detectives piled their coats into the fourth chair, pulled back the other three noisily, and sat. Smolovick reached into the pile of coats, extracted a faded manila folder with "William Smollett" printed on its dog-eared tab, and shoved it toward Ben.

"Pretty thin," he said. "But this is what we got."

Ben opened the folder and leafed through its contents.

"But first," grunted the big man, picking up the menu. "Let's eat."

CHAPTER 36

I n the dream, Ben is at his easel, facing a large canvas lavishly covered with brushstrokes and knife work he recognizes as his own but in an unfamiliar violent style and strident palette. With dismay, he realizes he has been commissioned to do this work and has somehow, madly, forgotten it. Now he is running out of time. Panic grips him, and he loads a brush with paint and frantically slushes at the canvas. But his every move is maddeningly slow— his oils seem stiff and unmalleable despite the thinner, and the paint on the canvas seems tacky. Then he hears rain hitting the window and understands that the air is laden with humidity. The work will not dry and he will not finish on time. But desperation spurs him on. Then he sees he's made the paint too thin, that it's running in some places, and he brushes and daubs furiously, but nevertheless it runs, sliding from the canvas. Then, incredulously, he detects another image beneath the underpaint—he has been painting over another picture! How could this be? He seizes a palette knife and scrapes at the canvas. The images are nothing he recognizes, but at a bottom corner, a name appears, the name Eleanor Ryan, in Nell's small, right-sloping script.

Ben pulled himself awake, mouth dry as dust, to a slurry sound he didn't recognize, to footsteps muted by carpeting, to a room he didn't know. He automatically reached for the Glock, its holster hanging from a drawer pull on the nightstand. Fingers on the weapon, he listened, trying to bring the room's murky shadows into focus. That gray rectangle there, a door, yes . . .

The room did a fade-in. Kalamazoo. Winnesaka. Kenechi and Smolovick. The night before coming back to Ben in scraps: Ben, mind heavy with unnamed worry, ordering a second martini for his empty stomach; Kenechi and Smolovick more sensibly deciding to wait. Mountains of Insalata and Pesce del Giorno, foothills of Pasta Primavera. A chunk of tiramisu the size of a brick. Four bottles of wine and after-dinner whiskeys.

He worked his mouth and, at last, stirred up a little moisture. He ran his tongue over his teeth, which felt as though they were wearing tiny sweaters. God! Never again! He seldom drank much and for good reason—he got drunk.

He didn't remember leaving the restaurant. His next recollection was riding back in a blizzard, Smolovick and Akundi in the front seat of the darkened car, talking quietly, Ben sprawled in back, watching the snow swirling toward the headlights like Van Gogh spirals and thinking dimly, *Omigod, Gallagher, you're losing it. You're out of control.*

And he remembered an earlier moment—was there such a moment?—when he belligerently announced, *I'll drive.* And was there a little skirmish, or wasn't there, when he tried to get the keys from Smolovick's hand, Smolovick saying coolly, *Not hardly, buddy,* and Ben collapsing in the back seat.

Ah, God. His cheeks went hot with shame.

He lay back carefully, his head feeling like an anvil waiting for the next ringing blow, testing his woolen tongue and sweatered teeth a further moment, getting his bearings.

The digital clock on the nightstand read 6:42. By his body clock and Central time, that made it 5:42. The room was still dark. He tossed back the blankets—glad to find he wore pajamas and not clothes—went to the window and pulled aside the heavy drapery and opaque vinyl night shield. And the room was *still* dark. He peered into a slate-colored semidawn. The steel gray light gave a lavender cast to the new snow, which lay on the city like a muffler, muting the sounds of sparse traffic below. He heard a clang in the alley and pressed his forehead to the cold glass trying to see the source of the sound. It was a windless morning, the air so still, Ben saw, that an inch or so of fresh snow was stacked undisturbed on the power lines.

He watched the gray city below him for a time, taking comfort in the silence, until he realized the room was frigid. He breathed experimentally into the gray light: He could see his breath.

The temperature controls were in a heating/cooling unit beneath the window. Ben lifted the little door to the controls and found the black pointer set to OFF. He turned it to HEAT/HIGH and pressed the power button; a blast of icy air rushed from the noisy fan. He dived back into the bed, got into his favorite fetal position, and pulled the blankets over his shoulders. He regretted the broken silence, the ugly sound of the fan, and its mistral-like breeze, but he thought he could stand it until the chill went off the room. He was used to compliant down pillows that conformed to the shape and weight of his head. This one was like a giant marshmallow. He rose on an elbow and punched it hard in the gut. It lay there and regrouped. Shoving it aside, he let his cheek sink to the mattress, his head cranking impossibly. Then, cursing, he grabbed the pillow and dragged it back beneath his head.

Thus he lay for a moment before remembering the soft, slurry sound that had wakened him. He turned on the bedside lamp, tossed back the blankets again, and went to the entry. The *Kalamazoo Gazette* had been shoved under the door and lay flat on the carpet. He dropped the newspaper on the desk and jumped back into bed, lay a moment, then hopped up again, turned off the heater and that damned fan, and crawled back under the blankets.

Wasn't he supposed to meet Kenechi and Smolovick downstairs?

He shoved himself over the king-size mattress until he could reach the phone and hit a button bearing a tiny symbol of a knife, fork, and spoon. A Middle Eastern chirp answered.

"I know breakfast is served downstairs, but what about coffee?" Ben asked. Yes, said the chirp, the coffee was downstairs, too. Christ.

"Okay, I'm coming down," Ben threatened. "But by God, it had better be fresh and it had better be strong."

He reached for his rumpled clothes from the night before, shoved bare feet into his loafers, and dragged a comb through his hair. It felt at once like an act of violence and like someone else's scalp.

The corridor was drafty and deserted. He punched the elevator button, heard it clank churlishly somewhere in the building's bowels, changed his mind, and pushed through the stairwell door. Holding the banister with one hand and his head with the other, he descended the three flights to the dining room.

First thing he saw: the coffee service on the opposing wall.

Second thing: Kenechi and Smolovick looking spiffy at a table strewn with breakfast remnants.

Ben took his steaming cup to their table, pulled out a chair and sat, rumpled, face mangled with sleep. He eyed their plates with a churn of stomach—cold toast crusts and congealed egg yolk.

"Am I late?"

The two detectives laughed. Kenechi was immaculate in sparkling white shirt and luminous gray suit, his black wool overcoat folded on an empty chair, black felt tam and black leather gloves stacked on his briefcase. Ben knew if he were closer, he'd smell a mélange of soap, shampoo, talc, toothpaste, and mouthwash. He looked at his bare wrist.

"What time is it?"

Both men answered at once: "Seven."

He sounded as grumpy as he felt. "Didn't we say half past?"

"I woke early," Kenechi said. "So I got dressed and came on down. Found John already here."

"The snow," Smolovick said. "Wanted to miss the rush."

Kenechi turned to Smolovick.

"Ben is cranky because he doesn't like to be late. Prides himself on being punctual."

Ben yawned hugely, jaw creaking and eyes watering, before responding.

"The good luck of the early bird and so forth."

"There's also, don't forget, the bad luck of the early worm," Smolovick rasped.

Ben took an experimental sip of the steaming amber fluid in his cup, screwed up his face, and set the cup back on the saucer.

Smolovick pointed to a folder on the table.

"I found some more poop on Smollett. And contact info on Otto Sonigson, the landlord for the place on Undermain. Village Apartments."

Ben opened the folder and sifted through yellowed pages of type and desiccated newspaper clippings, reading this page and that, only dimly aware of Kenechi and Smolovick's amiable chatter.

Smolovick was saying something Ben didn't catch as he closed the folder.

"We had a proverb in Africa," Kenechi responded. "Leave a log in the water as long as you like; it will never become a crocodile."

"Can the Ethiopian change his skin," Smolovick intoned, "or the leopard his spots?"

"Fun With Platitudes," Ben said, pushing the folder to the side. Kenechi and Smolovick were looking at him.

"Oh. My turn? Um . . . you can put kittens in the oven, but that don't make 'em muffins."

Kenechi's high-pitched laughter merged with Smolovick's trapped wasp, and they offered their palms for a high-five—

Kenechi's large and pinkly pale, and Smolovick's enormous and white. Ben raised his own palm and gave each one a lazy slap. Then he pressed his fingertips to his forehead.

"God," he said. "It hurts to laugh."

He turned on his chair and peered out a mullioned window, snow lying like confectioner's sugar in tiny drifts in the corners of each pane.

"When does it get light here?" he asked Smolovick. "I mean *does* it get light here?"

"Want some breakfast?" Smolovick said.

Ben threw him a look of loathing, tipped a big swallow of coffee into his mouth, and rose.

"I'm going to shower, and I'll be back here at . . . what time is it now?"

"Ten past seven," Kenechi said.

"I'll be back here at half past. Like we said. On the nose."

CHAPTER 37

Tuesday, February 25

The entry to 1160 Undermain was a narrow space fitted with incongruous Chinese red swinging doors sandwiched between two storefronts—Kwite Kleen Dry Cleaners and Ezio's Pizza. Village Apartments was a second floor of apartments directly over the dry cleaner and pizza joint. The drab little complex—circa 1920s or '30s, Ben guessed—included a drug store and a gift shop and was bounded at one end by a narrow street and at the other by an alley leading to a parking area.

Kenechi pushed the doors open with big black paws, saying over his shoulder, "You coming? Or just standing?"

The swinging doors at 1160 Undermain were tall and narrow, with small triangles of screened glass inserted too high for anyone to see through—except briefly, maybe, someone descending the stair. Over a surface pocked and pimpled by countless coats of paint, the doors wore a thick and impervious veneer of high-gloss, oil-based scarlet enamel.

They mounted the narrow stairs and paused at the top, waiting for their eyes to adjust to the dim hallway. Ben saw that stairwell and hall were lit by two bare bulbs, sixty watts max—one hanging over the stairs and another in a dingy-shaded wall sconce midway down the long corridor. He counted five apartments flanking the

hall. The building's fusty smallness, steep stairs, and narrow corridor suggested not just another decade, Ben thought, but another
era—the hip-hop music and television news incongruous behind
those antique doors. He rapped at apartment five, waited, rapped
again—louder this time—and listened while someone inside fum-
bled with deadbolt, chain, and latch. A bent reed of a man in his
seventies cracked the door a foot and peered at the detectives.

Ben showed him his badge. "Otto Sonigson?"

More apprehensive than curious, Sonigson took Ben's gold and
blue badge into his gnarled hands, lifted his spectacles and stared
at the badge closely with his naked eyes. He rubbed a nicotined
finger over the Texas state seal and, satisfied, handed it back to
Ben. Sonigson restored his glasses to the bridge of a nose so sharp
and prominent it seemed to proceed ahead of him like the prow
of a boat. He was slender and balding, down-like hairs atop his
spotted pate and a gray fringe above his long-lobed ears. He wore
a grayed undershirt; loose suspenders looped his hips.

"You're the owner and landlord of these apartments?" Ben
asked.

Sonigson looked wary, a look Ben had seen many times. A
look that said, *Shit!*

"My name is Gallagher. I'm a detective, and this is Detective
Akundi."

Shit! They've got me! Shit! Shit!

"We're from Texas, and we're investigating a murder. Could
we come in and talk to you for a minute?"

Sonigson blinked pale, red-rimmed eyes, Ben's words not com-
puting.

"Where you from again?"

"Texas. Arlington, Texas. We need to speak to you for just a
minute."

Sonigson moved back from the door, as if to close it, the fingers of his right hand wrapped high on the door's edge.

"I don't know a goddamn thing about any murder. And I sure as hell don't know a goddamn thing about any murder in Texas. You got the wrong man and the wrong place."

Ben found ample room for his toe in the doorway.

"No. You don't know anything about this murder. We know that."

He edged his foot in a bit farther, put his palm against the door and reassurance in his voice.

"It happened in Texas. We're tracking down acquaintances of the victim. He may have known one of your former tenants."

The man thought this over, relief gradually washing his features. He stepped back uncertainly, widening the space. Ben moved inside, Kenechi following.

"This is a Texas case, as I said," Ben repeated. "But there are Michigan connections—to a man who rented one of your apartments."

Sonigson motioned the detectives into the room and closed the door. They had stepped directly into a living room steeped in nicotine and as poorly lit as the hall. The landlord pointed to a brown vinyl sofa-and-chair arrangement in one corner involving the requisite two lamps, two end tables, and a coffee table. The table nearest the chair held a short pile of dog-eared magazines, a nearly empty package of unfiltered Camels, and a large and overflowing ashtray. The opposite corner was anchored by a large-screen color TV, tuned to the weather channel, but muted.

The three sat, Sonigson with difficulty, and Ben and Kenechi pulled out notebooks and pens.

Ben said, "We need to know anything you can remember about the people who rented your apartments in the early seventies."

Sonigson drew back.

"The seventies! Good Christ. I can't remember what happened yesterday."

"Why don't you just tell us a little about yourself first? You own the Village Apartments?"

"I do," he said. "And my parents before me: Rolf and Ingrid Sonigson. They had a little stake and came here from Sweden in 1925. Only in their twenties, but bought this place and managed to hang on to it through the Depression."

He shook a Camel from the pack and unfolded a book of matches.

"Pop ran a fixit service through the Depression, too—worked for food, or what have you, when folks had leaky pipes, but no money. Pert near furnished these apartments with stuff he took in trade. I was born then, too. 1932."

"How long have you run the business?"

"Since sixteen, when my dad died." He lit the cigarette and blew out a plume of blue smoke. "He was only fifty-two, heart attack. My mother died when I was thirty-seven, left everything to me."

"Wife? Children?'

"Me? Never." He tried a little laugh, but it came out a nervous hiccough.

"So . . ." Ben calculated. "You were sole owner and manager in 1971, then?"

"I was. Ma died in 1968."

Ben filled a page in his brown leather notebook with his neat vertical script, read what he'd written, wrote another sentence, and turned to Sonigson, who waited with palpable anxiety.

"You had a Sypinski family in apartment one in the early seventies. Gene and Marta Sypinski."

Sonigson ran a thin palm over his unshaven cheeks, his hand rasping audibly over the gray stubble.

"They had two boys, Frank and Peter," Ben offered.

The old man's pale eyes lit behind his lenses.

"Frankie and Petey, by Christ! Yes, I remember them. Good boys. Well, caused a speck of trouble, but they was boys after all."

He spoke around the cigarette, narrowing an eye against its spiraling smoke. "Usta throw stuff out their front windows on drunks going back and forth between the Komfy Kozy and the Swan Song, bars that usta be here. Had to laugh, myself. Damned if I wouldna done it, too, if I was their age. Shit, might do it now, if I had the energy."

"How long did they live here?"

Sonigson shrugged.

"What, several years?"

"Yeah, something like that. I saw the boys grow up a little, then their dad got a job at Kellogg's and they all moved to Battle Creek. All I know."

"You know anything about where they are now?"

"Ah, hell. No." Disappointed.

"We'll check it out," Ben said, and wrote something. "At that time, you also had a Manning Boyle here."

Sonigson slapped his bony thigh and laughed soundlessly.

"Boyle! Shit, old Boyle's still here."

He laughed again.

"Right next door, apartment four. I'm guessing forty years."

Ben and Kenechi exchanged glances.

"Old bachelor fella," Sonigson continued. "Retired. Keeps to himself. No family, no visitors. Pays on time, never a moment's trouble. Wish I had a houseful of old Boyles."

"He at home now?" Kenechi asked.

Sonigson shrugged again. "I don't keep track of my folks' comins and goins."

Ben turned to Kenechi, but Ken was already headed for the door, notebook in hand.

Ben resumed with Sonigson. "You also had a William Smollett."

The landlord stared at Ben for a split second.

"Willie Smollett, by Christ! I remember him. Smollett was murdered, by God—shot on those steps right out there!"

He pointed a yellow finger past Ben's shoulder, indicating the wall that separated his apartment from the stairwell.

"I haven't thought of that for ages."

Getting interested and comfortable now, Ben saw, and knew why. Whatever Sonigson had to hide, he now understood Ben cared nothing for it. He sat back, as if waiting for the next question on a quiz. Then he thought of something, hauled himself out of the brown vinyl chair and headed for the kitchen.

"Want a beer?"

Ben shook his head, his stomach taking a nauseating little whirl, hearing the refrigerator door slam, the *pffttt* of the beer can's pull tab. Sonigson returned, wiping his mouth with the back of his hand.

"Ahhh. Never too early for a beer, I always say."

"Mr. Sonigson," Ben began.

"Call me Soni," the landlord said affably, pronouncing it *SAH-nee*. "With Otto, friends of Soni Sonigson wouldn't know who you were talking about."

He took several pulls on the can of Bud, his Adam's apple bobbing audibly with each swallow.

"We know about Smollett's murder, Soni," Ben said. "But we want to hear everything you remember about it."

"I told the police everything I knew. Which was nothing."

"We'd like to hear it again. Everything."

"It figure into the thing you're looking at?"

"One way or the other. That's why we need to know anything you remember. No matter what it is."

"Well . . ." Soni Sonigson sat back to talk.

CHAPTER 38

Manning Boyle was a battered-looking man who seemed older than his midseventies, violet stains beneath red-rimmed eyes and clear tubing from an oxygen tank snaking to his nostrils.

"Yeah, I remember that night like it was yesterday," he told Kenechi. "But I ain't told it, not from that day to this."

Kenechi sat back a little, crossed one leg over the other and fixed his notebook on his thigh. He studied Manning Boyle with an implacable gaze.

"So today you tell."

Boyle returned his gaze beat for beat. "I thought the whole thing was over and done with. Never thought anyone'd come sniffing around after all this time."

"But here I am," Kenechi said, and the man gazed off into the distance so long that he added, "Sniffing."

Boyle sorted his thoughts. When he finally spoke, his voice was reedy and tremulous.

"The Smolletts had been out drinking. It was St. Patrick's Day. I'm Irish so I remember that. Those two drank a lot, and that was when they were friendly. Otherwise, they kept to themselves.

Sometimes they'd come home and rap on my door, ask me if I wanted a nightcap."

"And that happened that night?"

"Yeah. I went over there. Their place was just there—"

He pointed a thumb in the general direction of the door.

"In that apartment across the hall from mine. They left their door unlocked, and when I went in, there was a girl there—well, a young woman—I'd seen her around here before, but I didn't know how she fit in, thought she was maybe the babysitter. They talked a minute, I don't know what about, I was in the kitchen fixing a drink."

"Who was this young woman?"

"Never heard her name. She took a drink, but I got the feeling she was only interested in the baby."

Kenechi looked up from his notebook. "The baby?"

"The Smolletts' baby. She kept looking over at him, saying you think he's cold, hungry, like that. Once she looked at me and said, Have you heard him crying? But that baby cried all the time. I wasn't going to get into that."

Boyle plucked at his lower lip with a knobby thumb and index finger.

"Willie liked young girls. But they didn't like him—he was young enough himself, not much more than thirty, I'd guess, but sort of stuck in another era if you know what I mean."

"I'm not sure I do."

"Well, he didn't fit in, did he? We had a lot of university students renting these apartments in those days, and Willie always came on to the girls. But he was a world away from those students, this skinny guy in railroad clothes with a railroad job, and not even a high school education. I think he thought their world was forbidden to him. Made him want it even more."

Boyle reflected, and Kenechi waited.

"Anyway, Willie was coming on with all his might to that young woman. He had the radio on and kept flipping the dial—

You like this song? You like this song? Then he found the Top Forty and screwed up the volume, that radio blasting away—tunes like Simon and Garfunkel's 'Bridge Over Troubled Water' and the Beatles' 'Let it Be.' Then my favorite came on: 'Bobby McGee.' Janis Joplin singing it wild as a banshee. And I guess Willie liked it, too, because we both rocked out on our air guitars, yelling out the dah-dahs with Joplin."

Old Boyle's eyes sparked for just a second.

"I said I could remember it like it was yesterday, but I never did figure out what happened next, how it all came down. I remember Willie was saying something to this girl about being classy—he fancied he was some sort of ladies' man, but he had . . . Well, let me back up."

Boyle was quiet another long moment, eyes fixed on his hands, which were motionless in his lap. When he looked up again, his voice seemed stronger.

"You could almost call Willie handsome, but he had some kind of accident and one side of his face didn't match the other. Eyes didn't match, like. One eye glassy, sort of stared.

"Anyways, Willie Smollett was ugly sober and uglier drunk. Spoiling for a fight—that sort of guy—then a few drinks, and he'd be backslappin' all over the place, then just as fast, mean again, only meaner. Hung around the Komfy Kozy all the time, him and Moll. Had a handgun, a twenty-two, used to get drunk and wave it around from time to time. Good guy to stay away from."

Kenechi was writing fast in his bold scrawl of black ink, and Boyle paused to watch a moment. "So, where was I?"

Kenechi looked at his notebook, eyes running back over the words. "Smollett said something to the young woman about being classy."

Boyle looked pleased to hear his words retold accurately. "Right. Well, Willie liked class in a dame. Though you wouldn't know it by the Cantrell girl."

"Cantrell?"

"Moll."

"Smollett's wife?"

"Ah, I dunno if they was ever really married. But they had this baby, and Moll used Smollett's name. Moll was young enough, but she was from Willie's world. She . . ."

Boyle seemed lost for words.

"She suffered by comparison," Kenechi offered.

"Yeah. That's it. Anyway, Willie used to tell a story about how he had a crush on the smartest girl in the school. *Wouldn't give me the time of day, though,* he would say, like this was proof she had class. So he must have been telling that to this other gal, because I heard him say, *A real little lady, like you.*

"All of a sudden Moll was yellin' at the woman. First saying mind your own fucking business. But then something about going after my man right in front of my face. But then she settled right down to talking sweet, you know, like drunks do, and started talking about this gal's ring, wanted to see this ring. Kept saying, Come on, let me try it on. It was a special ring, you could tell, gold and onyx, like that, had some initials on the top, and I wasn't surprised when this gal said she couldn't get it off. So that pissed Moll off and she made a lunge for this gal. And then Willie drops Moll right in her tracks, hits her smack in the side of the head with his fist, and lets her lie there.

"This other gal goes all shocked looking and stares at me with great big eyes, I can still see 'em, and starts for the door, but then sort of whispers to me, I'm worried about the baby. And Willie says, Hey, don't go, finish your drink, ol' Moll here'll be just fine, just got a little exercised there.

"So Willie nudges Moll with the toe of his shoe, just a nudge, and she like comes to and starts screeching like you never heard, He's gonna kill me! Don't let him kill me! So Willie gives Moll a little punch, not a big one, not even with his fist, but with his open hand. And she turns the volume way up, and Willie gives her a kick on the backside. More for real now, because she's crawling away, and this other gal, she's throwing herself at Willie, screaming Stop! Stop! And Moll latches on to this other gal, puts her arms around her knees and bawls on her legs, all snot and tears, crying how she only wanted to try the ring on, she wasn't gonna keep it, and that gal reaches down to her. To—I don't know—help her, I guess. And Moll grabs this lady's hand and shoves her finger—the one with the ring—into her mouth and clamps down hard, all the time bleating and growling like an animal."

Kenechi looked up from his notebook, frowning. "She bit her?"

"You got it. She wants the ring. So now we're all screamin'. This other lady goes, Oh my God! And Willie yells, Let her go, goddammit! And Moll starts shaking the lady's hand like a puppy with a rag. Now Willie starts punching Moll for real, her nose crunching, and the blood—I don't even know whose blood anymore, Moll's or the lady's. All the time, Moll keeps her jaws clamped and keeps growling, sort of, and sort of laughing, teeth shut tight. The lady starts shrieking, She's biting it off!

"And I'm thinking the jaws are the strongest part of the human body and how trapeze folks hang from their teeth and twirl around. So now I know Willie's going to kill this bitch, and when she's dead, she'll still have that lady's finger between her teeth."

"Then what happened?" asked Kenechi.

"So the three of 'em are in this huddle, the lady screaming, Moll on her knees biting, Willie hitting her upside the head hard as he can, me on my knees now too, trying to try to get Moll to open her mouth. Then I see some real shiny black shoes walk up, and nice trousers, and I see a big ol' gun barrel touching down right on Moll's eyelid, a big clean hand with a nice gold watch and white cuffs and holding the gun. I don't even dare raise my head to see who this motherfucker is. Everybody stops screaming and moving for a second, and the guy in the shiny shoes says, real quiet: Open your mouth, or I'll blow your teeth out along with your brains. And Moll feels the gun on her eyelid and hears the guy pull back the hammer, and there must be something about a gun that sobers you up even when you're three sheets to the wind, because she snaps her mouth open like a crocodile. Then she falls back on the floor and lays there, crying and laughing and gagging, blood and slime on her, like she was in the ring for fourteen rounds."

Boyle took a minute to breathe.

"Then what happened?"

"Moll scuttles away like a fat cockroach, and I think she's got that lady's finger in her mouth, but no. She looks around, laughing like anything, and sticks out her tongue a little bit, and there's the ring, layin' on her tongue. I think, Goddamn! She got the ring! The lady's finger is already turning black, squirting, sort of, and off they go to the emergency. Right down to the bone, like an animal. I heard the human mouth is the dirtiest thing you can find."

"What happened to the man with the gun?"

"Like I said—off to the emergency. But a little later I'm in my place with the door open, and he comes back, looks in and sees me, and says he wants the ring. So we both go in there to Smollett's, the radio still blasting away—Three Dog Night singing 'Mama Told Me Not to Come,' and me thinking, No shit. Moll Smollett was about out of it but still pissed off, layin' back on the couch with blood all over her front, one tit hanging out and quivering like a jellyfish. She was muttering something at Willie about taking the ring from her. And Willie standing there, for some reason got his jacket and cap on, maybe going back to the bar, and maybe that's pissing Moll off, too. Willie breathin' hard, still wanting a fight, I can tell.

"This big guy—I guess he ain't afraid of nothin'—says, Give me the ring, Smollett. Willie starts to turn his back, and right then and there, the big guy grabs Willie by the neck, puts his knee in the middle of his back, and Willie lets out a scream like a woman."

Boyle let loose a phlegmy guffaw and coughed hard, then wiped his eyes and readjusted the plastic tubing in his nostrils.

"Don't make me laugh," he warned, and Kenechi shook his head.

"So Willie hangs on to the ring," Boyle resumed, "and this big guy drags him down and steps on his hand and Willie yells and grunts, Okay! and drops the ring. So the big guy picks it up, puts the gun in his pocket, and starts down the hall.

"So I'm thinking it's all over, and I go across the hall to my own apartment. Just as I'm closing the door, I see Willie running by, not making much noise—even with his big railroad boots—with a gun in his hand. Moll in the doorway, looking like something the cat drug in for sure, with that bloody face. And I think, Holy shit! and close the door. I hear scrabbling on the stairs, but nobody yelling or nothing, then I hear pop! and I think, Holy shit!

"I don't know what's happened, but it won't be good whatever, and here I was, putting my fingerprints all over the Smollett place, getting blood all over my shirt. After a while, I sneak open my door. I'd heard some noise in the hall, but now everything's quiet, and I see the Smollett's door wide open, so I tiptoe over there with a towel and wipe everything I touched, and even some stuff I didn't, and bring the glass I drank from back to my apartment."

"Who was in the Smollett place when you went in there?"

"Just Moll. Comin' out the bathroom with her eyes swoll almost shut."

"You weren't worried that she'd tell the police you'd been there?"

"Moll? Hell, would she even remember? Anyway, Moll was no friend of the police. Probably keep quiet just to spite them."

"What'd you do then? Go down the hall? The stairs?"

"No. But Willie's body must have been there, because pretty soon the cops were doing their deal, yellow tape and cameras and stuff, on the stairs."

"Why didn't you tell the police all this?"

"I already said. It was murder, man. I was with them. I had blood on me. I wasn't going to prison as an accessory. Or worse, a murderer."

"You're not worried about that now."

Boyle's eyes snaked toward his oxygen tank.

"I won't last long enough for it to matter. And if it came down like I think, it was self-defense. I thought the thing was over and forgotten. Never thought anyone would come nosing into it after all this time."

Boyle coughed into his hand and wiped a red smear from his palm with a tissue from the box on the table.

"The man with the gun," Kenechi said. "You didn't know who he was?"

"If I'm gonna say what I saw, it needs to be soon. Or I could sign something."

"The man with the gun."

Boyle hesitated.

"Did you know who he was?"

"Not then. Moll . . ."

Kenechi waited, pen poised, but Boyle was silent. Kenechi fixed his black eyes on the older man.

"Tell me," he ordered.

Boyle thought a minute. "Let's say I never knew."

"Tell me."

"Usta see stories about him in the paper. A good guy. Did a lot for this town. And did the world a favor, too, far as Willie was concerned. Willie was a no-account. Anyways, it was self-defense. Over the years, I came to believe things worked out fine just as they were."

"Tell me," Kenechi repeated. But he already knew.

"A lawyer. David Slaughter. Went by his middle name, though. Dayton."

CHAPTER 39

"**E**verything you can remember about Willie Smollett," Ben said to Soni Sonigson, who was beginning to look tired. "And we'll wrap it up for now."

Sonigson heaved himself to a standing position, flexed his knees, and moved to the kitchen, repeated the refrigerator door and *pfttt* sounds, and came back with another Bud, emitting a small belch on the way.

"Willie worked on the railroad," he said, settling himself again. "You need that?"

"Everything."

"Okay. So he worked on the railroad. His people were from Memphis. Told me they came to Michigan to find jobs in the auto plants, then spread out to the cereal plants in Battle Creek. Lots of cereal plants there, not just Kellogg's and Post. Fact, part of Battle Creek was called Postumville because of the cereal factories. Smelled like one big shitload of corn flakes."

He laughed suddenly.

"One time, Willie was going on about how he hated that town, how he hated *every* town, but especially how he hated Cereal City. He was drunk and didn't know what he was saying. He was trying to say, *All they got is snap, crackle, and pop.* Instead he said, *All they got is pop, snackle, and crap.*"

He laughed again, soundlessly, slapping his thigh.

"That was maybe the only funny thing Willie Smollett said in his whole life."

He lit a Camel and exhaled gustily, Ben fighting the urge to fan at the smoke.

"Anyway, lots of work over there for a guy like Smollett. Plenty of trains for hauling out all that stuff, especially in the east end. Train yards, switchyards, whatever.

"Willie liked trains. You wouldn't think so with what happened, but he did. The railroad was the only job I knew him to have. He always wore his railroad gear, even when he was laid off."

"Was he wearing railroad gear when he was killed?"

"I reckon."

Ben pulled a yellowed sheet of paper from a folder and read aloud: "Twill pants, navy sweater and jacket, billed cap, heavy woolen socks, black boots."

"Yeah, sounds right. Only thing different might be denim coveralls instead of twills. Mighta been dressed up that night."

"You said something happened that would make him dislike trains."

"He had a bad accident. Used to ride the rails. Find an empty boxcar, it would take you where you wanted to go if the railroad dicks didn't get you. They was mean bastards, gave you curbside justice, if you know what I mean. People think of railroad dicks as being in the '20s and '30s, but they were in operation right up through the '70s—probably still are.

"Anyway, Willie was in his teens, maybe twenty, when he jumped in a boxcar leaving Detroit"—pronouncing it *DEEtroit*—"and headed for the yards near the cereal factories in Battle Creek. Willie was waiting for the train to slow, but he saw some dicks and thought they saw him, so he jumped. Train was going a mite fast, which would of probably been all right, but he hopped out of that boxcar just in time to smash into a mail hook. It caught him on the left cheek, the hook coming out the eye socket. The dicks took him down, said his eye was laying out on his cheek. So what you was looking at, when you looked at Willie Smollett, was a young guy with a lot of plastic surgery.

"He was handsome in a way. Well, not handsome exactly, but interesting. He had a different look, intense but kind of paralyzed on the left side of his face. His smile was lopsided, not that he smiled much, and his left eye was odd—watery, kind of starey. Well, I'll tell you who he looked like, kinda," Sonigson said, a thought striking him. "Humphrey Bogart. That serious bloodshot look, you know? Only, look at the right side and it's this Bogart-looking guy, then he turns his head and scares the bejesus outta ya. Not that he was freaky or anything, but his left side . . . He said once when he was drunk that he didn't have any feeling in it.

"You'd think he wouldn't want anything to do with trains after that, but he did—spent his life on those rails, one way or the other."

He sighed heavily and stubbed out the cigarette.

"One more thing, Soni," Ben said

He pulled an old photo of Dayton from the pocket in his notebook.

"You ever see this man?"

Sonigson studied it, again pushing his spectacles up and peering at the photo with his naked eyes before handing it back and shaking his head, nothing readable in his face.

"Here's a more recent photo."

More decisive now, *No.*

Ben flipped the pages in his notebook to replace the photos and wrote, Sonigson watching. At length, Ben asked, "What became of Smollett's wife?"

"Ah, God, Moll lived in that same place since she was a girl, I guess. More'n thirty years, anyway. But she just up and left. Not that long ago."

"Forwarding address?"

"No, no. Nothing like that. Just gave notice, paid up, and left. I had to go out of town and when I got back, she was gone."

"What can you tell me about her?"

"I remember her back in the day, I can tell you. Willie's death didn't slow her down any. Well, she was young and liked to kick up her heels. Did plenty of after-hours entertaining, if you know what I mean. I used to wonder if that's where she got her money. I mean . . ."

"I know what you mean."

"She always seemed to have plenty. And never worked far as I know." He took another swig from the beer can. "But those were live and let live days. She paid her rent, and I stayed out of it."

"Then?"

"Then some older guy, some factory hand, moved in with her. And one day they got married. I could've dropped my teeth. Wasn't but a few weeks before I saw ol' Moll was preggers, so I knew then what was what. Not that she wanted babies. But the old man had some money, and he up and died after some years, and Moll was a widow again."

He drained the can and lit up again from the pack of unfiltered Camels, blew out a blue plume of smoke. Ben blinked, eyes already smarting from the building's pungent bouquet of odors.

"Still kicked up her heels, though. Yeah, had energy to burn, that gal, and she also had her old man's insurance money. And his pension money too, I guess, from what she said. But she got older like everybody else, and she maybe just plain tuckered herself out. She was always sort of a slow fish in shallow water, if you know what I mean."

"I don't think I do."

"Molly Cantrell wanted the deep end. Mebbe she figured the only way . . . for some reason, she couldn't swim alone, and she tried to latch on to one big fish after another. I reckon they just shook her off. Left her with nothing to hang on to but guppies like Smollett."

Ben wrote something in his notebook. "What was this older guy's name, the husband?"

Sonigson thought. "I don't rightly remember. I can always remember Smollett because of that murder. But . . ."

"Did Moll keep the Smollett name?"

"Nah, she went by her new husband's name. But I always just called her Moll." He screwed up his face. "Short name. Kinda odd."

"Could you check your rent receipts?"

"She always paid with cash."

Ben looked at him steadily.

"You'd still have records and receipts, no?"

He could feel the man freeze.

"Let's drop that for now," he said. "I can get the name."

Sonigson looked wary, and Ben felt him edging away.

"Soni. I'm not concerned with your financial arrangements or your dealings with the IRS. I'm concerned only with the people who lived in this building in the early seventies. Let me ask you . . ."

He hesitated, his mouth suddenly dry.

"Soni, you had another renter, a woman in apartment two, when Smollett was murdered."

Sonigson peered at him, shook his head. Sullen now, Ben saw.

"Dunno who that would be."

"Her name was Eleanor Ryan."

He shook his head.

"Young woman. She would have been a student at the university. At WMU."

He shook his head again. "I had a lot of university students over the years."

Ben relaxed a little. "She had a baby while she was here, a baby boy."

"Lots of girls had babies here, too. I don't remember any—what was that name?"

"Eleanor Ryan." He looked hard at Sonigson. "Her nickname was Nell."

Ben fished his mother's photo from the back of his notebook and handed it over without saying anything. Sonigson gave it the treatment—glasses, no glasses, a shake of head. But before that, Ben thought, a glimmer of recognition, quickly veiled.

"Those students all looked alike to me. Long hair, bell-bottom jeans, tee-shirts with peace signs . . ."

Sonigson thought some more, handed the photo back.

"Doesn't seem very long ago in a way. But I was young my-self then—I would have been, what . . . well, still in my thirties, y'see."

"Yes, I see."

Ben gratefully watched him take the last drag on what was left of his cigarette and stub it into the ashtray.

"You say she lived in apartment two?"

Ben nodded, heart dropping a little.

The old man thought. "Nope, guess not. Guess I can't help you there."

"I was mostly interested in what you could remember about her, and whether she knew the Smolletts."

"Guess not. I don't remember. Maybe she was quiet and stayed off to herself."

Yes, Ben thought. He pulled out a card and handed it over.

"Please keep this card, Soni, and if you think of anything more, let me know."

The older man took the card with quivering fingers and looked at Ben intently.

"I'll do that, Detective."

———

In the frigid hall, Ben checked his watch and stood for a second in the blended smells and sounds from five apartments: bacon grease, cigarettes, coffee, garlic, and—what, hair spray?—a game show on TV now, hip hop still playing behind another door, this time Ben recognizing Eminem's' "Lose Yourself." He looked to the left. Apartment two was at the top of the stairs. The hammered brass numeral on the door was askew. Ben saw it was missing its bottom screw, and he took a few quick steps, gave the brass numeral a tap with his index finger to make it hang straight.

Where I was born, he thought, *behind that door.*

He stood a moment, something nagging deep in his brain, something he should have asked Sonigson, and his cell phone rang. He pulled the phone from his pocket and looked at it. Then, staring at the phone as though it had come to life in his hand, he punched it off.

Nell. Not now, not fucking now!

Glancing at his watch, he turned and moved toward apartment four. Kenechi had been in there for nearly an hour. Either Manning Boyle had plenty to say, or he had killed Kenechi and was trussing the body.

Before he knocked, Ben heard Kenechi's voice on the other side of the door, an old man's laughter and some spasmodic coughing. The door opened, and Kenechi's figure loomed in the doorway, followed by a smaller, wizened-looking man with a pale but alert face and plastic tubes emerging from his nostrils.

Seeing Ben, Kenechi turned to the older man.

"Mr. Boyle, this is Detective Sergeant Ben Gallagher, my boss and head of detectives down in Texas."

Always careful to acknowledge hierarchy, Ben thought, taking Manning Boyle's cold hand. It was like grasping a bird's claw.

CHAPTER 40

Down the dim stairs, through the red doors, outside. They stood on the sidewalk for a second, stunned by light and cold.

"Christ!" said Ben, clapping a hand over his eyes and grabbing for his sunglasses.

The cloud cover had cleared, leaving behind one of those sunny winter days rare in overcast southwestern Michigan: icy air clean and still, sky a clear bright blue, sun flashing off the snow. Both men grabbed great lungfuls of fresh air and exhaled plumes of vapor that hung for a second before dissipating. Ben blew his nose and blinked his tearing eyes.

"Lethal combination in that place," he said. "Bacon, cigarette smoke, coffee, Ezio's pizzas. All mixed up with hair spray or furniture polish or whatever the hell it was. Your guy gives a whole new meaning to the term *infectious laugh*. If I lived in there, I'd be on oxygen, too."

Kenechi had his eyes closed and his face to the sun, arms outstretched, basking.

Ben smiled. "You love a brutal sun the way some people love a brutal god."

Kenechi gave him one of his looks. "I was raised with both." Then he said, "Probably perchloroethylene."

"Huh?"

"That smell."

"Dr. Akundi, how you do talk."

"That sharp, sweet smell? Dry cleaning fluid." He motioned toward the Kwite Kleen. "Also known as PERC or tetrachloroethylene. It's found in other stuff . . . some shoe polishes, for example. Used to be in typewriter correction fluid, don't know if they still make that. But lethal is right. Don't spend any time breathing it."

"Legal?"

"Only in small amounts. Happily, most people can smell even a little bit. But living above it . . . cancer, failed liver, kidneys, nervous system. Before that, confusion, memory loss."

"Ah!" Ben took another great breath, exhaled lustily. "Old Sonigson's memory seemed okay, though."

"Manning Boyle's, too. But he's on his way out and knows it. He's talking."

Ben snapped to attention. "What'd you get?"

Kenechi threw him a grin and paged through his notebook with a sturdy black index finger.

"Well, let's see," he said. "I got the St. Patrick's Day drinking party. And the brawl over the ring. And, oh, yeah, the struggle on the stairs."

He looked at Ben.

"And I got William Smollett's shooter."

They heard a scraping noise from above and a querulous voice cried, "Detective!" Ben looked up, squinting. Soni Sonigson had his head out the window, his fine, short, white hair lit with sun and swaying in the winter air like a baby's fringe. His wrung-out complexion looked even more etiolated in the sunlight than in his dim rooms. He leaned his elbow on the sill and looked at a small piece of paper in his right hand.

"That name you wanted. The guy Moll Smollett married."

"Yeah?"

Ben squinted up, one hand shielding his eyes from the blinding sun.

No excuse for being unprepared for Soni Sonigson's words, but that's what he was—unprepared.

———————————

To get to their rental car, Ben and Kenechi had to detour around a three-foot mound of soiled snow shoved to the curb by a snowplow. The midafternoon sun glinted off anything that would reflect: snow, storefront windows, auto windshields, brass fittings on a folded awning, the detectives' sunglasses. They got into the car and looked at each other.

"We need to get back," Ben said. "But we also need to talk to Sypinski."

He looked at his watch.

"No way we can get back to DFW tonight, especially with that leg from Kalamazoo to Chicago."

He considered.

"Let's split up. You stay here. I'll drive to Battle Creek and find Sypinski, while you brief Smolovick and bring Proudhorse and Hilda into the picture. Go ahead and see what time we can get out of here tomorrow. Any time after noon, in case I don't connect with Sypinski right away."

Kenechi nodded.

"Let's hold off on calling the chief. Leave him a message at the office when you know he's gone for the day; tell him it's been a productive trip, that we're coming back tomorrow. And leave your phone off."

Kenechi looked doubtful. "Shouldn't you call him?"

Worried about the hierarchy, Ben thought.

"You're leading this case, Ken," Ben reminded him.

Kenechi didn't mention that it was Ben the chief kept calling, just showed him a small smile and flipped back a few pages in his notebook.

"What about the woman in apartment two? Eleanor Ryan?"

Here was the moment, and Ben knew it. He contemplated the countless dust motes suspended in a shaft of sunlight slanting through the windshield and, pursing his lips, blew gently, stirring the motes into a small frenzy of agitation. He watched the motes—always there, breathing in and out with us. Unfelt, unknown.

And here was the moment, passing. The moment when Ben must say, *Eleanor Ryan is my mother.* Should have said it that day he'd read it in the report. But he hadn't, hadn't known what it meant. He still didn't know what it meant, and the moment was passing, passing right now, under his nose. He could say it, and it would stay with the two of them. He could say it, and Kenechi would give him that sidelong glance, his eyes turning to show their whites, showing he knew it wasn't a casual statement, that in an instant he knew it all—more than Ben himself dared know.

Ben imagined hearing it unfold, *She lived in apartment two when she was a university student. In fact, whaddya know and guess what—I was born there.* Now it was getting too big, a bigger story than he wanted out there. Still, here was the moment, and it was passing into this prolonged silence

Ben turned to his partner suddenly, and Kenechi waited, feeling it.

Ben said nothing.

Kenechi turned to him, a question in his eyes, and Ben gave a little shake of head.

So, not saying it. And just that fast, the moment stretched and slid . . . if not into forever, into too late. Just that fast, Detective Sergeant Ben Gallagher was on the wrong side of his rule of law.

CHAPTER 41

A ndrew pulled open the Cachet Day Spa's brass-framed glass doors. He'd spent another morning closeted with Tooley Deere and his ledgers, and he hoped to take Dollie for an early-afternoon bite. He'd heard about the burgers and fries down the street at a tiny bar-cum-cafe called the Ripe Olive. But Dollie wasn't at her usual post at the black marble counter.

He poked his head into the lobby.

"You know where Dollie is?" he asked Abner.

"Ain't she in there? She came out and got Zora off the sidewalk a little bit ago."

"Just tell her I came by. I'll be back in a while."

The Ripe Olive wasn't deserted, but it had the subdued feel of a bar in the afternoon. Andrew took a stool at the bar, where a large woman with skin the color of pale toffee tended both bar and cafe, solo and without hurry.

"What can I get for you?" she asked softly. Andrew thought she had a quietness about her. He looked up from the menu and smiled.

"Got any killer burgers?"

"All our burgers are killers." Her voice was like a warm shower.

"Which is the biggest killer of all?"

She didn't think long.

"Get the mushroom chiliburger with cheese and a batch of fries."

Andrew handed over the menu.

"I'll have the mushroom chiliburger with cheese and a batch of fries."

She rewarded him with a wide, white smile.

"I haven't seen you before. Are you new?"

"You could say that."

She turned back to her work. She'd take an order, pick up a phone and speak a few words, peer into a computer touch screen, and lay a long-nailed index finger on certain spots. At length, a small brown man in snug black pants and a short red waiter's jacket would emerge from a swinging door adjacent to the bar, a tray balanced on an upraised palm. He'd pivot and place the tray on the bar, where the large woman would examine it and bear it slowly, silently, to its destination.

Andrew watched this orchestration, wondering if each tray bearing a covered dish were his. A black man in a powder blue knit shirt, khaki pants, and mustard-colored gimme cap came in and took a stool. He and the large woman looked at each other.

"Hey, baby," she said, her voice soft and desultory.

The man grunted, and something like a conversation ensued. The man didn't order anything, and after a few exchanged words— *I been knowing him twenty years* and *yeah, you got that right*—he moved off the stool and left.

For some reason, the exchange reminded Andrew of his conversation with Dollie about the need to be connected, to belong.

The large woman saw him looking her way and came over, not rushing.

"You doin' okay?" she asked.

"Yeah," he said, meeting her eyes. "Sure."

"Your food'll be out. You from roun' here?"

He put a thumb over his shoulder. "I'm working at the Knowl-ton Arms."

"You have their buffet breakfast this mornin'?"

"Didn't."

"You should. It's good."

She looked at him a moment longer. She had small, clear brown eyes behind wire frames and short hair clipped all over into petal-like layers, each petal tip bleached a pale gold. A wig, maybe. It reminded Andrew of a rubber swim cap you might see in a 1940s movie featuring water ballet.

She said, "I'm Bernadette.'

He said, "I'm Andrew."

"But everybody call me Miz B."

"Glad to know you, Miz B."

"And I'm glad to know you, Andrew." Her voice was as thick and sweet as molasses. "Now you git yourself to that breakfast tomorrow, don't forget. Bacon, eggs, grits, redeye gravy."

"I'll do that, Miz B."

Her eyes roved his face again, as though memorizing his features, and she moved away on stealthy feet, taking her time.

His burger and fries came, and if they weren't the best he'd ever had, that's the way he'd remember them. When he was through, he tossed his napkin on the empty plate, laid a twenty on the bar, anchored it with a saltshaker, swiveled off the stool, and headed for the door.

Miz B. looked his way as he left.

"Bye, baby," she said. "Come back and see me now."

He felt he'd passed a test and was now part of Miz B's family, part of the community. He could come in, take a seat and not buy anything, like the man in the mustard-colored cap. They could pass a few words, and she'd call him "baby," and he could feel better for the exchange, like he belonged.

———————

When he got back to the Cachet, Dollie still wasn't at the black marble counter. Andrew pushed through the pink curtains to the shampoo room, where he found her scrubbing Zora Sanda's hair. The shapeless body of the older woman lay like a bag of feed on the shampoo chair, her head tilted into the black porcelain sink. Dollie, her rust-colored bell-bottoms protected with a deep pink nylon tunic, bent over Zora's inert figure, aiming a jet of warm water toward her scalp.

As Andrew watched, Dollie draped a black towel over Zora's wet hair and pulled the shampoo chair to its erect position. She gave Zora's towel-shrouded head a few good rubs, lifted the towel, and Zora emerged, her scalp sprouting a tangle of gray Medusa-like strands. More notable, Andrew thought, was Zora's broad face, currently covered with a paste-like substance the color of creamed spinach, two pale circles of flesh making bull's-eyes of her green irises.

Andrew laid a hand over his mouth.

"Let's rinse off your facial, Zora," Dollie said, "then we'll comb your hair."

Zora, seeing Andrew, flung up a forbidding hand.

"Oh! Andrew. We didn't see you." Dollie looked embarrassed. "We're using this quiet time to get Zora duded up."

"Take your time."

Dollie busied herself with a spritzer bottle and a handful of tissues, cleaning the muck from Zora's face, the older woman pulling faces and making unpleasant sounds—indicating, Andrew thought, that she might not want another facial real soon.

Dollie handed her a comb.

"Want to comb your hair?" she asked, giving Zora's meaty shoulder a pat and clunking away on tall sandals with wooden platform soles.

Zora moved to the mirror and studied her reflection. She tried to pull the comb through a thick hank of wet hair. Grimacing, she extracted the comb and began again, dragging the comb hard, yanking a little, yanking a lot, and then, with an odd exasperated sound that seemed a cross between a growl and a yelp, she gave herself three mighty whacks on the head with the comb.

"Here, no, don't do that," said Dollie, hurrying back. She took the comb from Zora, searched through a narrow drawer, and brought out a wider-toothed comb.

"Try this," she said.

When it seemed Zora would be able to comb the tangles from her hair without a tantrum, Dollie moved away again.

"Let's talk," Andrew said. He followed Dollie back through the pink curtains.

"It's about Zora," he said.

Dollie looked wary.

"I want to bring her in off the street," Andrew said.

She cocked her head.

"She should be somewhere safe. And she should have some responsibilities. She has some skills?"

"She has. Yes, she has, Andrew."

"What can she do?"

"Well. I mean—"

"She can follow directions, do simple work?"

"Yes! She's good at directions and following through. Dependable. Has a good memory for procedures." She looked at him. "What do you have in mind?"

"Putting her to work in the Knowlton. And letting her stay here. There's a handful of sleeping rooms on the second floor. Have you seen them?"

She shook her head.

"One is actually a small apartment. Has a refrigerator and kitchenette. Little sitting room, bedroom and bath. Wouldn't need much to fix it up. Zora could be on her own there."

Dollie's eyes brimmed, and she blinked and looked down. When she spoke, her voice was thick.

"Tell me you're not kidding."

"I'm completely serious. Why would you say that?"

"What do I do?"

"You're already doing it. Get her cleaned up. Help her buy some clothes. Get her off the religious handout kick. In fact, get her off her crazy stuff—which, frankly, I don't believe all the way anyway. It gets her attention on one hand and allows her to opt out on the other."

Dollie was looking at him round-eyed.

"What," he said.

"That's what I think, too, but I didn't know how to put it in words without making her sound even crazier."

"Tell her we need help and ask her if she wants a job. Room and board included. Show her the room; tell her it's hers. Make sure she knows what all that means, that she'll be responsible for herself."

"But will it be hers permanently, Andrew? Because if it isn't permanent—"

"I'm not being rash, Dollie. And this doesn't come out of the blue. I've thought about it a lot."

"Zora needs to belong, Andrew. She's a . . . a middle-aged orphan."

"You mean she's not Romanian?"

She grinned at him. "I mean—"

"I know what you mean, Dollie."

He resisted the impulse to wipe a smear of magenta lipstick from a front tooth.

"There's something else, Dollie."

She gazed at him expectantly. And, he recognized, adoringly. It almost took his breath away, the idea of it, and the responsibility . . . the responsibility of all of it—Dollie, the Knowlton and its staff and its residents, Nell and Ben. The moment firmed both his resolve and his understanding. He'd had no responsibility for a decade—at least no responsibility with *consequence*. He realized he wanted consequence, the consequence the free had and the unfree lacked.

"I want you to apply for assistant manager of the Knowlton, with an eye to becoming manager eventually."

She stared.

"I've been interviewing candidates, and not one has your skills with people or your coordination and follow-through."

She looked dumbstruck.

"I'm not being rash about this, either. I've thought it through, and I hope you'll consider it. Whatever happens . . ."

He didn't want to say *between us*, but he could tell she understood. "I need help. I need someone I can trust who has business experience and expertise, someone who can step in now and take over later. You'll need to finish your degree, but you were going to do that anyway."

"Both Zora and I are going to have to grow up."

"Zora, yes. But you're already there."

The phone rang at Dollie's elbow, startling her, and she answered it, her eyes never leaving Andrew's. She spoke a few words and handed him the phone.

"It's your mother."

He took the phone.

"Andrew. I'm worried about Ben."

"Why's that, Ma? He's fine."

"Have you talked with him?" she asked quickly.

"This morning."

"I want to talk to him, Andrew. I've called and called his cell. No answer."

"He's working, Ma. Probably turned it off."

"His cell rings and rings, then goes to voice mail. It's not like him to ignore a call. Ben doesn't do that."

He watched Dollie stalk out of the room on her tall sandals and return with a small red watering can.

"There's nothing to be concerned about, Ma. He's working."

Dollie tipped the long spout toward the white orchid on her marble counter and poured a thin stream of water into the silver container.

"Anyway," Andrew continued. "He and Kenechi will probably be coming back tomorrow."

"Oh?" She was silent for a moment, digesting that news, then said with an angry edge to her voice, "If you talk to him before he leaves, tell him to call me right away."

"Well. Okay, Ma. Anything wrong? Anything I can do?"

"No," she said quickly, her anger more pronounced. "I don't like my calls ignored. This is not like Ben, not like him at all. And I don't like that, either."

"Ma's in a grump," he told Dollie when he'd hung up. He laid the phone on the counter and went to where she stood. He took her and her watering can into his arms.

"Let me ask you, Dolls," he said softly. "Do you know Olive Oyl, Popeye's goil?"

CHAPTER 42

Ben stepped into the stale smoke-and-booze-smelling interior of the Last Resort on Battle Creek's Michigan Avenue and let his eyes adjust to the darkness for a minute. The big-nosed guy tending bar poured his tomato juice, added ice and lime, and said, sure, he knew Frankie Sypinski, used to work here, but why not ask Rayna Webb.

"Who's Rayna Webb?"

He pointed to a tall woman sitting at the bar with dingy gray skin and steel gray hair pulled into a ratty bundle atop her head. She stared at Ben's ID for a long time, then raised her eyes and slurred, "So?"

"I'm looking for Frank Sypinski."

"Whuh . . ."

"You know where I could find him?"

"Whah . . ."

"Just to talk. No problem."

She watched his lips in bewilderment, her own moving slightly, and without a sound, slid from the stool onto the floor in a heap of winter clothing. The big-nosed guy came from behind the bar with a towel and glass in his hands, and a bull of a man wearing a tan raincoat and a gray buzz cut showed up out of nowhere and stepped around Ben.

"I'll take care of it," the bull said. He grabbed the woman in the vicinity of her armpits, dragged her across the floor, and leaned her against the wall.

"She okay?" Ben asked.

"Just needs to rest."

He had a toothpick in his mouth and spoke around it.

"Besides, nothing's gonna happen to Rayna till they find a place to bury her liver."

The big-nosed guy went back behind the bar and drew a beer, and Ben, on a hunch, turned to the man with the toothpick.

"Sypinski?'

"Who wants to know?"

Ben showed his badge, Sypinski giving it only a glance. He took his beer to a table, and Ben followed him.

"I want to talk to you about March 17, 1971."

Sypinski looked at him sharply. "You're kidding."

"Not at all. Specifically, the night of March 17, 1971."

"St. Pat's. Sure, I remember that night," Sypinski said. "But I gotta tell you . . . This is old news—some of that night is lost in my mind, as it happens."

Ben looked at him.

"Coupla holes."

"Talk around the holes."

Sypinski shrugged. "Fine. Not that I haven't already. Police, shrinks . . ." He worked on a molar with the toothpick. "They called it the Potato Murder."

Ben looked at him.

"You know why?'

"Some potatoes were killed?" Ben said.

Sypinski had bloodshot brown eyes and a steady gaze.

"Good job you're not as dumb as you look."

"Okay. Why did they call it the Potato Murder?"

"We lived down the hall from the Smolletts—Ma, Dad, Petey. In apartment one, right at the top of the stairs. That night, my folks went out, and me and my brother Petey was supposed to be looking in on the Smollett baby, tiny little thing. I mean, Mrs. Smollett asked us to, because that woman, the Smolletts' friend who watched him sometimes, wasn't there yet. I don't know if she ever showed up. We did look in on him, but he was asleep at first. Began crying later, and we didn't know what to do. That lady, what in the hell was her name? I can see her in my mind's eye right now. Lady from Florida. Anyways, she didn't show, far's I know. A little later, the Smolletts came up the stairs, pie-eyed. And hateful, both of 'em."

"Who was this woman, the Smollett friend?"

"Ahhh . . ." He laid a couple of big fingers in the middle his forehead. "I don't remember. My memory . . . I don't think I could call her to mind."

He drained his beer mug and pushed it aside.

"Our place faced the street, and when the folks were gone, Petey and I used to watch the drunks going back and forth—our building was between two bars, the Komfy Kozy and the Swan Song, and we got the idea to tease the drunks. What'd you say your name was again?"

"Gallagher."

"You'd fit in here; buncha Irish in this part of town."

"You got the idea to tease the drunks."

"We'd tie something, a clothespin or what have you, to a string and hold it out the window, let it touch the drunk, then quick pull it back and watch the drunks swing around and swat the air. And we'd fall all over the room laughing."

The bartender came over, picked up the empty mug and raised it at Sypinski, who gave him a half-nod.

"When the fun wore out of that, we commenced throwing stuff at 'em. One night, one of those drunks fell into our swinging doors and passed out on our stairway. Like I said, our door was the first one on the landing, just to the left at the top of the stairs, and we heard him. We watched him through a crack in the door a while, then we begun throwing stuff down at him."

Ben looked up from his notebook.

"You know, whatever—wadded paper, buttons. A couple little bags of water. We threw down some stuff from the refrigerator."

"What kind of stuff?"

"Oh, you know, veggies. Carrots, celery, like that." He gazed into the middle distance, his hands quiet on the tabletop. "We liked to died laughing, but the guy didn't wake up. We found out we could sneak down there and go right up to him. He wouldn't wake up. Once he gave a big snore, and we almost shit our drawers, knocking each other down trying to get back upstairs. But when we peeked out the door again, he was just the same."

He grinned around the toothpick and shook his head. "Man oh man."

The big-nosed guy brought a full mug to the table and slid it toward Sypinski, who blew off some foam and took a large swallow.

"So?"

"Well, yeah, like anybody's guess, pretty soon it wasn't fun anymore. I mean, watching a guy sleep. So we just went on upstairs, left him there. He was gone next day."

He laughed.

"So next day Ma goes, *What the hell those carrots doin' on the stairs?*"

Ben put down his pen, and Sypinski read his expression.

"The reason I told you all that is because that's what happened the night of Smollett's murder. Or so we thought. My folks were gone for a little while, and we were listening to a couple new LPs. Jackson Five and Elton John—I remember that well enough. Petey loved the Jackson Five and Elton John. We heard a little commotion on the stairs while we were listening to them records, figured a drunk had stumbled in there again. So when it got quiet, we opened the door and took a peek, and sure enough. We threw some potatoes down on that guy, then I knew I had to go get them or Ma would be after us."

He told Ben, remembering it just fine around the holes.

The drunk lay sprawled on the stairs, cheekbone on the sixth step, elbow crooked above his head. Heavy boots, dark trousers, navy sweater and jacket, billed cap lying beside him.

He saw all that moving down in the dim light from the single bulb, hearing Petey's stifled giggles behind him, the volume turned down a bit on Michael Jackson singing "Mama's Pearl" in that sweet, high voice.

The potatoes lay all around. He paused several stair steps away, listening for the heavy breathing that would tell him the man was asleep. Or passed out.

Silence.

He crept down another step. A potato rested near the man's extended hand, and he reached for it, staring at the hand, watching for movement, and saw something beneath the fingers. A ring. He twisted his head and grinned up at Petey. Reached for the ring. Reached harder, touched it, closed his fingers around it.

And in that moment saw who it was—a flash of high cheekbone, angular jaw, a dark wound beneath the chin. Willie Smollett's lean face lay bad side down, blood staining neck and collar and pooling on the stair.

He gasped and jerked back, losing balance but catching the banister. Turning, he saw Moll Smollett teetering at the top of the stairs, glassy-eyed, hand on the rail, body swaying out over the stairwell as if to some internal rhythm. He scrambled up the stairs and past her, slamming the door, locking it, heart pumping, Petey wide-eyed.

Behind him, on the other side of the door, Moll was muttering.

He and Petey never said about the big guy they'd seen earlier on the stairs. Never said they'd burst from the apartment, roughhousing, and run straight into him. Or that he'd lifted them, one boy in each arm, and set them down a safer distance from the stair's edge. They'd looked up into his face, big head, perfect hair, rimless spectacles like John Lennon's. Mostly, his coat was soft against their cheeks, and he felt warm in the cold hall and smelled good. Later, Ma and Pa said don't say anything, it won't do any good, it'll just confuse things. Then old man Boyle said the same thing. So they didn't. They never said.

CHAPTER 43

Sypinski extended his legs and clasped his hands behind his head, his raincoat falling open over his barrel chest. Ben waited.

"The newspaper had a picture of Smollett's body, don't know how they got it with police all over the place. And there were those potatoes. The press thought it was some kind of Irish payback thing, called it the Potato Murder. Also, it happened on St. Pat's day. Beaucoup Irish around here, like I said, so that was a big deal.

"One of those newspaper stories . . ." Sypinski ran a hand over his gray buzz cut. "One of those stories said the killers probably used the potatoes to silence the gun. Said a potato is a cheap and popular silencer. Unprofessional, maybe, but it works. And nobody gets arrested for possession of a potato."

Ben stopped writing and sat back, shaking his head.

"Said it was maybe a message, maybe an Irish youth gang. But I lived over there, you know? And I never saw any Irish gangs. Too busy fighting among themselves to form a gang."

Ben smiled.

"Is that true?" Sypinski asked. "About potatoes being good silencers?"

"True. You fire into a raw potato, it's a good silencer. But it leaves chunks all around the body. You don't find whole potatoes lying around."

Sypinski pulled up an ankle and, showing a large expanse of hairy leg, tugged at his wadded sock.

"So that reporter was right. All this time I thought it was bullshit. But how many killers carry around potatoes in their pockets, you think? I mean—"

"Can you describe the ring?"

"Sure. I had it in my hand when I got back upstairs. Petey and I thought we should take it back, but by that time I was too scared. So we hid it. Never told anybody. Not even Ma or Dad. After that, things sorta go blank."

"You didn't give it to the police?"

"No, hell no." He reflected. "Never told them about it."

"What did it look like?"

"Gold. Black center. Had some initials on the top."

"Initials? What were they?"

Sypinski looked at him a minute, then shook his head.

"Where'd you hide it?"

He shifted in his tan raincoat. "Like I said, that's when things go blank."

"What happened to it, Frank? It's . . . it could be important."

"I think we hid it. I mean I know we hid it. I just don't know where. What happened is we moved. Ma knew something was screwy—the potatoes, you know, after the carrot thing. She didn't want us—"

He made a quick dismissive gesture with a beefy hand. "She and Dad packed us up and moved us over here to Battle Creek. Dad had a job here anyway."

His face closed.

"I know about your brother, Frank," Ben said.

"Ya think?"

"About the switchyard accident. About his death."

Sypinski flipped the toothpick away. "No, you don't."

"What don't I know, Frank?"

"What *do* you know, buddy?"

Ben waited.

"What you don't know is I was there. Nobody does. Another thing Ma and Pa kept secret."

He shifted his beer mug, leaving a wet trail on the tabletop.

"I was taking care of my little brother. *Supposed* to be taking care of my little brother. Like we were *supposed* to be taking care of the Smollett baby. I took Petey to play in the switchyard, and he got caught. A boxcar cut off his legs. Both of them. Bled to death even before the ambulance got there."

Sypinski leaned to the side, pulled a large, wrinkled handkerchief from his hip, wiped his eyes and blew his nose loudly.

"That's a lot to carry," Ben said.

He gave Ben a grave, unreadable look.

"Ya think?" he said again.

Ben thought, *I have a younger brother, too.* But he didn't say it.

"You don't know the half of it," Sypinski continued. "The folks both drank themselves to death. Don't bother to say it wasn't my fault."

"Frank. Would you agree to hypnosis?"

Surprised, Sypinski looked at him and laughed shortly.

"Shit, no."

"It's not the Svengali thing some people think. We use it with witnesses a lot, and it can sometimes retrieve a lost memory, I mean the details of a lost memory."

Sypinski drew back. "Oh yeah, Big Frank Sypinski's gonna get hisself hypnotized." He waggled his fingers at Ben. "I got you in my power. Wooo wooo."

"It's a way to get at repressed material. Might help you, too, Frank."

"No. After all these years? Fuck it—what's your name again?"

"Gallagher."

"Fuck it, Gallagher. What difference would the ring make?'

"Can't tell. Might help close a cold case."

"No way. I'm not doing it." He slapped the table. "Dixie Booth!"

"Come again?"

"Dixie Booth! That woman who was supposed to be taking care of the Smolletts' baby that night. Dixie Booth, goddamn, yeah. Had a stiff leg, hair frizzed up like a brush pile. Came from Florida. Lived down the block. I remember."

"Do you know what became of her?"

He scratched at the gray stubble on his scalp. "Probably died. She'd be like a hunnerd by now."

"Are you sure? We're talking only thirty years, and even relatively young adults seem old to a child."

But Sypinski was somewhere else.

"Dixie Booth," he said softly. "Can't believe I remembered. That's the first—"

He sat back, arms folded over his barrel chest, legs outthrust and crossed at the ankles, head tilted a little, nodding.

"Dixie Booth. Shit. I remember."

Rayna Webb moaned a little and lolled her head from side to side against the wall. Sypinski studied her at length, then turned his bloodshot gaze on Ben.

"You know what? That *wooo-wooo* thing. Set it up, what the hell. I'll do it."

CHAPTER 44

"Sorry about last night," Kenechi said the next morning when Ben called him. "I tried your room when I got in, but you weren't back. Then I went down to dinner, came back up here and fell asleep. When I woke, it was after midnight. I didn't want to bother you then."

"We were both tired," Ben said. "Anyway, no problem. I had dinner on the way back from Battle Creek, needed some time to think. Didn't get back to Kalamazoo till too late to bother you. My ass was dragging anyway, so I turned in."

"You feeling better now?"

"Much. Remind me never to have another hangover."

"Hang on a second."

Ben heard rustling in the background, and then Kenechi was back. "Got the flight info. There's a plane into O'Hare after noon. Leaves at 4:41, arrives 4:29. We gain an hour. But once we get to O'Hare, there are all kinds of flights into DFW—5:15, 5:50, 6:40."

"Cool."

"What are you up to? You see Sypinski?"

"I did. He's with me, in fact."

"Huh? In your room?"

Ben laughed.

"Where are you?" Kenechi asked.

"Right now I'm sitting on a vinyl divan in an office at the Ka-lamazoo PD."

"What's going on?"

"We're waiting for the police hypnotist." Ben looked at Frank Sypinski, waggled his fingers, and mouthed *wooo wooo*.

He could almost hear Kenechi blink.

"Who I think is coming down the hall as we speak." Ben peered through a plate glass window overlooking a corridor. "I'll clue you in later, Ken. By the way, the chief has been calling. I've let it go to messaging and haven't returned the calls. Has he called you?"

"Not yet."

"My mother's also been trying to get in touch with me, Kenechi, and I don't want to talk to her right now, either. So . . ."

Kenechi was silent, mulling that over, Ben knew.

"Want me to book the 4:41?"

"Yes. And if the chief calls—or Ma, for that matter—say we split up and that you haven't seen me. That I've been on the run."

"On the run." Kenechi's tone vested the words with more meaning than Ben had intended.

"Meantime," Ben continued, ignoring the question in Kenechi's voice, "have twelve cups of coffee. I just did, and you have no idea how it spruces up your nervous system."

Sypinski had vacated the vinyl sofa and was looking out the window, back to Ben. He turned with an expression Ben didn't understand.

"Let's go," Sypinski said, agitated.

"Go?"

"I remember. I remember everything. Don't ask me why. May-be Dixie Booth. Maybe because—"

He grabbed his jacket.

"I know where I put the ring."

––––––––––––––

Ben and Kenechi had lunch on the way to the airport before dropping the rental car at the Hertz place and boarding another fifty-seater to O'Hare. There was plenty of time to bring Kenechi up to date—or at least part way into the picture. *Most of the way*, Ben thought, salving his conscience for keeping his partner in the dark. As Ben was wrapping up, Kenechi listening with interest, Ben's cell rang. He looked at the display and sighed. Nell. He sent the call to the recorder, and immediately the phone rang again. Ben saw it was Chief Saenz.

"Shit," he said. Then punched OFF.

Kenechi raised his brows.

"Saenz. Third time he called."

"Better talk to him."

Ben chewed his thumbnail. He couldn't talk to Saenz. Not yet. Kenechi was looking at him, curious, his head cocked, when *his* cell phone rang. He dug it from an inside pocket in his black wool overcoat, checked the display, looked at Ben, and shook his head.

"Shit," Ben said again.

"Yes, sir," Kenechi said into the phone, eyes on Ben, then handed him the phone.

Saenz was so angry Ben didn't catch all the words. Skating on the edge. Don't be calling the office when you know I'm not there and leaving a message. You know my home phone. What the hell you doing up there that you have to hide from me? How damned dumb do you think I am?

"Chief, I'm sorry," he said. "We got some breaks in the case, but I didn't want to bother you with them until—"

"Since when am I bothered by hearing about breaks in a case? By hearing what it's my job and my right to know? And what the hell are you doing, Gallagher? Things falling apart up there, or coming together? *You* falling apart up there?"

You might say that, Ben thought.

"This isn't like you, Ben. The big thing, we could always depend on you."

Loyal team player, Ben thought, his tongue stuck to the roof of his mouth.

"Ben?"

"Yes."

"So say something."

Ben hesitated. "I'm the same as I always was."

Saenz was silent—puzzling, Ben knew, over the meaning of that inane statement.

"Chief, I—could we talk first thing tomorrow? They're getting ready to announce our plane," he lied.

"Tomorrow? What's the matter with tonight? When you get in. First thing."

"I've got to . . ." He fell silent. Got to *what*? Heart sinking, he hit OFF. Let Saenz think it was a dropped call. He couldn't have this conversation. Could he say yes, he was a team player, but he had other loyalties, another team? And keep his job? He had to talk to Nell first.

He felt Kenechi's stare.

"Can you turn off your phone, Ken?" he asked, and when his partner continued to look at him, his black brows raised, added, "I can't handle the chief right now."

"I can."

Ben understood that Kenechi was refusing to turn off his cell. Good for him. He didn't blame him a damn bit.

"You got any ideas for when he calls again?"

Ben exhaled gustily. "Tell him I vaporized. Tell him . . . whatever."

They had no trouble getting the 5:15 out of Chicago. Once again, the plane was crowded, and they had to sit apart, but at least they both had aisle seats.

Ben stowed his roll-on in the overhead for 14B and tucked his bomber jacket beside it. Kenechi was forward, settling himself in 9B.

Ben leaned his head on the rest and tried to empty his brain. He watched the passengers as they trundled by in their winter coats and backpacks, wheeling carryons toward the rear of the plane.

He took the airline magazine from the seatback pocket and turned to the crossword puzzle. The first space across needed a nine-letter word that contained the vowels *A*, *E*, *I*, *O*, and *U*, in that order. He pulled his pen from his pocket and printed "facetious" in the little squares. One down used the *F* in "facetious" to make a seven-letter word meaning something imagined. Ben pondered, counted, penned in "figment." He read through a few more clues with nothing coming to mind until he got to fourteen across. The clue asked, *A jaundiced view of idealism?* Seven letters, the first using the *N* from "figment." Ben printed "naiveté."

He thought of Nell, the chief reason he was trying to empty his brain. Idealism becomes naiveté becomes gullibility.

That right, Ma?

He closed the magazine and his eyes as the small plane racketed down the runway, picking up speed, struggling with gravity as it lifted and penetrated the sky with a less than orgasmic thrust.

Here's what I'm going to do, Ben thought. *I'm going to lie. I'm going to falsify my report. I'm going to say Eleanor Ryan is dead. She died of . . . of a drug overdose . . . an accident . . . a plane crash. No. Too traceable. I'll say she disappeared. Went somewhere on a student junket and never came back. To New Zealand . . . to Tibet . . . to the moon. Shit.* Self-disgust stuck in his chest like a handful of thorns, and with it, a razor-sharp realization that Saenz was right. He was not in control. He could not control this. There were primal rules.

He should have listened, should have let go, should have let the world turn as it would.

The plane negotiated some rough air for a bit, then banked and turned southward, a little away from the setting sun. And they were fully aloft, Ben with a nice view of Lake Michigan's white-capped waves before the plane tilted back to reveal a bruised horizon. He gazed out the window for a time, unwelcome thoughts stealing through the dark of his mind like rats through an attic, then unsnapped his seatbelt and rose, flexing his stiff knees. He tossed the magazine and its barely-worked crossword puzzle into the seat, hesitated, and walked unsteadily to 9B.

Kenechi had his head back, drowsing, but apparently felt Ben's presence at his shoulder because he opened his eyes and gazed at Ben.

Ben stooped to clear the overhead bins and spoke to the man in the window seat.

"Hey, buddy, this is my partner, and we have business to discuss. How would you feel about an aisle seat?"

The passenger looked blankly at Ben. He was a weathered man of uncertain age with a complexion the color of a dusty brick. For a moment, Ben thought he might not speak English, but the meaning of Ben's words suddenly dawned on him.

"Oh! You want to sit here."

"Trade for an aisle seat?" He jerked his thumb toward 14B. "Five rows back?"

"No problem," the man said, rising.

Kenechi rose as well and stepped into the aisle, let the man out and stepped back in, taking the window seat. Ben sat next to him, silent for a time, feeling his partner's gaze, turning to meet it.

"Ken." He leaned in close. "I've got to talk to you."

CHAPTER 45

It was dark when the plane set down on a runway between Dallas and Fort Worth, the sky stained to the east and west from the cities' reflected glare. Ben and Kenechi silently rode the airport bus to remote parking and parted, shaking hands.

"Let me know," Kenechi said, moving away in the eerie shadowless light of the parking lot's tall overheads.

Ben stood a minute, watching him go, then called after him, "If Jack Malone gets any part of this . . ."

It would be a disaster.

"I know," Kenechi tossed back. "Hurry. Call me as soon as you can."

Ben pulled into the drive in front of Nell's half an hour later. He let himself in and went up the stairs to the living room, where he found her on the ivory sofa, cozy in stocking feet and cream-colored sweater and slacks, a glass of red wine at her elbow, hair shining in the lamplight. A fire crackled in the fireplace, a Sibelius CD played quietly in the background, and she absent-mindedly stroked Bood, who lay with his head in her lap. When Bood saw Ben, he yipped and jumped off the sofa, dashed toward him.

Ben squatted to spare him the yo-yo antic of trying to spring Ben's six-feet-six. The little dog licked at Ben's cheek happily, and Ben rubbed his curls, warm from the fire.

Nell looked at him expectantly through tortoiseshell-reading glasses.

"You never called," she said, her tone grim.

"Where's Andrew?"

"He's with Dollie Varnes. They went to dinner."

He crossed the room and placed something on the table beside her wineglass.

She stared at it, whispered, "Oh my God," and leaned to pick it up, balance it on her palm. "My God. I never thought I'd see this again."

Still whispering, more to herself than to him, she examined the ring, its onyx stone emblazoned with the gold and diamond initials *ABC*, and slipped it onto the fourth finger of her right hand, over the mottled scars covering the knuckle.

"That was your mother's ring, I gather."

She nodded, still not looking at him, still not speaking, her head bent like a broken flower over the ring.

"Ana Brigh Casey," Ben said.

She replaced the ring carefully on the table and covered her face with both hands.

Ben took a step forward and pulled her hands away, but gently. "What happened on St. Patrick's Day in 1971, Ma? When I was six months old? Don't say you can't remember. The night Willie Smollett died. This ring was in his hand."

She was dead white.

"Moll Smollett almost bit your finger off trying to get that ring. Ma! I know! Goddammit, talk to me!"

Her cobalt eyes locked on his for a moment, then slid away. He had a sudden notion that he'd never known her, never seen her before.

"If you know all about it, what is there to say," she said, her voice flat. She sat up and put her feet on the floor. "The main thing, the *only* thing, Ben, is that no one else must know."

"Kenechi knows, Ma."

"How?"

"I told him."

"*You told him!*"

"I had to, Ma. Don't you see that? Anyway, he already knew. Knew something was wrong."

"Oh my God."

He placed his palms on the sofa arm and leaned in toward her.

"I'm walking away from this case, Ma. Maybe even away from my job. I'm—"

Her open hand flashed out and caught him square on the cheek. She had never struck him, and for a moment, pulling back, he was so shocked he didn't know what had happened.

"The case!" she cried, her eyes hot, blotches appearing on her cheeks. "The case! How dare you talk to me about the case when so much is at stake!"

"What exactly is at stake, Ma?"

"Everything is at stake!"

His cheek stung, and he had to resist the impulse to reach up and touch it.

"I don't know what you're talking about."

"No, I suppose you don't."

He sat on the sofa beside her, Bood making himself comfortable beside him. "Tell me. I can't protect you if I don't know. I might . . ." He was going to add that he might not be able to protect her anyway, but he left it unsaid.

The grandfather clock in the foyer chimed the half hour. She curled in on herself a little, like someone with a stomachache.

"Why couldn't you leave this alone?"

"Of course I couldn't. But let's say I could. Would others?"

She stared into the fire for a long moment, then took off her glasses, laid her book on the coffee table, and sat back. She took a wobbly breath.

"After that night," she began, her voice toneless, "I brought you and Andrew to Texas."

"Wait. Andrew wasn't born in Texas?"

Ben watched as she considered the question.

"I meant I brought you."

Ben's heart moved down, down, and down. "You're not a very good liar."

She leaned both elbows on her knees and rested her face in her palms, muffling her voice. "Be my son or be a detective, but be a detective somewhere else."

"How old were Andrew and I, Ma, when you brought us to Texas? I thought I was six months, but I guess not."

She looked trapped and stood abruptly, moving away toward the balcony, her arms wrapped about her like a shawl. He examined her in the silence, the fragile flesh at the corners of her eyes marked by faint pleats. And he saw the future. She would always be what she was now: slim and strong. But she would get older and smaller and slimmer. And maybe even stronger, given the chance. Her eyes would go deeper, the new lavender shades beneath them darkening into violet, the skin thinner, more fragile. He could see himself in her. And something else.

"Ma."

Under his scrutiny, he thought she breathed a faint *oh*, and he knew. Not everything, but enough to shift his internal landscape forever. Later, when he thought about it, thought about sitting there, heart thrumming in his chest, he'd recall a small almost audible *click* as the most important piece fell into place, altering everything. No, not that piece, this one. And it was as though he'd always known; that's how right it was, how tight the fit.

"Andrew isn't my brother."

It wasn't a question, so she didn't answer.

"He isn't my half brother, either."

She met his gaze at last, her trapped look falling away, leaving naked vulnerability.

"He's my son," she said. "And he's your brother."

He waited, his eyes on her face.

She sighed, a wistful sound.

"Tell me."

"He's not of our blood. Nevertheless . . ."

Her lips moved soundlessly; he guessed her mouth was as dry as his own.

"All those years . . ."

He fell silent now, knowing it would come. When she spoke, it was barely a whisper.

CHAPTER 46

"He was the baby down the hall, the Smollett baby, a tiny tiny baby, five or six weeks old. You were just six months old yourself. On that night, the Smolletts came home in their cups and asked me in for a drink. I could hear if you woke, through those paper-thin walls, so I went. To see if the baby was okay. He was always crying, breaking my heart . . ."

Tears spilled over her cheeks, and she brushed at them with both palms.

"After that incredible scene with Moll, I was in bed, and I heard him crying. My right hand was swathed in bandages from the ER. It was hurting, but I didn't want to take anything for the pain because I was nursing you. And my milk started to flow when the baby began crying, and he cried and cried and cried. I had to go to him, Ben. I loved him even before I ever saw him lying in that filthy apartment."

She gave a keening cry, and Ben half-rose, alarmed. But she waved him away.

"I got up and went down the hall. The door was wide open. I didn't know what was going on, what had happened.

"When I went in . . . I don't know how I had the nerve. But I went in. The baby was crying and I went in. I heard Moll in the bathroom. The door was closed, the water running, Moll probably trying to clean up a little, get the blood and muck off."

Nell ran out of words and wept silently, tears dripping onto her cream-colored sweater. Sibelius' violins soared in the background while Ben's heart sank even lower.

"What'd you do, Ma?"

"The baby was on a filthy cot, kicking and screaming. In nothing but a sodden diaper. Thin little blanket on the floor. In February, Ben. In Michigan. I touched him. His skin was cold. I picked him up. He smelled my milk and stopped crying and began hunting. Snuffling and pushing. Like a little animal."

She grasped both elbows with her hands, hugging herself.

"I can see him now, Benny, I will never forget—" Her chin quivered, and Ben could see her trying to gain control. "I took him. Maybe I told myself that it would be just for a little while, for the night. I don't remember. But when I took him, I took everything, everything that looked like a baby. There wasn't much. A bottle with sour milk in it, a couple of diapers, the blanket, a blue pacifier. A few other things.

"I left the door wide open when I left, just the way I found it. So they'd think anybody could have come in and got him. I nursed him. And I got a rubber glove over my bandages and bathed him and made him warm in your nightshirt and gown and diapers. And put him into bed with you, at the other end of the crib. Turned out he wasn't a baby who cried much at all. He was starving . . ."

Her voice broke, became a whisper again.

"He had bruises on his little back and legs, Ben. I think Willie—"

She burst into fresh tears, and Ben's own eyes filled. *Andrew!* Who couldn't catch a break. Except he *had* caught a break—he had caught Nell.

"Later I threw his stuff into the restaurant dumpster downstairs. They emptied it every morning."

They were silent for a long moment, the hall clock ticking, Ben seeing the tableau: the apartment across from the Boyle and Sonigson apartments, the dim hallway, the stairwell where Dayton and Smollett struggled and where the Sypinski boys chucked potatoes at a dead man.

"Why did you even live there, Ma? You could have lived anywhere."

"It was only a block from Benjamin's apartment. And after Benjamin was killed, I was lost, I thought I'd stay put for a while."

She sank onto the sofa and looked at him a long moment, her eyes catching fire.

"Who do you love most in the world, Ben?"

"What?"

"Who do you love most in the world?"

He shook his head.

"Andrew? Isn't it Andrew?"

"I suppose. So?"

Her gaze was intense. "Do you know why?"

"Do I know why *what*?"

She sighed.

"Do you know why you love him, why he's so important to you?"

"Are these trick questions?"

"You love him best because you've been taught to. Not just because he's your brother, or because he's loveable, or because he deserves to be loved. But because from the moment I laid him in your crib, I taught you to love him. I whispered it into your ear before you knew what the words meant, and kept whispering it. I told you he was your brother. That you must always love him. And take care of him. I poured that message into your ear for years."

"What's your point, Ma?"

"I wanted to be sure that someone would want this baby no one wanted. That he would be safe. If I weren't there. Or Dayt. Then there'd be you. And you never let me down. Until now."

She leaned forward.

"I'm saying—Ben, protect him now. No more bad breaks for your baby brother."

Ben sat rigid, silent, his throat tight. He felt sapped of reserves. After a long moment of heavy silence, he asked, "What happened after you took him?"

"The next morning, early, I called Dayton."

"Wait. Back to Dayt showing up with a gun the night before. I never knew Dayt to have a gun."

"Oh, he had guns from time to time. Not so much after he moved the firm downtown to a building with good security, but when it was in a solitary old building in an iffy part of town. All the partners kept guns in their desks in the old location, and they knew how to use them."

"How'd he happen to have it with him on that night?"

"He was working late and planned to stop by my place when he finished. I called and told him the Smolletts were drinking and in one of their rare friendly moods, and that I was going to their apartment to check on the baby. That baby had been sobbing nonstop, and I was frantic. Dayt knew how worried and upset I was, but he also thought Willie Smollett was a lunatic, so he said he'd go with me and asked me to wait till he came. He suspected the combination of Smollett and booze and Moll and me might be combustible. He was right. But I couldn't wait for him—I was too worried."

Ben nodded. "So when you called him the next morning?"

"I told him what I'd done, what this infant had already been through, what was in store for him, and that I wasn't going to let it happen."

She was calm now, grim.

"I named him. I gave him your father's middle name and your father's birthday. I made him your brother."

"What's his real name?"

"Andrew is his real name."

"You know what I mean."

"He was named after his father."

"William?" Ben said the name as if he'd never heard it. "*Willy? Billy?*"

"I guess." She waited, and when he said nothing, she asked, "What are you thinking?"

He dragged his mind back to the conversation.

"I'm not thinking. Or, yes, I am. I'm thinking you lied to me my whole life."

"Not *lied*."

"Yes. Lied." He felt as if his veins were flushed with ice water. "I will never trust you again."

She paled even more. "You're hurt. You've been kept in the dark, and you're hurt. And I don't blame you. But, Benny—I had no choice. I did what I did, and I'd do it again, and I can't and won't call it a mistake. Ben, I love you more than you could dream. I couldn't do without you, without your trust. Please say you'll get over this."

It was a naked and honest appeal, and Ben was astonished at how cold he felt in response, how numb. *Get over it?* My God!

"And I'm thinking of a song you used to sing to us." His voice was harsh. "Where have you been, Billy Boy, Billy Boy?"

She clasped her hands in her lap.

"And where has Billy been, Ma? State prison? We could sing it now, for irony."

Her color rose again abruptly, and her glance was withering.

"Huntsville was a fluke. Don't you dare suggest that saving him didn't save him."

He threw up a hand—perish the thought!—then placed it over his forehead.

"Do you have a headache?"

"A son of a bitch."

She left the room, returning with a glass of water and a small pill. He took it from her palm wordlessly and swallowed it with a gulp from the glass. Then he laughed mirthlessly.

"My God. How did you think you could get away with it, Ma?"

"What do you mean? I *did* get away with it! And I'd be getting away with it now if it weren't for my son, the detective."

"You committed a felony."

She stared at him for a split second, then laughed. *Laughed.*

"There were channels," he said, Saenz's words echoing in his head. "Andrew was abused. You could have proven it, adopted him. There's a process. You wouldn't have had to hide, to lie."

"Oh!" She fairly spat the word and turned to walk a tight circle in front of the fireplace.

"I know all about your channels! A process! Don't make me laugh! Ben Gallagher's worldview at its most Panglossian. Christ, Ben, who hasn't seen . . . you mean the process of victims continuing to be abused and even killed while the *process* grinds its way through the bureaucracy? You want felony? How about *that* for felony? You've seen your law, Ben, and its constant failure to protect. And so have I. Don't make me remember how many times."

"Ma. I do know. Trust me on that." Knowing how lame it sounded.

"Do you? I'm not so sure."

She broke into a fresh flurry of tears, but steadied herself again.

"Dayton helped me. He always helped me. Money wasn't a problem, thank God. Dayton got us out of there, covered our tracks, even came with us to Texas, set us up . . . and he got what we needed—the records, don't ask me how—whatever I needed to raise this baby. To give him a legitimate life as Andrew Gallagher, my son. And your brother."

She looked at him defiantly.

"The next day when the police came, I thought I might faint at the door. But Willie Smollett had been found dead on the stairs, and they wanted to know if I'd seen anything. I tried to be calm, and I had enough presence of mind to keep my bandaged hand out of sight. Not that it would mean anything necessarily—I just didn't want to raise any questions or suspicions. I told them the Smolletts had been partying the night before and that I'd gone down the hall briefly. But that I had an infant and had come back and gone to sleep and hadn't seen or heard anything after that."

"They believed you?"

She stared at him.

"It was the *truth*. At least most of it was. I didn't see Willie on the stairs, I mean his body. My shock was genuine, they could see that. But I got to be a good liar anyway, through the years, despite what you just said. I learned to be careful, not to say much, not to answer questions.

"I left Eleanor Ryan behind, Ben. No one ever knew me by Eleanor anyway, even though it was my real name, and I'd been using Benjamin's surname in the first place because I was pregnant and we planned to marry. Then I kept using it for just a little while longer, trying to keep some part of him, I guess. But then it was my best cover, that name. A name that had nothing to do with Nell Gallagher."

She sat again and took a shuddering breath, her eyes far away.

"I almost thought—this will sound irrational—I almost thought Andrew was God's gift to me. A consolation for losing Benjamin. Or as if Benjamin's energy had gone from the world for a bit and had returned in the soul of this infant, for me to keep and preserve."

She saw his expression.

"I said it was irrational. And that wasn't the most or the only weird thought I had. Grief makes you irrational, Ben. It makes you believe in magic."

"Then what? When the police came?"

"They were in the corridor with Moll. Her face was a swollen mass of bruises. Of course they were suspicious. They said, 'Willie Smollett beat you up.' And she gave them one of her big laughs and said, 'No shit, Sherlock. Worked that out, eh?' Then she realized what . . . she started screaming about her rights. Even jumped on one officer and scratched his face. They took her away screaming. She didn't say even once she had a baby or that he was missing, just blathered on about her rights. I don't know what happened after that. When they were gone, I paid Sonigson the rent, told him I had a sick relative in Seattle and had to leave. We left that afternoon."

"Why Texas?"

"Why not? Dayton had spent some time here. And his firm had business here. He thought it was good I had no connection to the state."

Her brow furrowed, and she closed her eyes.

"I never knew how Willie Smollett died, Ben. I always thought maybe Moll . . . until Friday. Dayt told me while you and Andrew were driving up from Huntsville. Told me he had terminal cancer. And that he'd caused Willie's death all those years ago.

"He said he and Willie struggled on the stairs, the gun between them. Said while he was trying to get the gun, Willie had wrested my ring from his pocket, then concentrated on trying to shoot him. Willie was pretty drunk, though. Dayt forced his hand back, and Willie pulled the trigger and shot himself under the chin."

Ben said, "We knew it was Dayt from what Manning Boyle told us."

"Manning Boyle," she whispered, remembering.

"But I have to ask you, Ma. Did you have anything . . . no, let me rephrase that. You had no knowledge of Smollett's death that night? You had nothing to do with it?"

Her eyes flew to his face, their vibrant blue flaring.

"I see," she said softly, continuing to gaze at him.

"Ma, I have to—"

"Oh, do you? Do you really *have* to?" She silenced him with a gesture. "I had no knowledge of it and nothing to do with it." Her tone was flat and cold. "What other questions do you *have* to ask, Ben? Did I kill Dayton?"

"Ma—"

"Oh, shut up, Ben! Just shut the fuck up!"

Her outburst was so uncharacteristic that he gaped at her, wordless.

"Killing! My God. My son has to ask if I'm a killer. Am I, Ben? Well, here's a question for you, goddammit. Are you the son I bore? Or are you just a cop now, nothing more, so used to suspecting everyone, trusting no one, that no one is exempt? You dare mention the word *trust* to me!"

"Yeah, let's just say I'm all out of blind faith in blind faith."

He almost said, *So sue me,* but his image, as she saw it, was beginning to emerge in his mind.

"I knew you were lying, Ma. What was I supposed to do?"

"You were supposed to trust!"

"In the face of all evidence to the contrary?"

"Yes, by God. That's what trust is! The very essence of it." Her voice quavered, and her eyes filled again. "As I have trusted you."

He felt too exhausted to respond. And he knew that whatever he offered in his defense would be taken in evidence against him. Rule of law? The goal of objectivity? Training? Procedures? No, no, and no. All that would only further infuriate her.

Sighing heavily, she rose and stood with her back to him.

"Dayt said that when he saw that wound, he knew Willie was dead and was so horrified he got out of there, not thinking, forgetting my ring. Said he never knew why the ring hadn't become an issue, but that it was just as well out of the picture, given those circumstances." She turned a little. "Where did you get it?"

"You remember the boys next door? The Sypinskis?"

She nodded.

"Frankie Sypinski took it. He hid it in an old velvet evening bag of his mother's, which she kept in a trunk and which he held on to after her death. Then his brother Petey was killed, and he got a block about the whole thing."

"All those years," she said, marveling.

"Why did Dayton tell you after all that time?"

"He was dying. He thought I had to know to protect myself and my boys. Moll had followed Dayt to Dallas, even to the Knowlton."

Ben nodded, and she added, "I thought he could keep us safe even if we stopped paying Moll's blackmail—for a little while at least, while I learned not to depend upon him and to be on my own."

"Blackmail?"

CHAPTER 47

Nell moved to one of the blue velvet chairs flanking the fireplace.

"Moll followed Willie when he ran down the hall with his gun, and she saw what happened on the stairs. Dayton didn't see her. Willie was dead, and he didn't want us mixed up in it. He knew he had to get away from the scene. He told me he'd thought my best defense would be innocence, and he figured we could handle whatever came out about the ring and my brawl with Moll."

"But Manning Boyle also knew Dayt had come back to confront Willie."

"Dayt said he had the idea— maybe it was just a hope—that Boyle wouldn't implicate him. And without Boyle, Moll would have no credibility, supposing she actually remembered that night's sequence of events.

"But none of that came up—the ring, the brawl, Dayton. No. Moll kept quiet because she smelled a chance to make money. She knew exactly who Dayton was. I'd introduced him when we ran into her in the hall, and the next time I saw her, she mentioned my 'well-heeled lawyer.' She was plenty drunk that night but not too drunk to scheme, to go down and retrieve Willie's gun. And Dayt's fingerprints."

"The police never found it, although they turned her place upside down. She was the prime suspect, according to the case file—pretty much the *only* suspect."

"Who knows where she stashed it. In any case, she had it, and she held it over Dayt's head. All those years she thought he paid her to keep her quiet about Willie. He would have faced that if I hadn't done what I did—he paid to protect *me*, and you and Andrew. But she'd upped the ante, and he wanted to cut her off—but that was a decision he felt I should make. He was dying and would soon be out of her reach, but he feared I might be dragged in somehow if she made good on her threat to expose him. He was also sure, so far anyway, that she hadn't a clue about me. A woman who took care of Andrew disappeared the same time Andrew disappeared, and Dayt thought maybe Moll supposed she took him." She gave a grim little laugh. "Not that she cared. *That* woman didn't have any money."

"Dixie Booth."

"You *have* been working hard."

She looked into the middle distance then back at him, intently.

"Talk to me, Ma."

"I didn't shoot Dayton, Ben." Her eyes were dark and cold. "Moll did."

"*What?* You know this?"

"I do know it. I saw it. After you and Andrew left Friday, I was—I couldn't settle down. I decided I'd go to your place, help Dayton, bring Bood back here. I got there a little after five, I guess. I used that extra remote for your garage door. I didn't see Moll's car in front, probably hidden behind the trees.

"I heard Dayton, his voice raised, as soon as I opened your kitchen door. I could hear what they were saying, and I knew who it was right away, that she'd followed him to your place. She had been trying to waylay him, and he'd been avoiding her, which of course set her into a rage. I could see them from your kitchen island—through the mirror in your foyer."

Ben nodded. He knew that reflection.

"Music was playing, too. It was one of your Verdi arias, and it helped mask the sound of the garage door. They didn't hear me come in. But Bood did. He came flying around the kitchen island and straight up into my arms the way he does—glad to see me but also frightened by the argument in the living room. I held him and calmed him, while they kept right on, both furious. Dayton told Moll her cash cow was dying. She didn't guess the meaning of that, of course."

Nell rested her head on the back of the blue velvet chair and closed her eyes tiredly, remembering. "He told her he'd seen to it that she'd spend the rest of her sorry life in jail. She scoffed. He told her he'd recounted the details of Willie Smollett's slaying and implicated her as an accomplice and a blackmailer in a letter to his lawyer. He told her he had thirty years of cancelled blackmail checks. That he'd always wondered if she was as stupid as she was greedy, and if it ever would occur to her that she should have demanded cash. There was no such letter, of course. Dayton would never have committed to paper anything about what happened that night that might lead to the truth about Andrew."

She swallowed hard. "Would you like a glass of wine, Ben? I would."

He rose, found the bottle in the kitchen, poured her a fresh glass, handed it to her, and again sat on the ivory sofa, looking at her.

"I was just about to slam the door and cry out: *Yoo hoo, Dayton! I'm here!* Or some such. I thought the intrusion would send that thieving Moll packing. But things went haywire before I could intercede. Suddenly Dayton's composure snapped, because he sprang across the room and grabbed Moll by the throat. I almost screamed, but he let go and flung her against the wall, where she must have fallen. I couldn't see her in the mirror.

"But she spoke, and she'd moved away, out of my view. Then the phone rang. The machine picked it up and it was you, Ben, checking to see if Dayt was still there. She said something like, "You'll go down with me." And Dayt said, "I've already gone down." I don't know what happened, but I heard Moll say, "You got that right." Then I heard a pop. I knew she'd shot him, Ben, even though I'd never heard a real gunshot. I was in . . . I don't know . . . shock, I guess, because I stood as if paralyzed for what seemed an eternity, Bood in my arms. I numbly realized that Moll . . . there was some rustling, I don't know . . . then she came into view again. I held my breath as she looked around the room and moved toward the front door. She picked up something from the table in your foyer—"

"Dayt's keys."

They sat in silence, each in private thought. The grandfather clock chimed again, softly, and the CD player whirred a little and started on a new disk. Nell rose, turned it off, and sat back down.

"I knew Dayton was dead," she said. "Moll wouldn't have left otherwise. That horrible soprano was still screeching. I crept into the living room where he lay and felt for a pulse. Of course, I was sobbing uncontrollably, and poor Bood was trembling in my arms. I stroked him a bit, then put him down, and he immediately lay beside Dayt, pressed himself against his leg and laid his head on his thigh. Then I knelt and kissed Dayt and talked to him." Tears coursed freely down her cheeks, but she didn't avert her face or brush the tears away. "I asked him what to do. I knew what he'd say, and I heard his voice as clearly as if he'd spoken. He said, *go, Nellie, run.*"

"Always a mistake to run, Ma."

"Is it? Whatever. I hated leaving Dayt, and I also hated leaving Bood. But things had to be as if I hadn't been there. How could I explain Bood if he were with me? Anyway, I knew from your phone message you were on the way. And Bood seemed to understand. I told him to stay, and he snuggled even closer to Dayt and watched me through his dreadlocks. He wasn't afraid anymore. He understood. So I ran. I ran just as Dayton had run all those years ago, and for the same reason. I did what Dayton would have wanted me to do."

"Let his murderer get away?" Ben said. It was an accusation, and his expression was hard and unapologetic.

So was hers. "If it had come to that, yes. Dayt was dying, Ben. But it wouldn't have come to that. I would have figured something out. I would have found a way to implicate Moll without implicating us . . ."

He nodded. It could be done.

"But," Nell added, "final analysis, Andrew's security and happiness are more important to me than what happens to Moll. And I don't apologize for that. You're the lawman, not me."

"So then what?"

"I opened the garage door and checked the drive behind your place. No one was in sight. I pulled out, turned south and scooted away, made a big loop, and headed back up to Fielder and the freeway and home. Then I waited. I didn't think or even feel. I just waited."

Ben put his fingertips on his closed eyelids and pressed.

"What are you going to do, Ben?"

"I have to think, Ma." His head was throbbing. "First I have to call Kenechi and the chief."

"Kenechi and the chief. Yes, that's the most important thing." She put her face in her hands, muffling her voice. "Sometimes I don't know you."

"*You* don't know me?" He poked himself in the chest with his thumb. "Looking back over the last week, Ma, I think I can say *I* don't know me." He stared glumly into the fire. "Or my family, for that matter. My impetuous brother gets out of prison and throws a guy out the window, right in front of me. He breaks and enters another guy's apartment. And the father I didn't have is murdered, an act my mother witnesses and keeps to herself. I throw a fit in front of the whole force, countermand direct orders, and withhold vital case information from my partner, my team, and my boss. And to top it all off, I find out my brother isn't my brother."

He tilted his head at her.

"The good news of the week, though, is that my mother isn't a murderer—just a kidnapper. God!"

Nell gaped at him. "Throw a guy out a window? Break and enter? What the hell are you talking about?"

He waggled a hand dismissively and rose, knees creaking, rolling his head a little to loosen his neck muscles. He fixed Nell with a blue stare.

"As I said, I'm going to call Ken and the chief. And you, Ma, *you* will plan on telling the law what you just told me. Beyond that—"

She gasped.

"I mean what you saw Friday. With Moll and Dayton. We'll have to think of a reason you didn't speak right away . . . probably shock and wanting to protect your family, especially Andrew, with his just being released from prison. I think we can finesse that. Beyond that, I don't know."

"But—"

"Not now, Ma. Please."

He took out his phone.

"Ben—"

"Not now. Let me do my job. Or my former job. Just for now. I'm going to have to go to the station, talk with the chief and Kenechi, get an arrest warrant."

He saw her face.

"And try not to worry too much. I don't know what time I'll be back, but I'll call. We'll talk later, figure it out."

"Big trouble," she whispered, as if to herself.

He bent and took her hand. It felt small and cool and listless in his, and his own hopelessness grew with her silence. But then she looked up and leaned forward to take him in her arms. Where he stayed, bent and awkward, until she released him.

"Will you help me, Ben?" she asked, her voice faint. "Andrew can never know. Whatever else." She started sobbing wildly. "We can't have him hurt, not after Huntsville."

He picked up Bood and deposited him in her lap.

"Will you?" she repeated. Ben had never seen anyone look so haunted.

"Ma, you know I'll do whatever I can. I just don't know—"

He punched in a number on his speed dial.

She fell silent, wrapping her arms around Bood and trying unsuccessfully to compose herself. Ben went downstairs and made his calls. Then he hurried through the unlit courtyard and past the cars parked along the drive—shadowy, hunkering shapes in the darkness, like an Edward Hopper painting.

CHAPTER 48

Ben was already waiting in the lobby of the Knowlton Arms when Kenechi arrived on Thursday morning, himself nearly an hour early. Ben had been there since the promise of dawn streaked the horizon, alone and all nerve ends in the early morning hush of the lobby, holding with damp palms *The Dallas Morning News* he'd taken from a table in the lobby, pretending to read. He'd arrived even before Abner, who'd come in briskly, thin cheeks polished, hair in grooves sharp enough to have been made with a gardening fork, gray rump-sprung uniform neatly pressed. Abner had peered around Ben's newspaper.

"Mr. Ben?"

Ben could see his mind working, could see him preparing to bustle. Police business!

The element of surprise. They needed that. Surprise and fear. Hell, they needed a confession. Let Moll hesitate, take time to think, figure it out, and Nell would end up in the witness chair. And who knew where that would take them. Nell wasn't a good liar despite her claims to the contrary. He felt blood pulsing in his temples, the remnants of yesterday's headache.

Kenechi, spruce in black leather cap and black poplin raincoat, crossed the lobby and sat heavily in the gray velvet chair opposite Ben's.

"Thought I might get here before you, have time for coffee," he rumbled, rubbing the pale palms of his big black hands together. They rasped like old leather. "You been here all night?"

"Feels like it. Get your coffee. I'm watching the elevator and stairwell. No one's come down. So she's up there. Least her car's here. But go ahead—Andrew's not here yet. Best if the person in control of the property goes up with us."

Kenechi disappeared and came back with two steaming Styrofoam cups, Andrew striding through the lobby's back entrance at the same moment. Ben examined Andrew as if seeing him for the first time and shoved his thoughts away, hard.

Kenechi set the coffee cups on the low table.

Ben felt the tension in the two men.

"Let's just go," he said, waving at the coffee and turning to Kenechi, "Got your cuffs?"

Kenechi patted his pocket. "Think she'll run?"

Ben looked toward the ceiling. "Where's she going to run to?"

Kenechi and Andrew took the elevator to the third floor, Ben the stairs, and they met at the door, skin prickling with excitement. They knocked twice, and after a long pause, Jimmy Snipes answered with a heavy scowl but no surprise—having looked through the peephole, Ben knew. Ben saw he was nearly dressed despite the early hour—stuffing a stiff white shirt into black pants and buckling the gold fitting on his black belt, shoeless feet sheathed in scarlet socks.

"Well, lookee here first thing in the morning. You bring the Jimster some croissants? Or should I open the window, do my trapeze act?"

"Glad to see you didn't lose your balls on your last flight, Jimster," Ben said. "We'll do breakfast another day. Is your mother here?"

"Ma?" He backed up and opened the door. "Why?"

"Tell her we're here to see her, Jimmy."

"She doesn't like to get up early."

"Nevertheless."

"I don't . . ." Jimmy turned and crossed the hall hesitantly to one of the closed doors, looking back at them. He opened the door and turned back to them, surprised. "She's not there."

"Do you know where she might have gone?" Ben asked.

Confused, Jimmy pulled open the closet door.

"Her coat's gone. Purse, too."

He looked at them, immediately apprehensive but trying to hide it.

"Ah declare, if Miz Moneypenny abandoned her baby boy, least she could leave her wallet. Always making out she's broke. Try to get a nickel of her shitload of money, though! Miz Molly by Golly! But—"

As though realizing he was babbling, he stopped and tried a grin, but tremulous, Ben thought, as though on the verge of tears.

Jimmy had a thought and rushed to the first door again, snatched it open, disappeared briefly, and came back, face washed with relief.

"Clothes in there. Suitcase, too."

He had another thought and ducked into the closet, ran his hand around a small shelf.

"No keys."

Apprehensive again.

"I don't—she doesn't like to get up early."

Ben and Kenechi exchanged glances, simultaneously guessing where Molly Snipes was at the mention of keys. The men took leave of an anxious Jimmy, who followed them uncertainly to the elevator and watched them step inside, watched the doors close, watched the light on the dial above the elevator climb to the fifth floor and stop. He hesitated a moment, then headed for the stair-well door.

The three men stepped off the elevator and moved quickly, quietly, up the handful of carpeted stairs leading to Dayton Slaughter's foyer, the detectives drawing their weapons. The tape was still in place, the ivory doors closed.

"Stay back," Ben whispered to Andrew, who was taking a key from his pocket. "Let's try it first."

The knob turned easily, silently, in Ben's hand, and the door opened. Ben turned to Andrew, placed a palm gently against his chest, and signaled him to stay. He and Kenechi slipped soundlessly under the yellow tape and stepped into the foyer.

The radiators were clunking in the sealed and stuffy apartment, but a cold and freshening breeze emanated from the living room, where Ben could see sheer curtains billowing away from an open window. He also could see Moll's maroon coat draped over a nearby sofa arm. Moll herself, unaware of their presence, was in Dayton's office, seated at his desk, its drawers open, their contents piled in her lap and strewn at her oxford-clad feet. She had the blurred-edged, blowsy look of an aging Renoir whore in the apartment's subdued light, head bent over a stack of folders in her lap, intent on a sheet of paper in her blunt fingers.

Ben watched her for a split second, then spoke her name. She startled so badly that the files slid from her lap and fell in a heap on the carpet. She jumped up and wheeled on them, mouth a small *O* emitting an indecipherable sound.

"Still looking for the letter, Moll? Didn't find it on your earlier search, did you."

Her eyes fell to the Glock semiautomatic in Ben's hand.

"Stand right there," he ordered.

She was stock-still, face blanching.

"Molly Snipes, a.k.a. Moll Smollett," Ben continued quietly but clearly, wanting no subtlety, wanting every advantage, "you're under arrest for the blackmail and murder of David Dayton Slaughter."

She raised a hand a couple of inches, as if to ward off his words, but was otherwise motionless, her eyes never leaving his face.

"You have the right to remain silent," Ben added, "but anything you say may be held against you in a court of law."

She gave her dusty-looking curls a small toss. "You'd have better luck with a charge of breaking and entering," she responded, her voice breathless but defiant.

"But you had a key, didn't you, Moll. Dayton's key. You took it from the table in my foyer after you shot him."

She looked wary and uncertain, and Kenechi advanced carefully, handcuffs out of sight in his left hand. Her hazel eyes, magnified by the lenses in the amber plastic frames, darted from Ben to Kenechi. She stared at them a moment longer, her breathing quick and shallow, her beefy shoulders dropping, but thinking, thinking, Ben could tell. She considered, then glanced at him and quickly lowered her gaze, pale lashes almost hidden in the flesh overhanging her eyes.

"I'll need my coat," she said tonelessly. Then, in an appeal to Kenechi, "If you're going to put those handcuffs on me, please let me put on my coat first."

Ben held up a hand. "Just a minute."

He stepped into the living room and picked up the maroon coat from the sofa arm and went through the pockets, bringing out a gold ring bearing a key and an enameled gold and red shield emblazoned with the scrolled numerals 601. He showed it to Kenechi and to Andrew, who had edged into the room, then pocketed it and examined the contents of Moll's handbag.

"Where's Dayton's money clip, Moll?" he asked. "His Rolex?"

She waited without responding, and he stood back from the doorway and signaled her to pass.

Slowly, thoughtfully, she entered the living room, took up the woolen coat and shrugged into it, grasping the straps of her handbag and fitting them over her shoulder. Her gaze grazed Ben's cheek and went past him, lips moving, and Ben thought in that suspended moment that she saw something, that she whispered *Jimbo*. Then, with an inscrutable expression, an amber flame burning behind her eyes, she went perfectly still, as if for a split second's assessment, as still as a trapped creature gathering strength. And Ben knew. But couldn't move. Or . . . *was* it that he couldn't move? Or just that he didn't?

Moll pivoted and dashed across the room toward the open window, moving with surprising speed considering her bulk, Andrew shouting and closing the distance between them at the same instant she hurtled through the open space, taking some of the wooden frame and glass with her in an explosion of sound. It was Andrew who grabbed at her first, his right hand closing on a handful of shoulder pad, her bag slipping from her shoulder, straps looping Andrew's hand as she went over the sill. Kenechi was rushing to the window, too, and—improbably—Jimmy, screaming, face contorted. Then Ben was there as well, reaching for all his might, but his fingertips only grazed Moll's broad back as she turned in Andrew's grasp, her hazel eyes touching Andrew's hazel eyes before the weight of her was too great for his fistful of maroon wool and down she went into the gray morning, down, down, to lie on the sidewalk in the Knowlton's pooled light, her maroon wool coat covering her like a lake of blood.

By the time they made it to the street, Jimmy was already there, kneeling beside his mother, his sharp knees in their sharp creases on the cold sidewalk, his face strewn with tears. He was ineffectually trying to wipe blood from her nostrils with his scarlet pocket silk, and now and again rocking back on his heels to sob, "Mommy."

Molly Snipes lay face down, one arm outflung and the other bent unnaturally beneath her, head slightly turned, unseeing eyes flat as glass, spectacles shattered and askew beneath her cheek, a red stain widening on the sidewalk beneath her head.

Ben, Andrew, and Kenechi stood back, letting Jimmy have his goodbye, but Abner moved to go to him. Ben put a restraining hand on his arm.

"Let him be a minute."

Abner worked his thin lips and blinked back tears. "Boy's havin' a bad time there," he said.

"Let him be a minute, Ab. You can't help him right now."

CHAPTER 49

Rolando Saenz stood with a knot of officers in the patrol briefing room when Ben and his team got back from lunch on Friday afternoon. He called to them immediately.

"*Doctor* Gallagher! *Doctor* Akundi! Detective Proudhorse! Detective Cloy!"

"Oh shit," Hilda whispered.

They filed into the room, and the chief approached them, his glistening black hair a little awry. Then he turned so he spoke partly to them and partly to the room.

"One week ago, y'all ran with the bit in your teeth. Especially the first two days and especially you, Ben."

The four detectives stood awkwardly, waiting to see where this was going to go, knowing it couldn't be good.

The chief turned fully to the patrol room, everyone listening intently, eyes alternately on Chief Saenz and on the four detectives.

"Five days ago, I agreed to give Ben and his team a week to work this case, thinking I'd probably be giving it to another team at the end of that week. But I had a little hunch and decided to follow it."

Even under these tense circumstances, Ben felt like smiling. *Had a little hunch.* Rolando Saenz, master of spin!

Saenz looked sternly at the four detectives standing beside him.

"And my hunch paid off. In five days, they solved this case and would have made an arrest if the perp hadn't offed herself. Not only that, but they also solved and closed another murder case out of state, a cold case more than thirty years old."

The chief was silent for a long moment, looking at the patrol room expectantly, then added with emphasis, "In five days."

Ram Ratzlaff rose and put his long hands together in a slow clap and the others followed his lead, somberly—until they lost the beat and it fell apart. But it was long enough for Kenechi and Proudhorse to lower their heads and for Hilda to swipe at her eyes. Long enough for Ben's heart to swell and for his lips to tug into a smile. Rolando Saenz. A piece of work. Not that Ben was faulting him. Was his version a reconstruction? Maybe not!

Saenz put a hand on his shoulder to steer him away from the others.

"You're not going to can me," Ben said.

The chief smiled. "How can I continue to take credit for your successes if I can you? Still, you skated real close to the edge, Ben. And I know why. But don't do it again."

Ben looked at him closely, trying to read his face.

"Have you—I mean, what do you . . . You been talking to Kenechi?" Ben felt a crushing disappointment.

Rolando's expression sharpened. "Akundi knew. Ah. He's not a talker, then. Not that I thought he was."

"Then—?"

"Ay yi yi—you think I'm stupid? Some things you know. Some you're told. Others you guess. You think I don't read the case files? That I don't remember the flag on your mama's stairs and your daddy Benjamin Ryan?" He lowered his voice to its usual volume and pitch. "Now I didn't know Nell was a nickname for Eleanor, and that's a fact. But I looked it up."

Ben stared at him.

"You think I put two and two together and get twenty-two?" He leaned a little closer. "All I'm saying is you could have talked to me. I'm not just your chief; I'm your friend."

Ben was touched. "I guess I'm not a talker, either."

"Yeah, well, snap out of it. You and your buddy, Ken Akundi, too. Both ya." The chief ran a hand through his gelled hair. "Have you met my mother, Ben?"

"What? Your mother? Yes."

He drew nearer and lowered his voice a little more. "Did you know she's illegal?"

"Well." Ben almost smiled. Didn't everyone? He thought of Rolando Saenz's mother, once a young Mexican widow who'd sneaked into the United States to put three children through school on her proceeds as a maid, now a bent brown woman with a lined face and callused, reddened hands.

"Well," he said again.

Saenz aimed a hard look at Ben. "You could have trusted me. That's all I'm saying. And I'm trusting you. When I leave this job—if I leave this job—I'd like you to be in place behind me. But that's nothing we have to talk about right now."

Trust, Ben thought. Getting a little theme going here. He watched the chief's back as he walked away, and felt the heaviness slide from his shoulders and roll away. Helluva guy, really. He moved down the corridor toward his office.

Ramsey Ratzlaff was waiting outside his door. "Got a minute?"

"Sure, take a seat."

Ramsey sat, the midafternoon sun streaming through the blinds and slicing his long face into slats, like an Escher drawing.

"I'd like to join your team, Ben," he said. "Sometime, when you have a place."

Ben put on his poker face.

"I know you don't think much of me," Ram continued. "I'm a redneck, don't come from white-collar stock. But I'm a good cop. I never said this to you, but I thought what you did with Jack Malone was exactly the right thing. I respect it. And I've said so out there." He put a thumb toward the patrol room. "I couldn't have done it. I'm a good cop, but not that good."

He averted his lean face for a moment, then met Ben's eyes.

"Malone's an asshole. Crooked as a corkscrew. But he won't bother you again."

Ben studied him. "You know this."

"I do."

More silence passed between them. Then Ramsey shook his head.

"I know more than I want to know about Jack Malone. More than *he* wants me to know, too. And he's keeping a low profile from now on."

Ben absorbed that. "I guess I owe—"

"No," Ramsey said. "It's for everyone, not just you. Jacko's a negative force."

Ben tried not to look surprised. Okay, he thought, I can be wrong. And others can be right.

"I'd like to have you on the team, Ram," he said. "I'll mention it to the chief."

"I already did. He said to talk to you."

"Oh. Well, then."

When the door closed on Ram Ratzlaff, Ben sat squinting and plucking at his lower lip. Okay, he could be wrong. Even if he was right ninety percent of the time, he thought with a small wry smile. Something he needed to remember. He heard a tentative peck at his door and looked up. Kenechi, Proudhorse, and Hilda were milling around in the corridor. He beckoned and they filed in, Kenechi carrying a fourth chair in one hand and a paper-clipped sheaf of papers in the other.

He slid the papers toward Ben. "My official report."

Proudhorse and Hilda exchanged expressionless glances.

"So Molly Snipes had been blackmailing Slaughter all that time," Hilda said.

Ben squared up the pages of Kenechi's report and slipped them into a folder.

"For more than thirty years. Since Willie Smollett's death. Then followed him lock, stock, and barrel to the Knowlton. Leased some space so she could continue to be a pain in the ass."

"I'm surprised he let her stay there."

Ben shrugged. "Dayt was just another renter when she showed up. He wouldn't have renewed the lease, that's for sure. But then he learned he was dying, so—"

"So he cut her off," Proudhorse said.

"But why kill him?" Hilda asked. "What does that get her?"

"I understand perfectly," Proudhorse said. "Anyway, don't go to a nutso for logic."

"Avarice," Ben said. "Or who knows. She might not have believed him. All she could see was the caboose on her gravy train. She flew into a fury."

"People who are out of control don't consider consequences," Kenechi said. "She didn't. Not then, and not when she jumped."

"I understand perfectly," Proudhorse said.

"And Smollett," Hilda said. "That was self-defense. Slaughter was a lawyer. He had to know he could've gotten off."

Ben kept his thoughts to himself. *He couldn't risk my mother. Or Andrew.*

Kenechi spoke up. "Dayton Slaughter was well-placed in the community. Would he want the scandal? And money was the least of his problems. Like most blackmail victims, he thought the truth would cost him more than the blackmail."

Ben sent a grateful glance Kenechi's way, and his partner met his gaze calmly.

"Yeah, but—"

"I understand perf—" Proudhorse said.

"Oh!" Hilda laughed and gave him a little shove toward the door. "Okay, Geronimo here got some 'splainin' to do."

Kenechi remained sitting when Proudhorse and Hilda left the room, then reached over and pushed the door closed.

"Why didn't Molly Snipes make a fuss about her missing baby?" he asked.

"Ma says Moll no doubt thought he was with Dixie Booth. Not that Moll cared. But Dixie did that often—took him home with her. Apparently she cared about him. Must have been the only one." Ben's throat tightened. "Sypinski said Dixie was supposed to take care of him that night, but she never showed. Moll was probably too wasted even to remember. But Ma said he cried steadily for a long time. Until she couldn't stand it any more."

They were silent, Kenechi toying with his fountain pen and Ben drawing angular, crosshatched doodles on a scratch pad.

"And later?"

"No money in it. Moll didn't want the baby anyway. Cramp her style. So a stone best left unturned. And Dixie Booth had conveniently disappeared."

Kenechi raised his brows.

"Not really. She was ill—maybe that's why she didn't show the night of the St. Pat's party. She went back to Florida to live with relatives and died there less than a year later."

"Never knowing the role she played in that drama."

"Never knowing," Ben agreed. "You could say the same about Moll. When she followed Dayt to Texas, she ended up a stone's throw from not only her baby—now a man—but also from her baby's kidnapper. And from endless dollars—Ma would've paid anything. But Moll never knew. Thanks to Dayton."

"He was a good man."

Ben nodded, eyes stinging.

"How's your mother now?"

"Ragged. Scared. It'll be a long while before she can relax, I guess."

"She can, can't she?"

"Relax? Well, yes. Hell, yes. Not that I'm easy with it."

Kenechi nodded.

"A kidnapper, Ken. Jesus Christ."

"Why is it the word scares you more than the act?"

Ben thought that over. "The word defines the deed, Ken. And it defines the letter of the law. She broke the letter of law, which I swore to uphold."

"Sometimes, by transgressing on the letter, we most truly keep the law. I mean law with a capital L—its spirit."

"An old African proverb?"

Kenechi capped his pen, stuck it in his pocket, and turned toward the door.

"Conjured up four centuries ago by a dead white guy named John Milton."

"Ken?"

Kenechi turned.

"I thought you'd feel you had to . . . It's a felony. I mean—"

"I know what you mean. And I don't take *felony* lightly, Ben, even if it is just language."

"But? And?"

"Do you have anything to fear from me? Not now. Not ever."

Ben was ashamed his partner had read him so easily. His mind drifted to that moment when he'd looked at Andrew, and the words *Moll's baby* suddenly sank in. But they were still just words, and they finally didn't signify—*finally* didn't signify. In that moment since the seamless puzzle of his life ripped apart and rebuilt itself, new pieces appeared out of nowhere and snapped snugly into place of their own accord. *Andrew and I are the same age. He wasn't born a year and five months after me, but only five months. His name wasn't Andrew. We didn't have the same father, right. But we also didn't have the same mother! Ponder that . . .*

Ben felt a smile prick at his lips, and he marveled. In a moment, everything changed—in another moment, it didn't matter. Things weren't what he thought, and it didn't matter. It didn't signify! What's the difference if it's *brother* or *half-brother* or *no-brother?* Just language. A brother is a brother is a brother.

Kenechi had been watching him intently, and now he tossed off one of his falsetto laughs.

"Nietzsche said a chalked streak stops the hen."

Ben knew the words, and their import. "Overstepping a chalked line has no consequence," he said. "The line here is not imaginary. It's more than chalk."

"And you're more than a chicken."

Ben smiled. "I'll think that over later."

Kenechi sat again, on the edge of the chair, elbows on Ben's desk, chin on clasped hands, onyx eyes calm.

"Ben, your brand of idealism doesn't get you where you want to go, not if you want to practice it on this planet."

"No?"

"No."

"Where does it get me?"

"You hear the one about the guy who wants to join the Communist party? And his future comrades interview him?"

Ben shook his head.

"So this guy wants to join a Communist group and his comrades ask, *If you had two houses, would you give one to the group?*

"*Of course,* he replies.

"*And if you had two cars,* they ask, *would you give one to the group?*

"*Naturally,* he says.

"*And what if you had two shirts?*

"*No way,* he says.

"*What?* They ask in surprise. *Why not?*

"*Because,* the man says, *I have two shirts.*"

Ben smiled. "Point being?"

"The point being . . . the point of the law. Live on the planet, Ben—some lines really are drawn in chalk. Reassure your mother. And be at ease. The point of the law is justice. You don't have to lose your shirt."

"That kind of thinking can lead to outrageous rationalizations."

Kenechi dismissed that with a shrug.

"I believe the rule of law is satisfied."

"So I just . . . *forget* it?"

Kenechi stood and stretched and grunted, raising his big black fists toward the ceiling.

"Forget what?"

CHAPTER 50

Sunday, March 9, 2003

Andrew, red-gold hair gleaming in the clean, bright light of noon, stood on the walk in front of number twenty-two and looked down McKinney toward Ben and Bood, returning from a last-chance visit to the little park down the street.

"Bood! Hey, buddy!" Andrew called, jingling the keys to Nell's Prius. "Wanna ride in the car?"

Bood threw his whole weight into tugging at his harness and leash, trying hard to break into a run, Ben lengthening his own long strides to accommodate him.

This was a new Bood, this Bood jumping into Andrew's arms, this groomed and polished and perfumed Bood. Ben thought the whole of him shone like metal in the sun. His black dreadlocks were brushed and shortened, the tangle of curl on his muzzle tamed to a proper arch and bow of mustache and beard, the shag of his torso clipped close in tiny velvety waves, and the long, silky fringe of his tail swept the air like an ostrich plume. As a final touch, he wore a new black leather harness and leash—and around his neck a black silk scarf bedecked with little figures embroidered in bright green.

"Ma's about ready," Andrew said, pulling his face away from Bood's pink tongue. "Ben. I've been wanting to say . . . thank you for helping me face myself the night Dayton was killed."

"What do you mean?"

"When I had the guilts. When I thought it was universal pay-back. God taking his due."

"It was crazy."

"But I really thought it. At least right then. I guess that was the single lowest moment of my life—except when I heard the judge pronounce sentence on me. I mean the moment when I felt the most worthless, the most like I didn't belong."

Ben shook his head. "God, Andrew."

"I was on overload anyway. But you promised it would have nothing to do with me, and I'm glad you were right. I have enough to live with."

Nell closed the door on number twenty-two, locked it, and approached her sons. Andrew dumped Bood into her arms and headed for Nell's car, Ben watching him move down the walk.

Nothing to do with me. Everything to do with him! Andrew's words had struck Ben with the enormousness of Nell's secret and the necessity of keeping it. Secrets and lies, snares and traps. Ben had always sensed the destructive force of secrets and lies, and his work had underlined that lesson—terrible things happened because someone tried to protect a secret, or failed to. Secrets and lies, always a betrayal to someone—a burden to the sharers and an exclusion to the rest. Ben would feel that exclusion without know-ing its source—he *had* felt that exclusion—and he knew Andrew would, too.

He realized Nell was watching him watch Andrew, and he turned to meet her anxious eyes. An observer might have said they studied each other, but it was more than that. It was an ex-change. Abruptly, the anxiety faded from Nell's expression and her face was suffused with love—love blended with understanding and guilt and sorrow.

Ben moved the few feet separating them and took her hand. She held it hard.

"It'll be okay, Ma," he whispered. "We'll be okay."

Nell laughed at Bood wriggling in her arms and straightened his scarf.

"What are these little green figures? Oh, shamrocks! That Dollie."

"I can't believe Dollie groomed him—and in the Cachet," Ben said, imagining Bood in one of the salon's black leather chairs, his ruined dreadlocks littering the marble floor. "I wonder what the other patrons thought."

"They thought it was cute. Dollie did him proud for Dayt's ceremony." She turned her face to the sun. "I'm so glad we've seen the last of February."

The stubborn weather system had blown out of northeast Texas during the night and headed for Arkansas, pulling warm, dry air in its wake.

"Dayt always arranged to spend some of March and April here," she said. "He thought March was Michigan's worst month and Texas' best."

"Ma," Ben said. "You know an M. J. Kildare?"

She looked at him blankly.

"M. J.? Sure, Martha. Why?"

"Message slip on Dayt's desk."

"She heads the interior design firm that's refurbishing the Knowlton. A diva. Dayton called her brilliant but pesky. She's Andrew's problem now."

"Horse-faced woman? Wears a sort of psychedelic wardrobe?"

Nell laughed. "Andrew said the same thing. Called her horse-faced woman with a whinny-like voice."

"That night at Chez Dee. You looked behind me and went white. When I turned, I saw that woman. I thought you were reacting to her."

Nell fondled Bood's head. "She was there, yes. But the person I saw over your shoulder was Moll. She was in the entryway, looking at the menu posted on that easel. I nearly fainted—I thought she was going to come in, sit down, see all of us sitting together. I didn't know what to do, whether she'd see me, recognize me, and put things together. But she just looked at the menu and left."

Andrew brought Nell's Prius around. Ben unleashed Bood, who was trembling with joy, and he and Bood climbed into the back, after Nell, leaving the passenger seat for Dollie. Andrew looked at Nell in the rearview mirror.

"You get this Toyota to match your eyes, Ma?" He transferred his attention to Ben. "I moved the passenger seat all the way up to give you more leg room, Ben."

Even so, Ben's long legs were sharply bent and sharply angled.

"You like this color?" Nell asked Andrew. "It's called brilliant blue pearl."

"Dollie said she'd wait in front of the Knowlton," Andrew said, backing up and pulling into the McKinney traffic. "She also said Jimmy Snipes came round to give her another chance. He told her he'd be livin' large without his mother to cramp his style."

Ben smiled. "Handling his grief."

"Bless him, I say," Nell said. "What must his life have been like, living with that terrifying woman."

"I guess his dad was no picnic, either, from what Dollie says," Andrew added. "But Moll banked three decades of pension checks, so Jimmy will get something nice from Thatcher Snipes, after all."

Nell tossed her head. "As I said, bless him."

"She also had a large Hummel collection," Andrew put in. "Worth a fortune, apparently."

Ben remembered the figurine on the coffee table that Jimmy had nudged with his foot to torment his mother.

"He'll probably blow it all on flashy silk hankies," Andrew said.

Half brothers, Ben thought, still trying to absorb it. *Not Andrew and I, but Andrew and Jimmy Snipes.* He had an absurd desire to laugh. Jimmy Snipes, family. An ostensible heir in the Gallagher family estate through his relationship to Andrew. Wouldn't *that* have thrilled Molly Snipes! Except that Andrew was stolen, never legally adopted. And neither Jimmy nor Andrew was of the Gallagher bloodline—therefore, per stirpes, neither was an heir.

All that felt like trouble—big trouble, as Nell would say—and Ben pushed those thoughts away.

Andrew pulled onto Elm, following JFK's motorcade route, sailed through several lights, and waited for the left-turn signal on Houston. He turned his head toward them, the sun lighting his sandy lashes.

"Something about that woman—"

"You met her?" Ben asked in surprise. "I mean besides when she jumped?"

"She was in the Cachet when I got my hair cut. What I remember about her is she came up to the counter where I was standing and just . . . shoved me aside. Like I wasn't there. Like I was invisible. She gave me bad vibes. Do you believe in that sixth-sense stuff?"

Ben, feeling Nell tense, put a hand on hers and stared at the back of his brother's head a second before answering.

"I guess we intuit things about people all the time."

"Except *now* I know that I was standing next to a killer. *Dayton*'s killer. God! No wonder I got bad vibes."

Nell took a breath, relaxed a little.

"But you've stood next to plenty of killers in prison," Ben said.

Andrew laughed and turned left onto Houston.

"I got bad vibes from them, too."

"What's happening at the Knowlton?" Ben asked.

"Turns out Tooley Deere's going to be with us a while. The Hyatt manager was set to retire at the end of the month, but there's some financial snafu, and he needs to stay out the year. So Tooley's delaying his move. Good deal for everybody. Especially me."

"Gives you time to find a good manager."

"Yeah," he said. "I think I know what I want to do there, though. Meantime, I'll help Tooley manage the property. Be good for me."

Ben started to speak, but Nell laid a hand on his arm.

"It's your place," she said.

"My place," Andrew echoed. He pointed toward the Knowlton and put on his blinker. "There she is, that dark-haired lass in the red plaid horse blanket and stilts."

He pulled to the curb and Dollie, carrying Snazzy, clacked across the walk in her tall yellow shoes. Andrew leaned over to open the passenger door, and she got in, turning to give Ben and Nell a high-wattage magenta smile.

"You sure it's okay to bring Snaz?"

Andrew leaned to kiss Dollie's cheek, and something outside caught his attention.

"What's Zora doing?"

Zora Sanda's broad back was to them, her head swathed in a bandanna. She was vigorously sweeping the walkway under the red canopy, kicking up a small cloud of dust.

"Sweeping the stoop like a hausfrau," he said ruefully. "Good thing it's Abner's day off—he'd have a stroke. I'd better—"

Dollie opened her door and jumped out. "Let me."

Dollie approached Zora, and the older woman turned, her big face smothered in something resembling green spackle, eyes rimmed in pale circles. With a grin, Dollie turned toward the Toyota Prius, where the others watched, and sent a merry glance heavenward. Then she took Zora's arm and disappeared briefly into the Knowlton. Zora went along peaceably, but she turned at the door and sent Andrew a dark look.

Dollie crossed the sidewalk and hopped back into the car. "She understands now not to do that."

"Zora's a work in progress," Andrew told Ben and Nell. "She's on like a twelve-hundred-step program."

"She's still irked at Andrew," Dollie said. "He asked her what rhymed with *discombobulate*."

Andrew pulled away from the curb. "Soon's we get away from this traffic, I'm going to give Ben the ride of his life."

"No, you're not," Nell said.

"I got him in back where I won't have to see him slamming on the invisible brakes."

"You'll still be able to hear me scream," Ben said.

Dollie spoke over her shoulder. "I've never scattered anyone's ashes before."

"Today," Ben said, "we're just going to sleuth out the perfect place for Dayton."

"They haven't released the body yet," Nell said. "But that's okay. We'll do the memorial this month and the ashes in April— during the height of bluebonnet season."

"Do you have a spot in mind?" Dollie asked.

"On our spring drives down to Huntsville, Dayton used to point out some hilly stretches where the bluebonnets were like seamless carpets along both sides of the I-road. A lot of cars would pull over, and folks would go walk among the blooms. We did that, too. It was stunning. I'll never forget—" She broke off, voice wobbling. "I wish we'd see some bluebonnets today."

"Too early, Ma," Ben said.

"What I want to do is find one of those spots, then leave the I-road and explore the nearby back roads. Find a quiet and perfect place for Dayton's ashes. He'd like that."

Andrew glanced at Dollie. "What'd you do to your hair, Dolls? I love it."

"I left off the products." Dollie looked back at Nell. "I'm going to be twenty-four pretty soon. And I'll have my business degree. So I should change my image. Maybe one day look as lovely as you."

They turned left off Young Street and left again, moving past the book depository, past the grassy knoll, and headed for open country.

Nell leaned forward, her lips close to Dollie's ear, and whispered, "You are so lovely just as you are, Dollie. Don't you know that?"

Dollie's eyes met Nell's, and her bright face almost crumpled. Then she rose in her seat, turned on her knees, and opened the horse-blanket coat. Under the red plaid, she wore an old tee from Nell's trunk. Across its breast was a faded peace sign.

"Way to go, Dollie!" Nell said.

So they sped down the highway, the sun glinting off the Toyota's shining hood, Andrew's left hand on the wheel and right hand warm on Dollie's knee, Snazzy on the console staring at Bood, Bood in Ben's lap staring back, Nell's face relaxing, Ben sitting back, taking it all in—a passenger, his brother at the wheel.

"Crapola," Nell said after a while, her eyes searching the landscape. "No wildflowers."

"It's too early, Ma," Ben said again.

Dollie turned and gave them one of her sunrise smiles.

"But soon. They're just below the surface."

And so they were. Bluebonnets. Even now warming in the soil and pressing toward the light, unfurling their colors.

ACKNOWLEDGMENTS

I offer my grateful thanks:

To Detective John Murrell of the Arlington, Texas, Police Department, both for reading the completed manuscript of *Chalk Line* and for his valuable counsel. The Arlington PD desk officers were unfailingly gracious in fielding impromptu questions, and the Arlington Police Academy was helpful as well.

To Mike Viesca of the Texas Department of Criminal Justice in Austin for crime/sentence and Huntsville educational program information. The TDCJ's Sal Caruso of Review and Release, Parole Division, helped me understand parole procedures and provisions. And I am especially indebted to the TDCJ's Michelle Lyons for repeatedly, clearly, and interestingly answering my questions.

To Robert L. Berry, formerly Chief of Detectives, Summit County Sheriff's Office, Utah, for help with forensics, gun-tracing, and other ATF procedures.

To Marion Street Press' Jim Schuette and Kel Winter, and to my editor, Lorna Gusner, whose savvy questions made *Chalk Line* a better novel.

To Joe Delio for his detailed on-the-road description of the drive to Huntsville in mid-February.

To my dear first readers: Paul LaRocque, Ralph Langer, Keeta Auton, Mary Brolley, Linda Swift, Bruce DeSilva, and Doug Swanson—and to the members of the Dallas-Fort Worth Writers Workshop, who listened . . .

And last, but by no means least, to all my friends who for a decade never forgot to ask: *What's going on with your book?*

Paula LaRocque

READING GROUP GUIDE

1. The term "chalk line" has multiple meanings—for example, a line drawn around a corpse, or a tool that uses a string coated with chalk to make a straight line. Another meaning is suggested by the prefacing quotation from Friedrich Nietzsche: "A chalk streak stops a hen"—a reference to chickens that won't step over a chalked line because they perceive the line as a real barrier. How do those various meanings make *Chalk Line* a meaningful title for this novel?

2. What does Nell mean when she says: "Ben Gallagher's world view at its most Panglossian?"

3. Ben says he no longer has blind faith in blind faith; Nell says the very essence of trust is trusting *despite* the evidence. Are there differences between the kind of trust Nell is talking about and what Ben calls blind faith? What are those differences?

4. Kenechi Akundi's question, "Who's completely bad?" suggests not only that people are often inconsistent and contradictory, but also that black/white thinking is flawed thinking. How else does the novel denounce "black/white" thinking?

5. What does Kenechi hope to convey when he tells Ben the joke about the wannabe Communist's responses to the Party's questions?

6. In Ben's professional life, he is in a sense torn between love and duty—between art and law. What does this dichotomy tell us about Ben's character?

7. What's the meaning of the reference to Ben as "passenger" in the final chapter?

8. Chapter 41 is a quiet but pivotal chapter in terms of Andrew's character development. What's the meaning of his scene with Miz B at The Ripe Olive? His discussion with Dollie afterwards? Do the two scenes connect? How? What does the author imply by writing: "His burger and fries came, and if they weren't the best he'd ever had, that's the way he'd remember them"?

9. How has Ben changed by the end of the novel? Andrew?

10. Orphans or orphan-hood is a recurrent theme in the novel, both literally and figuratively. Where does this theme appear, either actually or symbolically, and how does it reinforce some of the novel's deeper meanings?

11. A common archetype in art, literature, and psychology is that of the Mother Goddess—both good and evil. The Great Mother archetype loves, feeds, nurtures, and protects her young, while the Wicked Mother archetype withholds such care. The latter may ignore or abuse her young, or even devour them (often symbolically rather than actually). Who are the principal "mother figures" in *Chalk Line*? How do they represent the good and evil archetypes, and how does the presence of each enrich and deepen the meaning of the other?

12. It's said that all worthwhile and enduring art is moral at its heart. Is that true of *Chalk Line*? How does the novel resolve the fact that a major and sympathetic character breaks the law and not only escapes punishment but is also protected by those sworn to uphold the law?